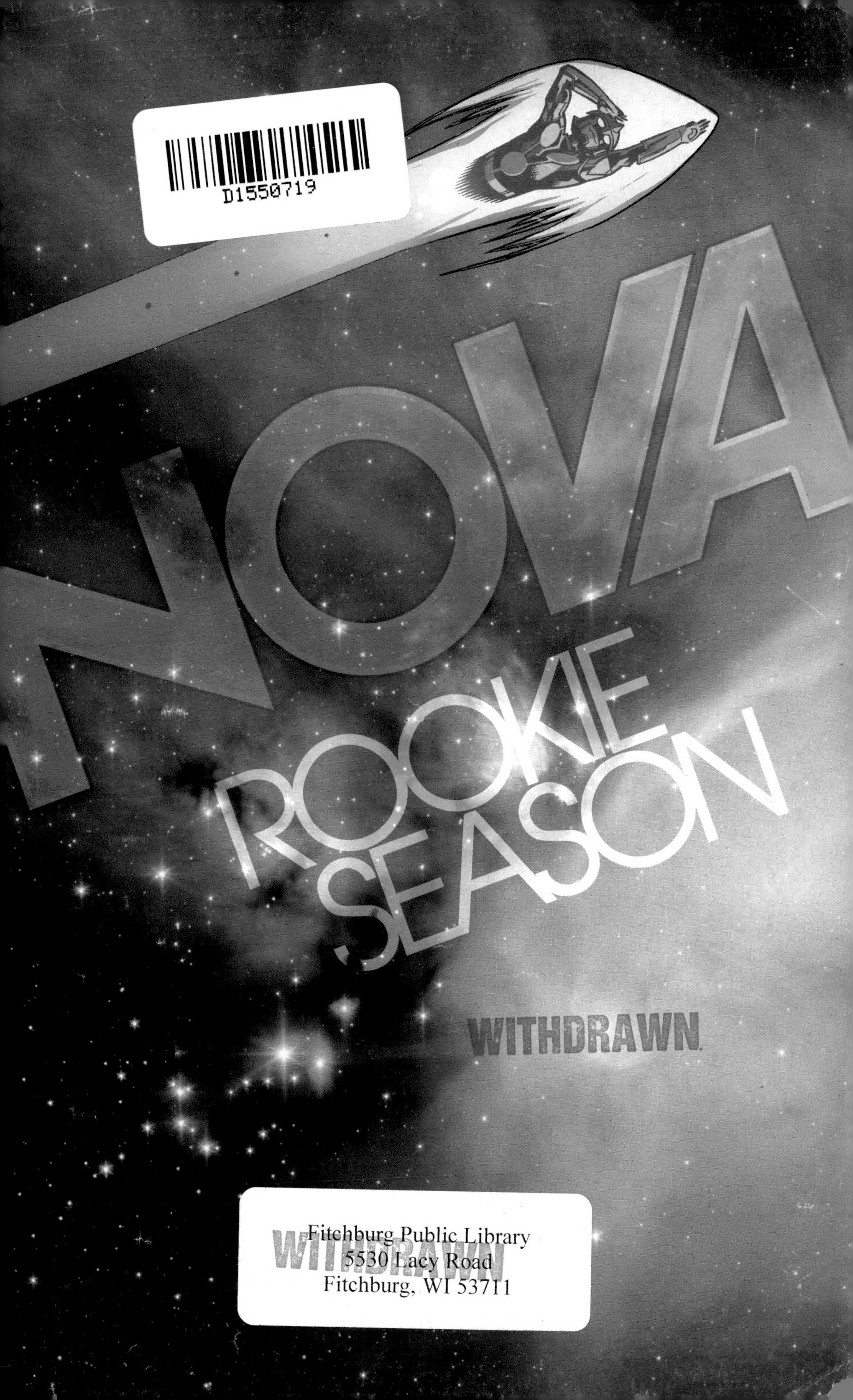
NOVA
ROOKIE SEASON

ROOKIE SEASON

WRITER   ZEB WELLS

ISSUES #6-9
PENCILER   ED McGUINNESS
INKER   JUAN VLASCO
COVER ART   ED McGUINNESS, DEXTER VINES & MARTE GRACIA

ISSUE #10
PENCILERS   CARLO BARBERI & DAVID LOPEZ
INKERS   JOHN LIVESAY, DAVID LOPEZ & TERRY PALLOT
COVER ART   ED McGUINNESS & MARTE GRACIA

COLORIST   DAVID CURIEL
LETTERS   COMICRAFT'S ALBERT DESCHESNE
ASSISTANT EDITORS   ELLIE PYLE & DEVIN LEWIS
EDITOR   STEPHEN WACKER

COLLECTION EDITOR   JENNIFER GRÜNWALD
ASSOCIATE MANAGING EDITOR   ALEX STARBUCK
EDITOR, SPECIAL PROJECTS   MARK D. BEAZLEY
SENIOR EDITOR, SPECIAL PROJECTS   JEFF YOUNGQUIST
SVP PRINT, SALES & MARKETING   DAVID GABRIEL

EDITOR IN CHIEF   AXEL ALONSO
CHIEF CREATIVE OFFICER   JOE QUESADA
PUBLISHER   DAN BUCKLEY
EXECUTIVE PRODUCER   ALAN FINE

NOVA VOL. 2: ROOKIE SEASON. Contains material originally published in magazine form as NOVA #6-9 and #10. First printing 2014. ISBN# 978-0-7851-6839-3. Published by MARVEL WORLDWIDE, INC., a subsidiary of MARVEL ENTERTAINMENT, LLC. OFFICE OF PUBLICATION: 135 West 50th Street, New York, NY 10020. Copyright © 2014 Marvel Characters, Inc. All rights reserved. All characters featured in this issue and the distinctive names and likenesses thereof, and all related indicia are trademarks of Marvel Characters, Inc. No similarity between any of the names, characters, persons, and/or institutions in this magazine with those of any living or dead person or institution is intended, and any such similarity which may exist is purely coincidental. **Printed in the U.S.A.** ALAN FINE, EVP - Office of the President, Marvel Worldwide, Inc. and EVP & CMO Marvel Characters B.V.; DAN BUCKLEY, Publisher & President - Print, Animation & Digital Divisions; JOE QUESADA, Chief Creative Officer; TOM BREVOORT, SVP of Publishing; DAVID BOGART, SVP of Operations & Procurement, Publishing; C.B. CEBULSKI, SVP of Creator & Content Development; DAVID GABRIEL, SVP of Print & Digital Publishing Sales; JIM O'KEEFE, VP of Operations & Logistics; DAN CARR, Executive Director of Publishing Technology; SUSAN CRESPI, Editorial Operations Manager; ALEX MORALES, Publishing Operations Manager; STAN LEE, Chairman Emeritus. For information regarding advertising in Marvel Comics or on Marvel.com, please contact Niza Disla, Director of Marvel Partnerships, at ndisla@marvel.com. For Marvel subscription inquiries, please contact 800-217-9158. Manufactured between 1/3/2014 and 2/17/2014 by R.R. DONNELLEY, INC., SALEM, VA, USA.

10 9 8 7 6 5 4 3 2 1

LEGO and the Minifigure figurine are trademarks or copyrights of the LEGO Group of Companies. ©2013 The LEGO Group. Characters featured in particular decorations are not commercial products and might not be available for purchase.

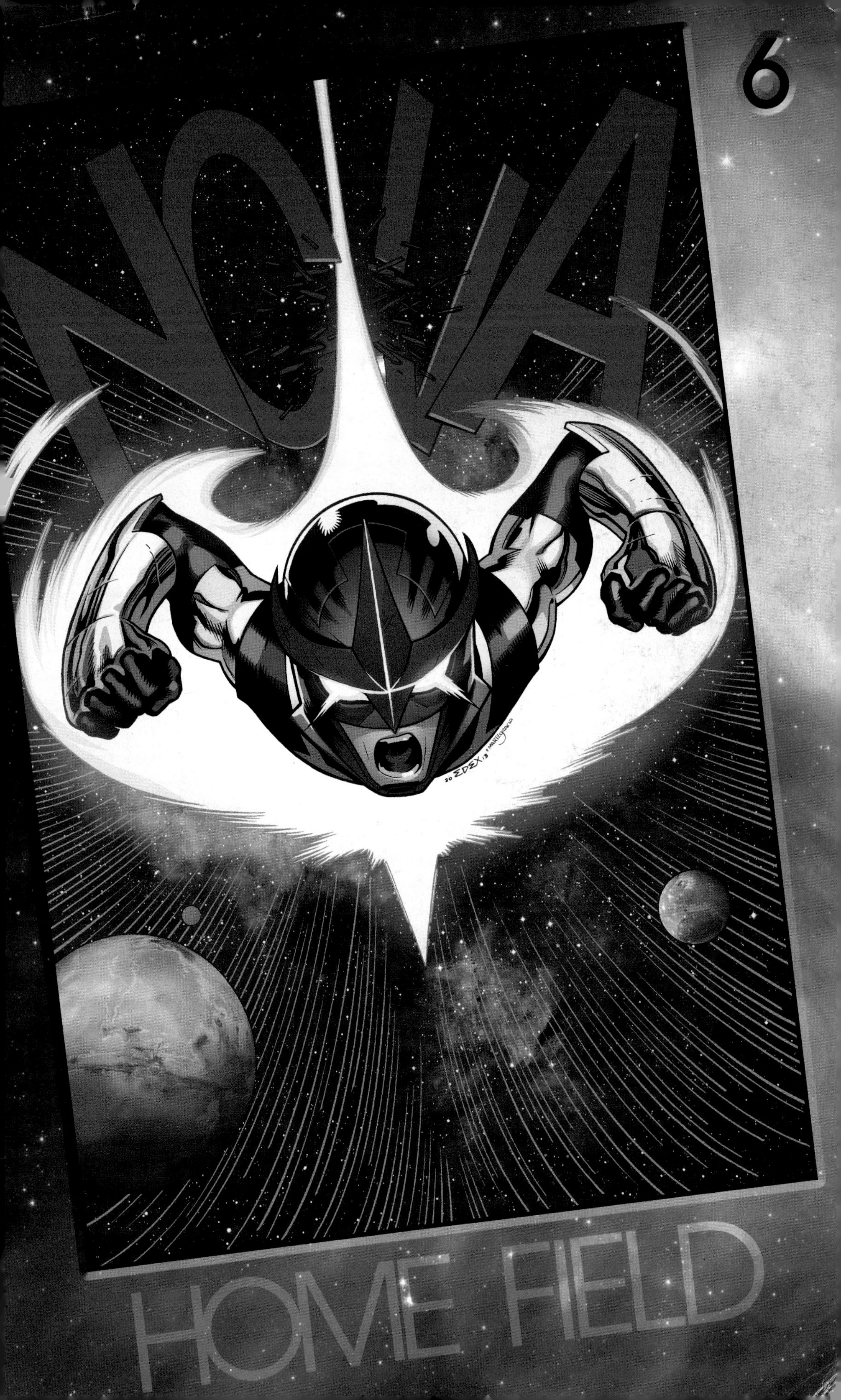

6
NOVA
HOME FIELD

PREVIOUSLY...

Things have been *CRAZY* for small-town Arizona kid *SAM ALEXANDER* lately. In just a few weeks, he has discovered that his missing father was a member of the *NOVA CORPS*, become a *NOVA* himself, explored outer space with galactic guardians *ROCKET RACCOON* and *GAMORA*, fought aliens, helped *THE AVENGERS* defeat the *PHOENIX FORCE*, and been invited to join the team by the one and only *THOR*!

Sam's ready to become the newest member of the Avengers. He just has to get permission from one person first...

...his *MOM*.

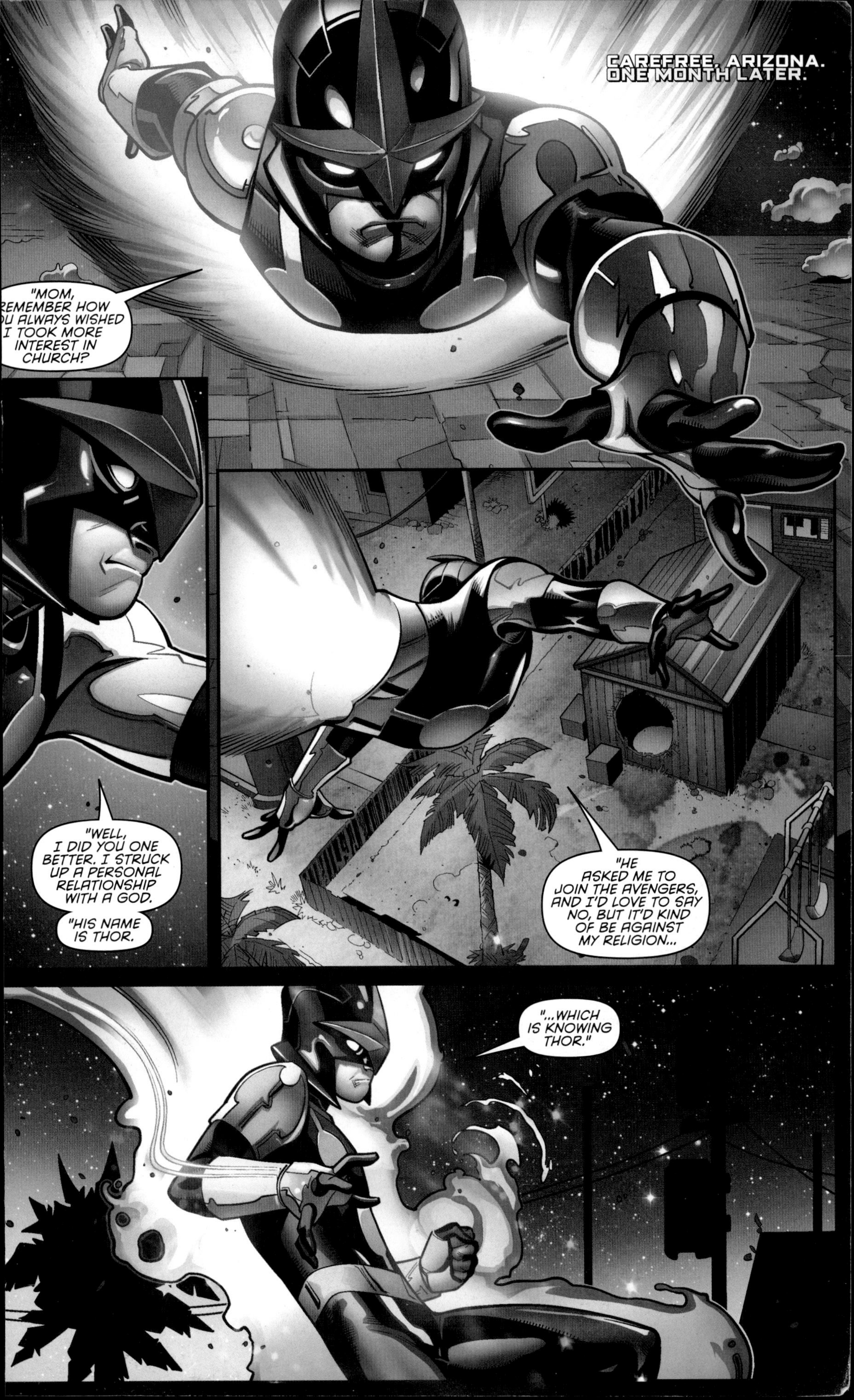
CAREFREE, ARIZONA. ONE MONTH LATER.
"MOM, REMEMBER HOW YOU ALWAYS WISHED I TOOK MORE INTEREST IN CHURCH?
"WELL, I DID YOU ONE BETTER. I STRUCK UP A PERSONAL RELATIONSHIP WITH A GOD.
"HIS NAME IS THOR.
"HE ASKED ME TO JOIN THE AVENGERS, AND I'D LOVE TO SAY NO, BUT IT'D KIND OF BE AGAINST MY RELIGION...
"...WHICH IS KNOWING THOR."

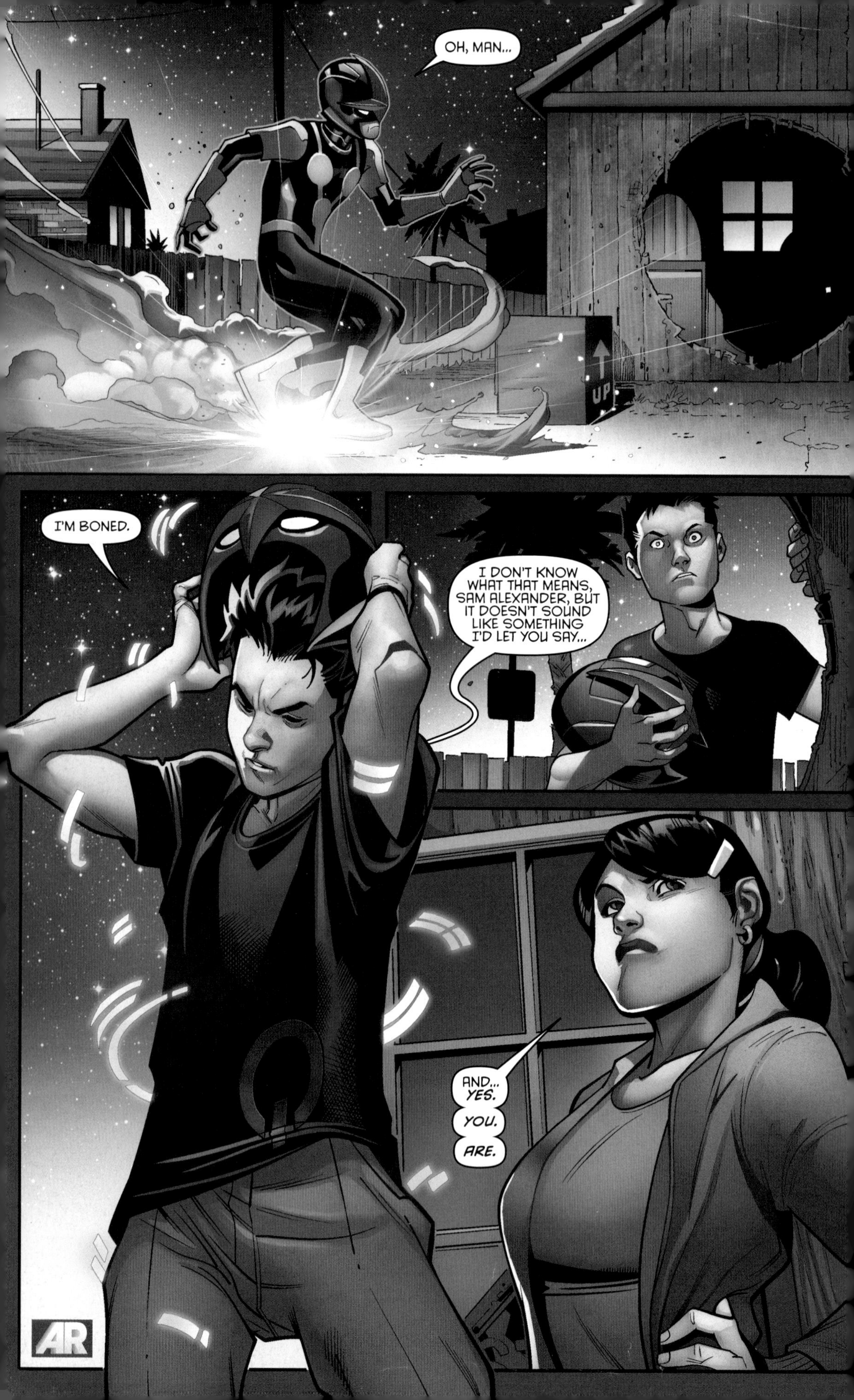
OH, MAN...
I'M BONED.
I DON'T KNOW WHAT THAT MEANS, SAM ALEXANDER, BUT IT DOESN'T SOUND LIKE SOMETHING I'D LET YOU SAY...
AND... YES.
YOU.
ARE.

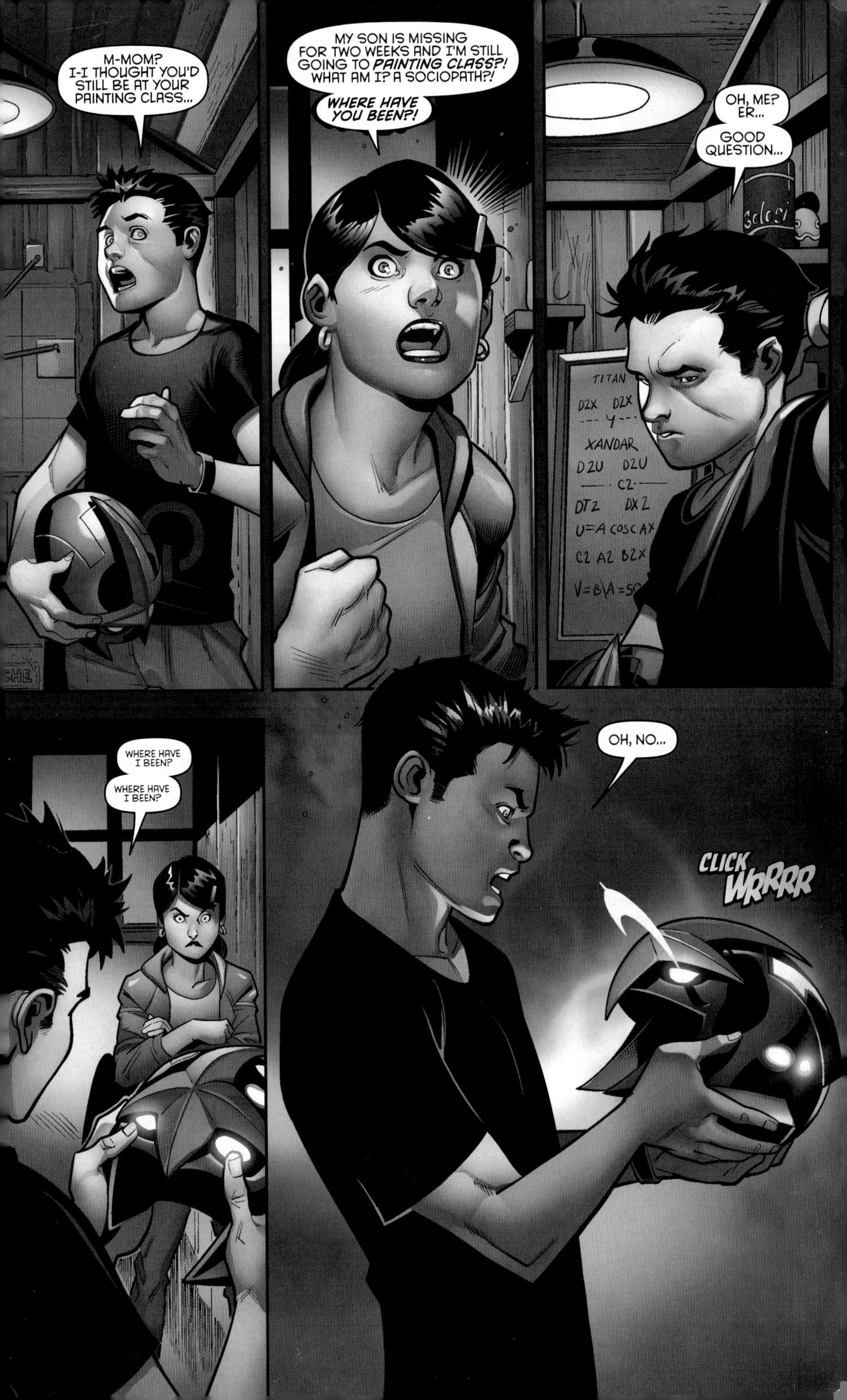
M-MOM? I-I THOUGHT YOU'D STILL BE AT YOUR PAINTING CLASS...
MY SON IS MISSING FOR TWO WEEKS AND I'M STILL GOING TO PAINTING CLASS?! WHAT AM I? A SOCIOPATH?!
WHERE HAVE YOU BEEN?!
OH, ME? ER...
GOOD QUESTION...
TITAN
D2X D2X
Y
XANDAR
D2U D2U
C2
DT2 DX2
U=A COSCAX
C2 A2 B2X
V=B\A=5
WHERE HAVE I BEEN?
WHERE HAVE I BEEN?
OH, NO...
CLICK
WRRRR

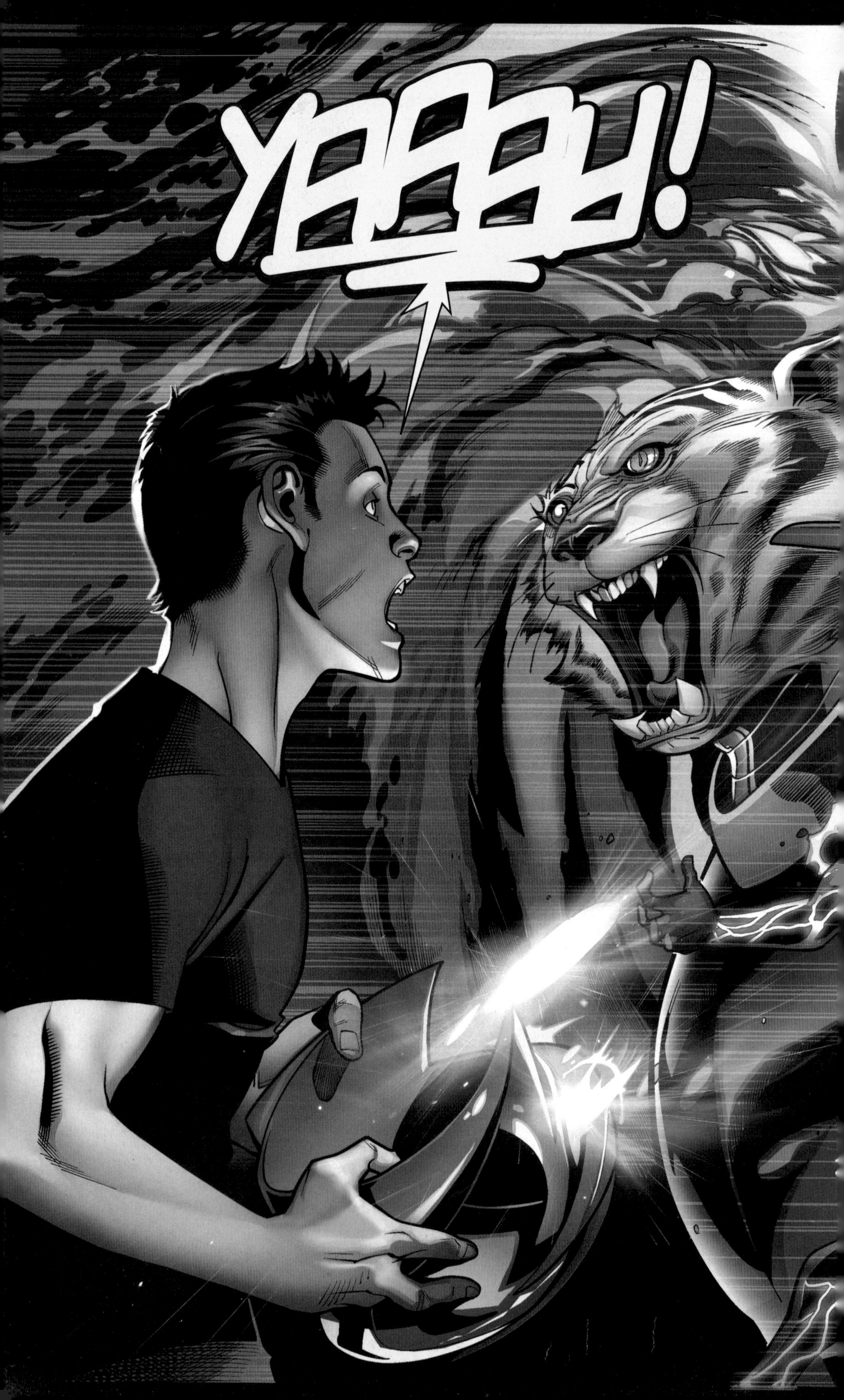
YAAAH!

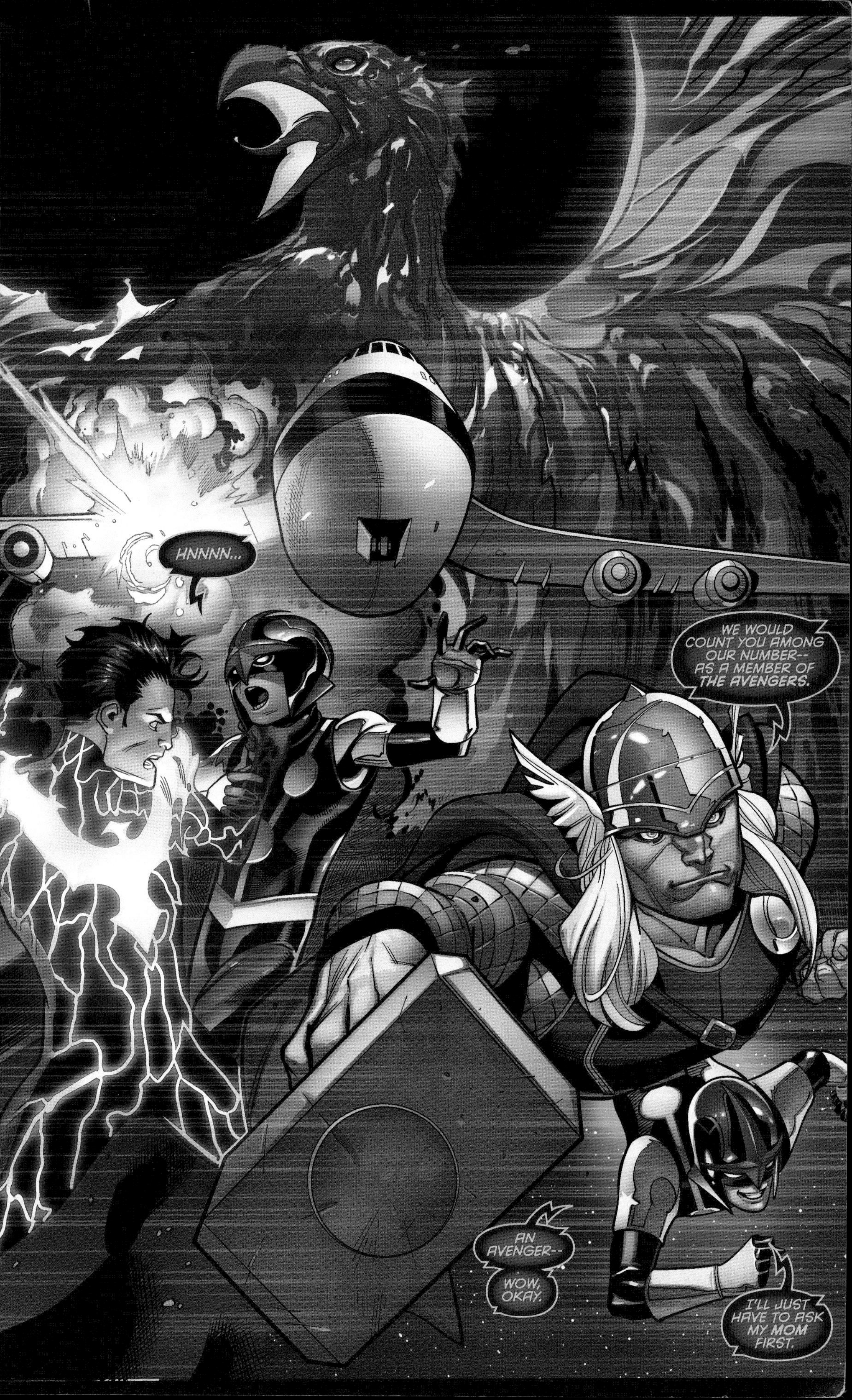
HNNNN...
WE WOULD COUNT YOU AMONG OUR NUMBER-- AS A MEMBER OF THE AVENGERS.
AN AVENGER--
WOW, OKAY.
I'LL JUST HAVE TO ASK MY MOM FIRST.

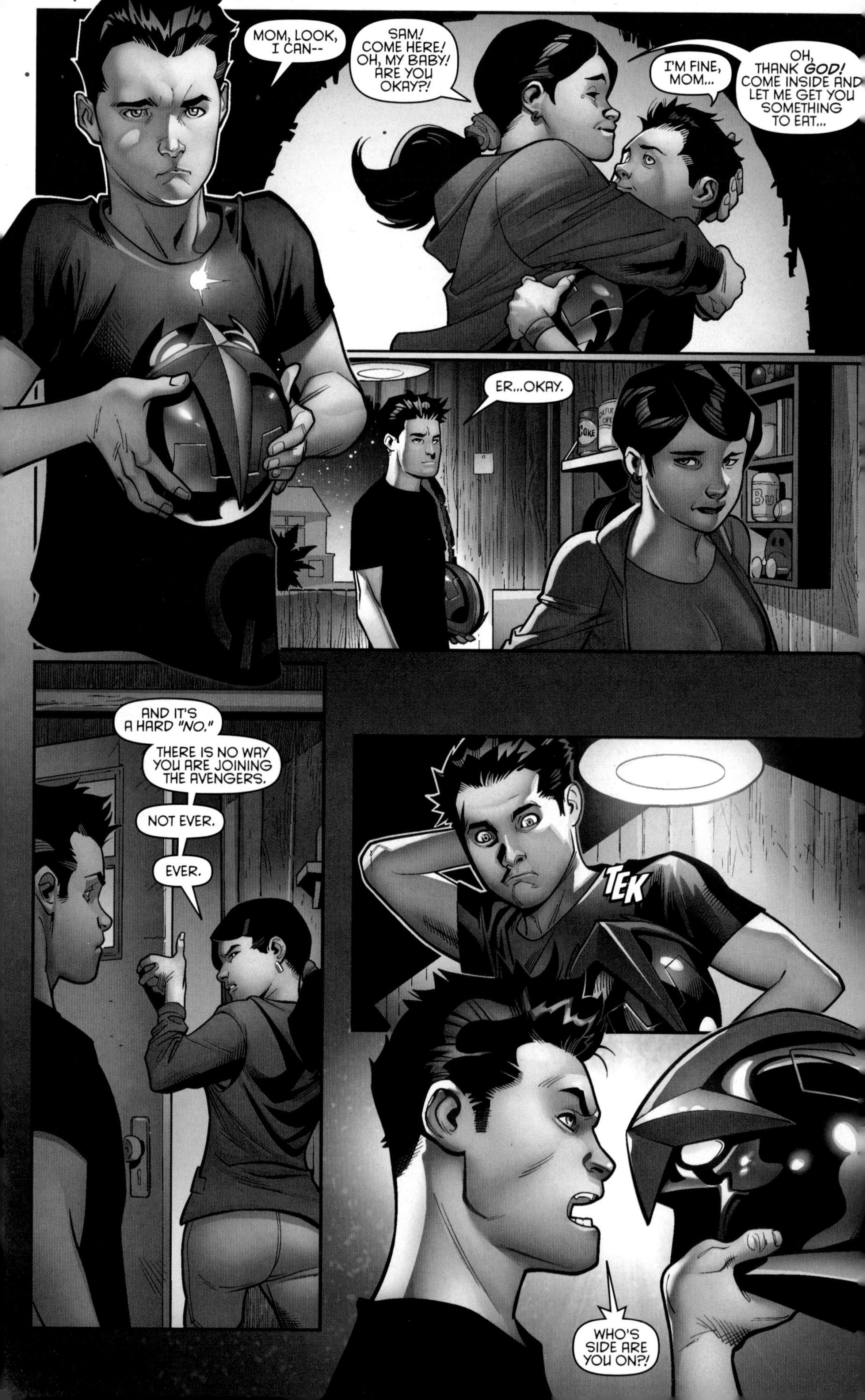
MOM, LOOK, I CAN--
SAM! COME HERE! OH, MY BABY! ARE YOU OKAY?!
I'M FINE, MOM...
OH, THANK GOD! COME INSIDE AND LET ME GET YOU SOMETHING TO EAT...
ER...OKAY.
AND IT'S A HARD "NO."
THERE IS NO WAY YOU ARE JOINING THE AVENGERS.
NOT EVER.
EVER.
TEK
WHO'S SIDE ARE YOU ON?!

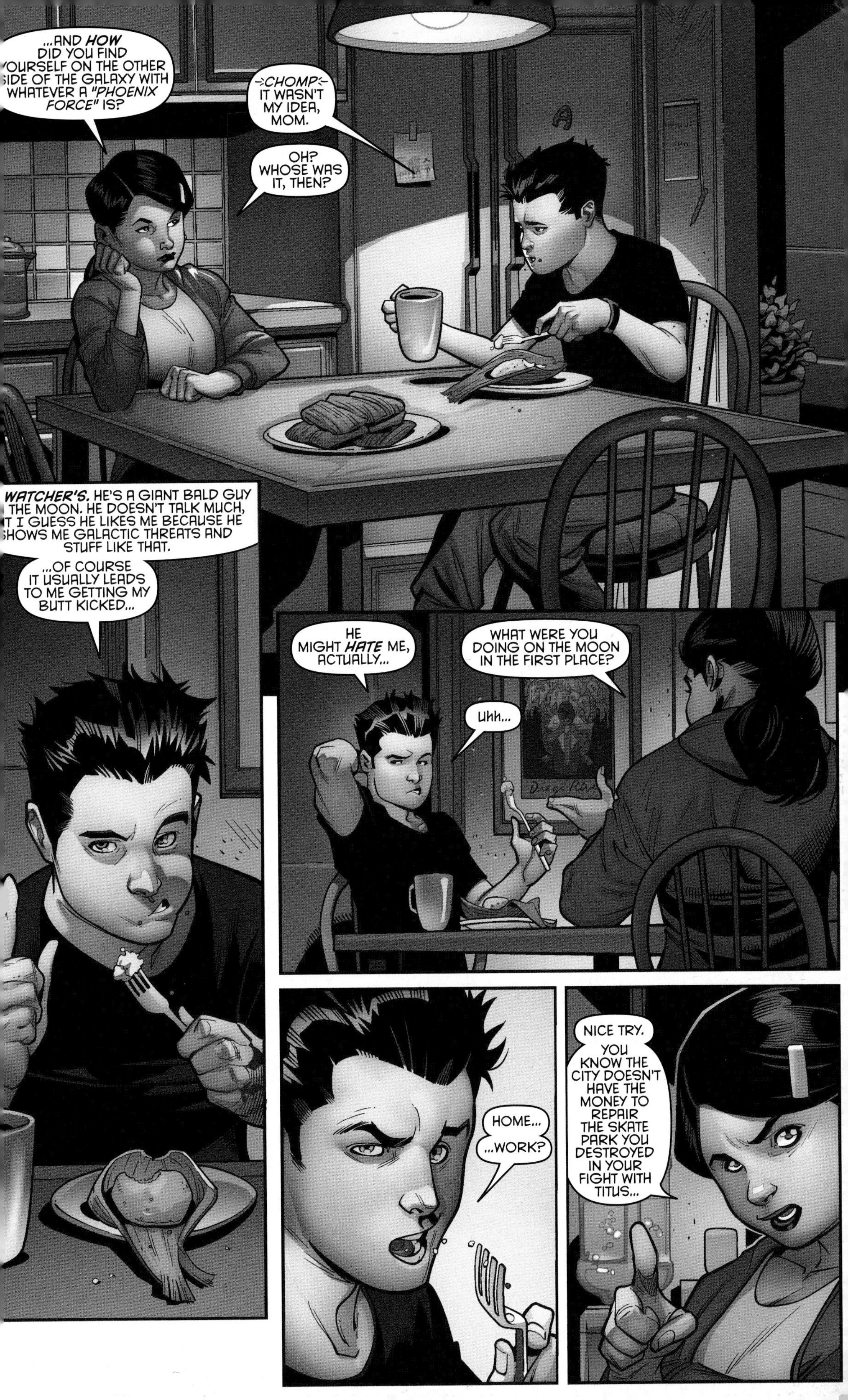
...AND HOW DID YOU FIND YOURSELF ON THE OTHER SIDE OF THE GALAXY WITH WHATEVER A "PHOENIX FORCE" IS?
-CHOMP- IT WASN'T MY IDEA, MOM.
OH? WHOSE WAS IT, THEN?
WATCHER'S. HE'S A GIANT BALD GUY THE MOON. HE DOESN'T TALK MUCH, T I GUESS HE LIKES ME BECAUSE HE SHOWS ME GALACTIC THREATS AND STUFF LIKE THAT.
...OF COURSE IT USUALLY LEADS TO ME GETTING MY BUTT KICKED...
HE MIGHT HATE ME, ACTUALLY...
WHAT WERE YOU DOING ON THE MOON IN THE FIRST PLACE?
Uhh...
HOME... ...WORK?
NICE TRY.
YOU KNOW THE CITY DOESN'T HAVE THE MONEY TO REPAIR THE SKATE PARK YOU DESTROYED IN YOUR FIGHT WITH TITUS...

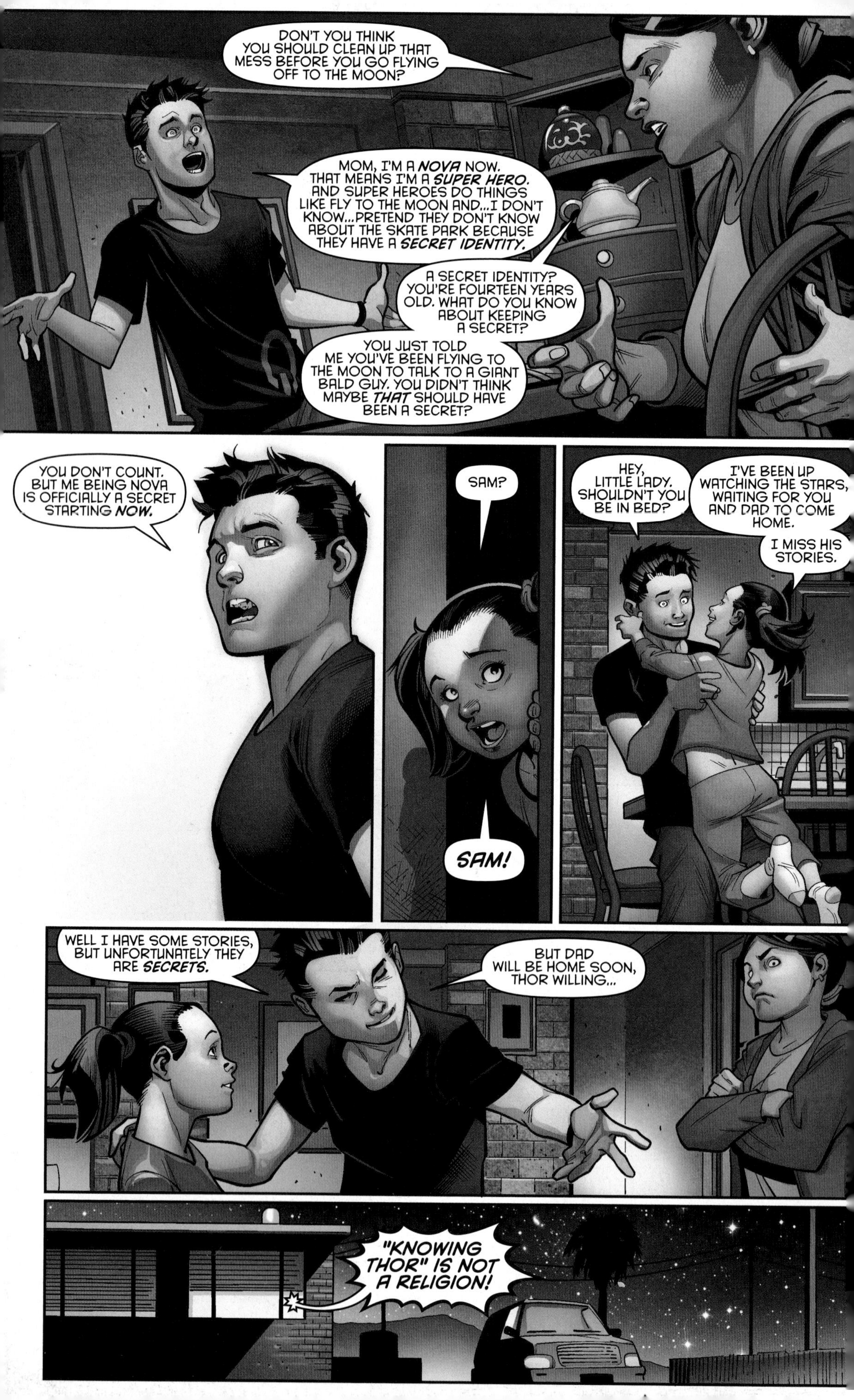
DON'T YOU THINK YOU SHOULD CLEAN UP THAT MESS BEFORE YOU GO FLYING OFF TO THE MOON?
MOM, I'M A NOVA NOW. THAT MEANS I'M A SUPER HERO. AND SUPER HEROES DO THINGS LIKE FLY TO THE MOON AND... I DON'T KNOW... PRETEND THEY DON'T KNOW ABOUT THE SKATE PARK BECAUSE THEY HAVE A SECRET IDENTITY.
A SECRET IDENTITY? YOU'RE FOURTEEN YEARS OLD. WHAT DO YOU KNOW ABOUT KEEPING A SECRET?
YOU JUST TOLD ME YOU'VE BEEN FLYING TO THE MOON TO TALK TO A GIANT BALD GUY. YOU DIDN'T THINK MAYBE THAT SHOULD HAVE BEEN A SECRET?
YOU DON'T COUNT. BUT ME BEING NOVA IS OFFICIALLY A SECRET STARTING NOW.
SAM?
SAM!
HEY, LITTLE LADY. SHOULDN'T YOU BE IN BED?
I'VE BEEN UP WATCHING THE STARS, WAITING FOR YOU AND DAD TO COME HOME.
I MISS HIS STORIES.
WELL I HAVE SOME STORIES, BUT UNFORTUNATELY THEY ARE SECRETS.
BUT DAD WILL BE HOME SOON, THOR WILLING...
"KNOWING THOR" IS NOT A RELIGION!

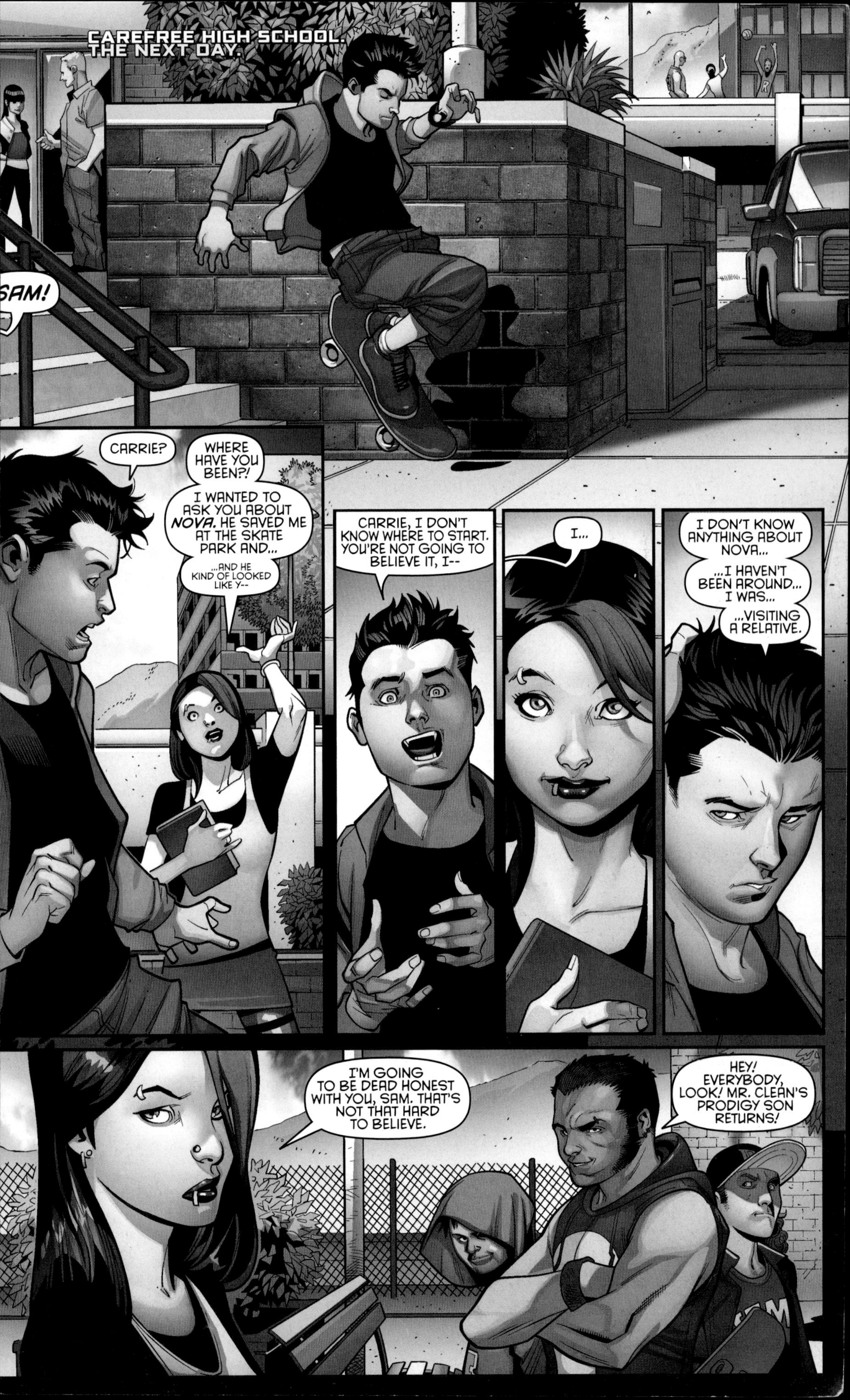
CAREFREE HIGH SCHOOL. THE NEXT DAY.
SAM!
CARRIE?
WHERE HAVE YOU BEEN?!
I WANTED TO ASK YOU ABOUT NOVA. HE SAVED ME AT THE SKATE PARK AND...
...AND HE KIND OF LOOKED LIKE Y--
CARRIE, I DON'T KNOW WHERE TO START. YOU'RE NOT GOING TO BELIEVE IT, I--
I...
I DON'T KNOW ANYTHING ABOUT NOVA...
...I HAVEN'T BEEN AROUND... I WAS...
...VISITING A RELATIVE.
I'M GOING TO BE DEAD HONEST WITH YOU, SAM. THAT'S NOT THAT HARD TO BELIEVE.
HEY! EVERYBODY, LOOK! MR. CLEAN'S PRODIGY SON RETURNS!

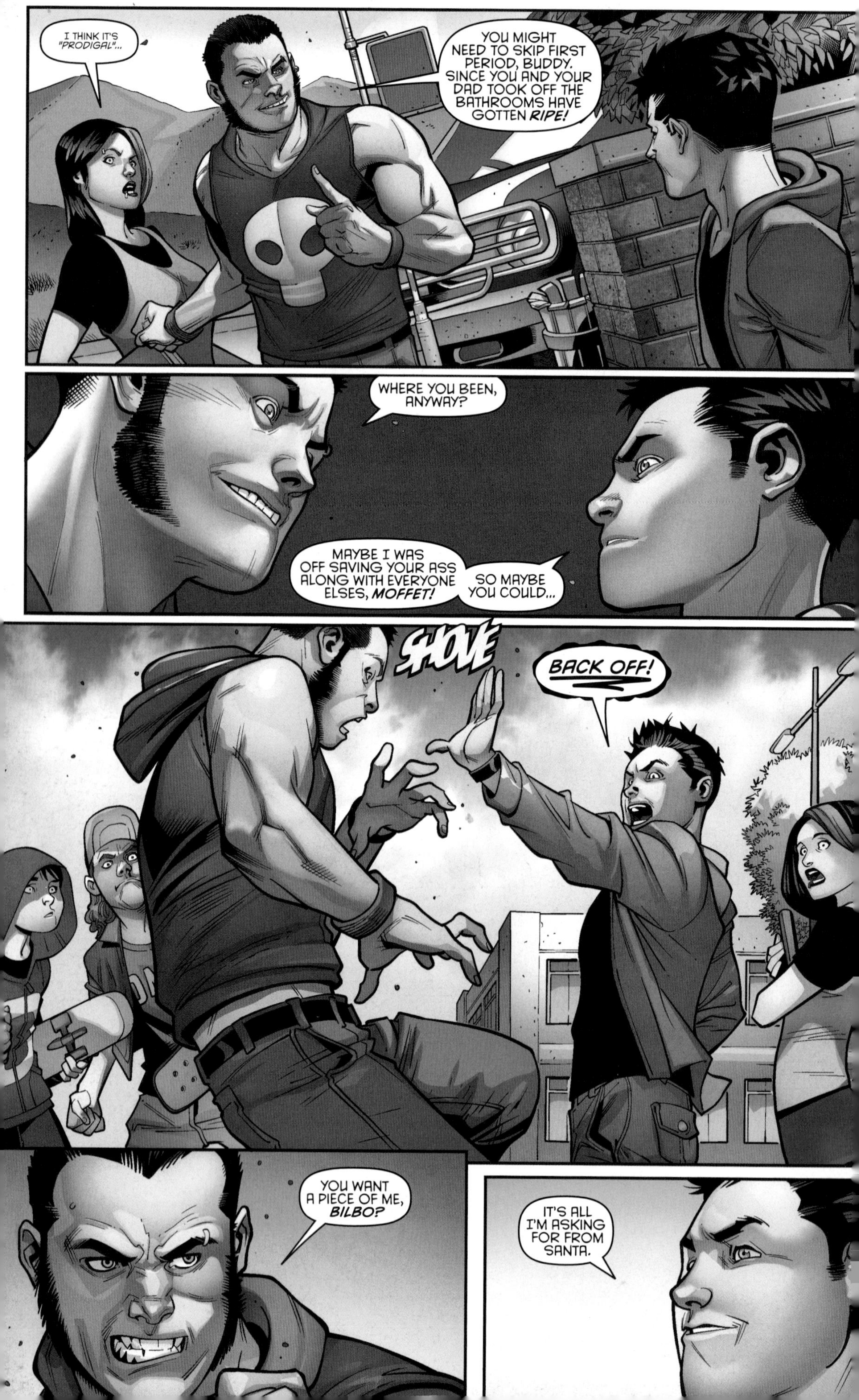
I THINK IT'S "PRODIGAL"...
YOU MIGHT NEED TO SKIP FIRST PERIOD, BUDDY. SINCE YOU AND YOUR DAD TOOK OFF THE BATHROOMS HAVE GOTTEN *RIPE!*
WHERE YOU BEEN, ANYWAY?
MAYBE I WAS OFF SAVING YOUR ASS ALONG WITH EVERYONE ELSES, *MOFFET!*
SO MAYBE YOU COULD...
SHOVE
BACK OFF!
YOU WANT A PIECE OF ME, *BILBO?*
IT'S ALL I'M ASKING FOR FROM SANTA.

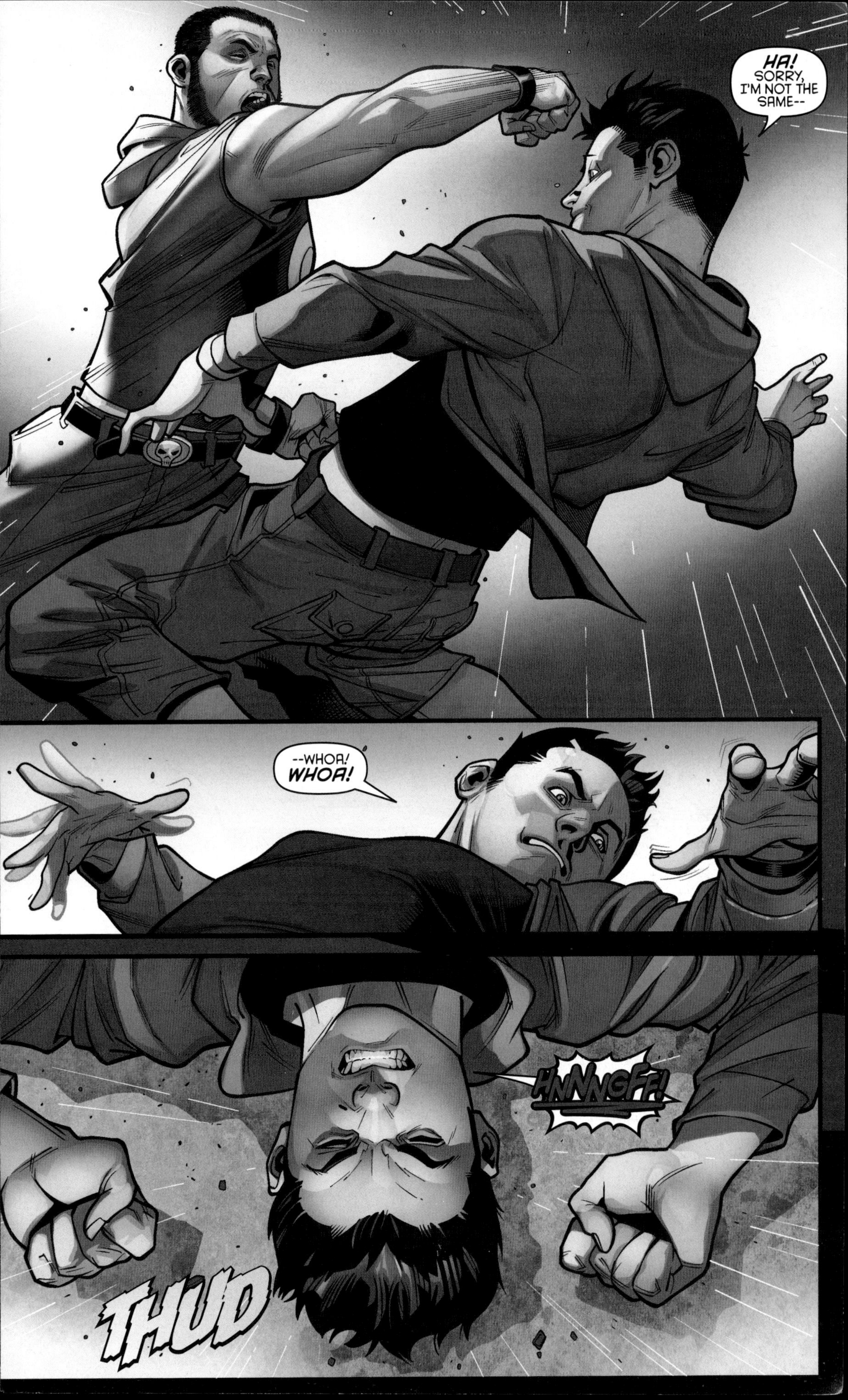
HA! SORRY, I'M NOT THE SAME--
--WHOA! WHOA!
HNNNGFF!
THUD

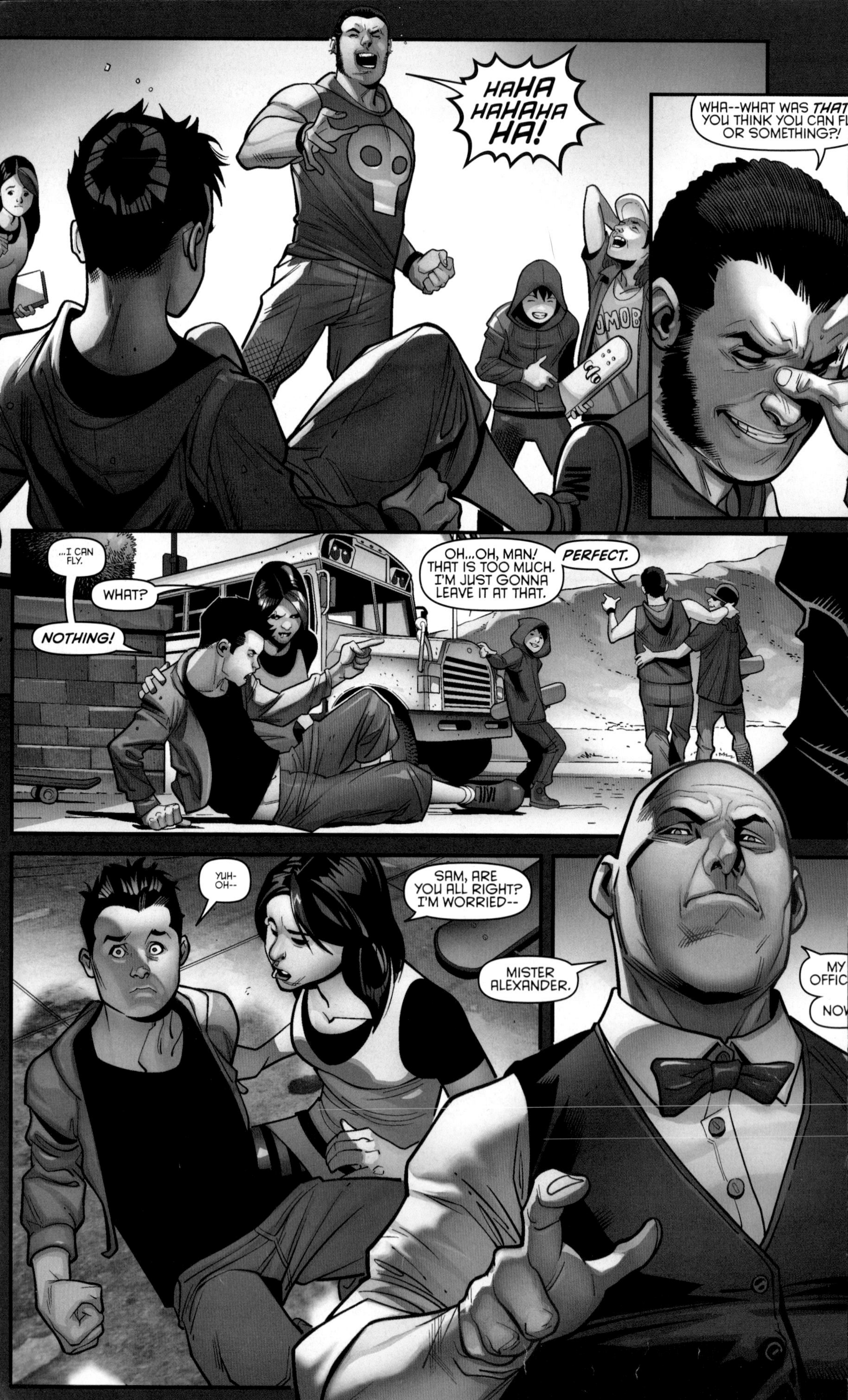

HAHA HAHAHA HA!
WHA--WHAT WAS THAT YOU THINK YOU CAN FL OR SOMETHING?!
...I CAN FLY.
WHAT?
NOTHING!
OH...OH, MAN! THAT IS TOO MUCH. I'M JUST GONNA LEAVE IT AT THAT.
PERFECT.
YUH-OH--
SAM, ARE YOU ALL RIGHT? I'M WORRIED--
MISTER ALEXANDER.
MY OFFIC
NOW

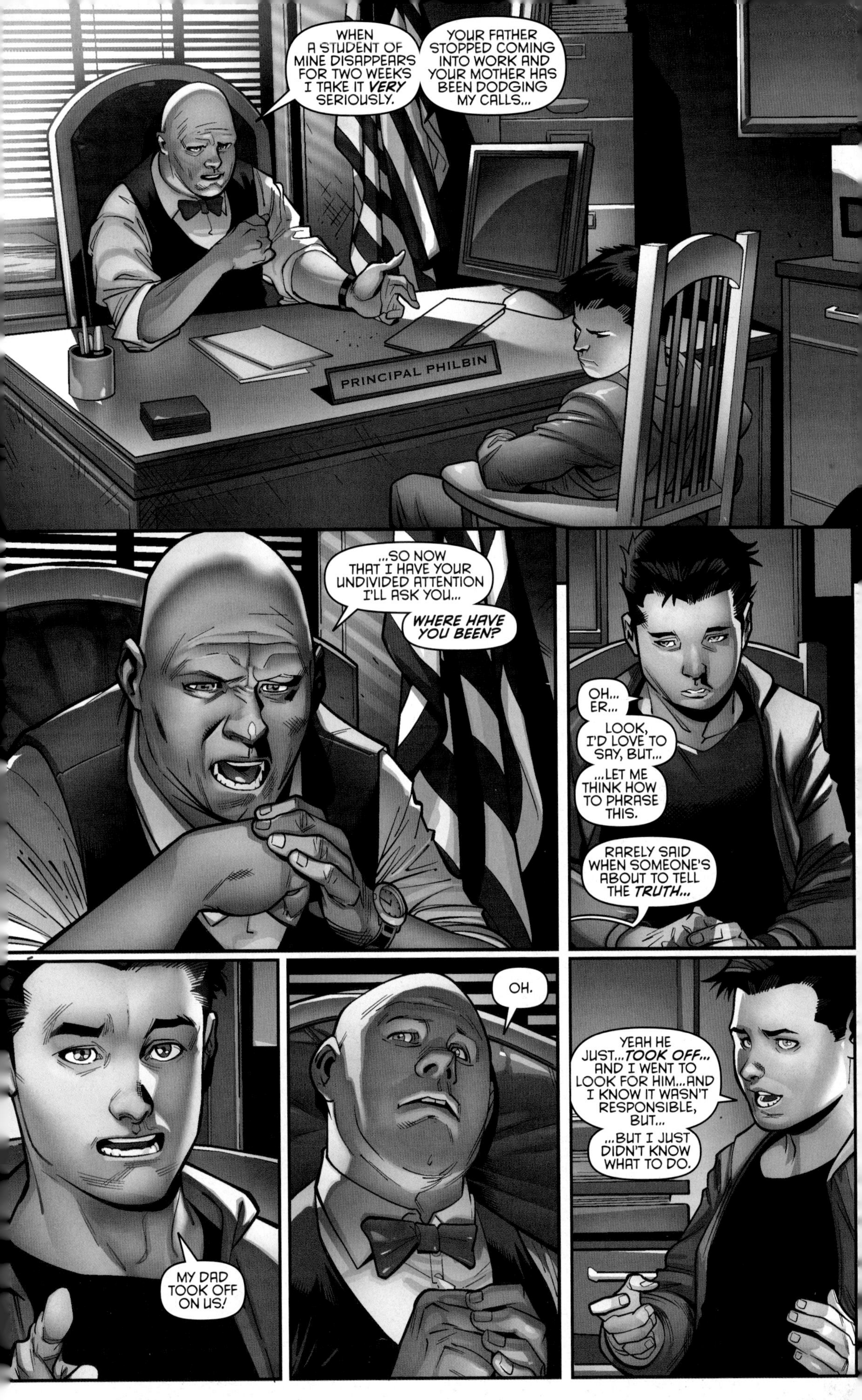
WHEN A STUDENT OF MINE DISAPPEARS FOR TWO WEEKS I TAKE IT VERY SERIOUSLY.
YOUR FATHER STOPPED COMING INTO WORK AND YOUR MOTHER HAS BEEN DODGING MY CALLS...
PRINCIPAL PHILBIN
...SO NOW THAT I HAVE YOUR UNDIVIDED ATTENTION I'LL ASK YOU...
WHERE HAVE YOU BEEN?
OH... ER...
LOOK, I'D LOVE TO SAY, BUT...
...LET ME THINK HOW TO PHRASE THIS.
RARELY SAID WHEN SOMEONE'S ABOUT TO TELL THE TRUTH...
MY DAD TOOK OFF ON US!
OH.
YEAH HE JUST...TOOK OFF...AND I WENT TO LOOK FOR HIM...AND I KNOW IT WASN'T RESPONSIBLE, BUT...
...BUT I JUST DIDN'T KNOW WHAT TO DO.

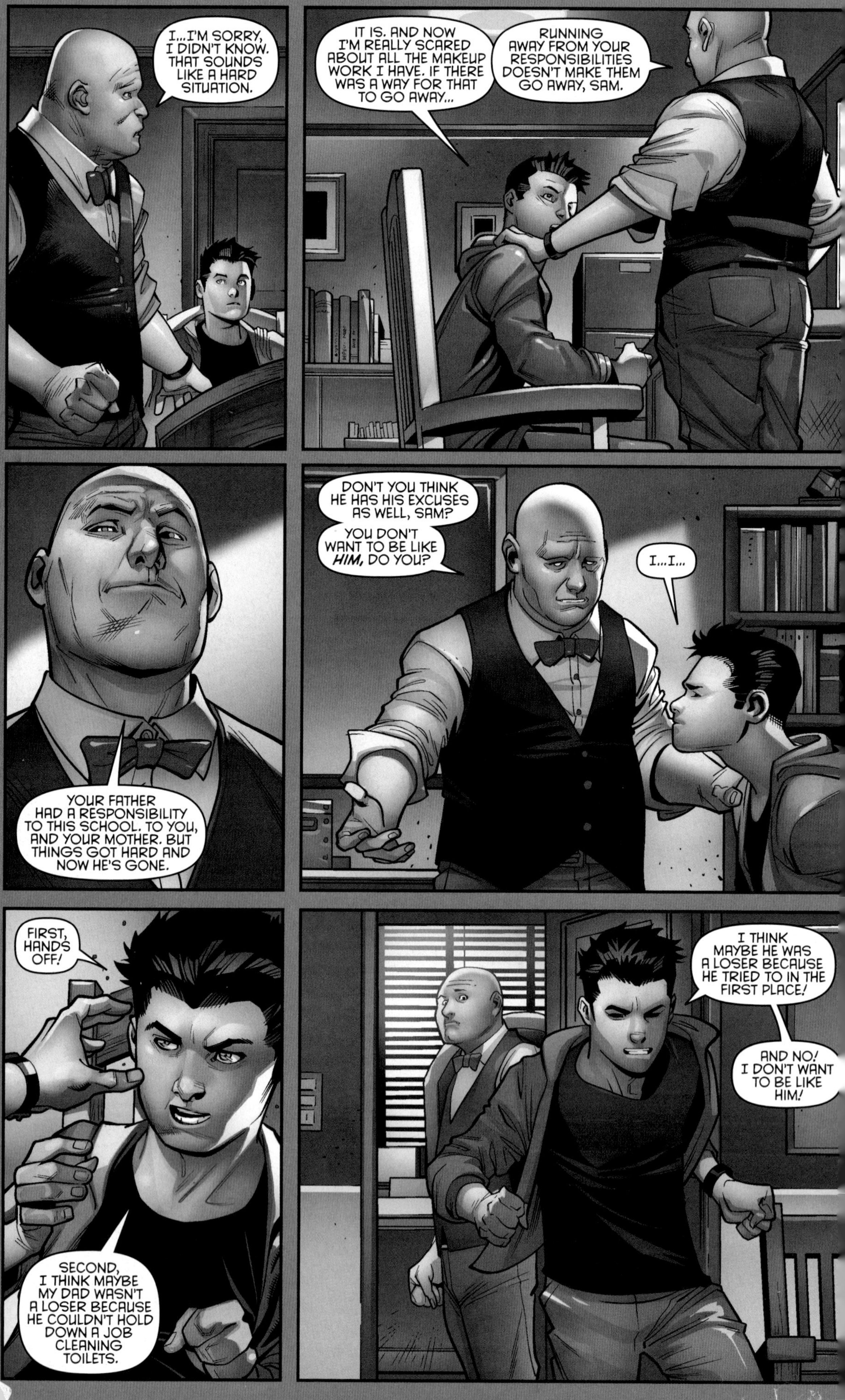
I...I'M SORRY, I DIDN'T KNOW. THAT SOUNDS LIKE A HARD SITUATION.
IT IS. AND NOW I'M REALLY SCARED ABOUT ALL THE MAKEUP WORK I HAVE. IF THERE WAS A WAY FOR THAT TO GO AWAY...
RUNNING AWAY FROM YOUR RESPONSIBILITIES DOESN'T MAKE THEM GO AWAY, SAM.
YOUR FATHER HAD A RESPONSIBILITY TO THIS SCHOOL. TO YOU, AND YOUR MOTHER. BUT THINGS GOT HARD AND NOW HE'S GONE.
DON'T YOU THINK HE HAS HIS EXCUSES AS WELL, SAM?
YOU DON'T WANT TO BE LIKE *HIM,* DO YOU?
I...I...
FIRST, HANDS OFF!
SECOND, I THINK MAYBE MY DAD WASN'T A LOSER BECAUSE HE COULDN'T HOLD DOWN A JOB CLEANING TOILETS.
I THINK MAYBE HE WAS A LOSER BECAUSE HE TRIED TO IN THE FIRST PLACE!
AND NO! I DON'T WANT TO BE LIKE HIM!

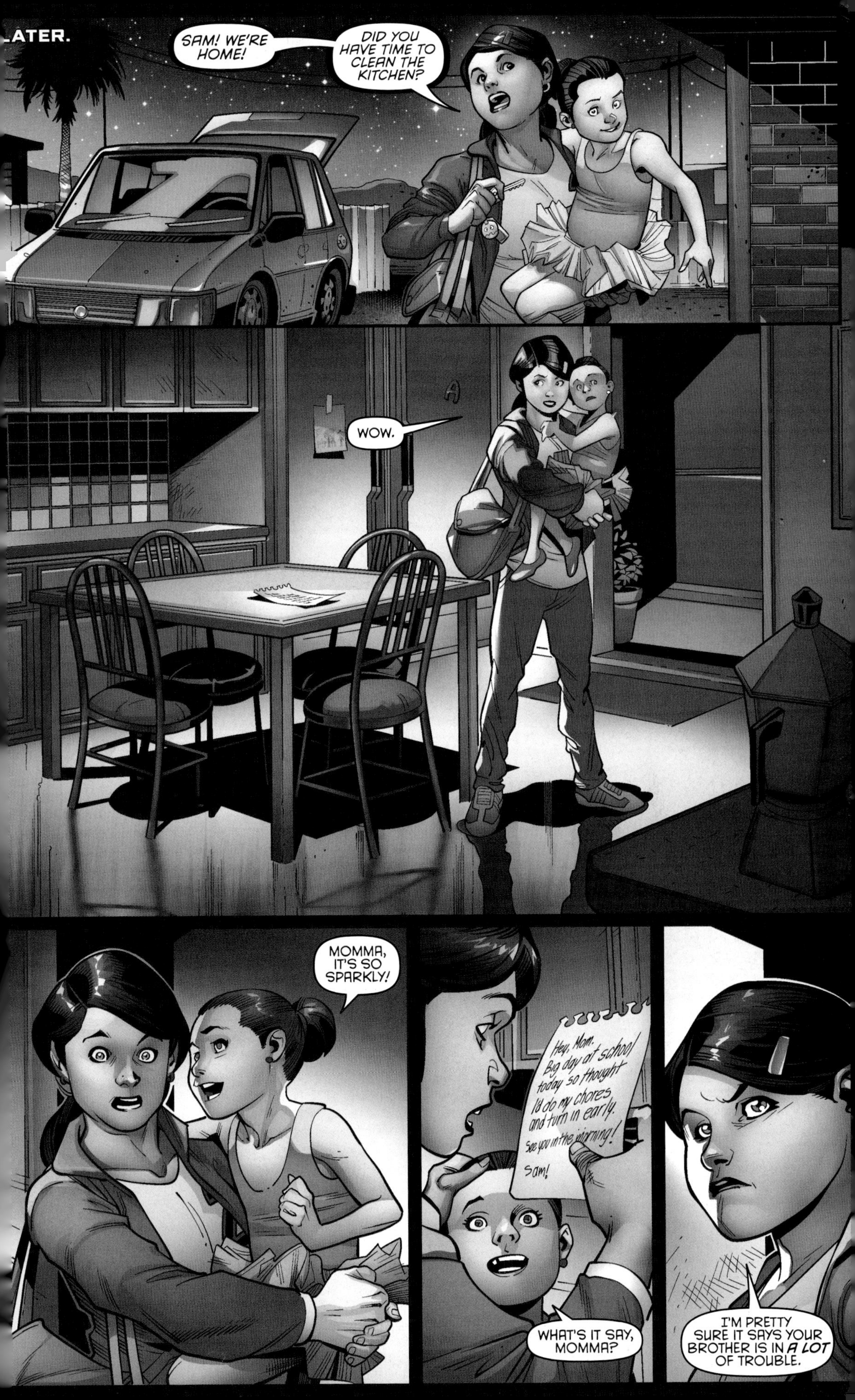
LATER.
SAM! WE'RE HOME!
DID YOU HAVE TIME TO CLEAN THE KITCHEN?
WOW.
MOMMA, IT'S SO SPARKLY!
Hey, Mom.
Big day at school today so thought I'd do my chores and turn in early.
See you in the morning!
Sam!
WHAT'S IT SAY, MOMMA?
I'M PRETTY SURE IT SAYS YOUR BROTHER IS IN A LOT OF TROUBLE.

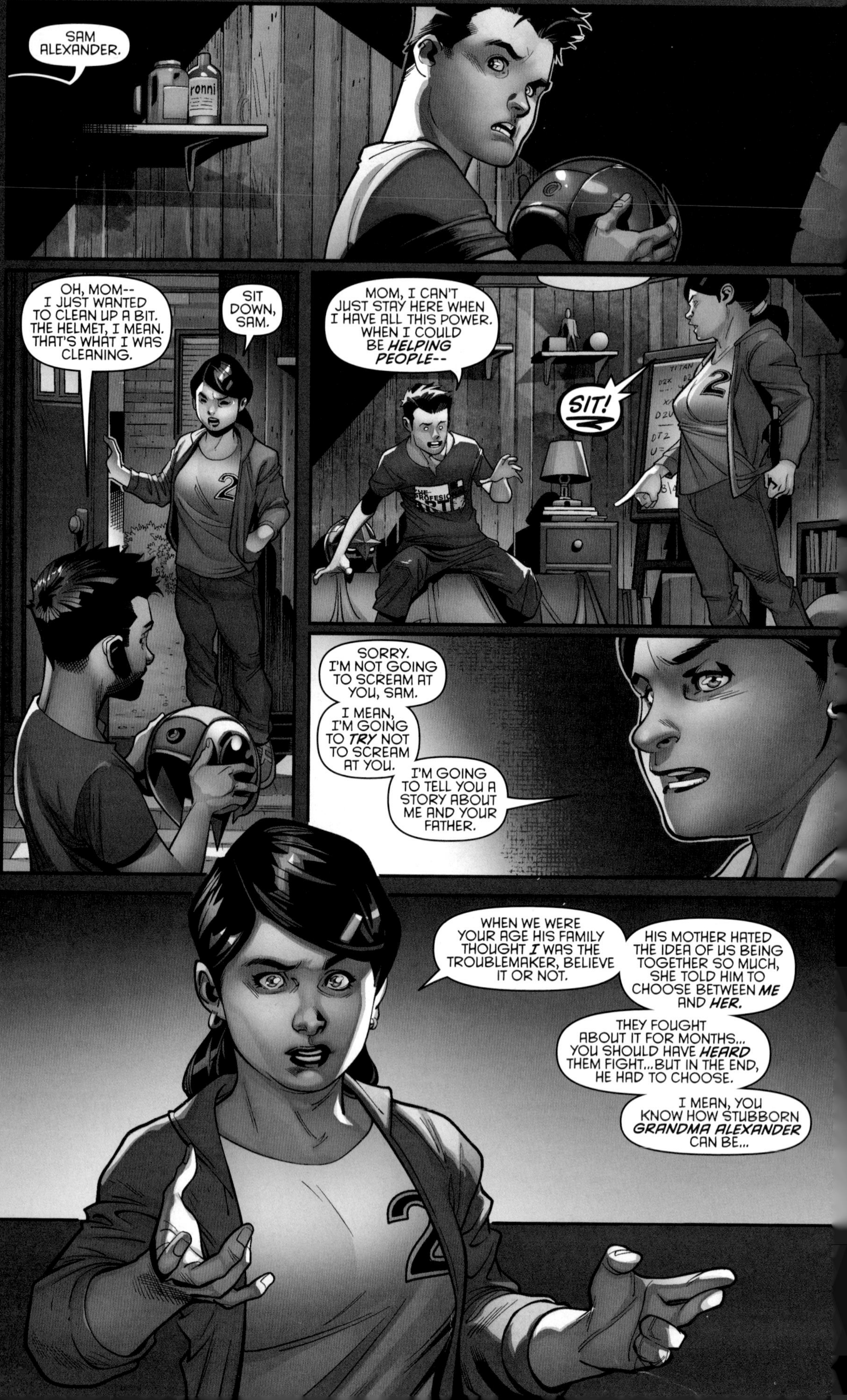
SAM ALEXANDER.
OH, MOM-- I JUST WANTED TO CLEAN UP A BIT. THE HELMET, I MEAN. THAT'S WHAT I WAS CLEANING.
SIT DOWN, SAM.
MOM, I CAN'T JUST STAY HERE WHEN I HAVE ALL THIS POWER. WHEN I COULD BE HELPING PEOPLE--
SIT!
SORRY. I'M NOT GOING TO SCREAM AT YOU, SAM.
I MEAN, I'M GOING TO TRY NOT TO SCREAM AT YOU.
I'M GOING TO TELL YOU A STORY ABOUT ME AND YOUR FATHER.
WHEN WE WERE YOUR AGE HIS FAMILY THOUGHT I WAS THE TROUBLEMAKER, BELIEVE IT OR NOT.
HIS MOTHER HATED THE IDEA OF US BEING TOGETHER SO MUCH, SHE TOLD HIM TO CHOOSE BETWEEN ME AND HER.
THEY FOUGHT ABOUT IT FOR MONTHS... YOU SHOULD HAVE HEARD THEM FIGHT...BUT IN THE END, HE HAD TO CHOOSE.
I MEAN, YOU KNOW HOW STUBBORN GRANDMA ALEXANDER CAN BE...

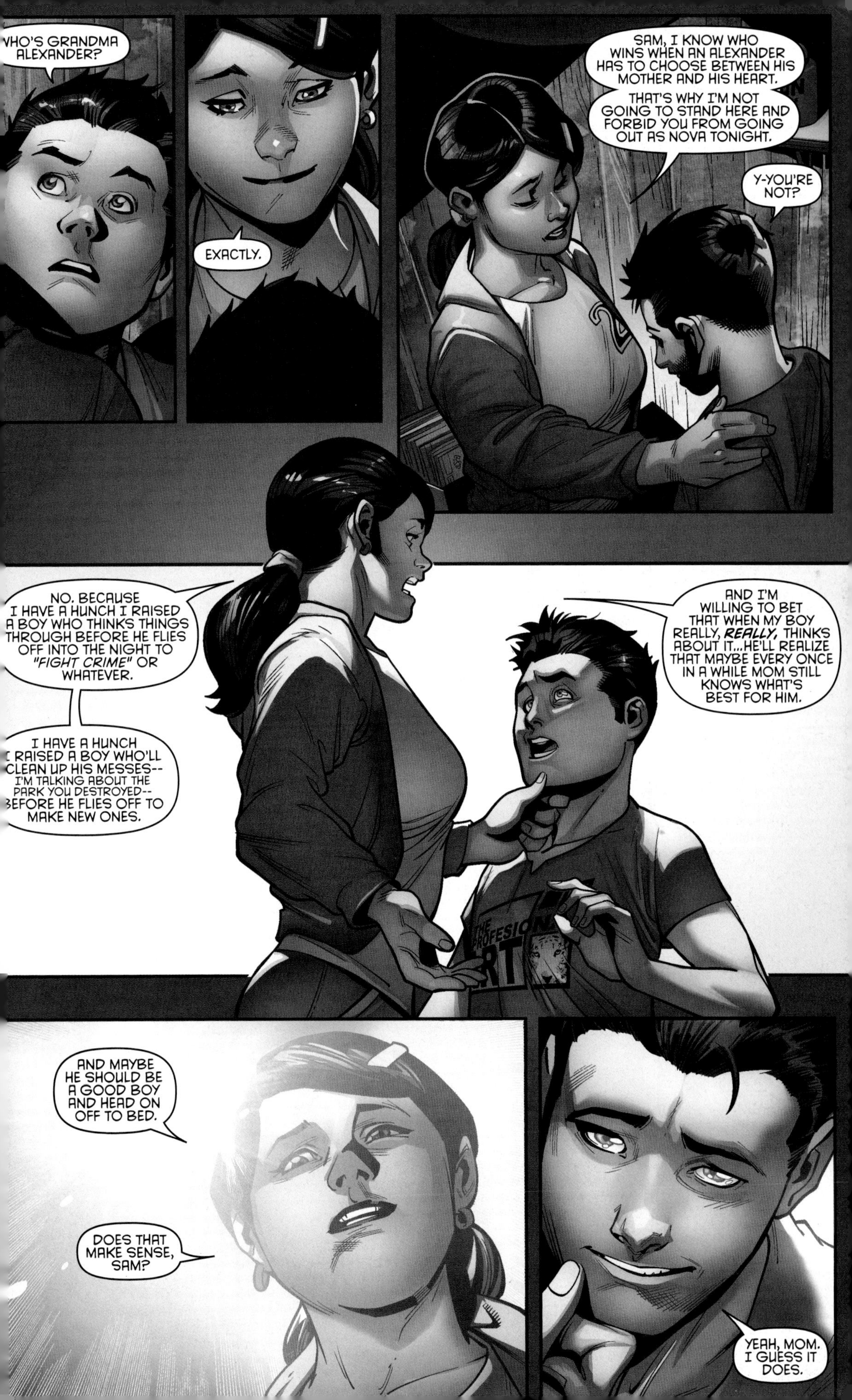
WHO'S GRANDMA ALEXANDER?
EXACTLY.
SAM, I KNOW WHO WINS WHEN AN ALEXANDER HAS TO CHOOSE BETWEEN HIS MOTHER AND HIS HEART.
THAT'S WHY I'M NOT GOING TO STAND HERE AND FORBID YOU FROM GOING OUT AS NOVA TONIGHT.
Y-YOU'RE NOT?
NO. BECAUSE I HAVE A HUNCH I RAISED A BOY WHO THINKS THINGS THROUGH BEFORE HE FLIES OFF INTO THE NIGHT TO "FIGHT CRIME" OR WHATEVER.
I HAVE A HUNCH I RAISED A BOY WHO'LL CLEAN UP HIS MESSES-- I'M TALKING ABOUT THE PARK YOU DESTROYED-- BEFORE HE FLIES OFF TO MAKE NEW ONES.
AND I'M WILLING TO BET THAT WHEN MY BOY REALLY, ***REALLY,*** THINKS ABOUT IT...HE'LL REALIZE THAT MAYBE EVERY ONCE IN A WHILE MOM STILL KNOWS WHAT'S BEST FOR HIM.
AND MAYBE HE SHOULD BE A GOOD BOY AND HEAD ON OFF TO BED.
DOES THAT MAKE SENSE, SAM?
YEAH, MOM. I GUESS IT DOES.

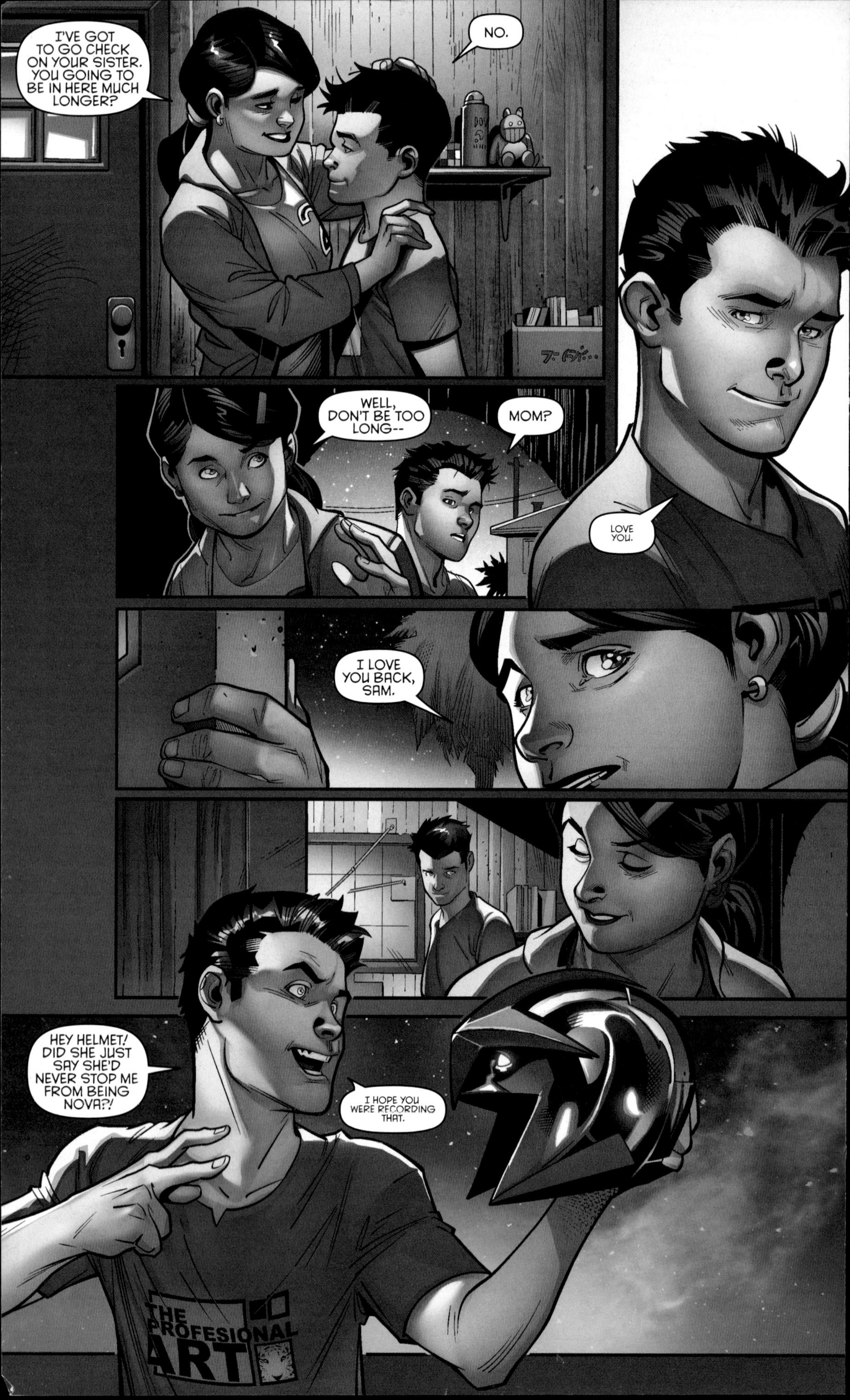
I'VE GOT TO GO CHECK ON YOUR SISTER. YOU GOING TO BE IN HERE MUCH LONGER?
NO.
WELL, DON'T BE TOO LONG--
MOM?
LOVE YOU.
I LOVE YOU BACK, SAM.
HEY HELMET! DID SHE JUST SAY SHE'D NEVER STOP ME FROM BEING NOVA?!
I HOPE YOU WERE RECORDING THAT.
THE PROFESIONAL ART

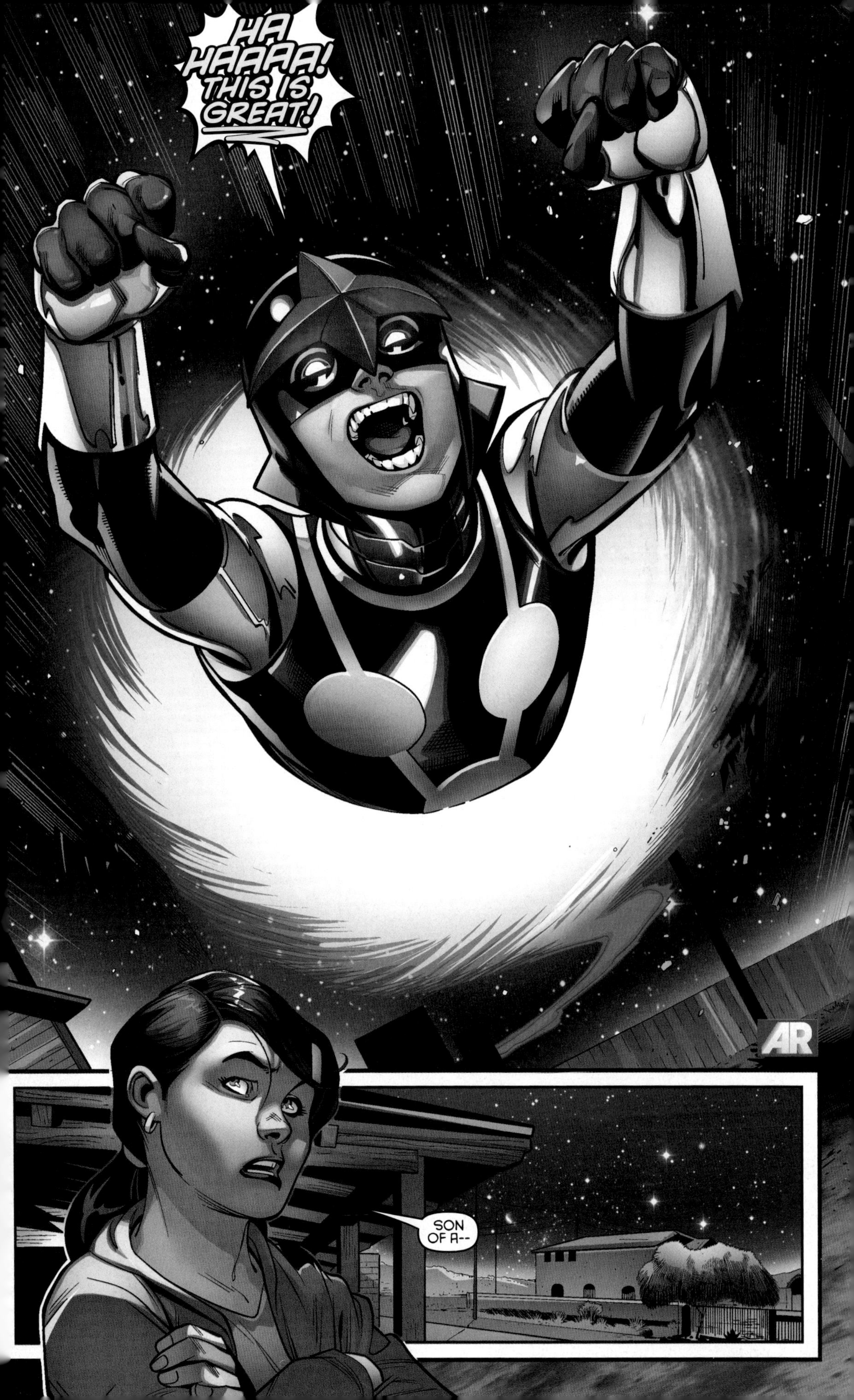
HA HAAAAA! THIS IS GREAT!
SON OF A--

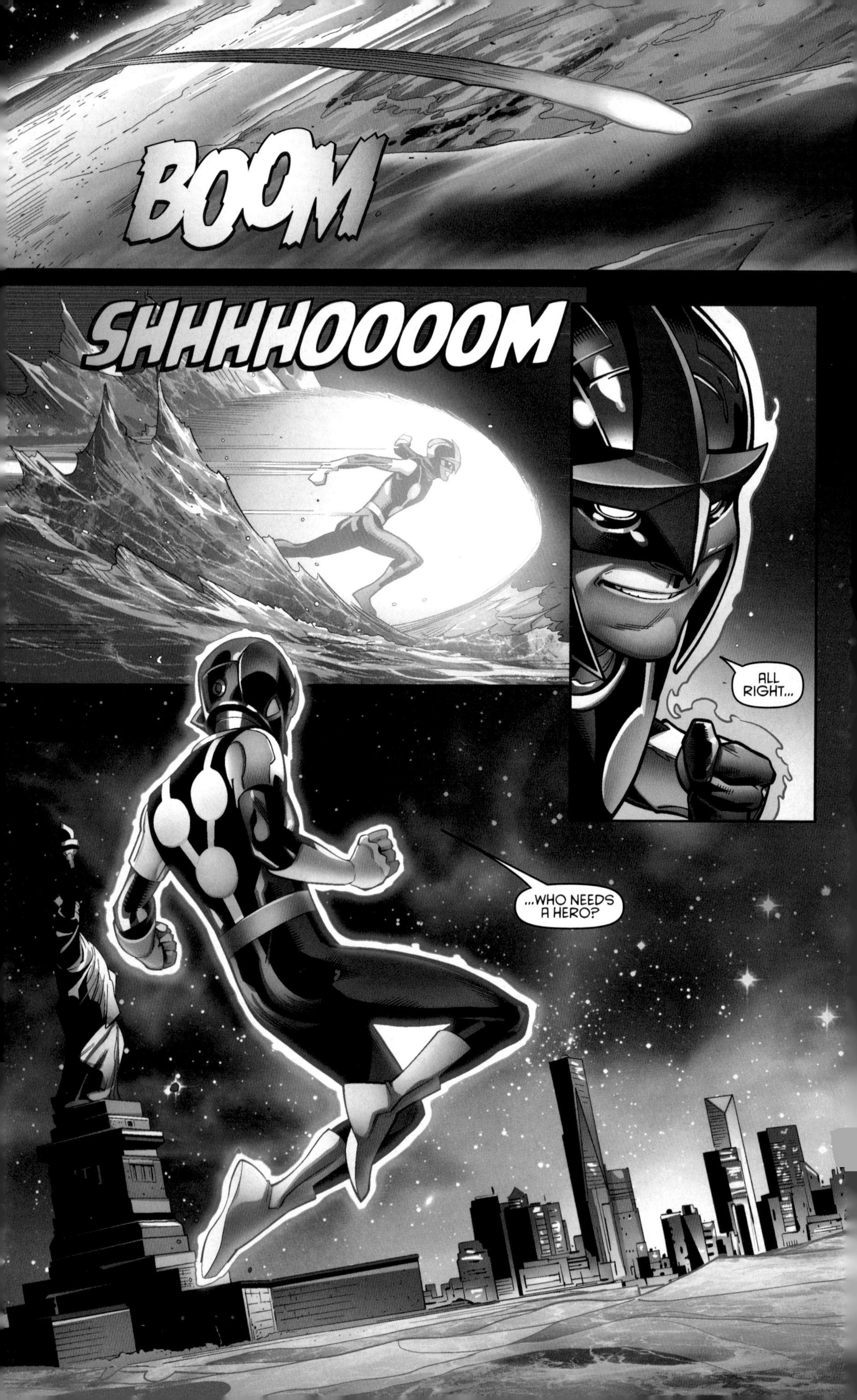
BOOM
SHHHHOOOOOM
ALL RIGHT...
...WHO NEEDS A HERO?

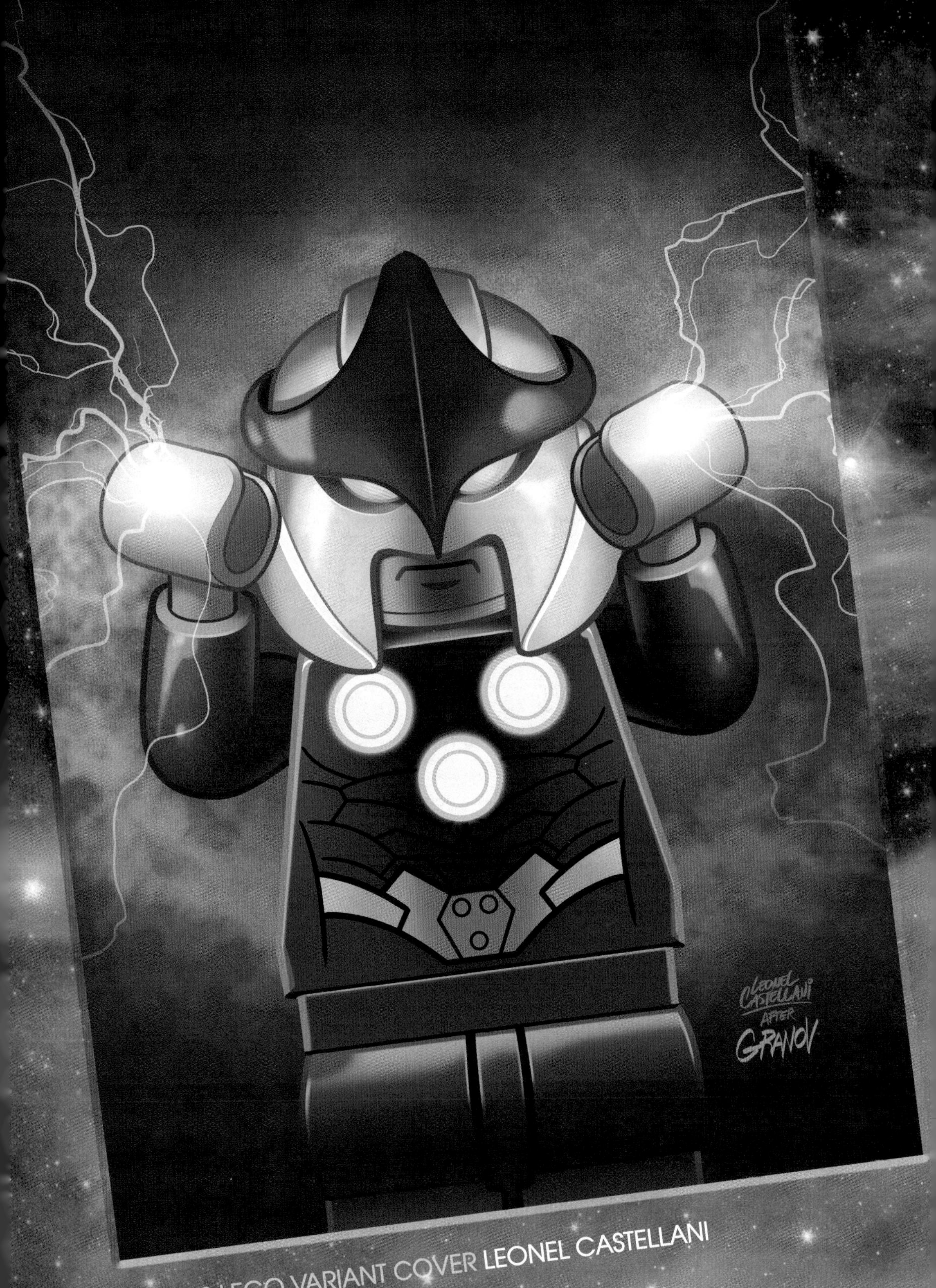
LEONEL CASTELLANI
AFTER
GRANOV

ISSUE #8 LEGO VARIANT COVER LEONEL CASTELLANI

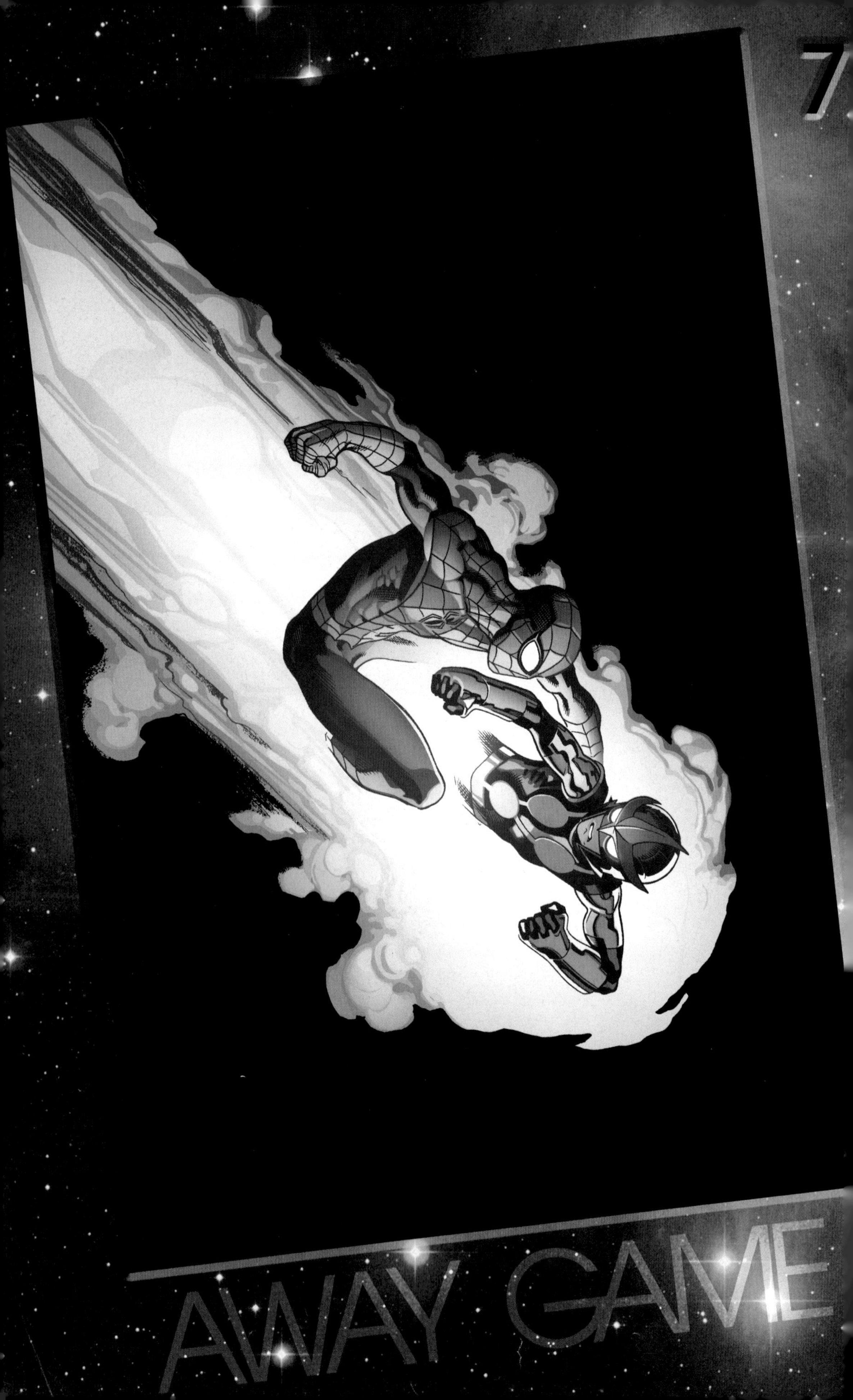

7
AWAY GAME

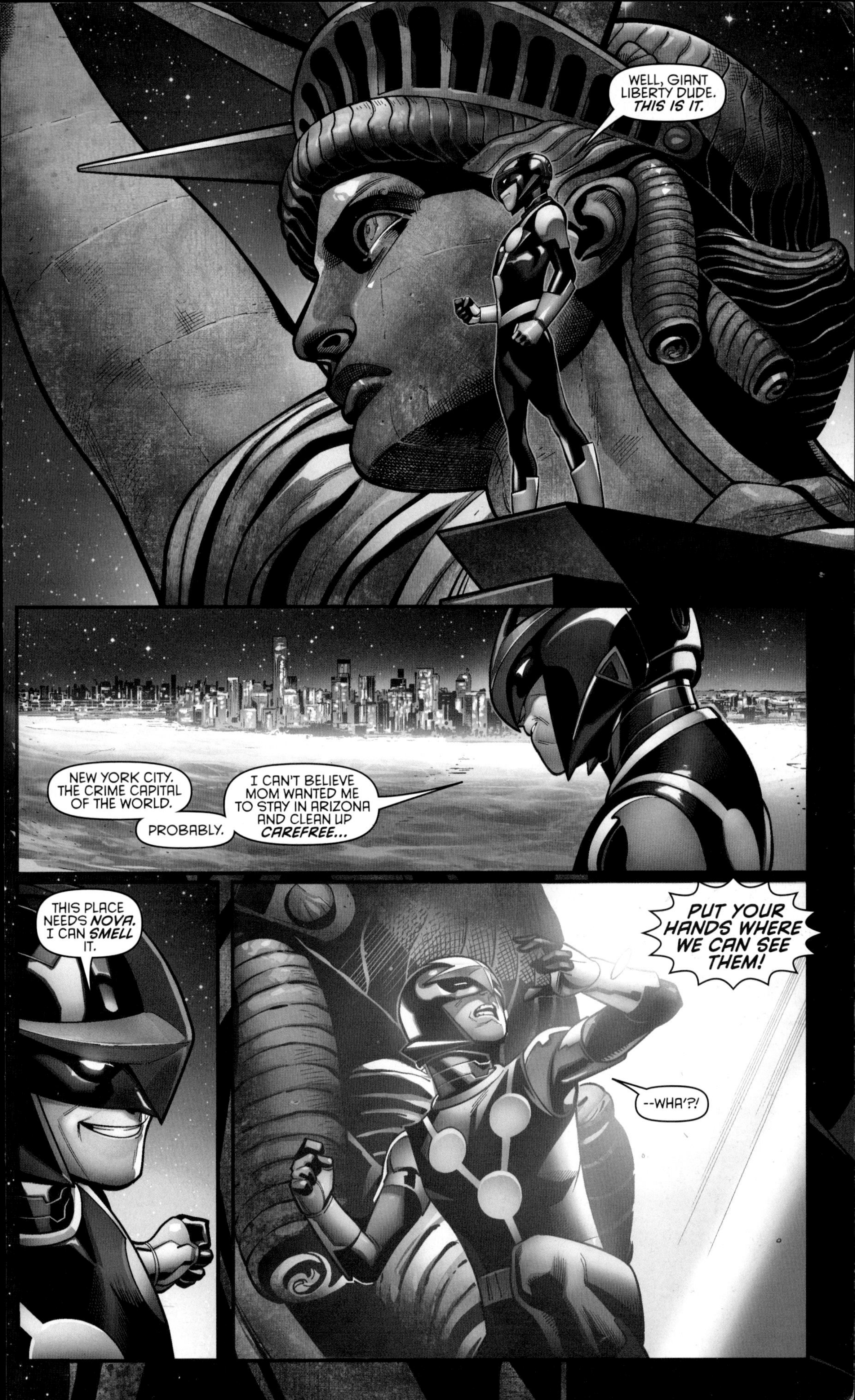
WELL, GIANT LIBERTY DUDE. THIS IS IT.
NEW YORK CITY. THE CRIME CAPITAL OF THE WORLD.
PROBABLY.
I CAN'T BELIEVE MOM WANTED ME TO STAY IN ARIZONA AND CLEAN UP CAREFREE...
THIS PLACE NEEDS NOVA. I CAN SMELL IT.
PUT YOUR HANDS WHERE WE CAN SEE THEM!
--WHA'?!

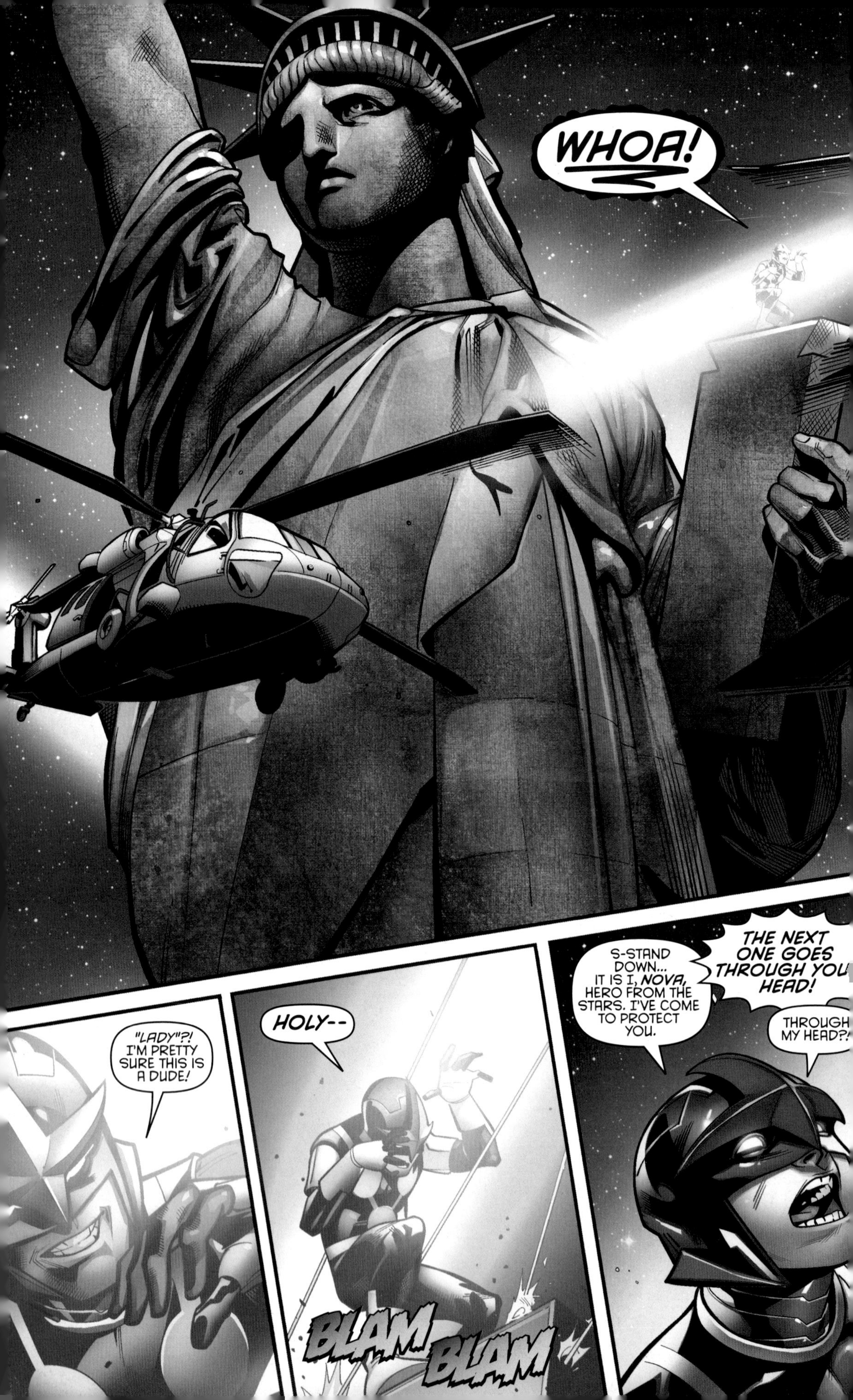
WHOA!
"LADY"?! I'M PRETTY SURE THIS IS A DUDE!
HOLY--
BLAM
BLAM
S-STAND DOWN... IT IS I, NOVA, HERO FROM THE STARS. I'VE COME TO PROTECT YOU.
THE NEXT ONE GOES THROUGH YOUR HEAD!
THROUGH MY HEAD?!

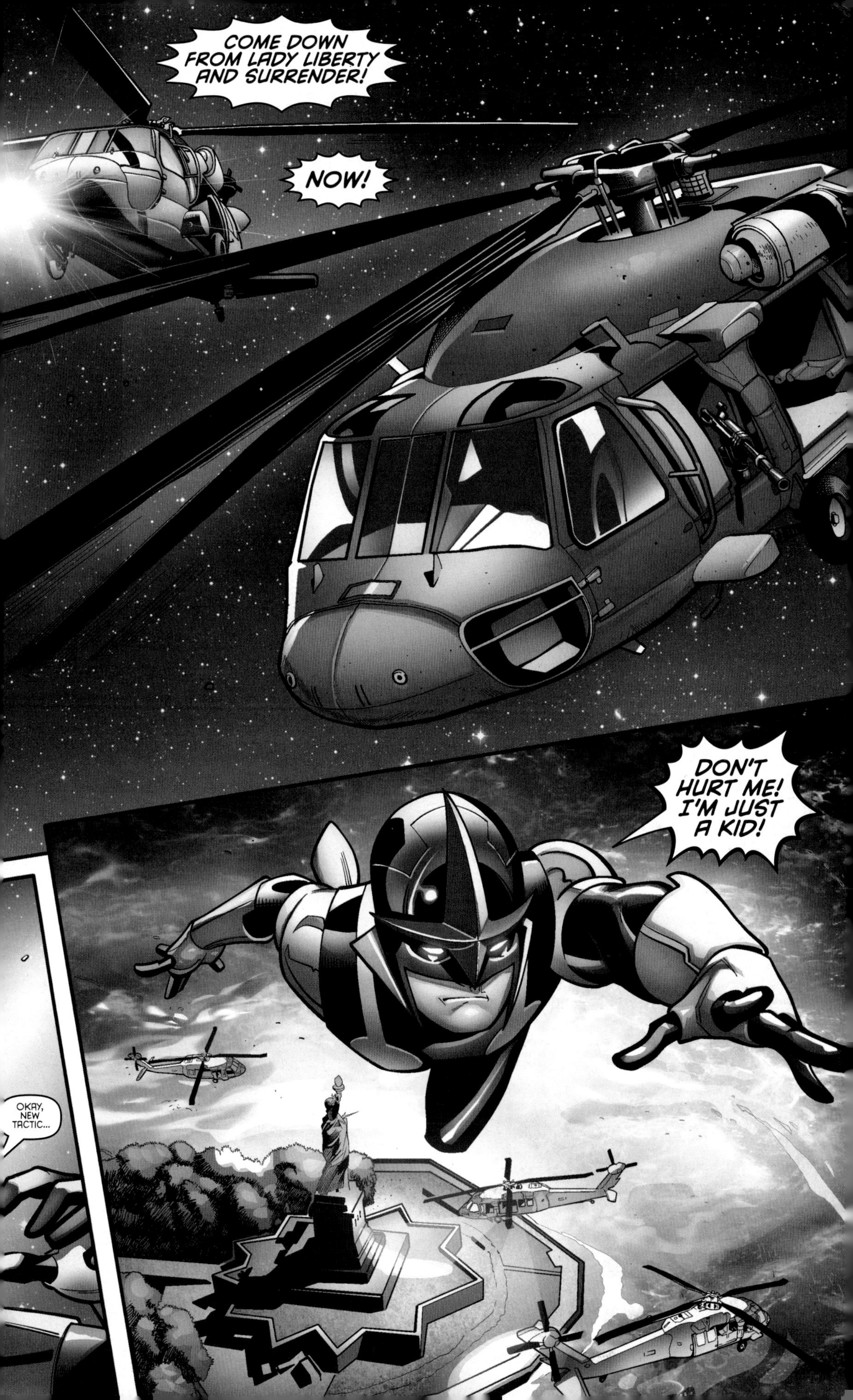
COME DOWN FROM LADY LIBERTY AND SURRENDER!
NOW!
DON'T HURT ME! I'M JUST A KID!
OKAY, NEW TACTIC...

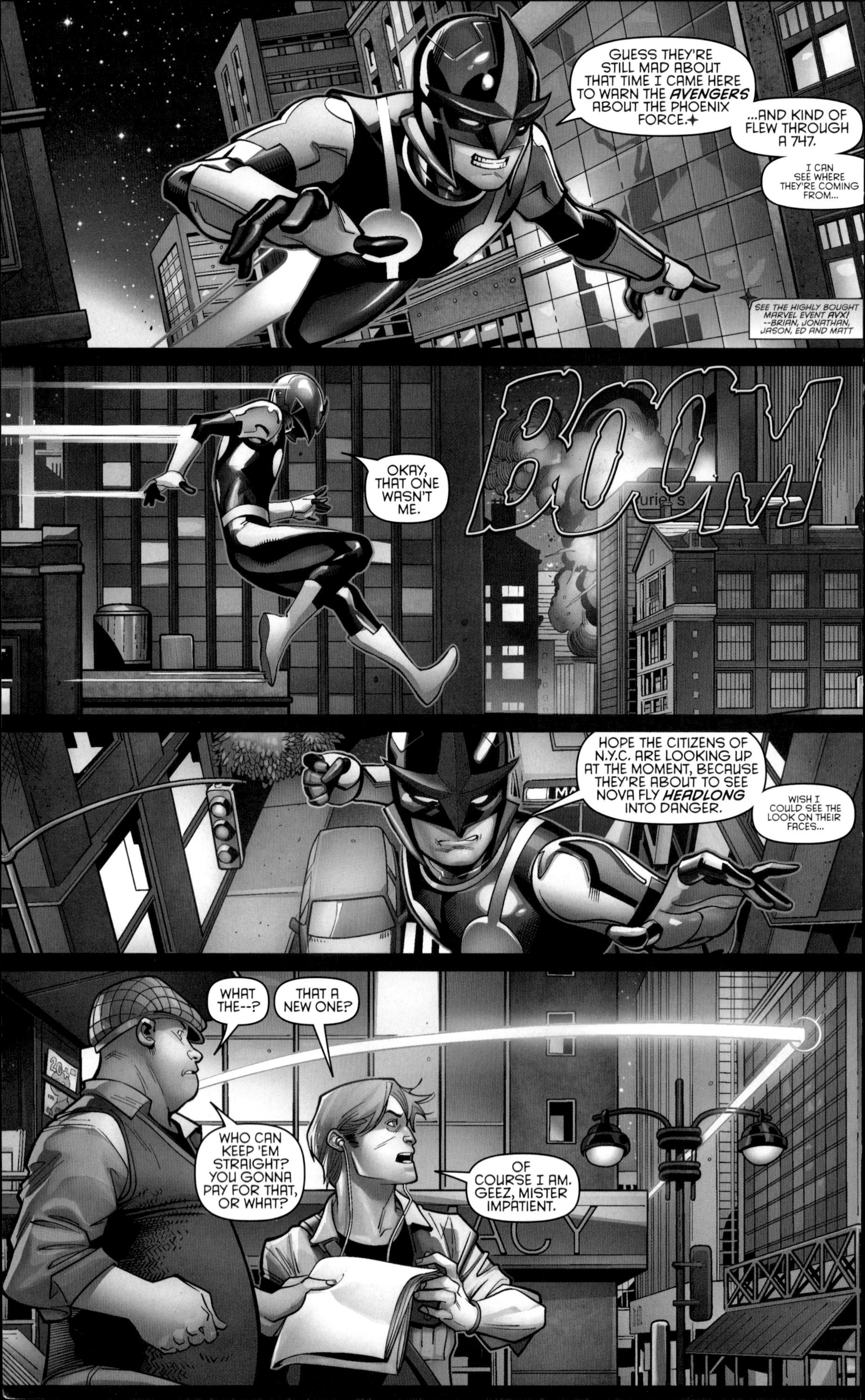

GUESS THEY'RE STILL MAD ABOUT THAT TIME I CAME HERE TO WARN THE *AVENGERS* ABOUT THE PHOENIX FORCE.✦
...AND KIND OF FLEW THROUGH A 747.
I CAN SEE WHERE THEY'RE COMING FROM...
✦SEE THE HIGHLY BOUGHT MARVEL EVENT *AVX!* --BRIAN, JONATHAN, JASON, ED AND MATT
OKAY, THAT ONE WASN'T ME.
BOOM
HOPE THE CITIZENS OF N.Y.C. ARE LOOKING UP AT THE MOMENT, BECAUSE THEY'RE ABOUT TO SEE NOVA FLY *HEADLONG* INTO DANGER.
WISH I COULD SEE THE LOOK ON THEIR FACES...
WHAT THE--?
THAT A NEW ONE?
WHO CAN KEEP 'EM STRAIGHT? YOU GONNA PAY FOR THAT, OR WHAT?
OF COURSE I AM. GEEZ, MISTER IMPATIENT.

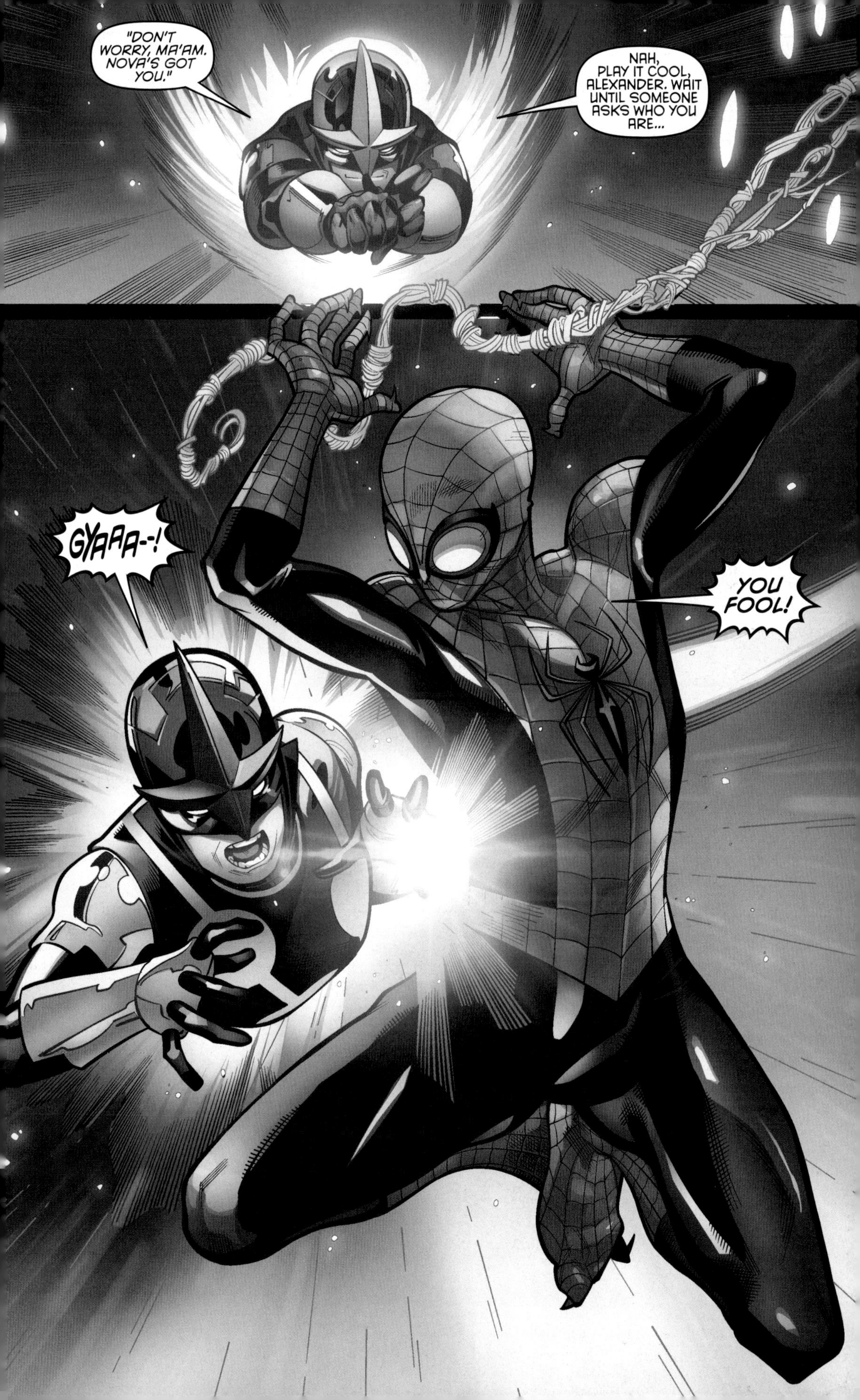
"DON'T WORRY, MA'AM. NOVA'S GOT YOU."
NAH, PLAY IT COOL, ALEXANDER. WAIT UNTIL SOMEONE ASKS WHO YOU ARE...
GYAAA--!
YOU FOOL!

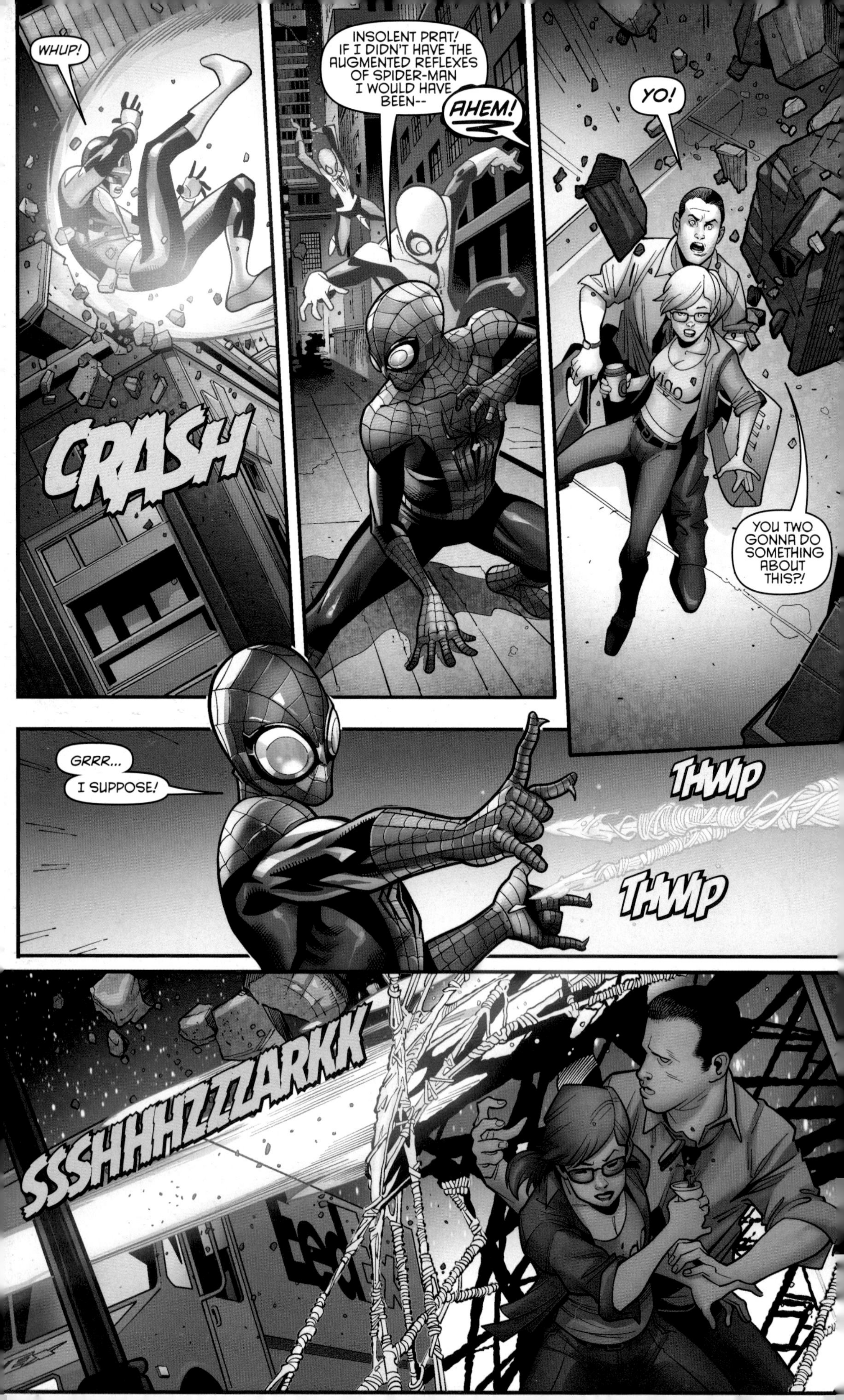
WHUP!
CRASH
INSOLENT PRAT! IF I DIDN'T HAVE THE AUGMENTED REFLEXES OF SPIDER-MAN I WOULD HAVE BEEN--
AHEM!
YO!
YOU TWO GONNA DO SOMETHING ABOUT THIS?!
GRRR... I SUPPOSE!
THWIP
THWIP
SSSHHHZZZARKK

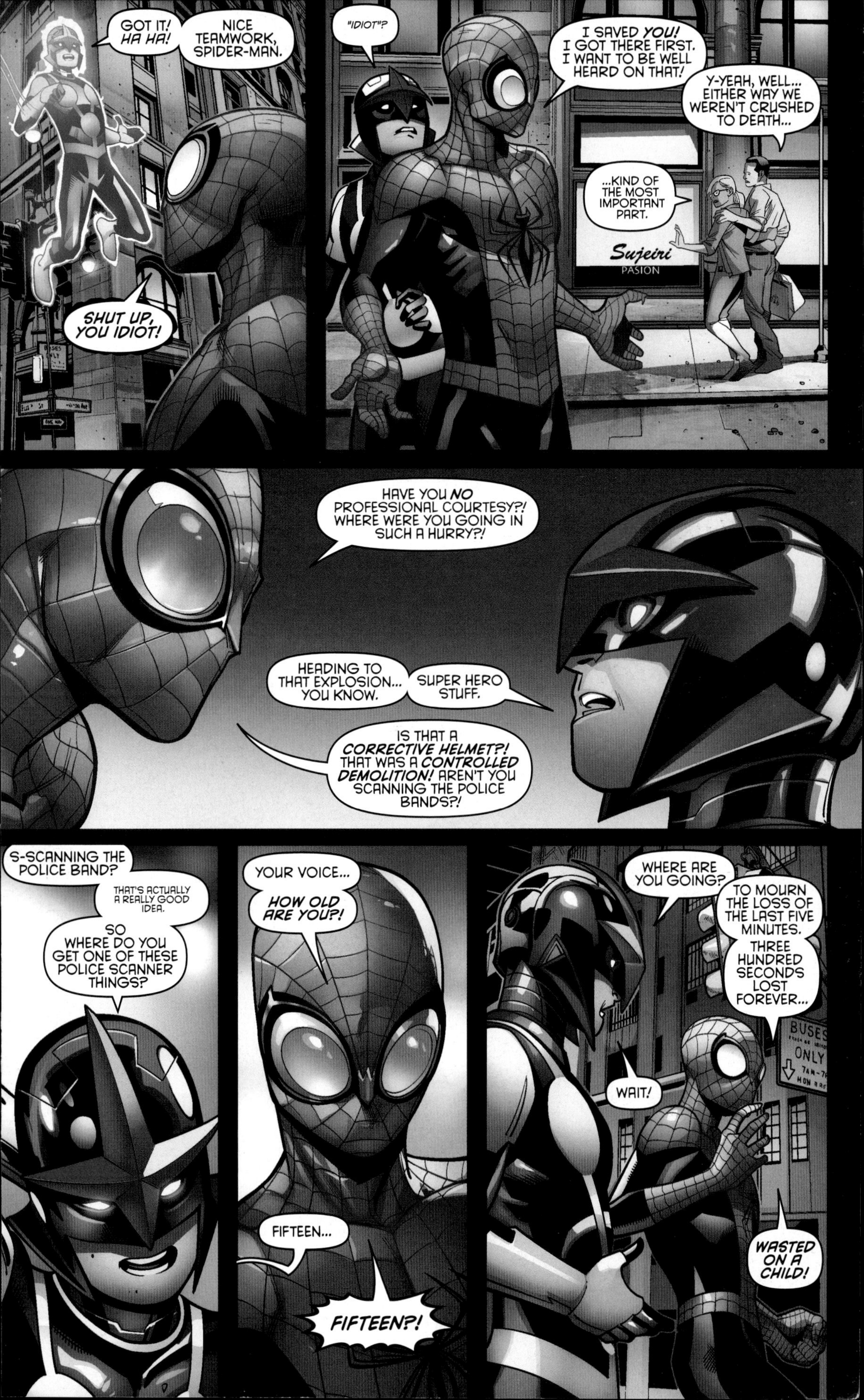

GOT IT! HA HA!
NICE TEAMWORK, SPIDER-MAN.
SHUT UP, YOU IDIOT!
"IDIOT"?
I SAVED YOU! I GOT THERE FIRST. I WANT TO BE WELL HEARD ON THAT!
Y-YEAH, WELL... EITHER WAY WE WEREN'T CRUSHED TO DEATH...
...KIND OF THE MOST IMPORTANT PART.
Sujeiri
PASION
HAVE YOU NO PROFESSIONAL COURTESY?! WHERE WERE YOU GOING IN SUCH A HURRY?!
HEADING TO THAT EXPLOSION... YOU KNOW.
SUPER HERO STUFF.
IS THAT A CORRECTIVE HELMET?! THAT WAS A CONTROLLED DEMOLITION! AREN'T YOU SCANNING THE POLICE BANDS?!
S-SCANNING THE POLICE BAND?
THAT'S ACTUALLY A REALLY GOOD IDEA.
SO WHERE DO YOU GET ONE OF THESE POLICE SCANNER THINGS?
YOUR VOICE...
HOW OLD ARE YOU?!
FIFTEEN...
FIFTEEN?!
WHERE ARE YOU GOING?
TO MOURN THE LOSS OF THE LAST FIVE MINUTES.
THREE HUNDRED SECONDS LOST FOREVER...
WAIT!
WASTED ON A CHILD!
BUSES
ONLY

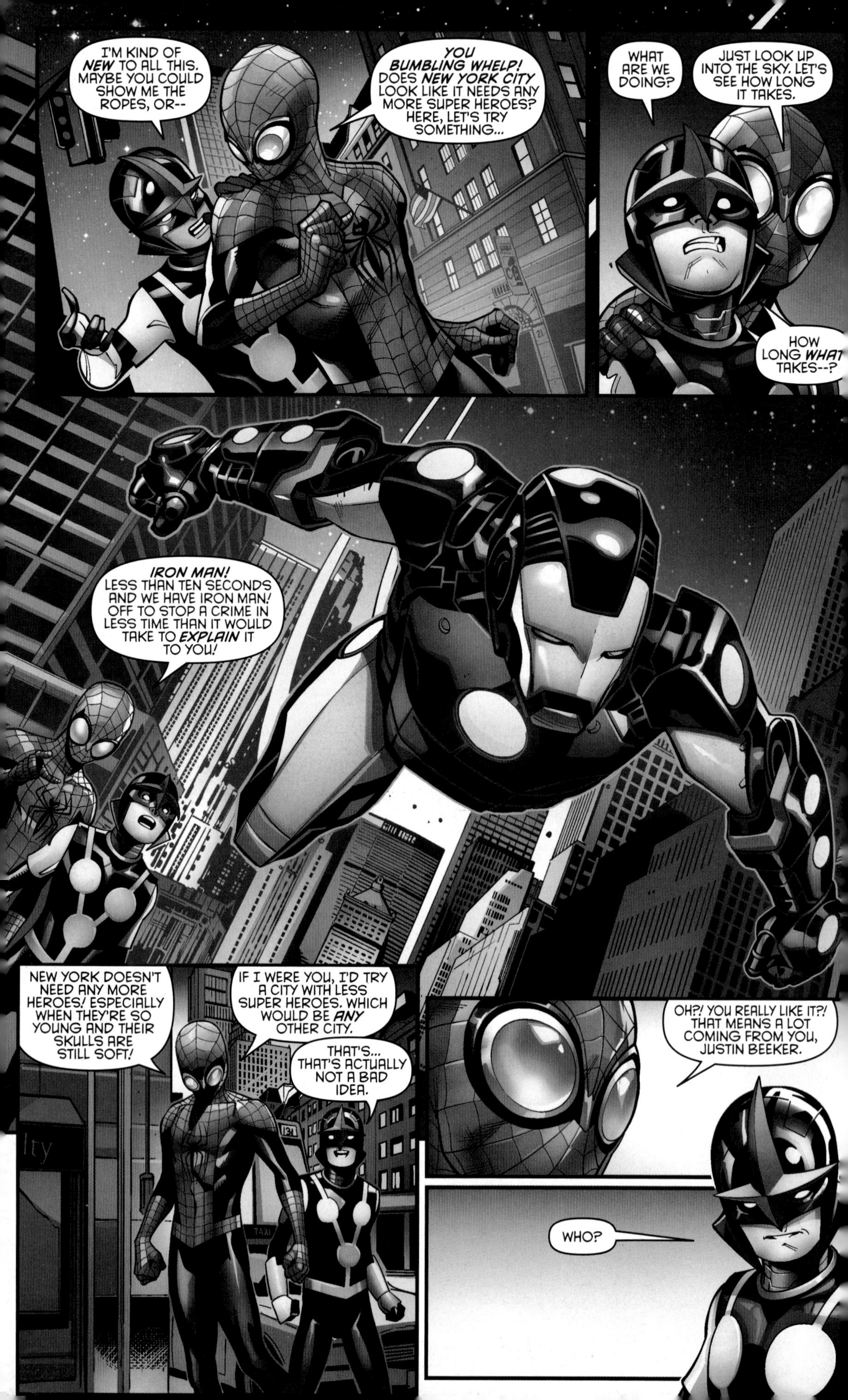
I'M KIND OF NEW TO ALL THIS. MAYBE YOU COULD SHOW ME THE ROPES, OR--
YOU BUMBLING WHELP! DOES NEW YORK CITY LOOK LIKE IT NEEDS ANY MORE SUPER HEROES? HERE, LET'S TRY SOMETHING...
WHAT ARE WE DOING?
JUST LOOK UP INTO THE SKY. LET'S SEE HOW LONG IT TAKES.
HOW LONG WHAT TAKES--?
IRON MAN! LESS THAN TEN SECONDS AND WE HAVE IRON MAN! OFF TO STOP A CRIME IN LESS TIME THAN IT WOULD TAKE TO EXPLAIN IT TO YOU!
NEW YORK DOESN'T NEED ANY MORE HEROES! ESPECIALLY WHEN THEY'RE SO YOUNG AND THEIR SKULLS ARE STILL SOFT!
IF I WERE YOU, I'D TRY A CITY WITH LESS SUPER HEROES. WHICH WOULD BE ANY OTHER CITY.
THAT'S... THAT'S ACTUALLY NOT A BAD IDEA.
OH?! YOU REALLY LIKE IT?! THAT MEANS A LOT COMING FROM YOU, JUSTIN BEEKER.
WHO?

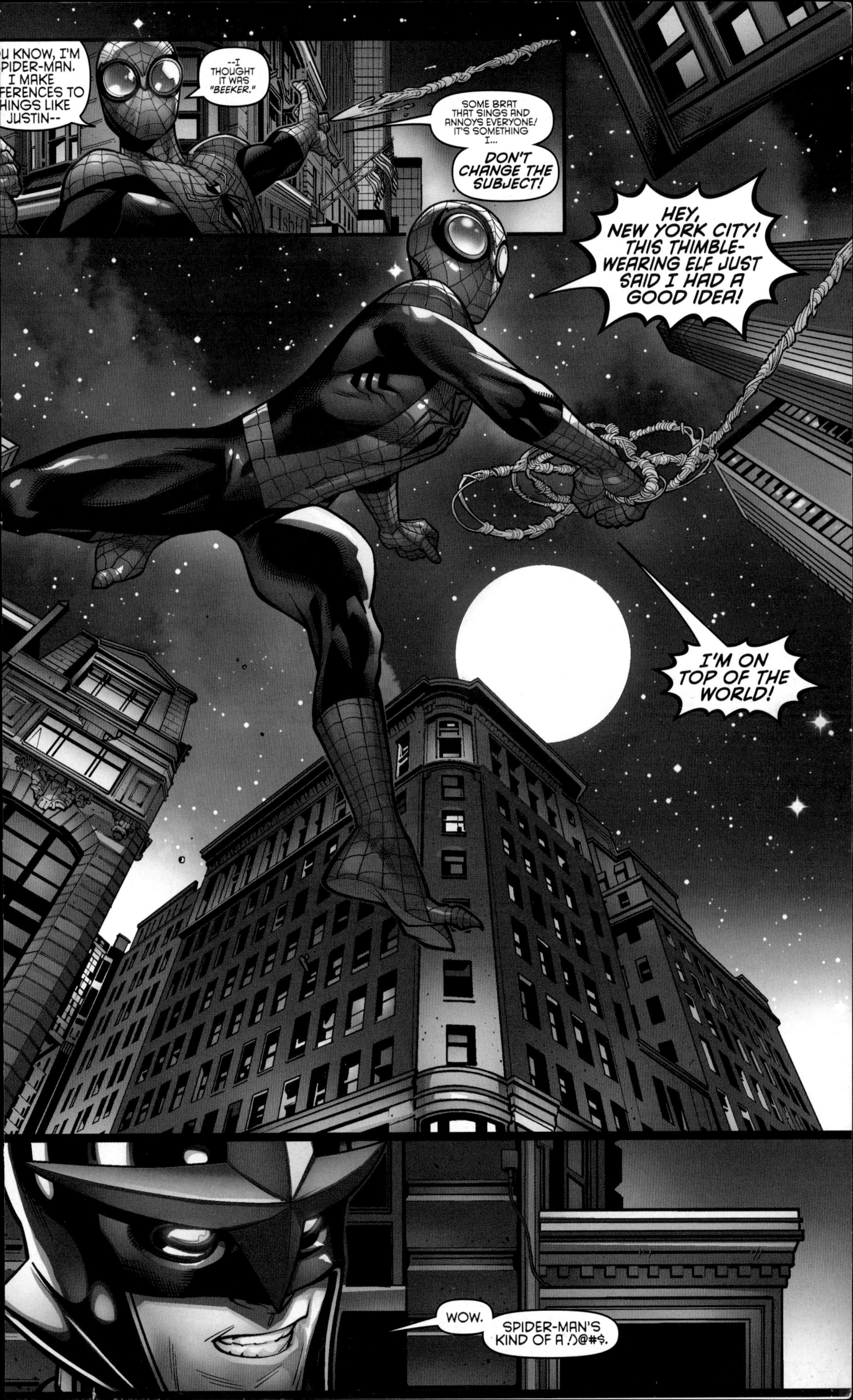

U KNOW, I'M SPIDER-MAN. I MAKE FERENCES TO HINGS LIKE JUSTIN--
--I THOUGHT IT WAS "BEEKER."
SOME BRAT THAT SINGS AND ANNOYS EVERYONE! IT'S SOMETHING I...
DON'T CHANGE THE SUBJECT!
HEY, NEW YORK CITY! THIS THIMBLE-WEARING ELF JUST SAID I HAD A GOOD IDEA!
I'M ON TOP OF THE WORLD!
WOW.
SPIDER-MAN'S KIND OF A !)@#$.

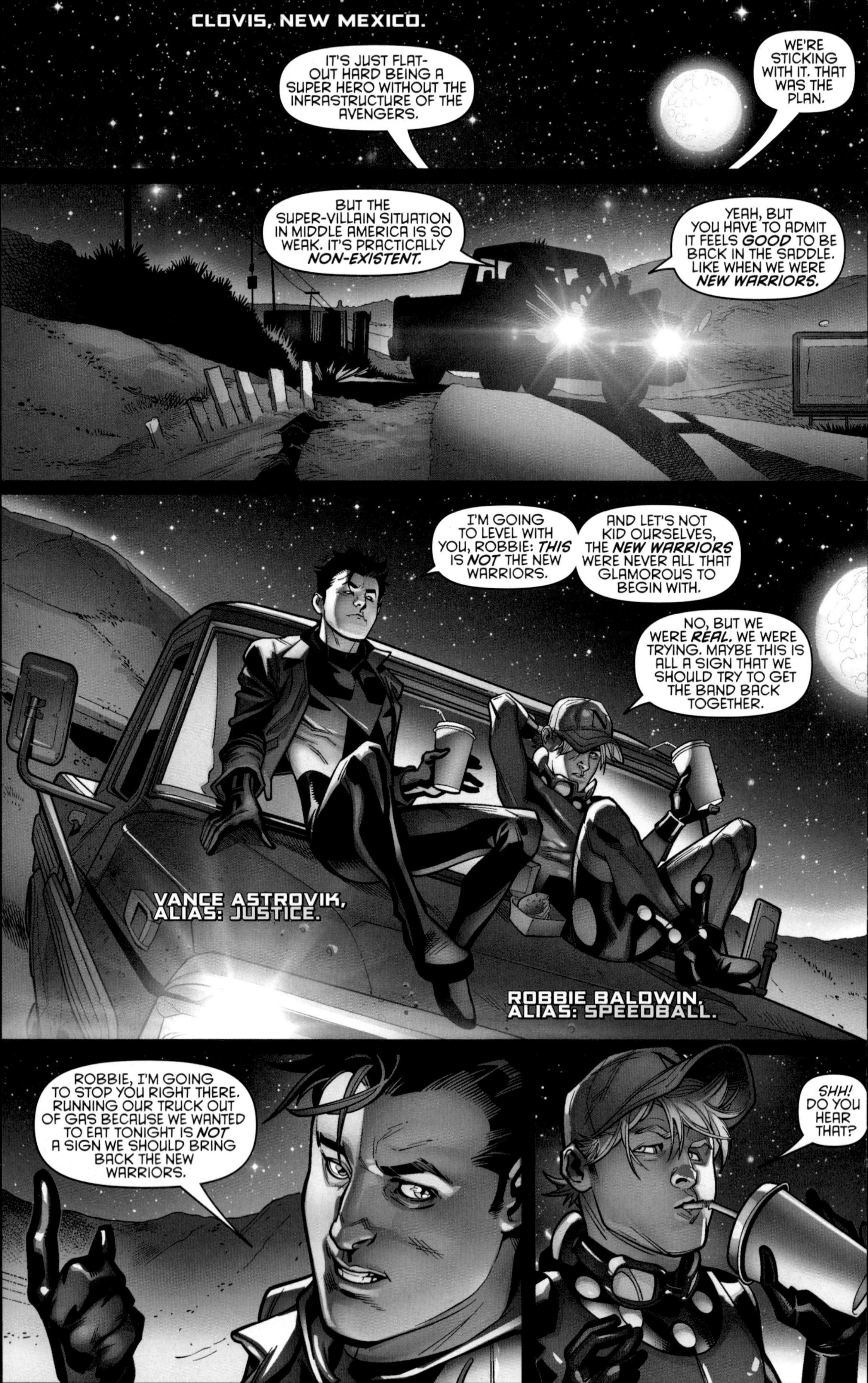
CLOVIS, NEW MEXICO.
IT'S JUST FLAT-OUT HARD BEING A SUPER HERO WITHOUT THE INFRASTRUCTURE OF THE AVENGERS.
WE'RE STICKING WITH IT. THAT WAS THE PLAN.
BUT THE SUPER-VILLAIN SITUATION IN MIDDLE AMERICA IS SO WEAK. IT'S PRACTICALLY NON-EXISTENT.
YEAH, BUT YOU HAVE TO ADMIT IT FEELS GOOD TO BE BACK IN THE SADDLE. LIKE WHEN WE WERE NEW WARRIORS.
I'M GOING TO LEVEL WITH YOU, ROBBIE: THIS IS NOT THE NEW WARRIORS.
AND LET'S NOT KID OURSELVES, THE NEW WARRIORS WERE NEVER ALL THAT GLAMOROUS TO BEGIN WITH.
NO, BUT WE WERE REAL. WE WERE TRYING. MAYBE THIS IS ALL A SIGN THAT WE SHOULD TRY TO GET THE BAND BACK TOGETHER.
VANCE ASTROVIK, ALIAS: JUSTICE.
ROBBIE BALDWIN, ALIAS: SPEEDBALL.
ROBBIE, I'M GOING TO STOP YOU RIGHT THERE. RUNNING OUR TRUCK OUT OF GAS BECAUSE WE WANTED TO EAT TONIGHT IS NOT A SIGN WE SHOULD BRING BACK THE NEW WARRIORS.
SHH! DO YOU HEAR THAT?

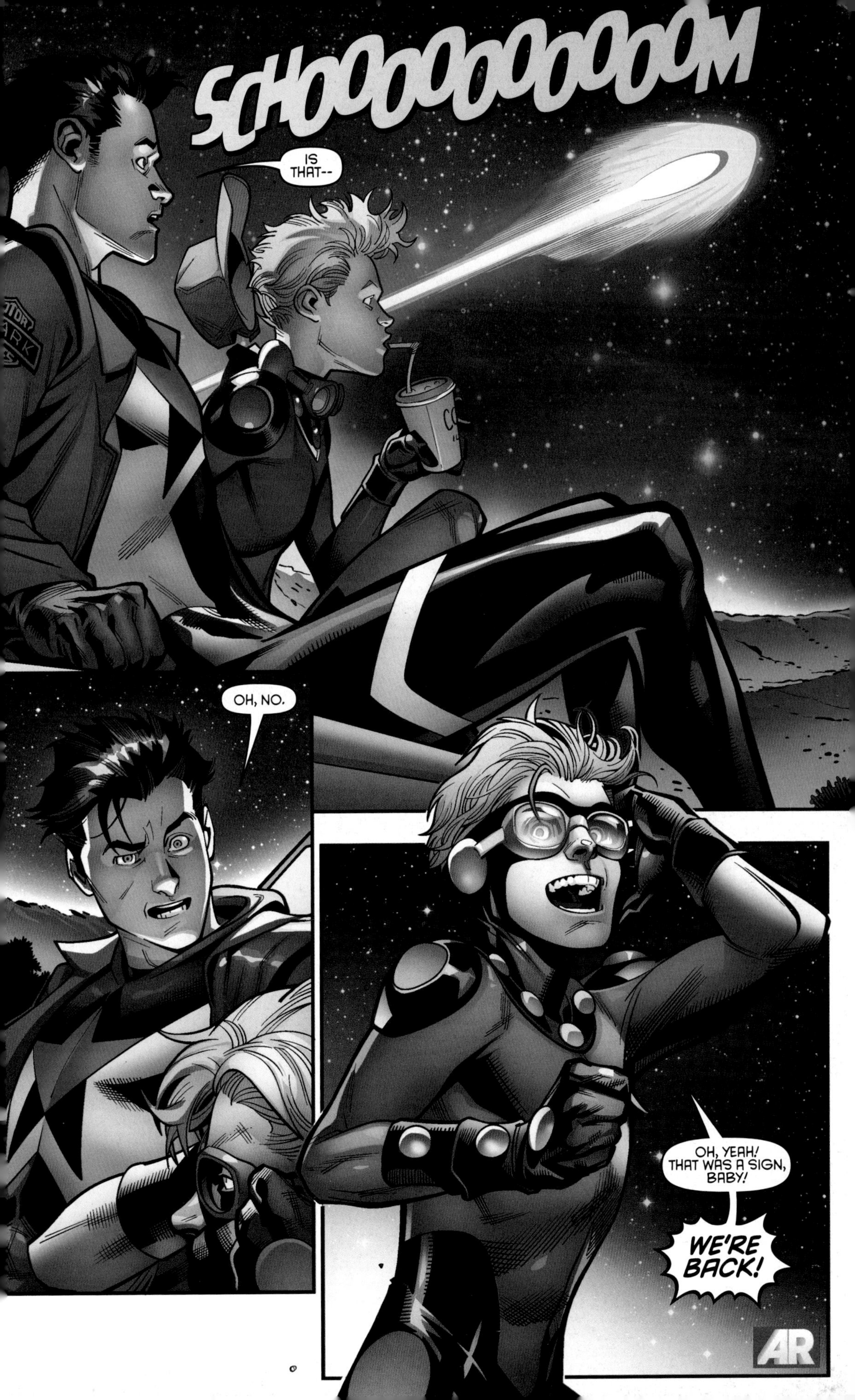
SCHOOOOOOOOOM
IS THAT--
OH, NO.
OH, YEAH! THAT WAS A SIGN, BABY!
WE'RE BACK!
AR

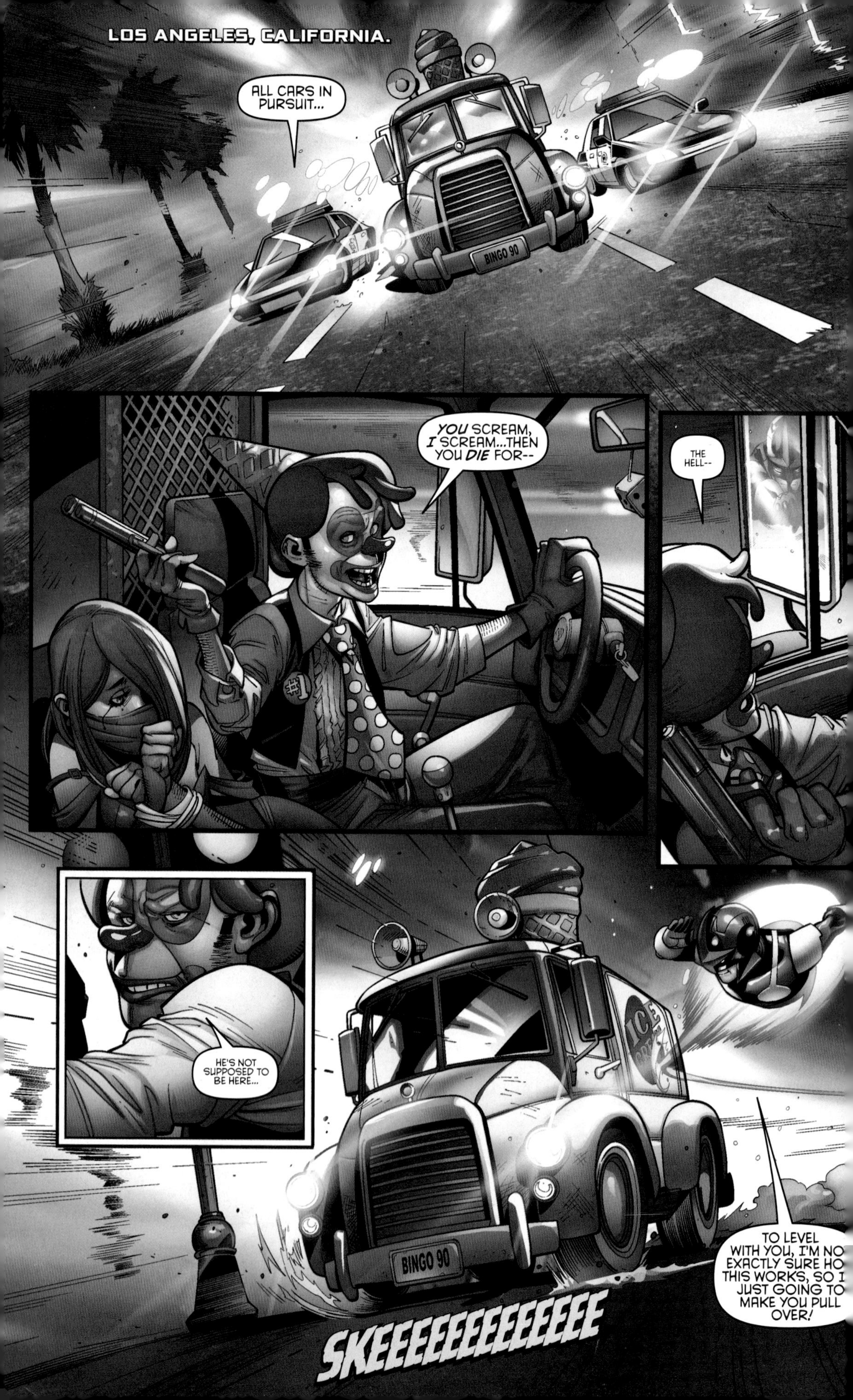
LOS ANGELES, CALIFORNIA.
ALL CARS IN PURSUIT...
BINGO 90
YOU SCREAM, I SCREAM...THEN YOU DIE FOR--
THE HELL--
HE'S NOT SUPPOSED TO BE HERE...
BINGO 90
TO LEVEL WITH YOU, I'M NO EXACTLY SURE HO THIS WORKS, SO I JUST GOING TO MAKE YOU PULL OVER!
SKEEEEEEEEEEEEE

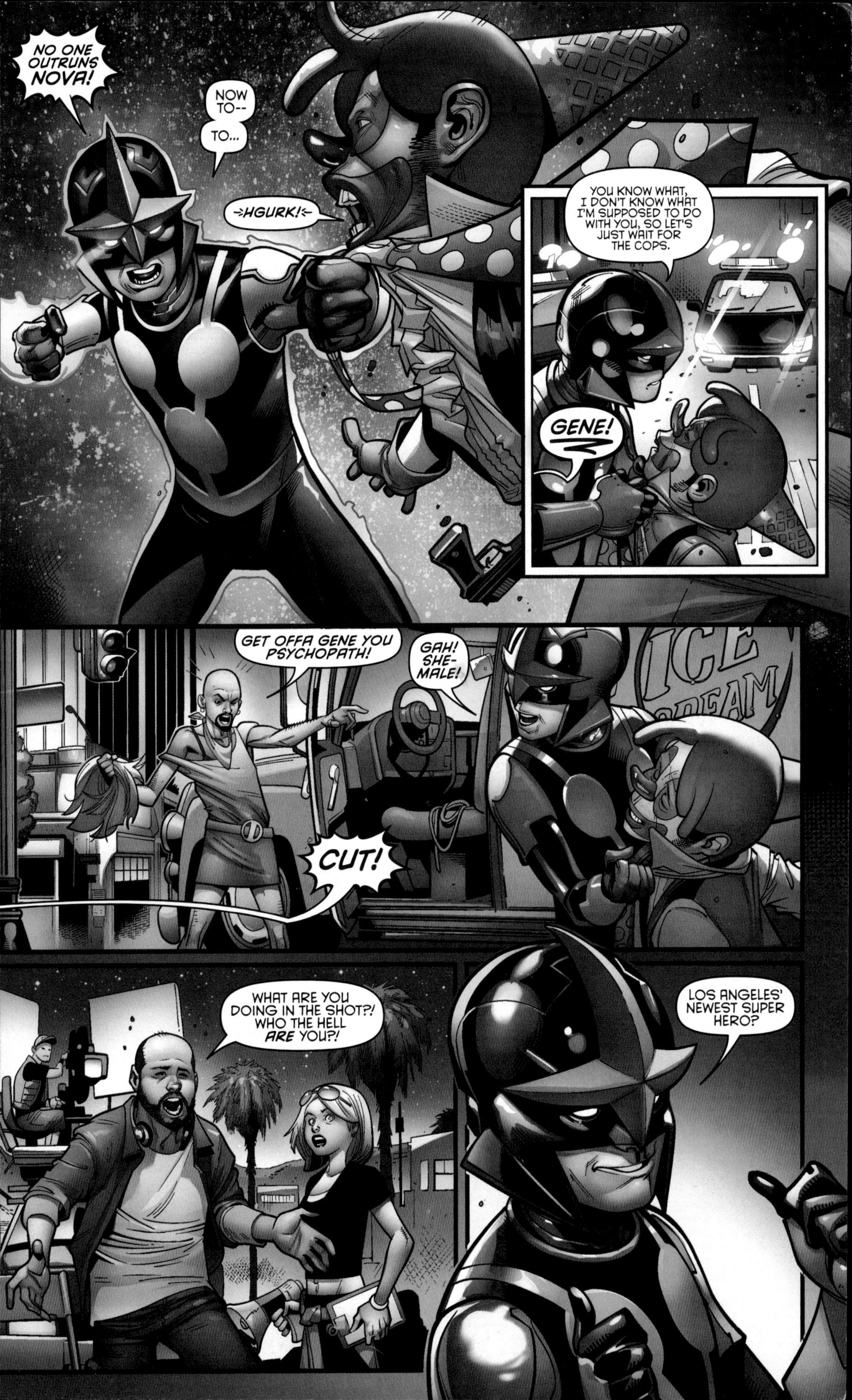
NO ONE OUTRUNS NOVA!
NOW TO--
TO...
-HGURK!-
YOU KNOW WHAT, I DON'T KNOW WHAT I'M SUPPOSED TO DO WITH YOU, SO LET'S JUST WAIT FOR THE COPS.
GENE!
GET OFFA GENE YOU PSYCHOPATH!
GAH! SHE-MALE!
ICE CREAM
CUT!
WHAT ARE YOU DOING IN THE SHOT?! WHO THE HELL ARE YOU?!
LOS ANGELES' NEWEST SUPER HERO?

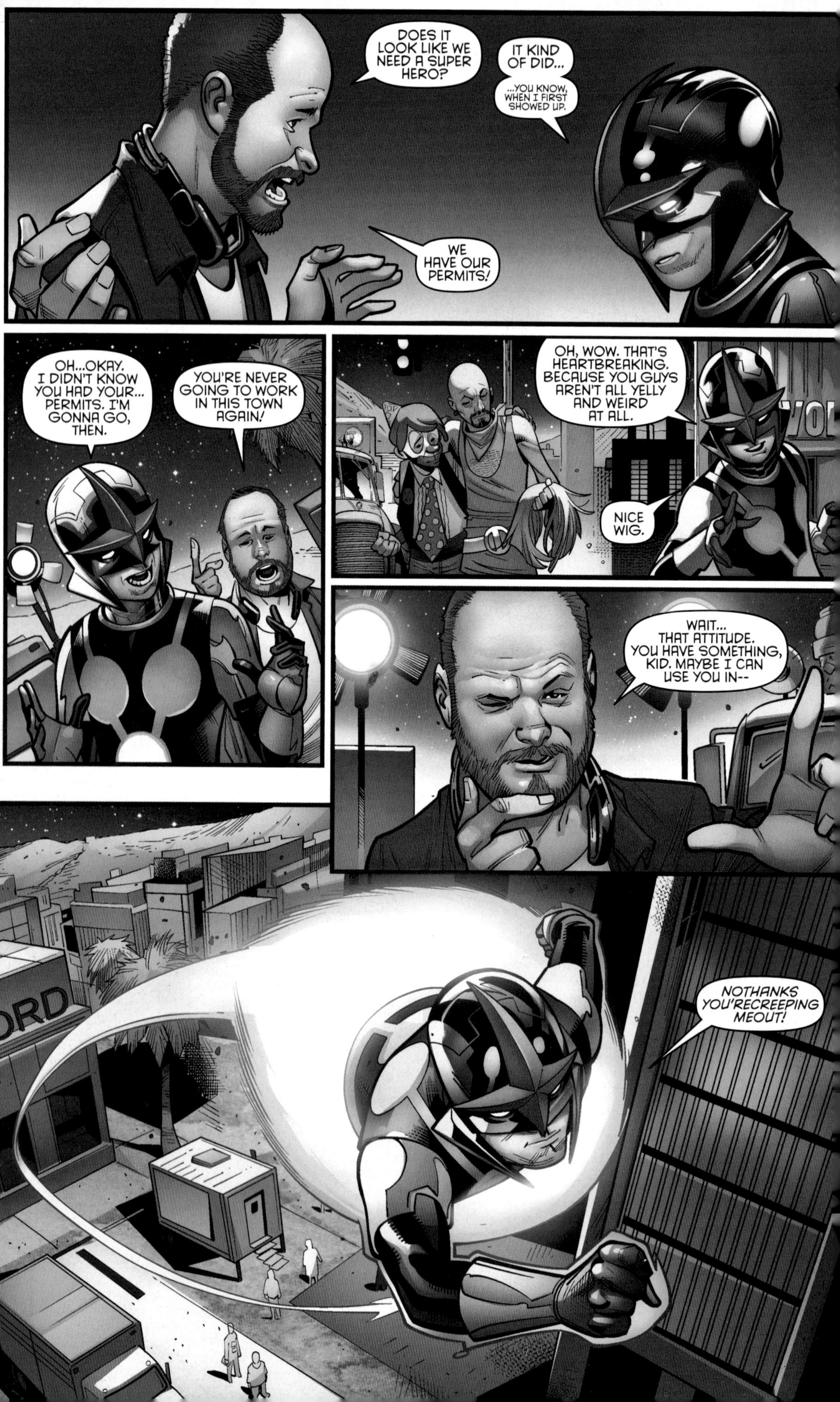
DOES IT LOOK LIKE WE NEED A SUPER HERO?
IT KIND OF DID...
...YOU KNOW, WHEN I FIRST SHOWED UP.
WE HAVE OUR PERMITS!
OH...OKAY. I DIDN'T KNOW YOU HAD YOUR... PERMITS. I'M GONNA GO, THEN.
YOU'RE NEVER GOING TO WORK IN THIS TOWN AGAIN!
OH, WOW. THAT'S HEARTBREAKING. BECAUSE YOU GUYS AREN'T ALL YELLY AND WEIRD AT ALL.
NICE WIG.
WAIT... THAT ATTITUDE. YOU HAVE SOMETHING, KID. MAYBE I CAN USE YOU IN--
NOTHANKS YOU'RECREEPING MEOUT!

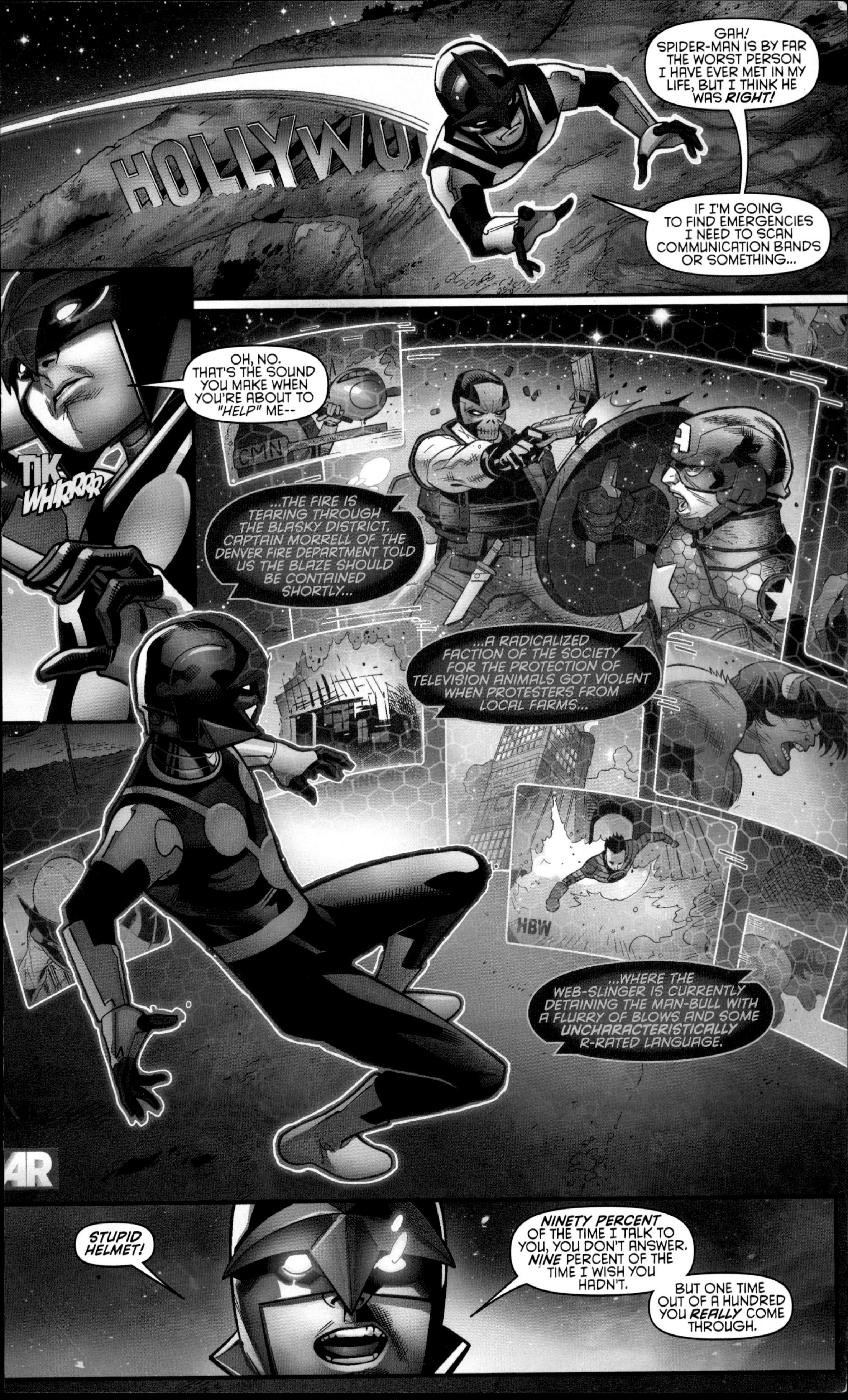
GAH! SPIDER-MAN IS BY FAR THE WORST PERSON I HAVE EVER MET IN MY LIFE, BUT I THINK HE WAS *RIGHT!*
IF I'M GOING TO FIND EMERGENCIES I NEED TO SCAN COMMUNICATION BANDS OR SOMETHING...
OH, NO. THAT'S THE SOUND YOU MAKE WHEN YOU'RE ABOUT TO *"HELP"* ME--
TIK
WHRRRR
CMN
...THE FIRE IS TEARING THROUGH THE BLASKY DISTRICT. CAPTAIN MORRELL OF THE DENVER FIRE DEPARTMENT TOLD US THE BLAZE SHOULD BE CONTAINED SHORTLY...
...A RADICALIZED FACTION OF THE SOCIETY FOR THE PROTECTION OF TELEVISION ANIMALS GOT VIOLENT WHEN PROTESTERS FROM LOCAL FARMS...
HBW
*...WHERE THE WEB-SLINGER IS CURRENTLY DETAINING THE MAN-BULL WITH A FLURRY OF BLOWS AND SOME **UNCHARACTERISTICALLY** R-RATED LANGUAGE.*
STUPID HELMET!
NINETY PERCENT OF THE TIME I TALK TO YOU, YOU DON'T ANSWER. ***NINE*** PERCENT OF THE TIME I WISH YOU HADN'T.
BUT ONE TIME OUT OF A HUNDRED YOU ***REALLY*** COME THROUGH.

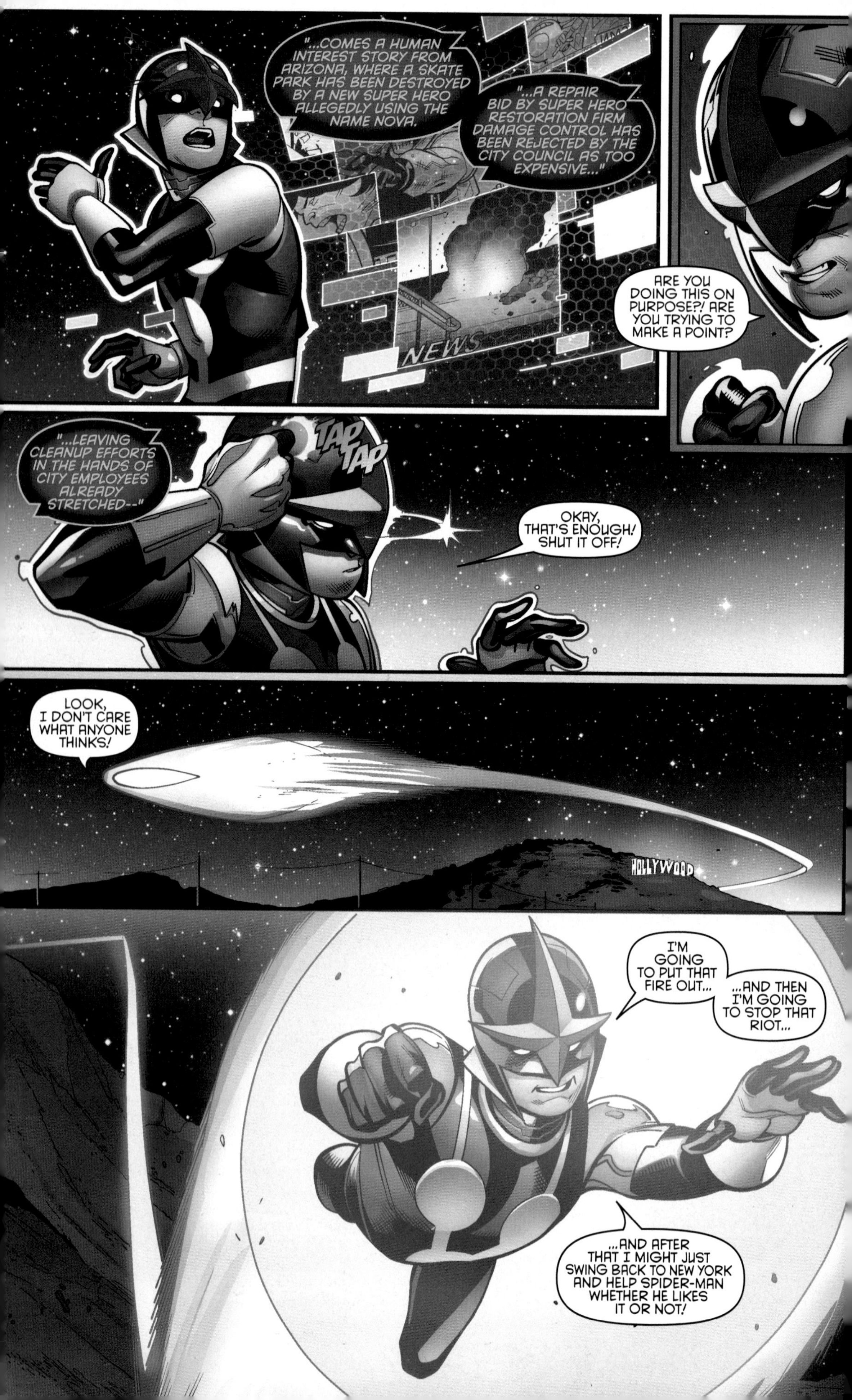
"...COMES A HUMAN INTEREST STORY FROM ARIZONA, WHERE A SKATE PARK HAS BEEN DESTROYED BY A NEW SUPER HERO ALLEGEDLY USING THE NAME NOVA.
"...A REPAIR BID BY SUPER HERO RESTORATION FIRM DAMAGE CONTROL HAS BEEN REJECTED BY THE CITY COUNCIL AS TOO EXPENSIVE..."
NEWS
ARE YOU DOING THIS ON PURPOSE?! ARE YOU TRYING TO MAKE A POINT?
"...LEAVING CLEANUP EFFORTS IN THE HANDS OF CITY EMPLOYEES ALREADY STRETCHED--"
TAP TAP
OKAY, THAT'S ENOUGH! SHUT IT OFF!
LOOK, I DON'T CARE WHAT ANYONE THINKS!
HOLLYWOOD
I'M GOING TO PUT THAT FIRE OUT...
...AND THEN I'M GOING TO STOP THAT RIOT...
...AND AFTER THAT I MIGHT JUST SWING BACK TO NEW YORK AND HELP SPIDER-MAN WHETHER HE LIKES IT OR NOT!

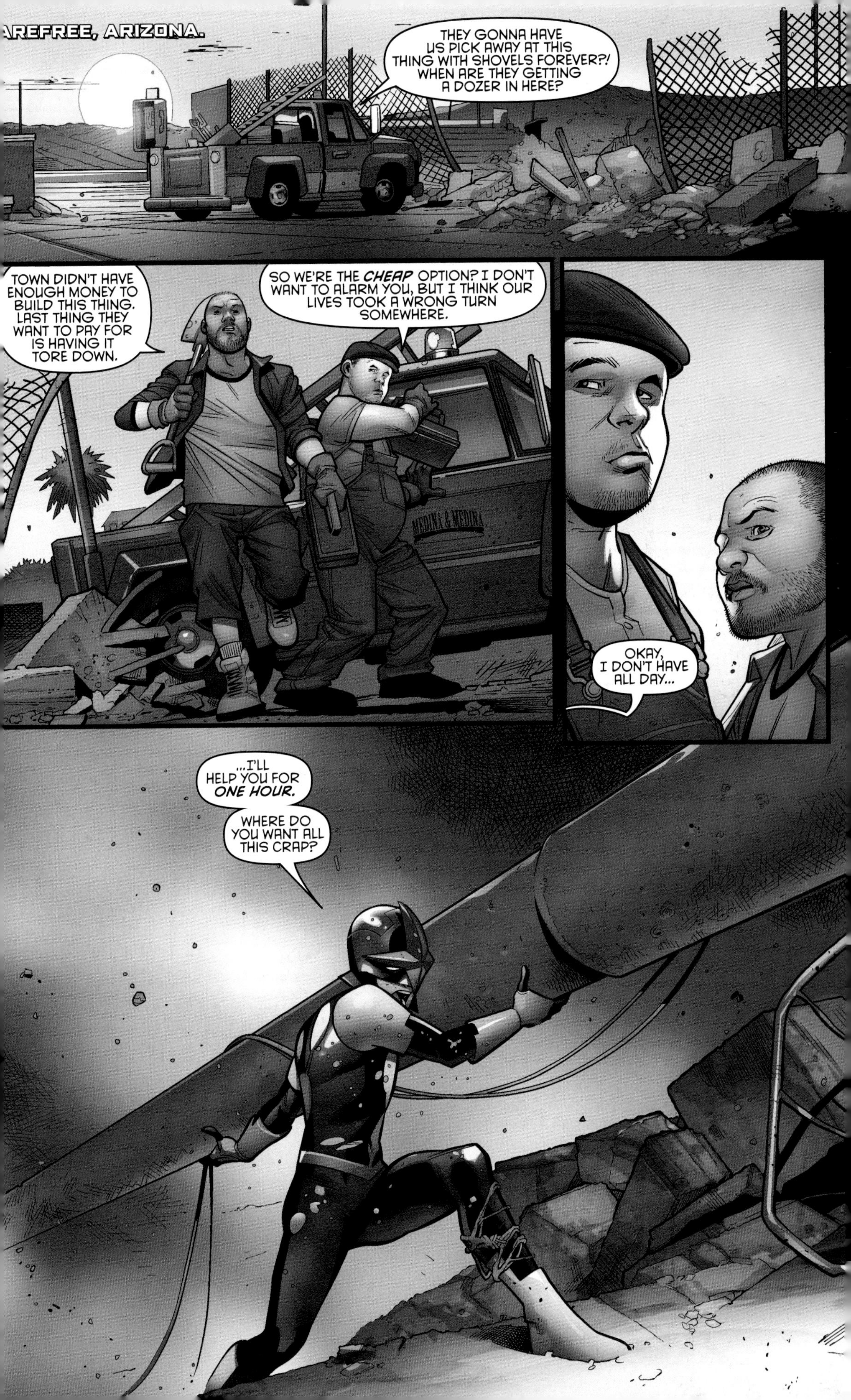
AREFREE, ARIZONA.
THEY GONNA HAVE US PICK AWAY AT THIS THING WITH SHOVELS FOREVER?! WHEN ARE THEY GETTING A DOZER IN HERE?
TOWN DIDN'T HAVE ENOUGH MONEY TO BUILD THIS THING. LAST THING THEY WANT TO PAY FOR IS HAVING IT TORE DOWN.
SO WE'RE THE CHEAP OPTION? I DON'T WANT TO ALARM YOU, BUT I THINK OUR LIVES TOOK A WRONG TURN SOMEWHERE.
MEDINA & MEDINA
OKAY, I DON'T HAVE ALL DAY...
...I'LL HELP YOU FOR ONE HOUR.
WHERE DO YOU WANT ALL THIS CRAP?

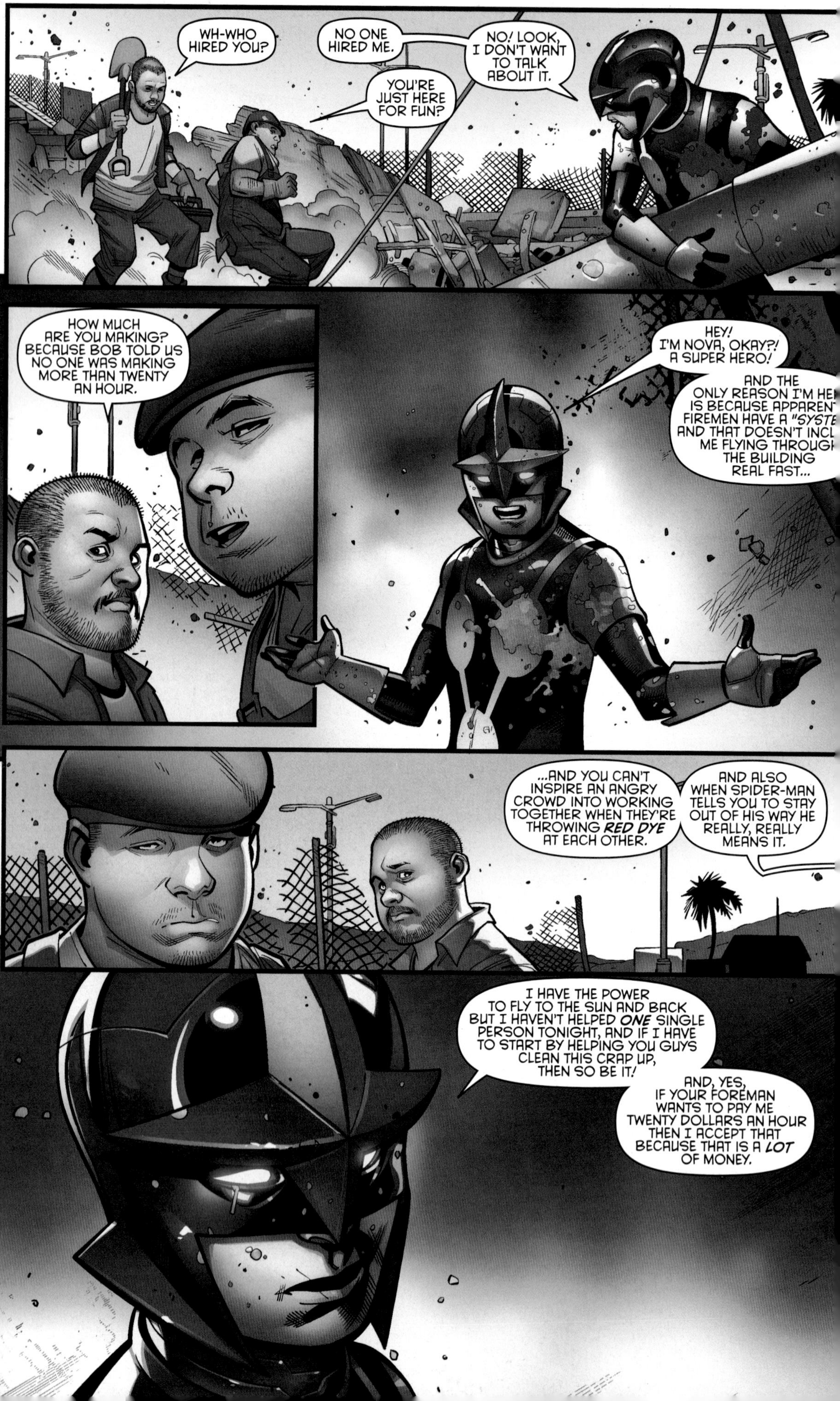
WH-WHO HIRED YOU?
NO ONE HIRED ME.
YOU'RE JUST HERE FOR FUN?
NO! LOOK, I DON'T WANT TO TALK ABOUT IT.
HOW MUCH ARE YOU MAKING? BECAUSE BOB TOLD US NO ONE WAS MAKING MORE THAN TWENTY AN HOUR.
HEY! I'M NOVA, OKAY?! A SUPER HERO!
AND THE ONLY REASON I'M HE IS BECAUSE APPAREN FIREMEN HAVE A "SYSTE AND THAT DOESN'T INCL ME FLYING THROUG THE BUILDING REAL FAST...
...AND YOU CAN'T INSPIRE AN ANGRY CROWD INTO WORKING TOGETHER WHEN THEY'RE THROWING RED DYE AT EACH OTHER.
AND ALSO WHEN SPIDER-MAN TELLS YOU TO STAY OUT OF HIS WAY HE REALLY, REALLY MEANS IT.
I HAVE THE POWER TO FLY TO THE SUN AND BACK BUT I HAVEN'T HELPED ONE SINGLE PERSON TONIGHT, AND IF I HAVE TO START BY HELPING YOU GUYS CLEAN THIS CRAP UP, THEN SO BE IT!
AND, YES, IF YOUR FOREMAN WANTS TO PAY ME TWENTY DOLLARS AN HOUR THEN I ACCEPT THAT BECAUSE THAT IS A LOT OF MONEY.

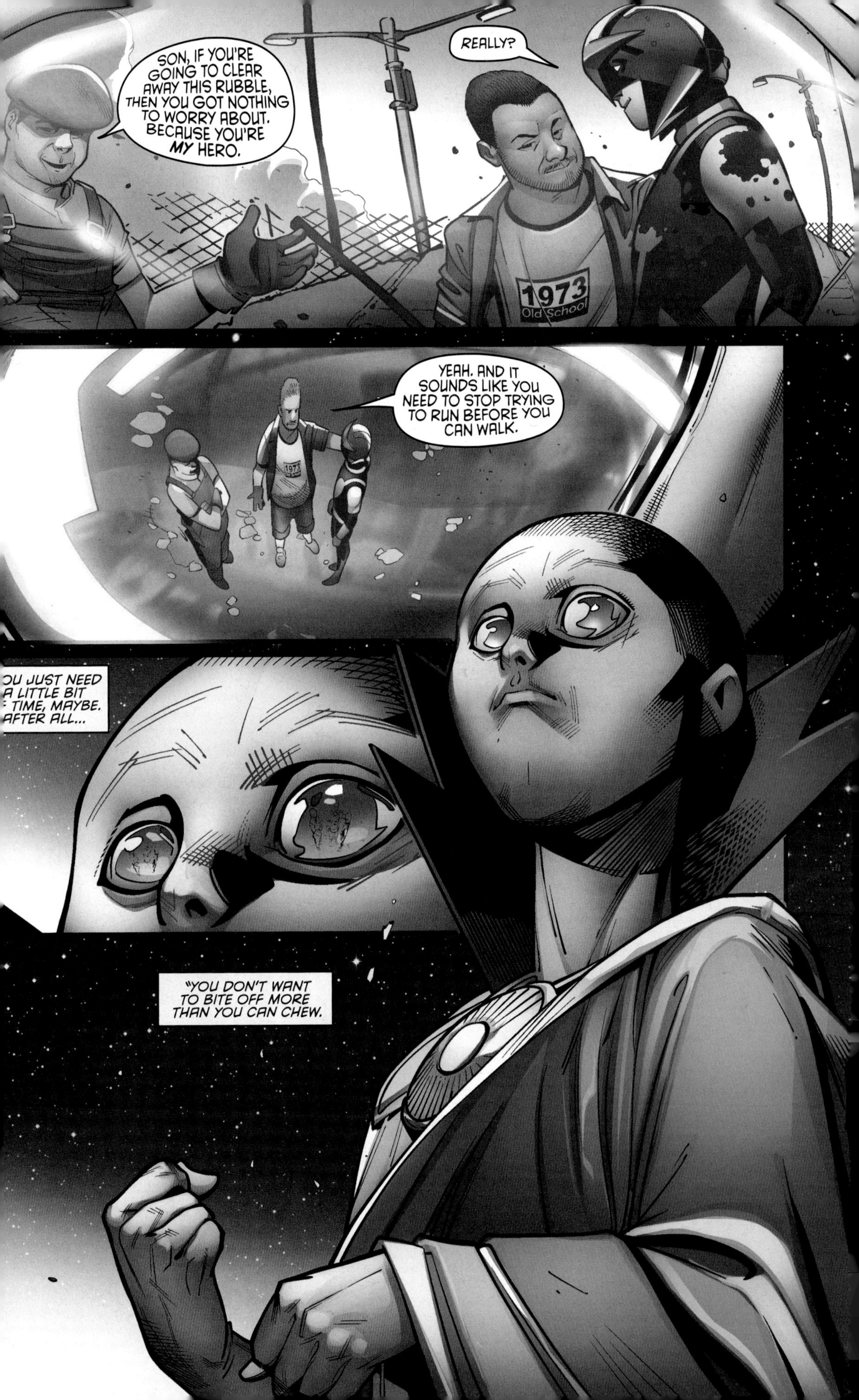
SON, IF YOU'RE GOING TO CLEAR AWAY THIS RUBBLE, THEN YOU GOT NOTHING TO WORRY ABOUT. BECAUSE YOU'RE MY HERO.
REALLY?
1973 Old School
YEAH. AND IT SOUNDS LIKE YOU NEED TO STOP TRYING TO RUN BEFORE YOU CAN WALK.
1973
OU JUST NEED A LITTLE BIT F TIME, MAYBE. AFTER ALL...
"YOU DON'T WANT TO BITE OFF MORE THAN YOU CAN CHEW.

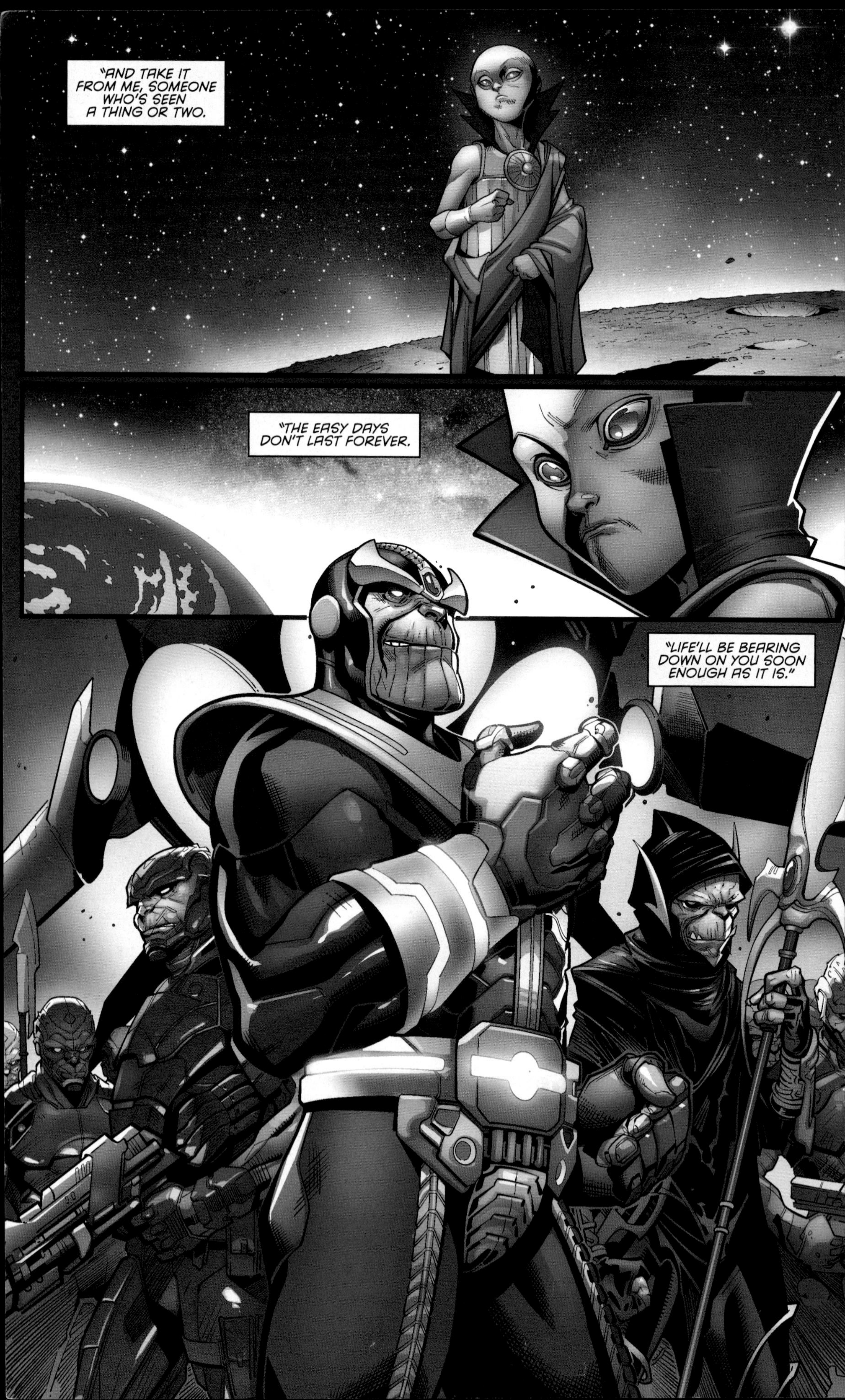
"AND TAKE IT FROM ME, SOMEONE WHO'S SEEN A THING OR TWO.
"THE EASY DAYS DON'T LAST FOREVER.
"LIFE'LL BE BEARING DOWN ON YOU SOON ENOUGH AS IT IS."

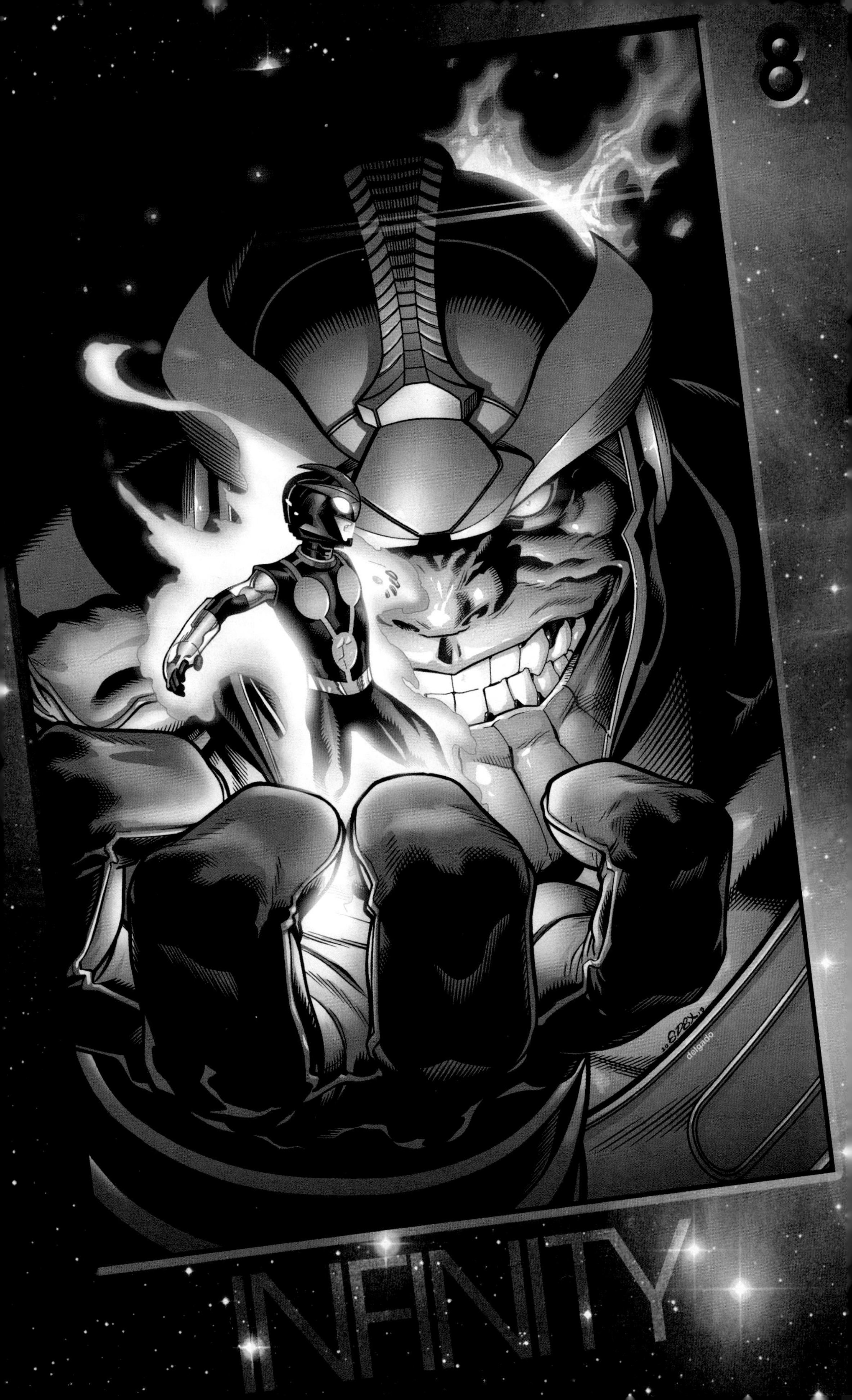
8
delgado
INFINITY

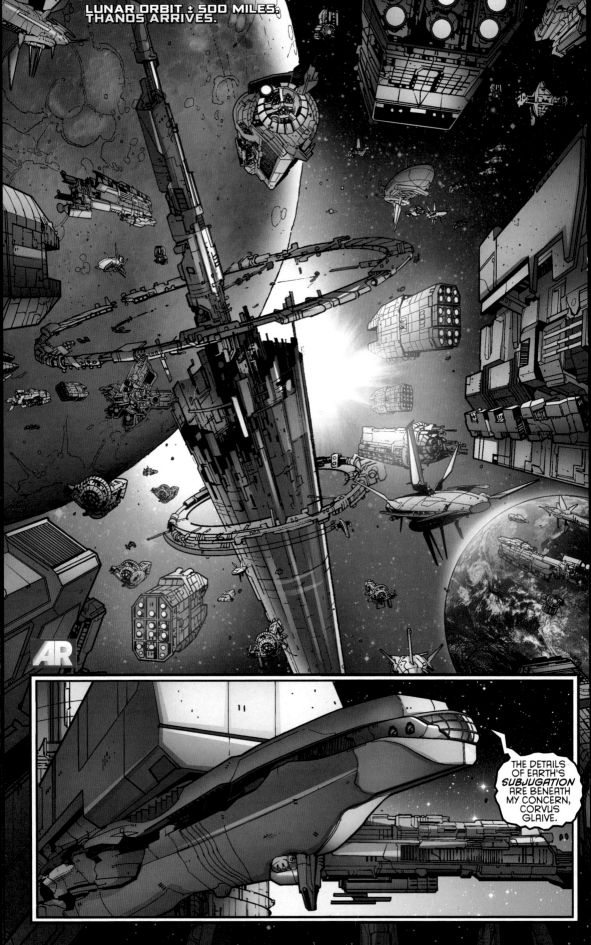

LUNAR ORBIT ± 500 MILES.
THANOS ARRIVES.

THE DETAILS OF EARTH'S *SUBJUGATION* ARE BENEATH MY CONCERN, CORVUS GLAIVE.

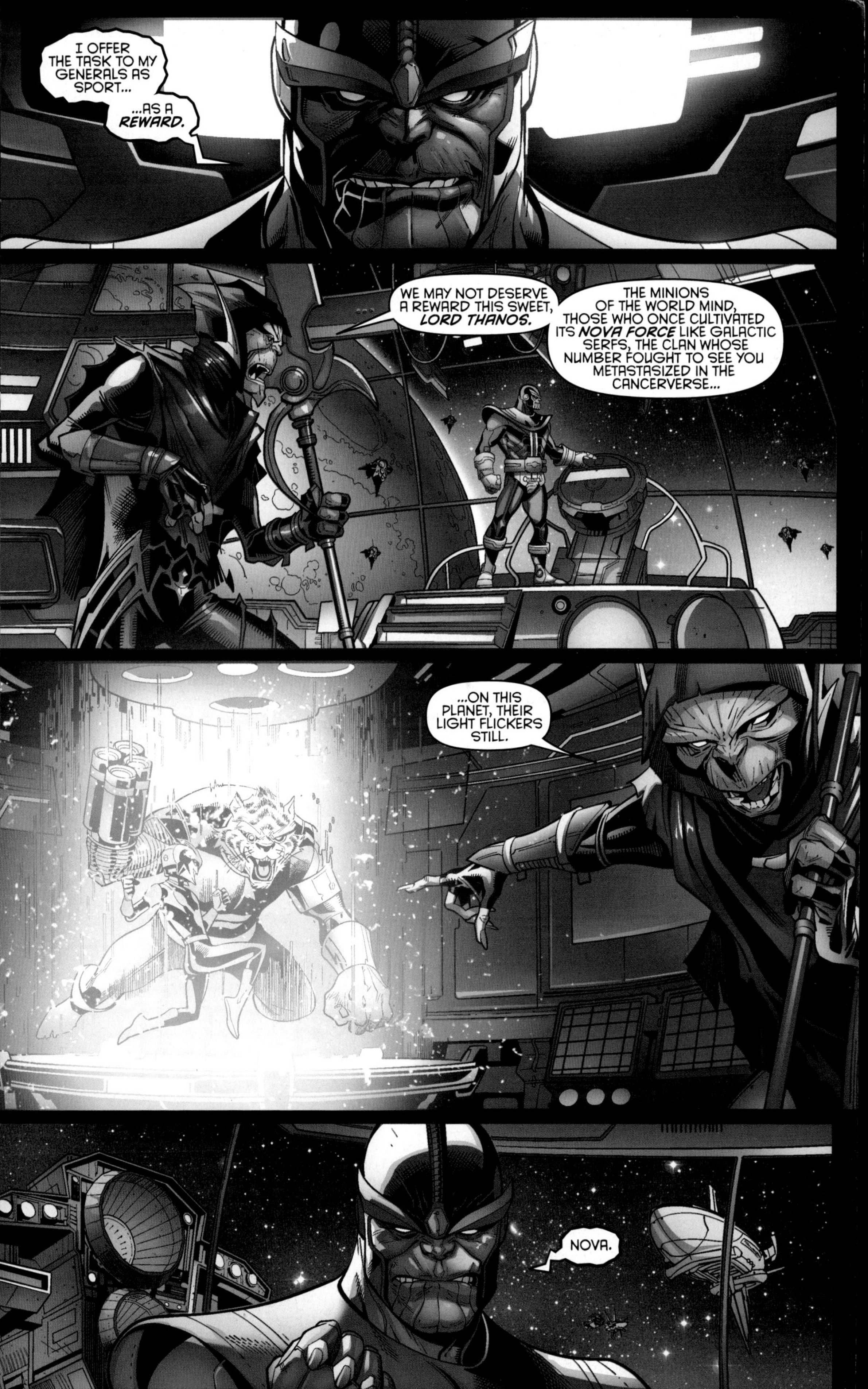
I OFFER THE TASK TO MY GENERALS AS SPORT...
...AS A *REWARD.*
WE MAY NOT DESERVE A REWARD THIS SWEET, *LORD THANOS.*
THE MINIONS OF THE WORLD MIND, THOSE WHO ONCE CULTIVATED ITS *NOVA FORCE* LIKE GALACTIC SERFS, THE CLAN WHOSE NUMBER FOUGHT TO SEE YOU METASTASIZED IN THE CANCERVERSE...
...ON THIS PLANET, THEIR LIGHT FLICKERS STILL.
NOVA.

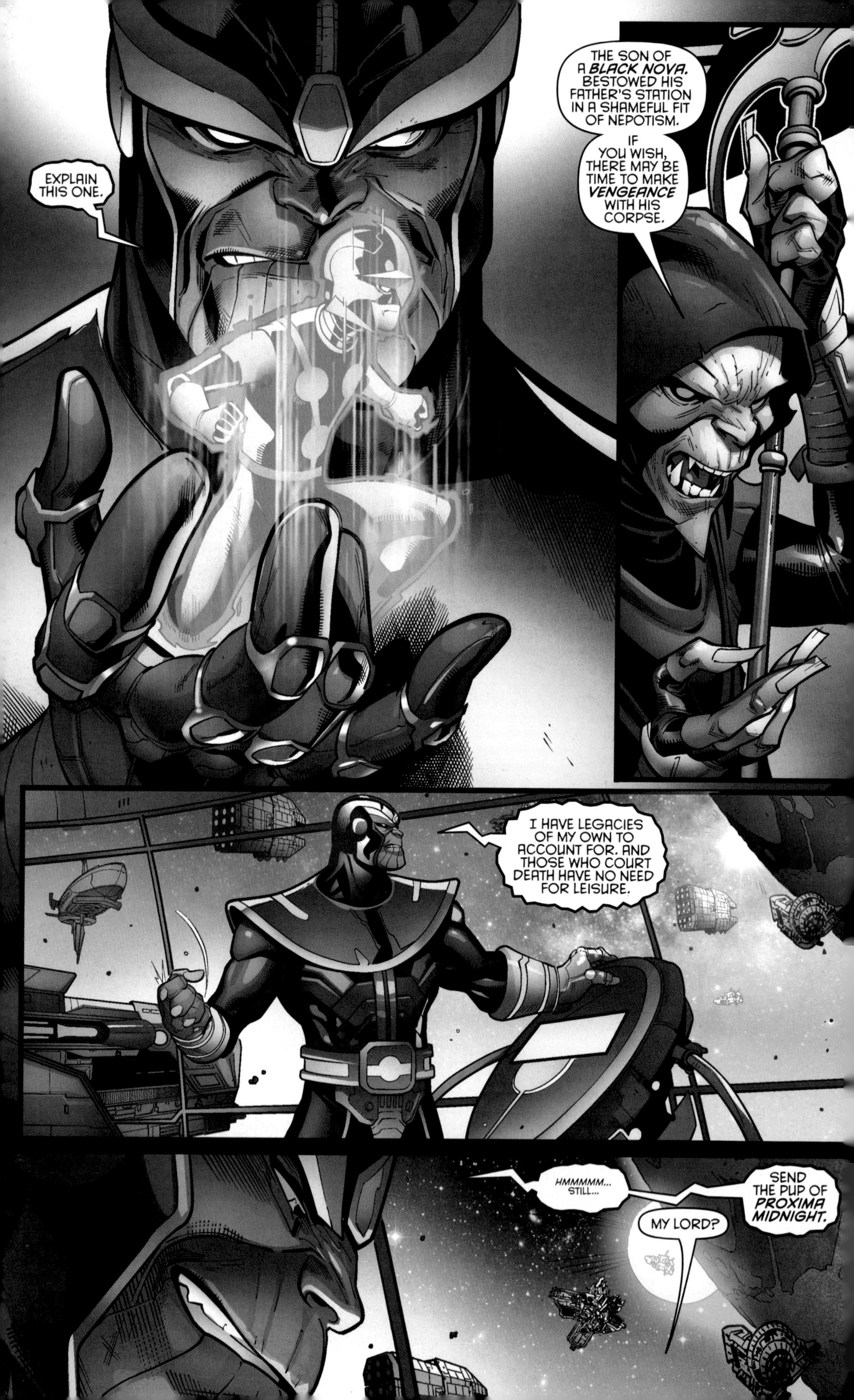
EXPLAIN THIS ONE.
THE SON OF A *BLACK NOVA*. BESTOWED HIS FATHER'S STATION IN A SHAMEFUL FIT OF NEPOTISM.
IF YOU WISH, THERE MAY BE TIME TO MAKE *VENGEANCE* WITH HIS CORPSE.
I HAVE LEGACIES OF MY OWN TO ACCOUNT FOR. AND THOSE WHO COURT DEATH HAVE NO NEED FOR LEISURE.
HMMMMM... STILL...
SEND THE PUP OF *PROXIMA MIDNIGHT*.
MY LORD?

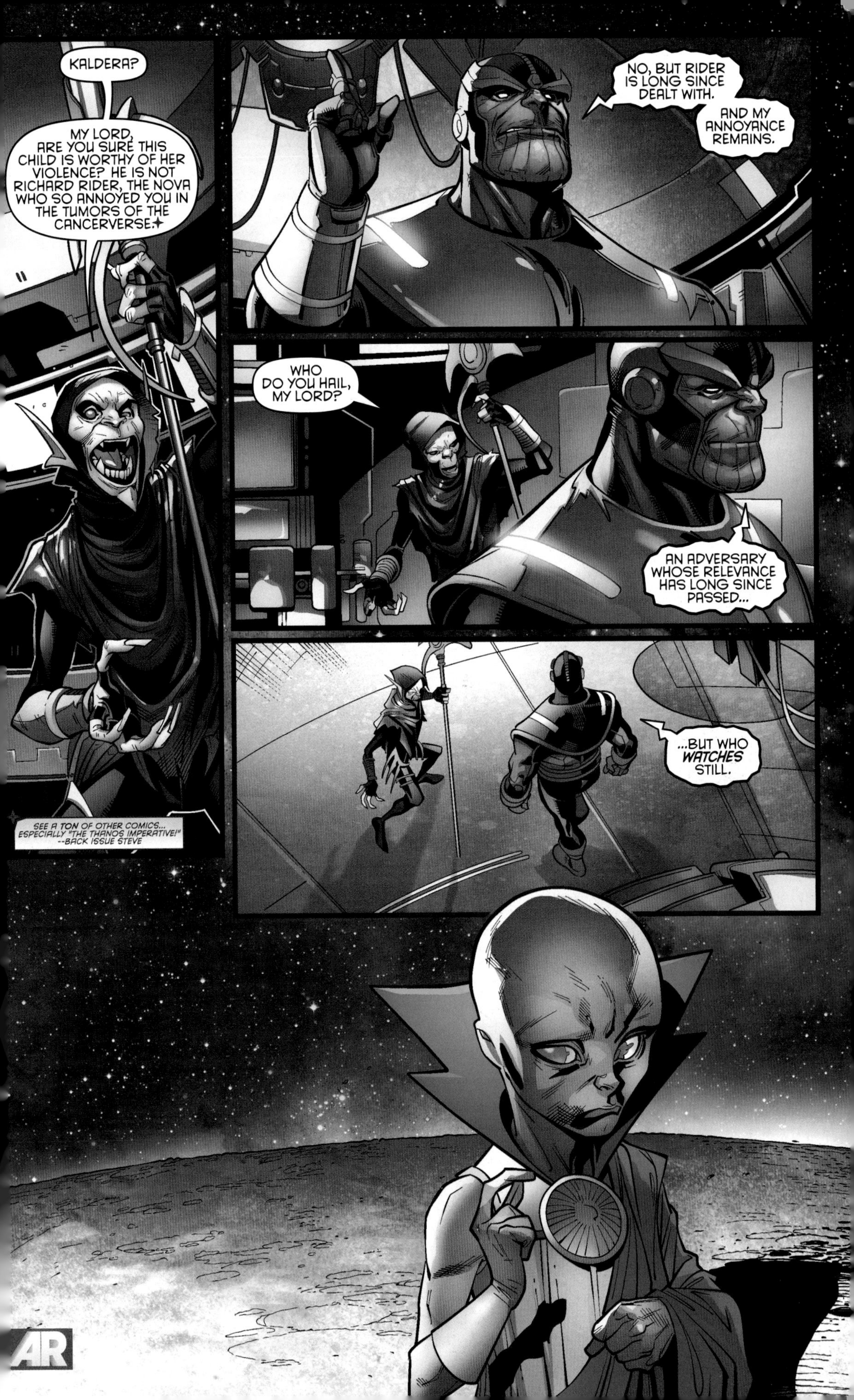
KALDERA?
MY LORD, ARE YOU SURE THIS CHILD IS WORTHY OF HER VIOLENCE? HE IS NOT RICHARD RIDER, THE NOVA WHO SO ANNOYED YOU IN THE TUMORS OF THE CANCERVERSE.✦
NO, BUT RIDER IS LONG SINCE DEALT WITH.
AND MY ANNOYANCE REMAINS.
SEE A TON OF OTHER COMICS... ESPECIALLY "THE THANOS IMPERATIVE!" --BACK ISSUE STEVE
WHO DO YOU HAIL, MY LORD?
AN ADVERSARY WHOSE RELEVANCE HAS LONG SINCE PASSED...
...BUT WHO *WATCHES* STILL.
AR

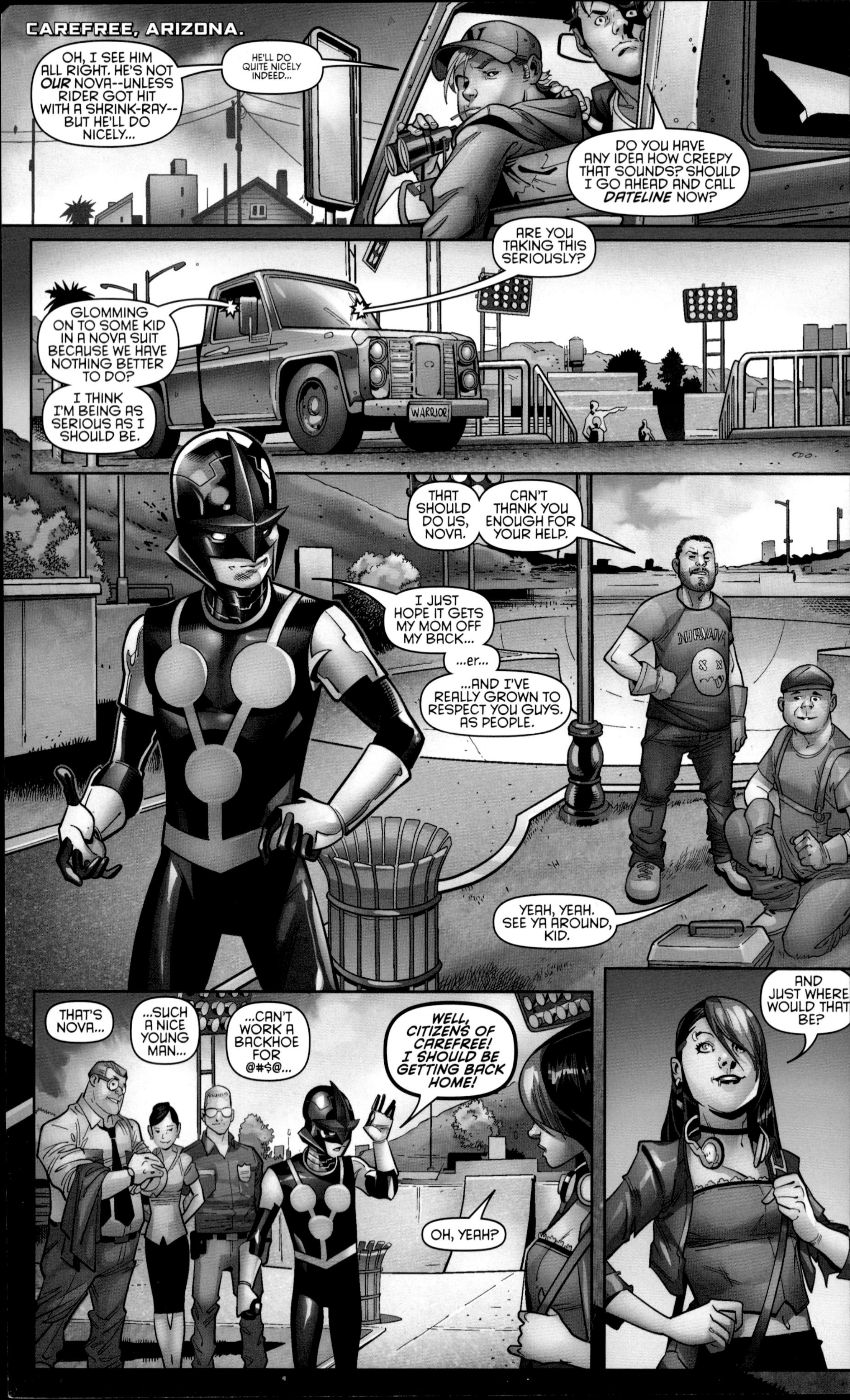
CAREFREE, ARIZONA.
OH, I SEE HIM ALL RIGHT. HE'S NOT OUR NOVA--UNLESS RIDER GOT HIT WITH A SHRINK-RAY--BUT HE'LL DO NICELY...
HE'LL DO QUITE NICELY INDEED...
DO YOU HAVE ANY IDEA HOW CREEPY THAT SOUNDS? SHOULD I GO AHEAD AND CALL DATELINE NOW?
ARE YOU TAKING THIS SERIOUSLY?
GLOMMING ON TO SOME KID IN A NOVA SUIT BECAUSE WE HAVE NOTHING BETTER TO DO?
I THINK I'M BEING AS SERIOUS AS I SHOULD BE.
WARRIOR
THAT SHOULD DO US, NOVA.
CAN'T THANK YOU ENOUGH FOR YOUR HELP.
I JUST HOPE IT GETS MY MOM OFF MY BACK...
...er...
...AND I'VE REALLY GROWN TO RESPECT YOU GUYS. AS PEOPLE.
YEAH, YEAH. SEE YA AROUND, KID.
THAT'S NOVA...
...SUCH A NICE YOUNG MAN...
...CAN'T WORK A BACKHOE FOR @#$@...
WELL, CITIZENS OF CAREFREE! I SHOULD BE GETTING BACK HOME!
OH, YEAH?
AND JUST WHERE WOULD THAT BE?

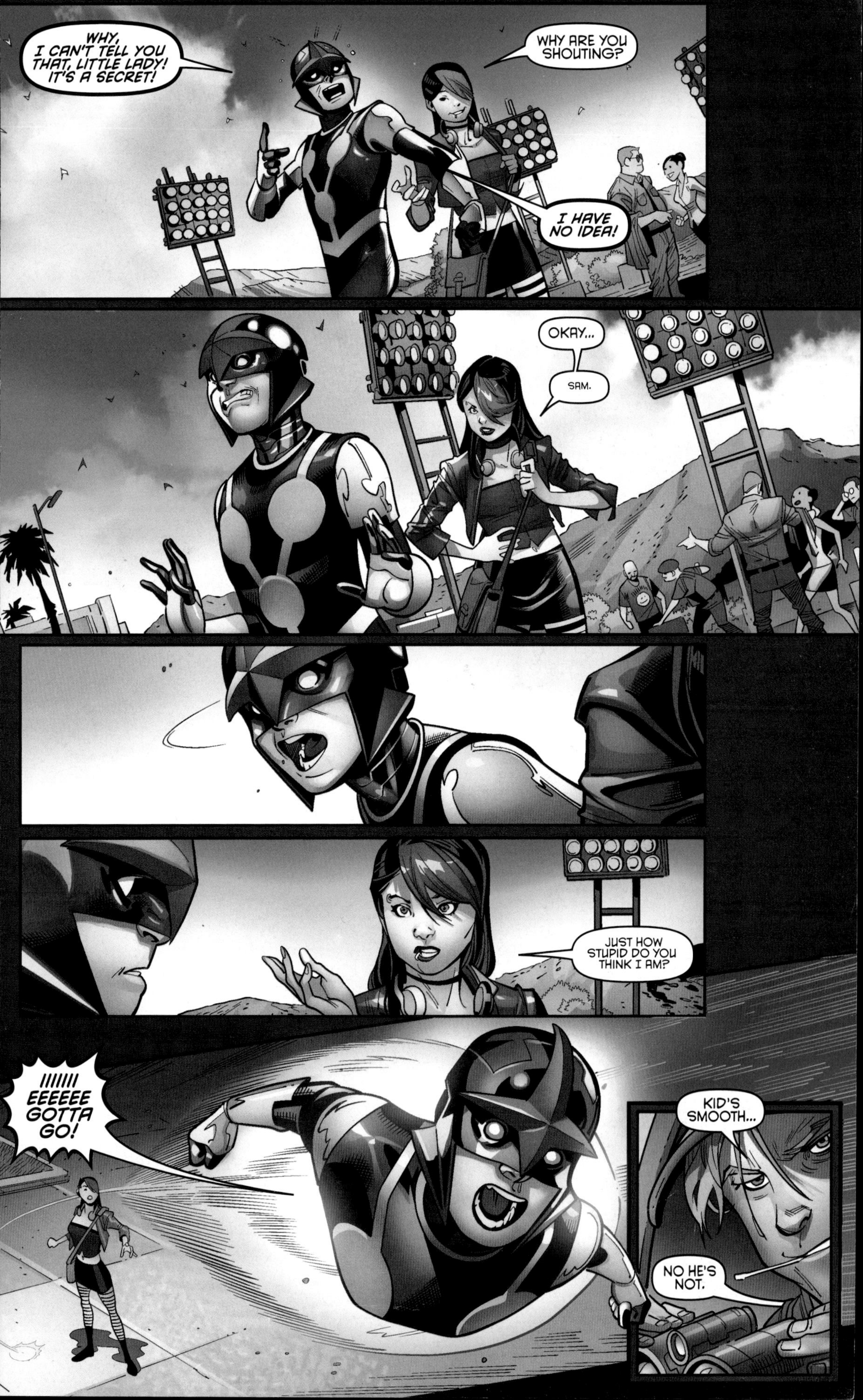
WHY, I CAN'T TELL YOU THAT, LITTLE LADY! IT'S A SECRET!
WHY ARE YOU SHOUTING?
I HAVE NO IDEA!
OKAY...
SAM.
JUST HOW STUPID DO YOU THINK I AM?
IIIIII EEEEEE GOTTA GO!
KID'S SMOOTH...
NO HE'S NOT.

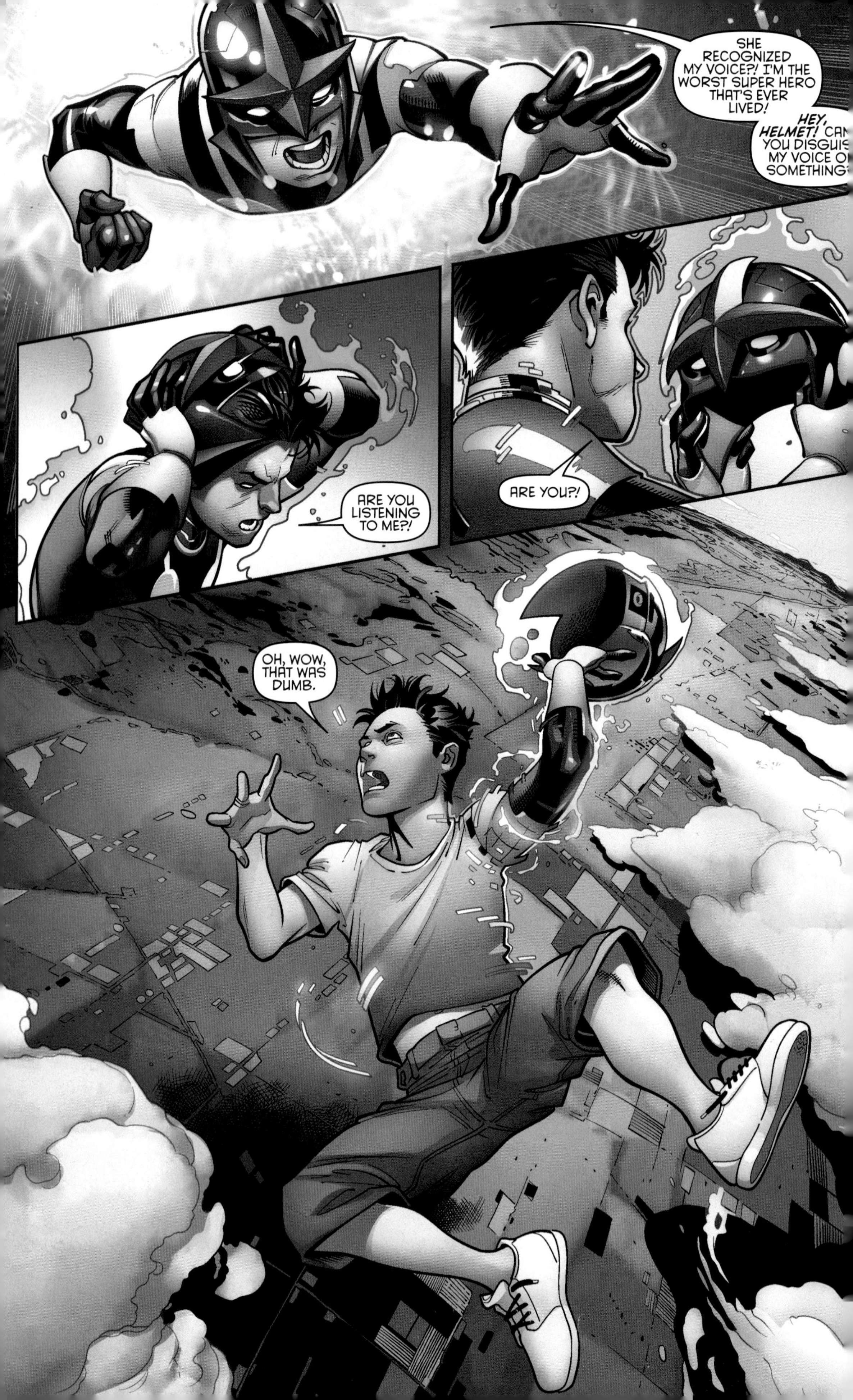
SHE RECOGNIZED MY VOICE?! I'M THE WORST SUPER HERO THAT'S EVER LIVED!
HEY, HELMET! CAN YOU DISGUIS MY VOICE O SOMETHING
ARE YOU LISTENING TO ME?!
ARE YOU?!
OH, WOW, THAT WAS DUMB.

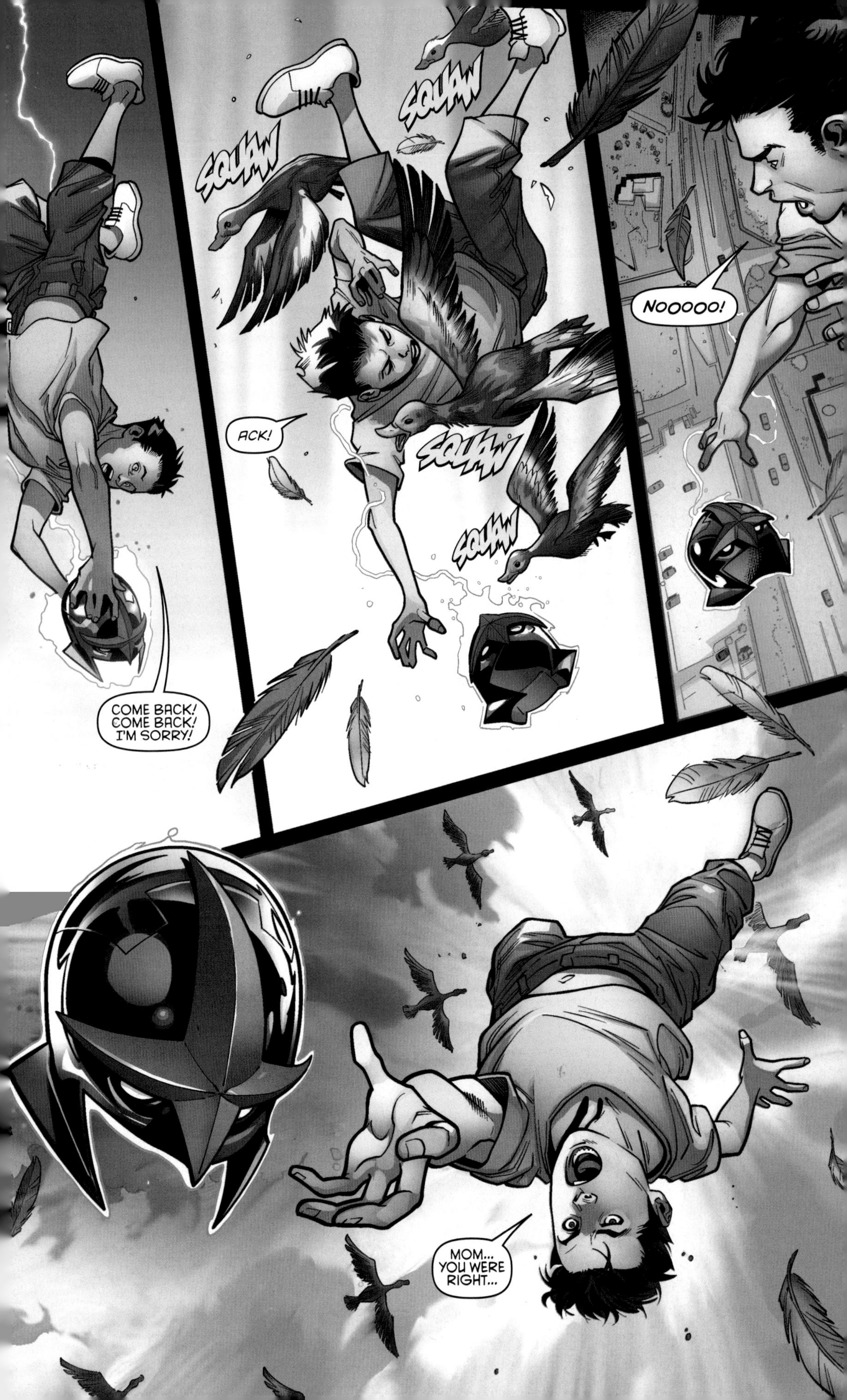
COME BACK! COME BACK! I'M SORRY!
SQUAW
SQUAW
ACK!
SQUAW
SQUAW
NOOOOO!
MOM... YOU WERE RIGHT...

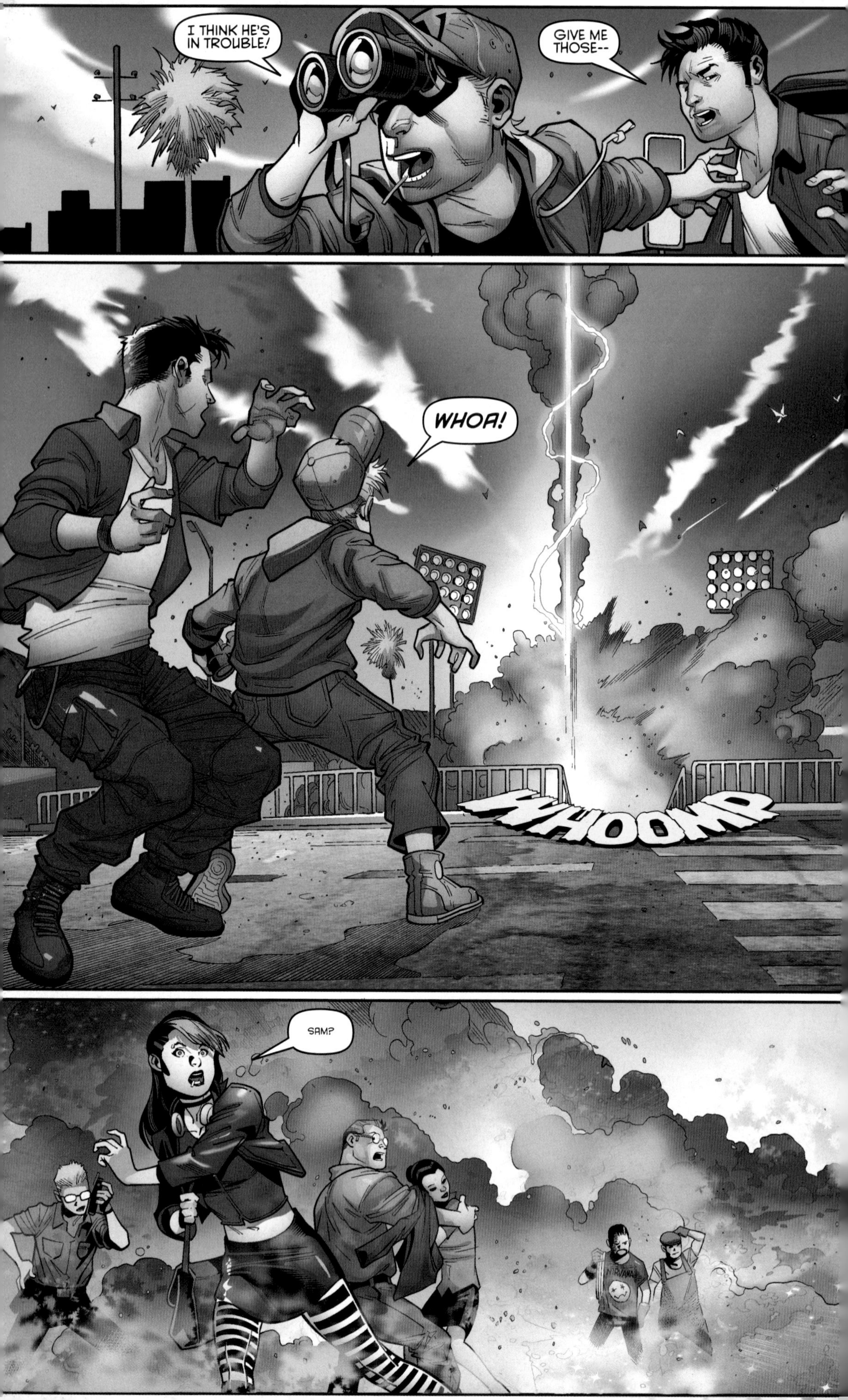
I THINK HE'S IN TROUBLE!
GIVE ME THOSE--
WHOA!
WHOOMP
SAM?

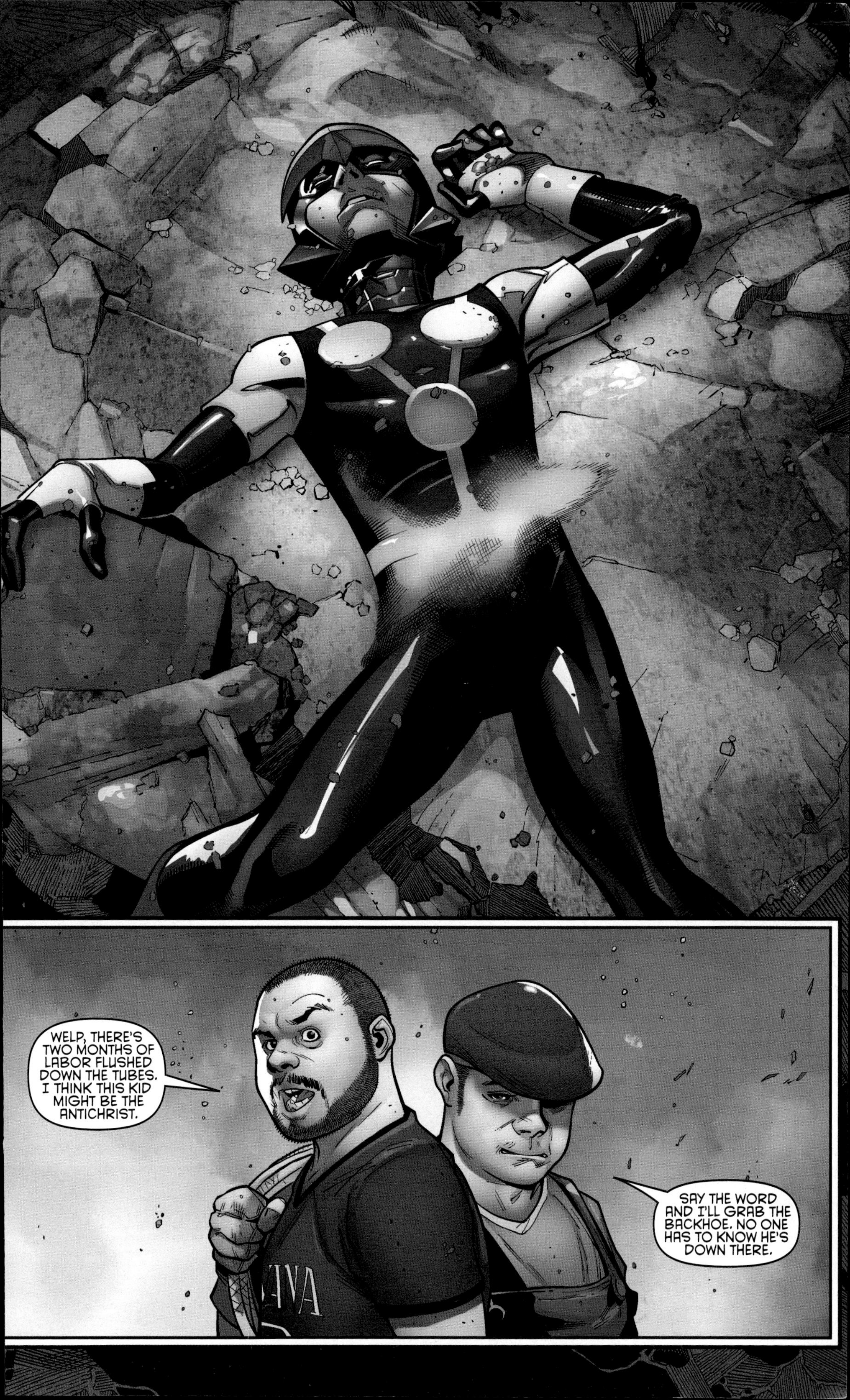
WELP, THERE'S TWO MONTHS OF LABOR FLUSHED DOWN THE TUBES. I THINK THIS KID MIGHT BE THE ANTICHRIST.
SAY THE WORD AND I'LL GRAB THE BACKHOE. NO ONE HAS TO KNOW HE'S DOWN THERE.

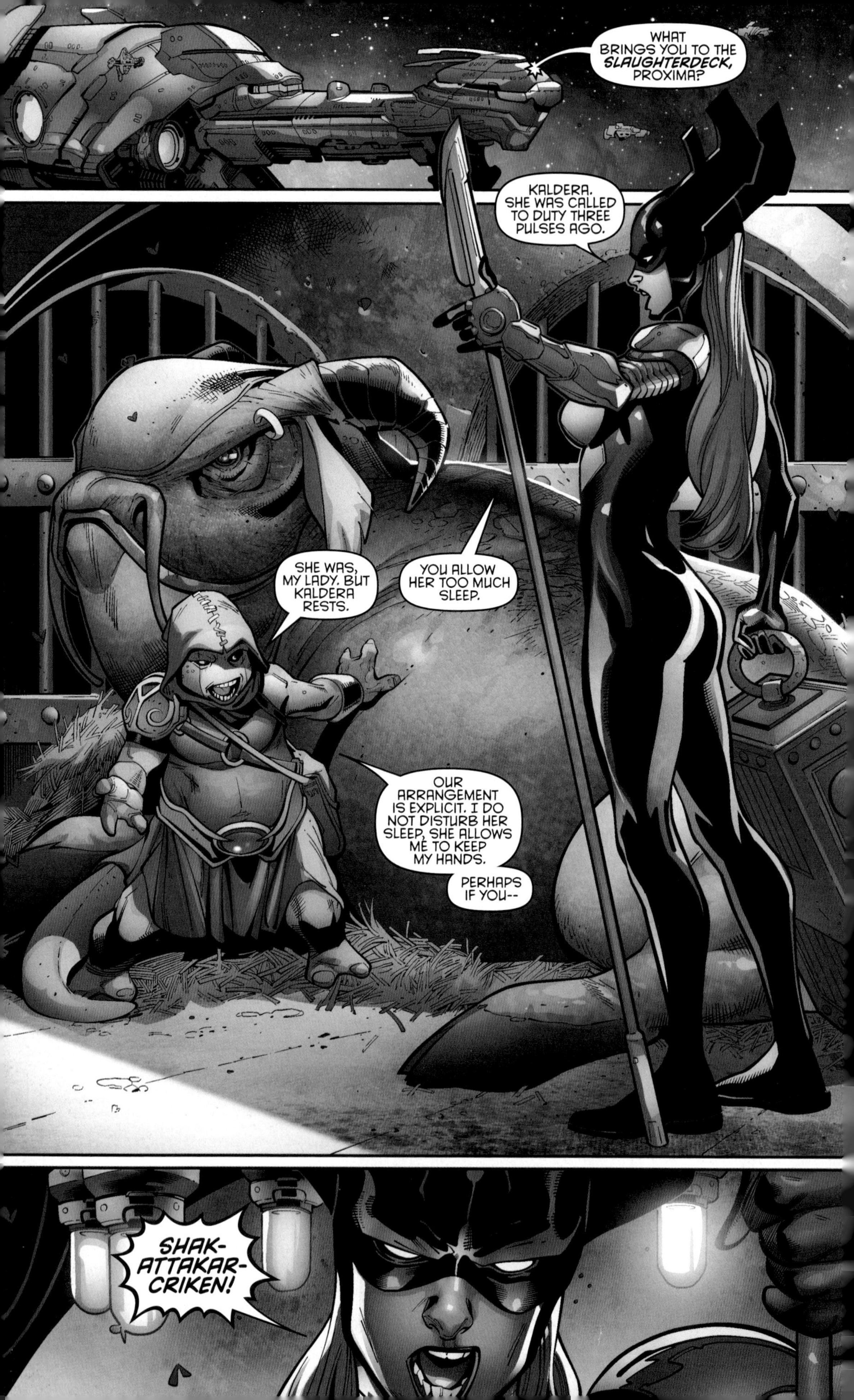
WHAT BRINGS YOU TO THE *SLAUGHTERDECK*, PROXIMA?
KALDERA. SHE WAS CALLED TO DUTY THREE PULSES AGO.
SHE WAS, MY LADY. BUT KALDERA RESTS.
YOU ALLOW HER TOO MUCH SLEEP.
OUR ARRANGEMENT IS EXPLICIT. I DO NOT DISTURB HER SLEEP, SHE ALLOWS ME TO KEEP MY HANDS.
PERHAPS IF YOU--
SHAK-ATTAKAR-CRIKEN!

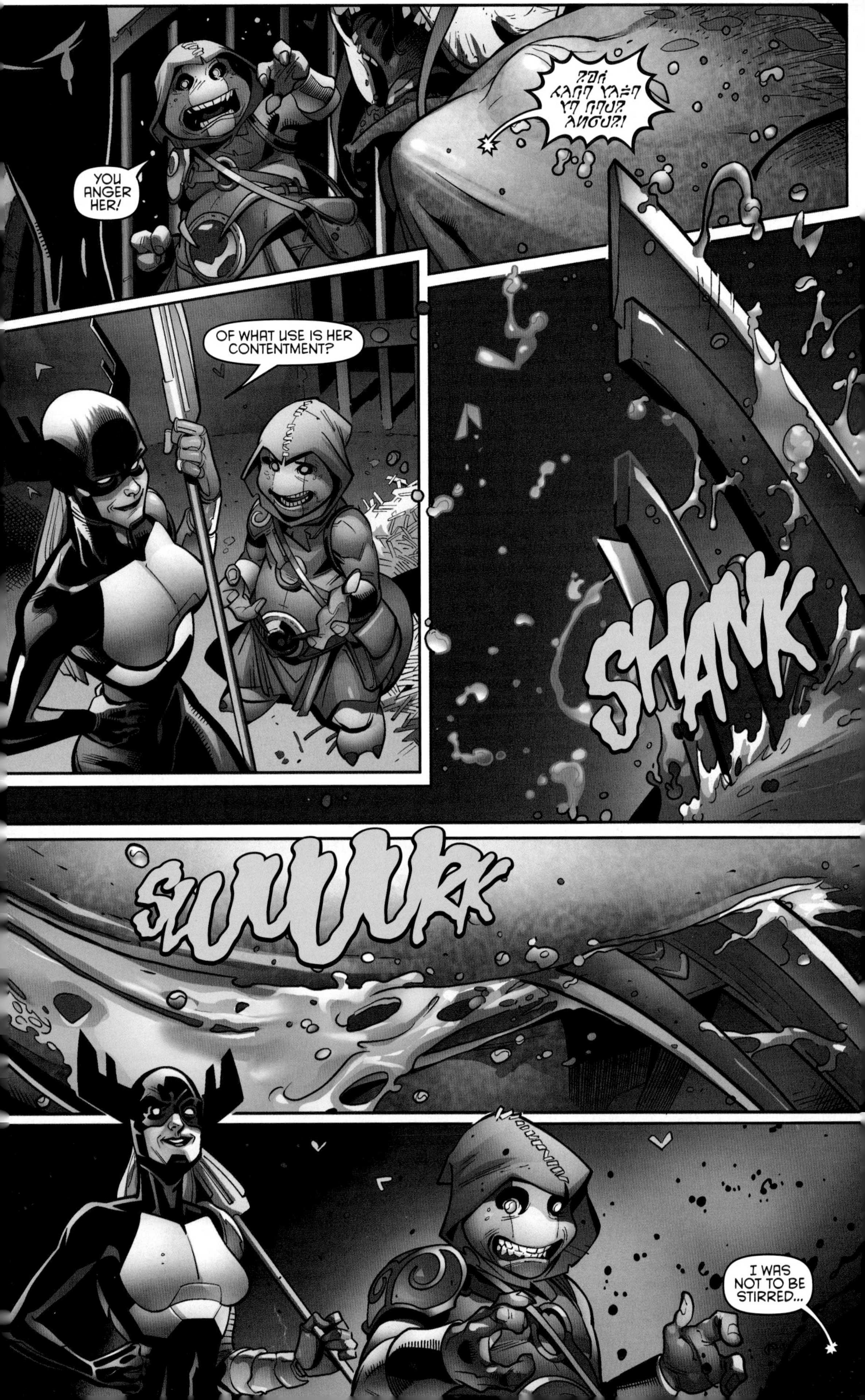
YOU ANGER HER!
OF WHAT USE IS HER CONTENTMENT?
SHANK
SLUUURK
I WAS NOT TO BE STIRRED...

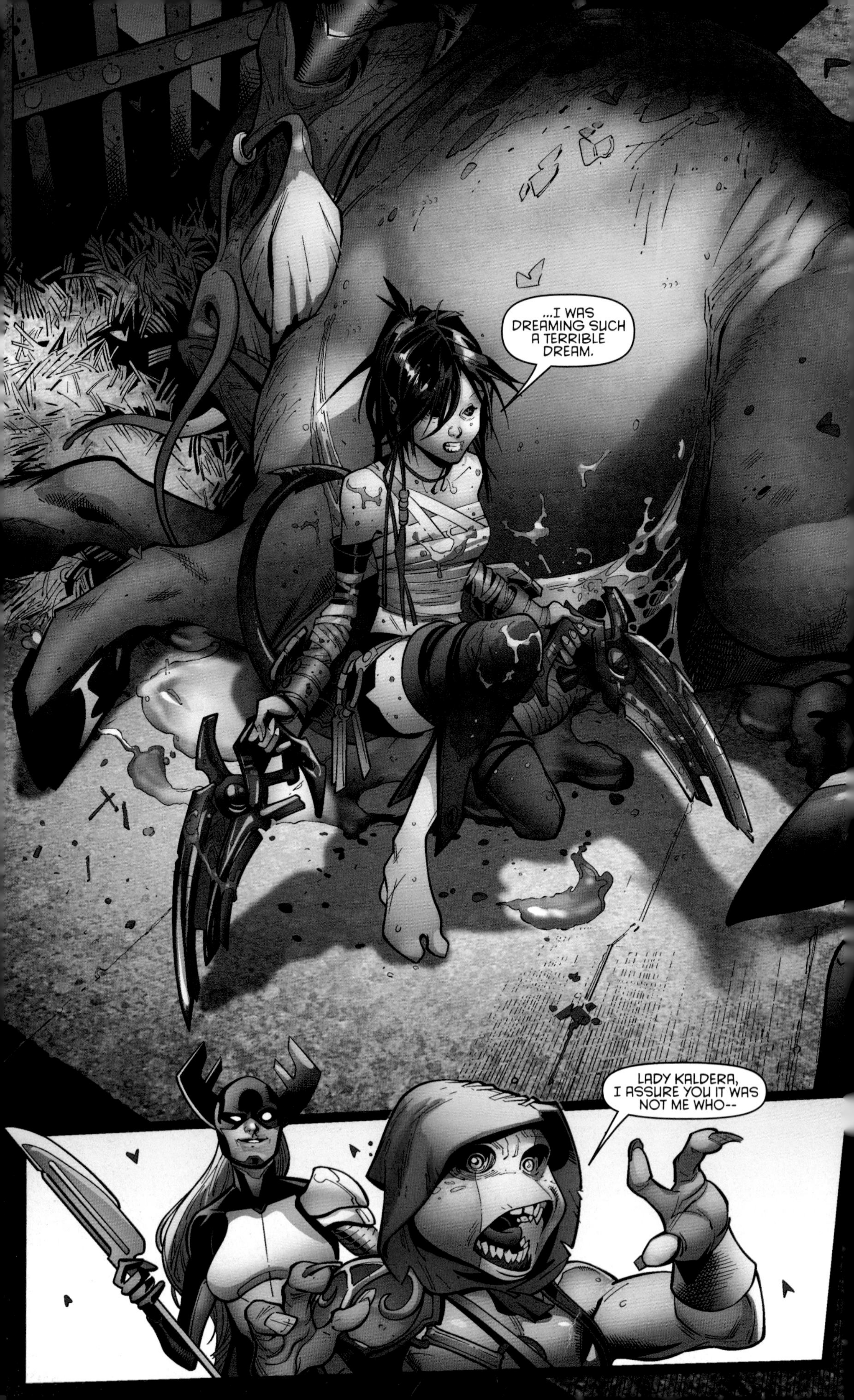
...I WAS DREAMING SUCH A TERRIBLE DREAM.
LADY KALDERA, I ASSURE YOU IT WAS NOT ME WHO--

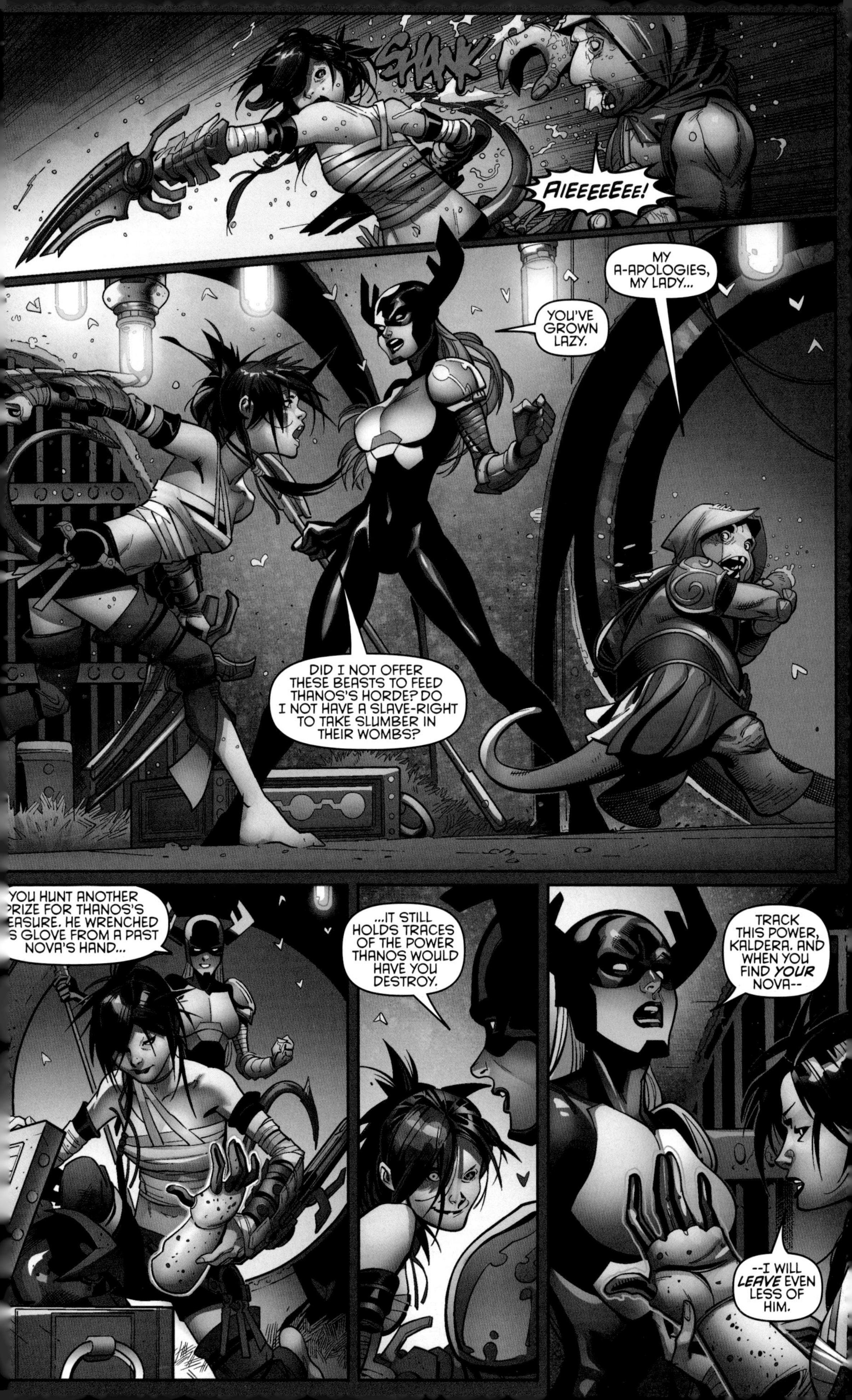
SHANK
AIEEEEEEee!
YOU'VE GROWN LAZY.
MY A-APOLOGIES, MY LADY...
DID I NOT OFFER THESE BEASTS TO FEED THANOS'S HORDE? DO I NOT HAVE A SLAVE-RIGHT TO TAKE SLUMBER IN THEIR WOMBS?
YOU HUNT ANOTHER PRIZE FOR THANOS'S EASURE. HE WRENCHED S GLOVE FROM A PAST NOVA'S HAND...
...IT STILL HOLDS TRACES OF THE POWER THANOS WOULD HAVE YOU DESTROY.
TRACK THIS POWER, KALDERA. AND WHEN YOU FIND YOUR NOVA--
--I WILL LEAVE EVEN LESS OF HIM.

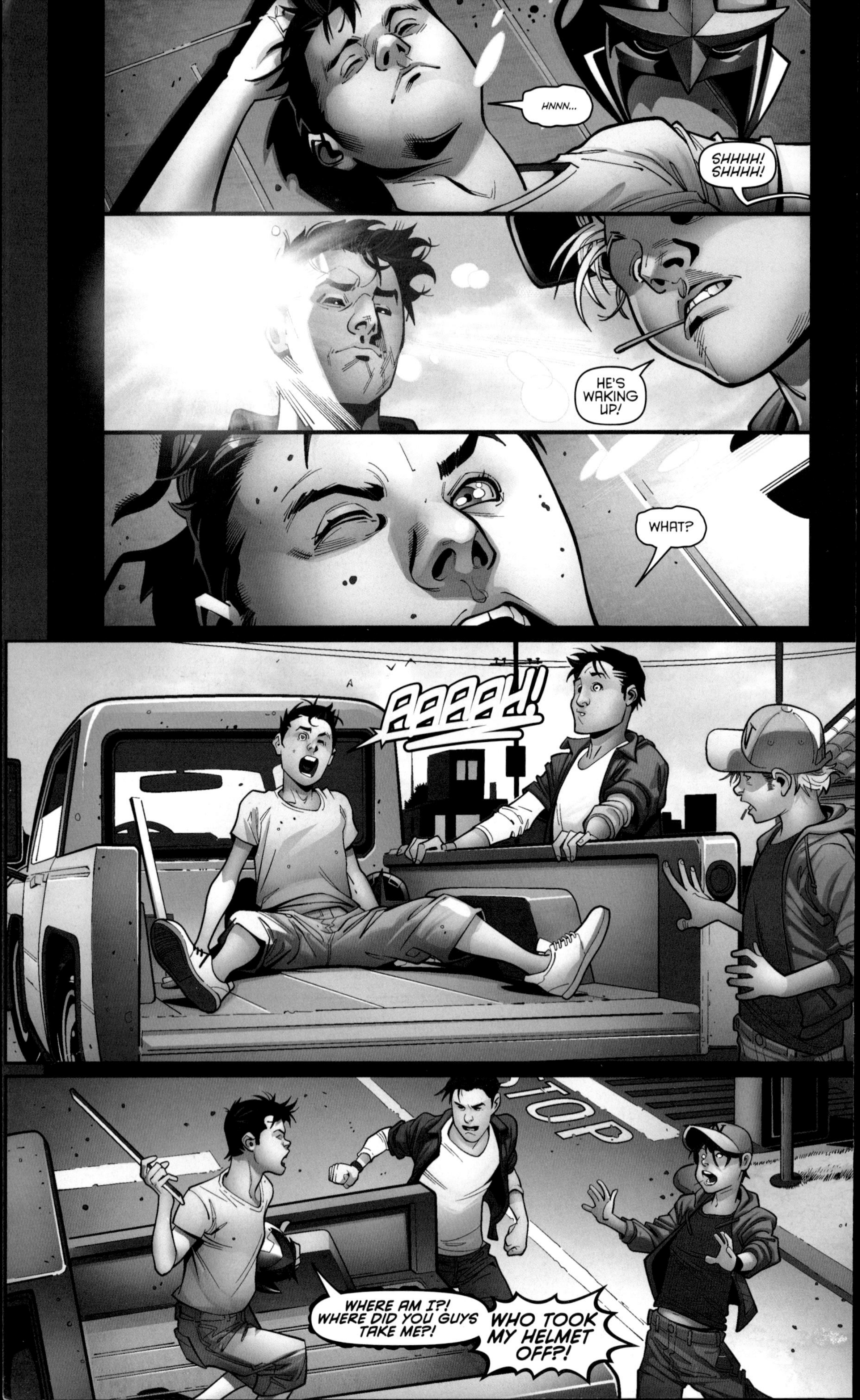
HNNN...
SHHHH! SHHHH!
HE'S WAKING UP!
WHAT?
AAAAH!
WHERE AM I?! WHERE DID YOU GUYS TAKE ME?!
WHO TOOK MY HELMET OFF?!

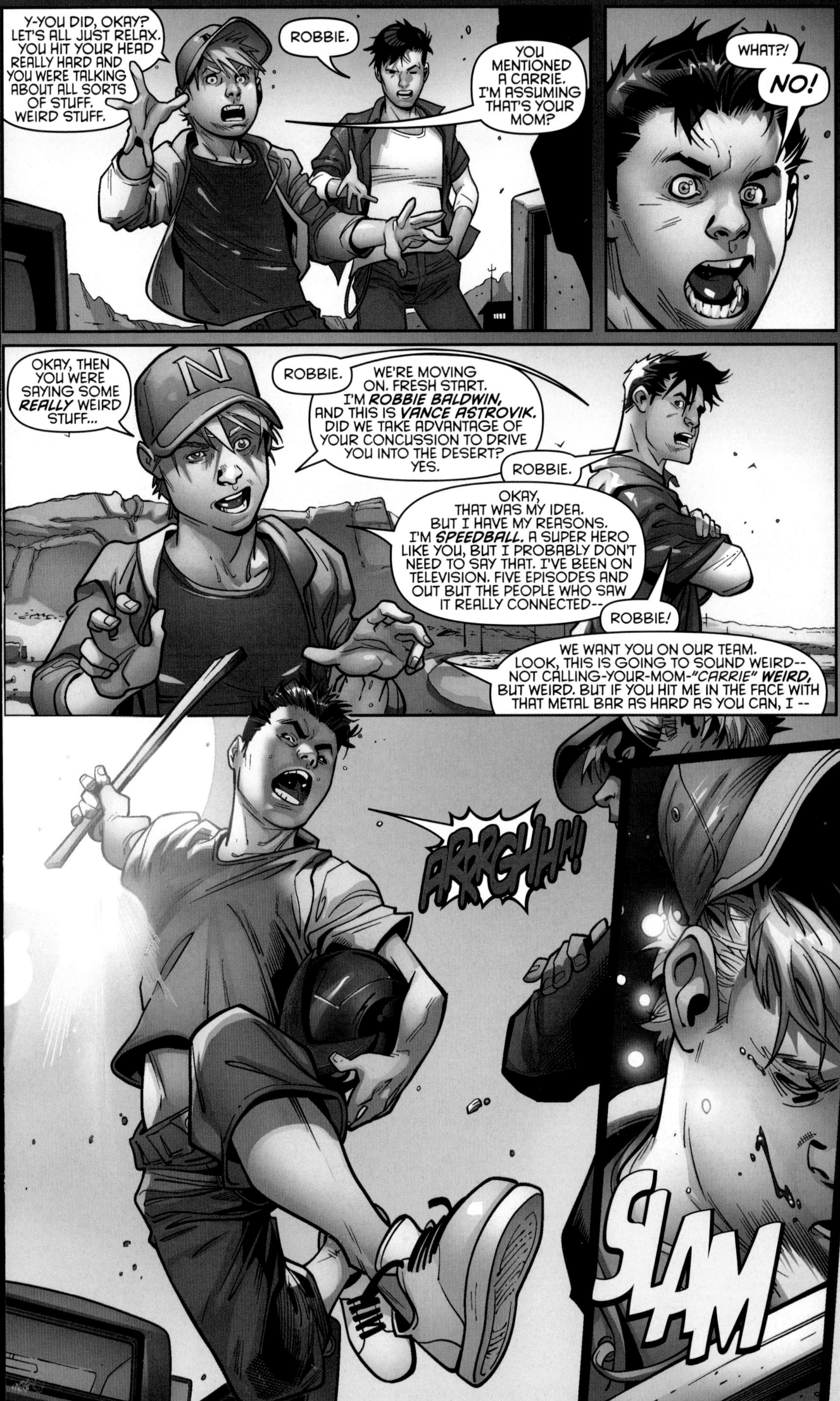

Y-YOU DID, OKAY? LET'S ALL JUST RELAX. YOU HIT YOUR HEAD REALLY HARD AND YOU WERE TALKING ABOUT ALL SORTS OF STUFF. WEIRD STUFF.
ROBBIE.
YOU MENTIONED A CARRIE. I'M ASSUMING THAT'S YOUR MOM?
WHAT?!
NO!
OKAY, THEN YOU WERE SAYING SOME REALLY WEIRD STUFF...
ROBBIE.
WE'RE MOVING ON. FRESH START. I'M ROBBIE BALDWIN, AND THIS IS VANCE ASTROVIK. DID WE TAKE ADVANTAGE OF YOUR CONCUSSION TO DRIVE YOU INTO THE DESERT? YES.
ROBBIE.
OKAY, THAT WAS MY IDEA. BUT I HAVE MY REASONS. I'M SPEEDBALL. A SUPER HERO LIKE YOU, BUT I PROBABLY DON'T NEED TO SAY THAT. I'VE BEEN ON TELEVISION. FIVE EPISODES AND OUT BUT THE PEOPLE WHO SAW IT REALLY CONNECTED--
ROBBIE!
WE WANT YOU ON OUR TEAM. LOOK, THIS IS GOING TO SOUND WEIRD-- NOT CALLING-YOUR-MOM-"CARRIE" WEIRD, BUT WEIRD. BUT IF YOU HIT ME IN THE FACE WITH THAT METAL BAR AS HARD AS YOU CAN, I --
ARRRGHHH!
SLAM

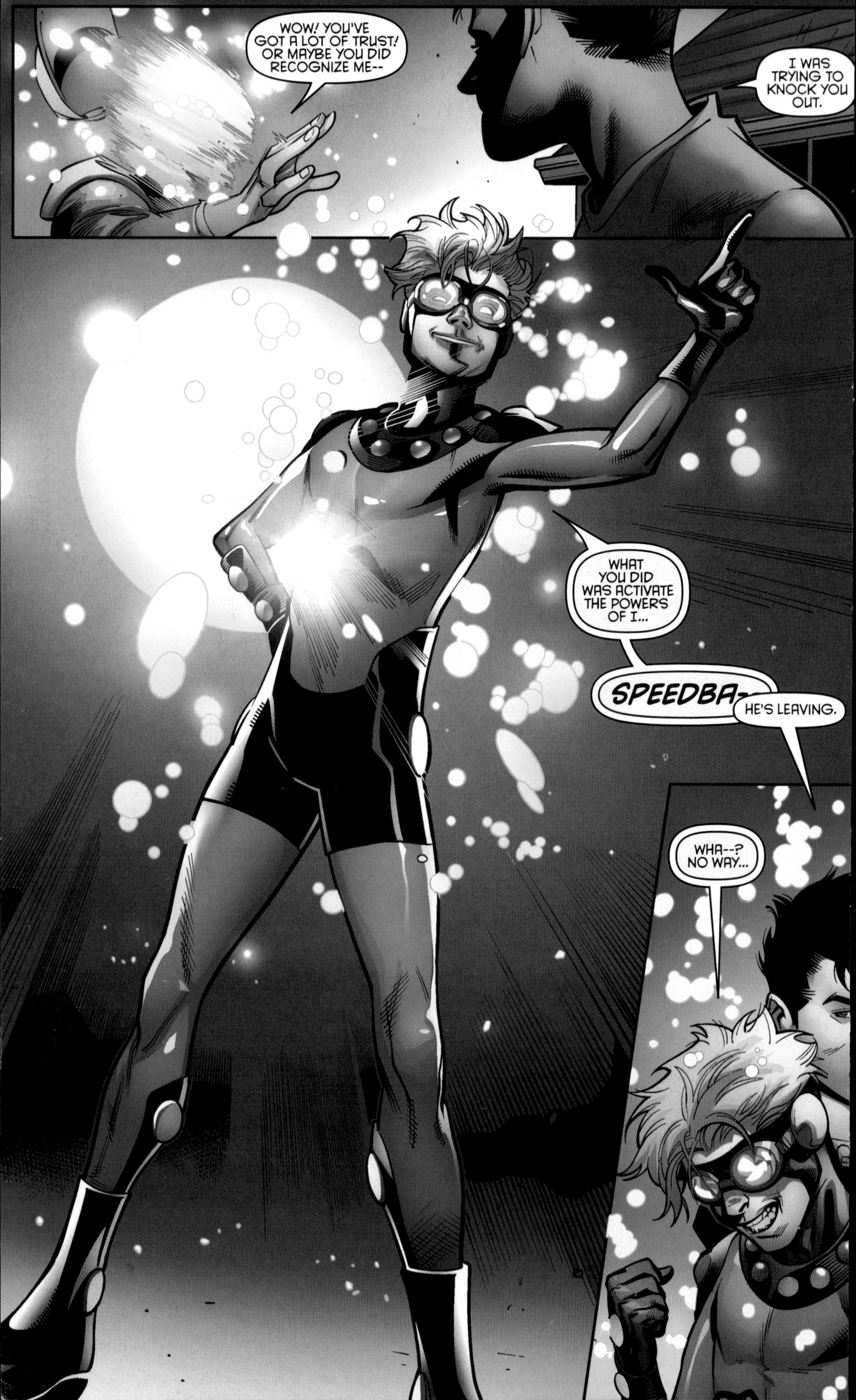
WOW! YOU'VE GOT A LOT OF TRUST! OR MAYBE YOU DID RECOGNIZE ME--
I WAS TRYING TO KNOCK YOU OUT.
WHAT YOU DID WAS ACTIVATE THE POWERS OF I...
SPEEDBA--
HE'S LEAVING.
WHA--? NO WAY...

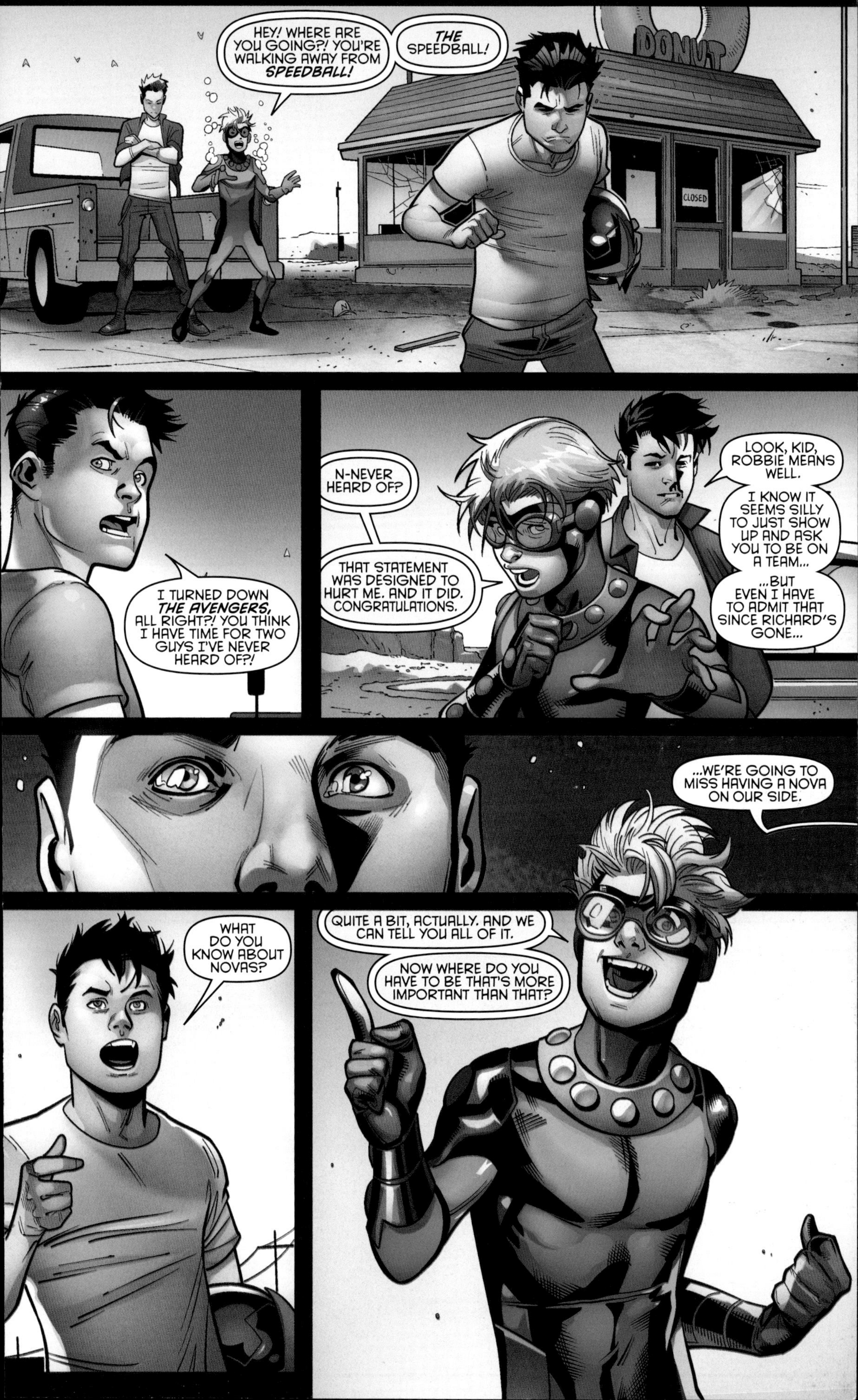
HEY! WHERE ARE YOU GOING?! YOU'RE WALKING AWAY FROM SPEEDBALL!
THE SPEEDBALL!
DONUT
CLOSED
I TURNED DOWN THE AVENGERS, ALL RIGHT?! YOU THINK I HAVE TIME FOR TWO GUYS I'VE NEVER HEARD OF?!
N-NEVER HEARD OF?
THAT STATEMENT WAS DESIGNED TO HURT ME. AND IT DID. CONGRATULATIONS.
LOOK, KID, ROBBIE MEANS WELL.
I KNOW IT SEEMS SILLY TO JUST SHOW UP AND ASK YOU TO BE ON A TEAM...
...BUT EVEN I HAVE TO ADMIT THAT SINCE RICHARD'S GONE...
...WE'RE GOING TO MISS HAVING A NOVA ON OUR SIDE.
WHAT DO YOU KNOW ABOUT NOVAS?
QUITE A BIT, ACTUALLY. AND WE CAN TELL YOU ALL OF IT.
NOW WHERE DO YOU HAVE TO BE THAT'S MORE IMPORTANT THAN THAT?

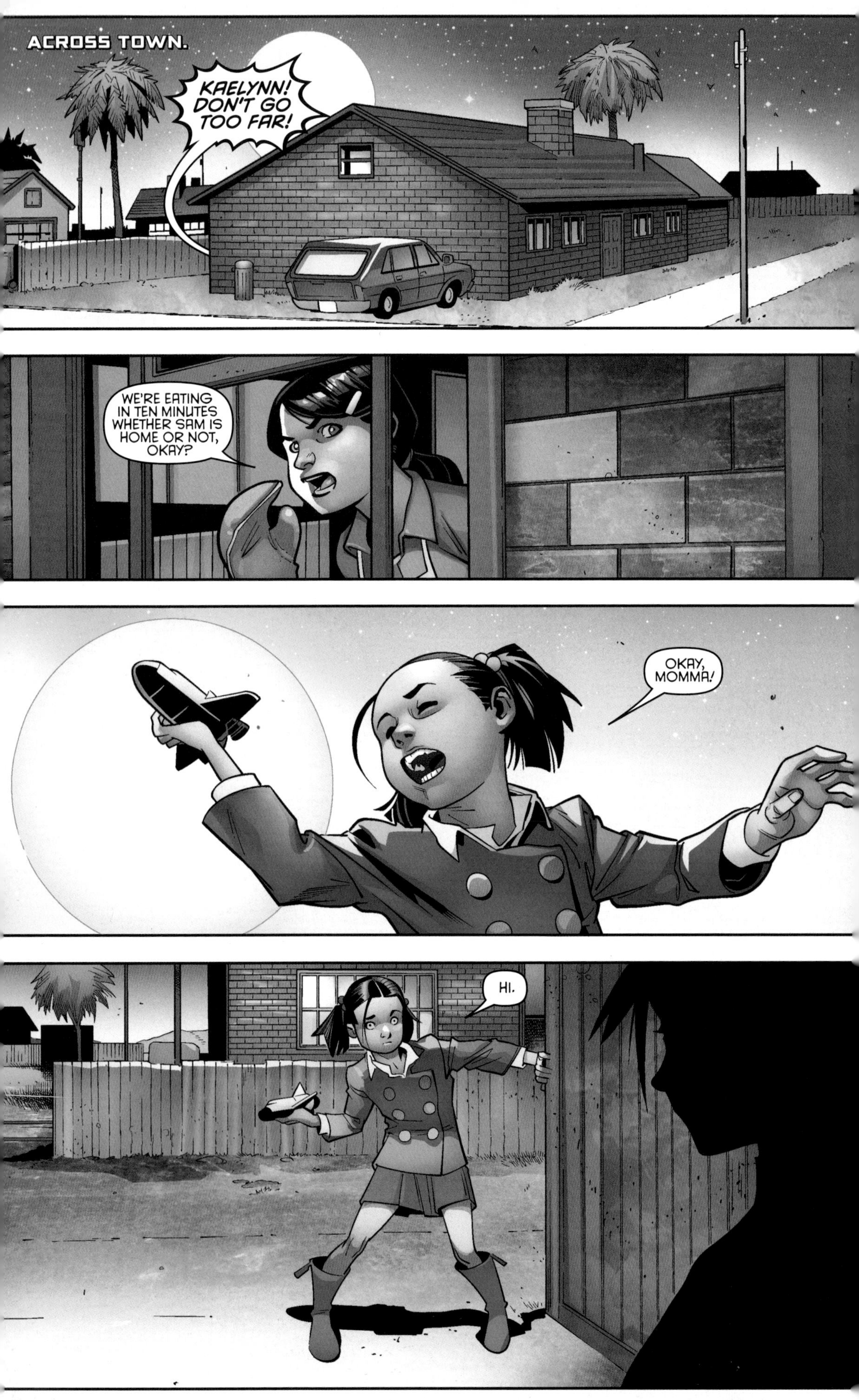
ACROSS TOWN.
KAELYNN! DON'T GO TOO FAR!
WE'RE EATING IN TEN MINUTES WHETHER SAM IS HOME OR NOT, OKAY?
OKAY, MOMMA!
HI.

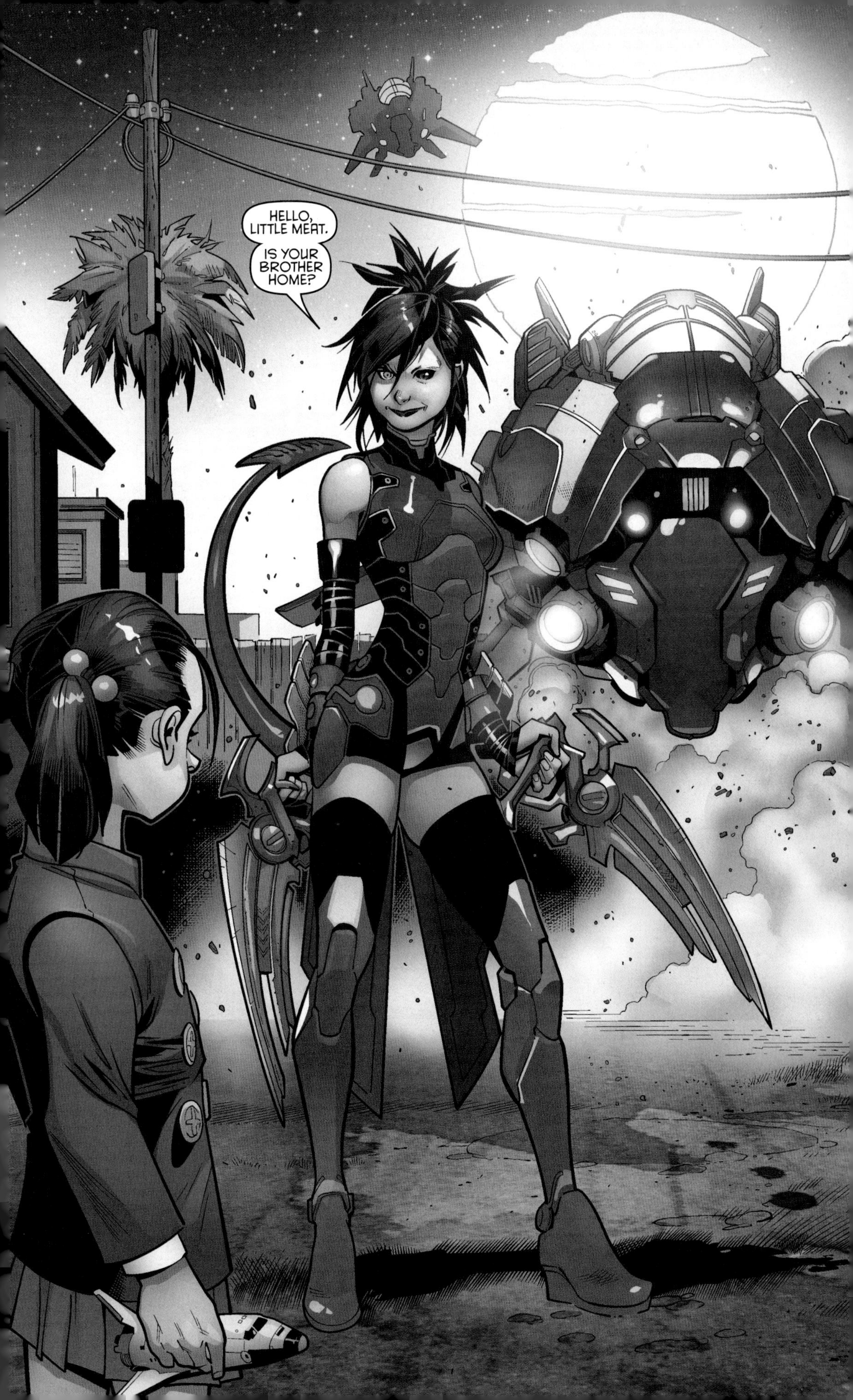
HELLO, LITTLE MEAT.
IS YOUR BROTHER HOME?

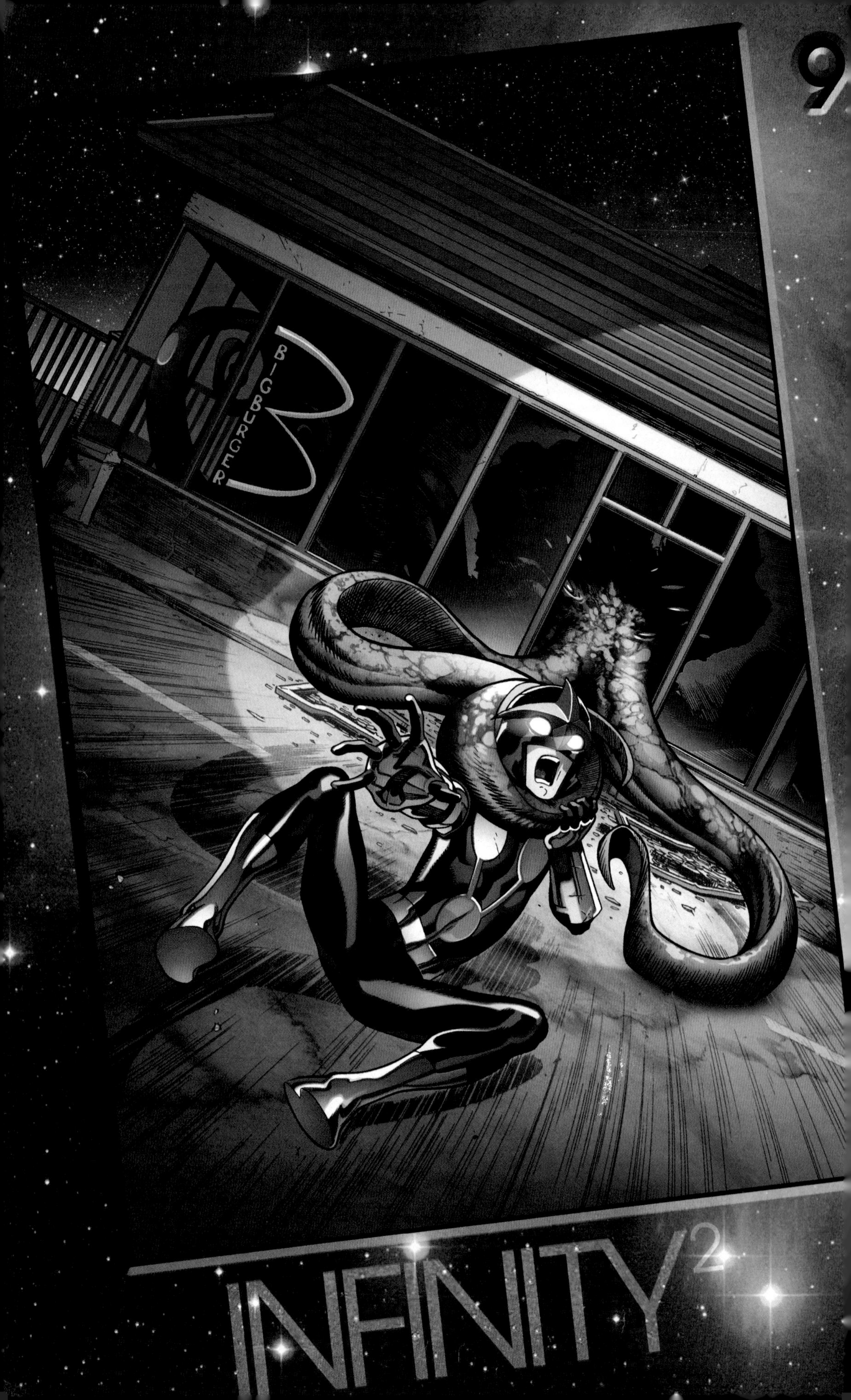
9
BIGBURGER
INFINITY²

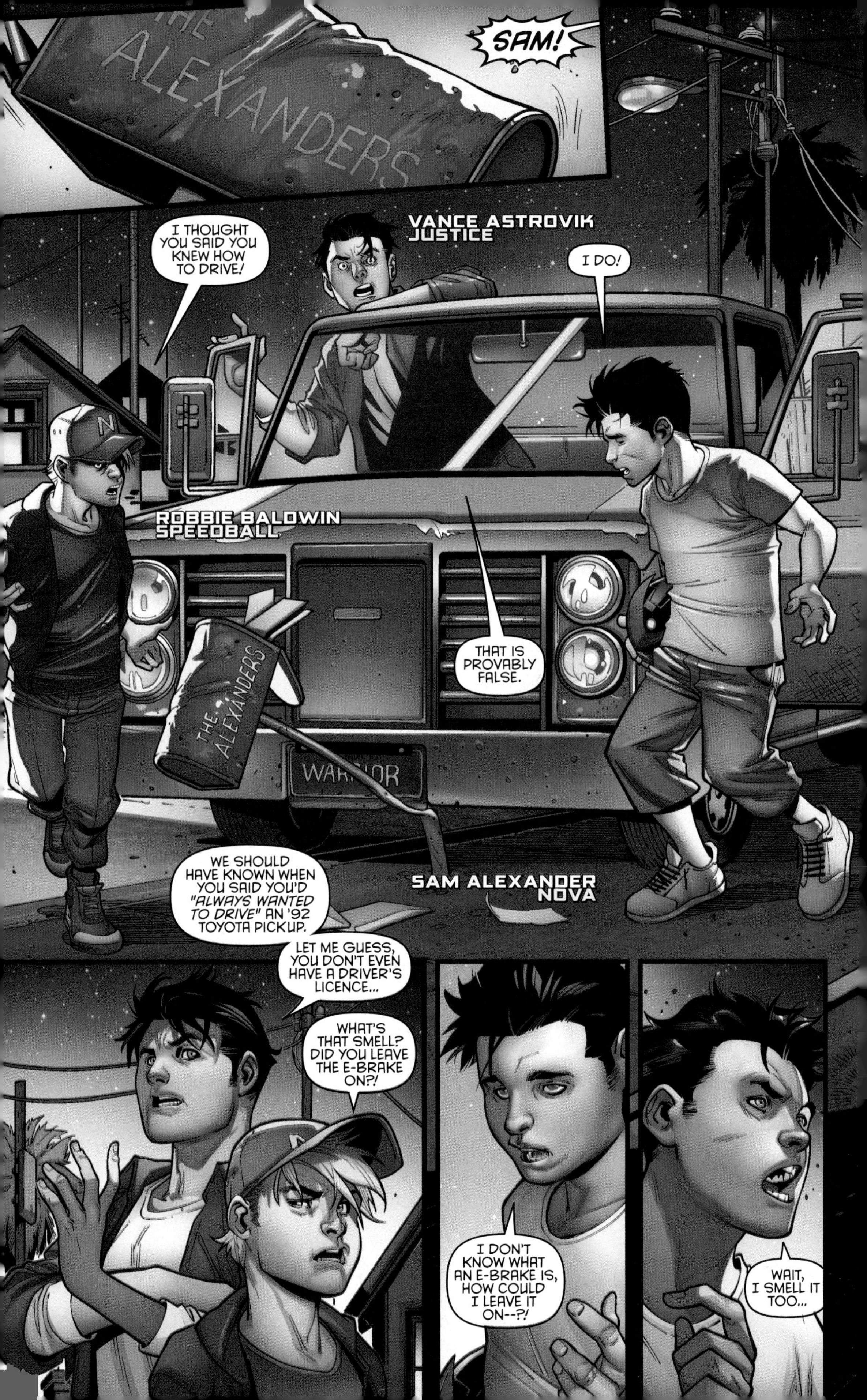
SAM!
THE ALEXANDERS
VANCE ASTROVIK JUSTICE
I THOUGHT YOU SAID YOU KNEW HOW TO DRIVE!
I DO!
ROBBIE BALDWIN SPEEDBALL
THAT IS PROVABLY FALSE.
THE ALEXANDERS
SAM ALEXANDER NOVA
WE SHOULD HAVE KNOWN WHEN YOU SAID YOU'D "ALWAYS WANTED TO DRIVE" AN '92 TOYOTA PICKUP.
LET ME GUESS, YOU DON'T EVEN HAVE A DRIVER'S LICENCE...
WHAT'S THAT SMELL? DID YOU LEAVE THE E-BRAKE ON?!
I DON'T KNOW WHAT AN E-BRAKE IS, HOW COULD I LEAVE IT ON--?!
WAIT, I SMELL IT TOO...

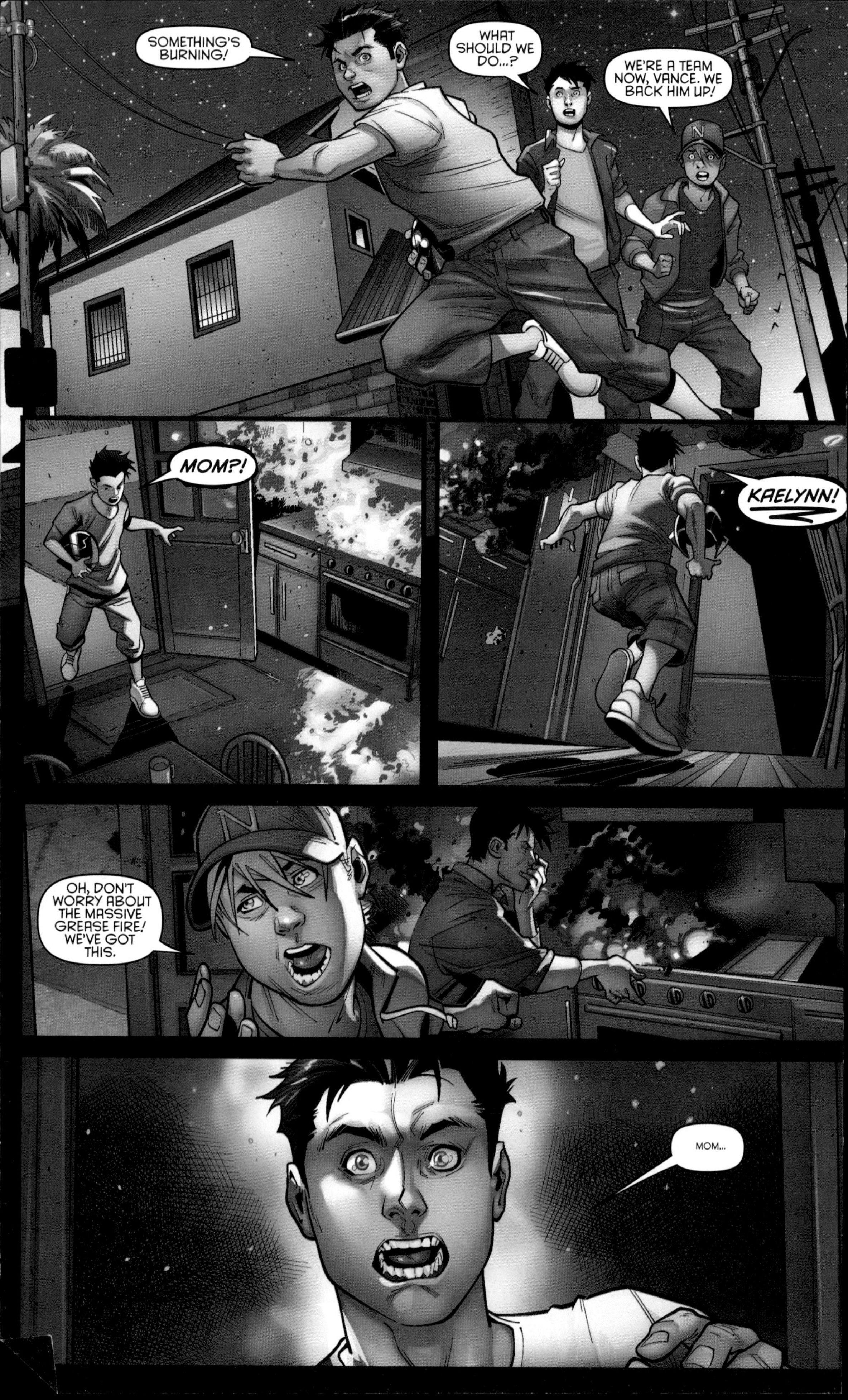
SOMETHING'S BURNING!
WHAT SHOULD WE DO...?
WE'RE A TEAM NOW, VANCE. WE BACK HIM UP!
MOM?!
KAELYNN!
OH, DON'T WORRY ABOUT THE MASSIVE GREASE FIRE! WE'VE GOT THIS.
MOM...

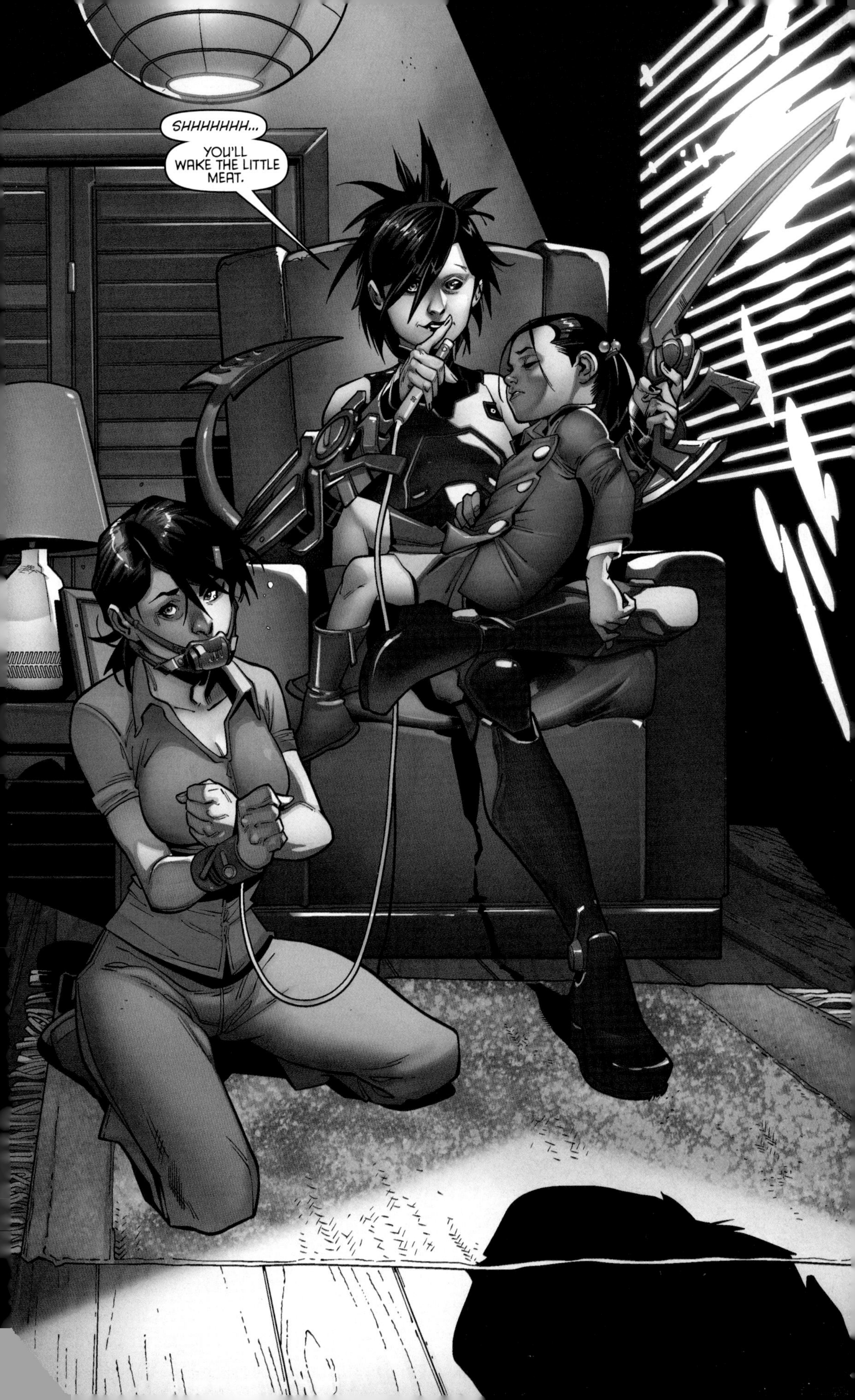
SHHHHHHH...
YOU'LL WAKE THE LITTLE MEAT.

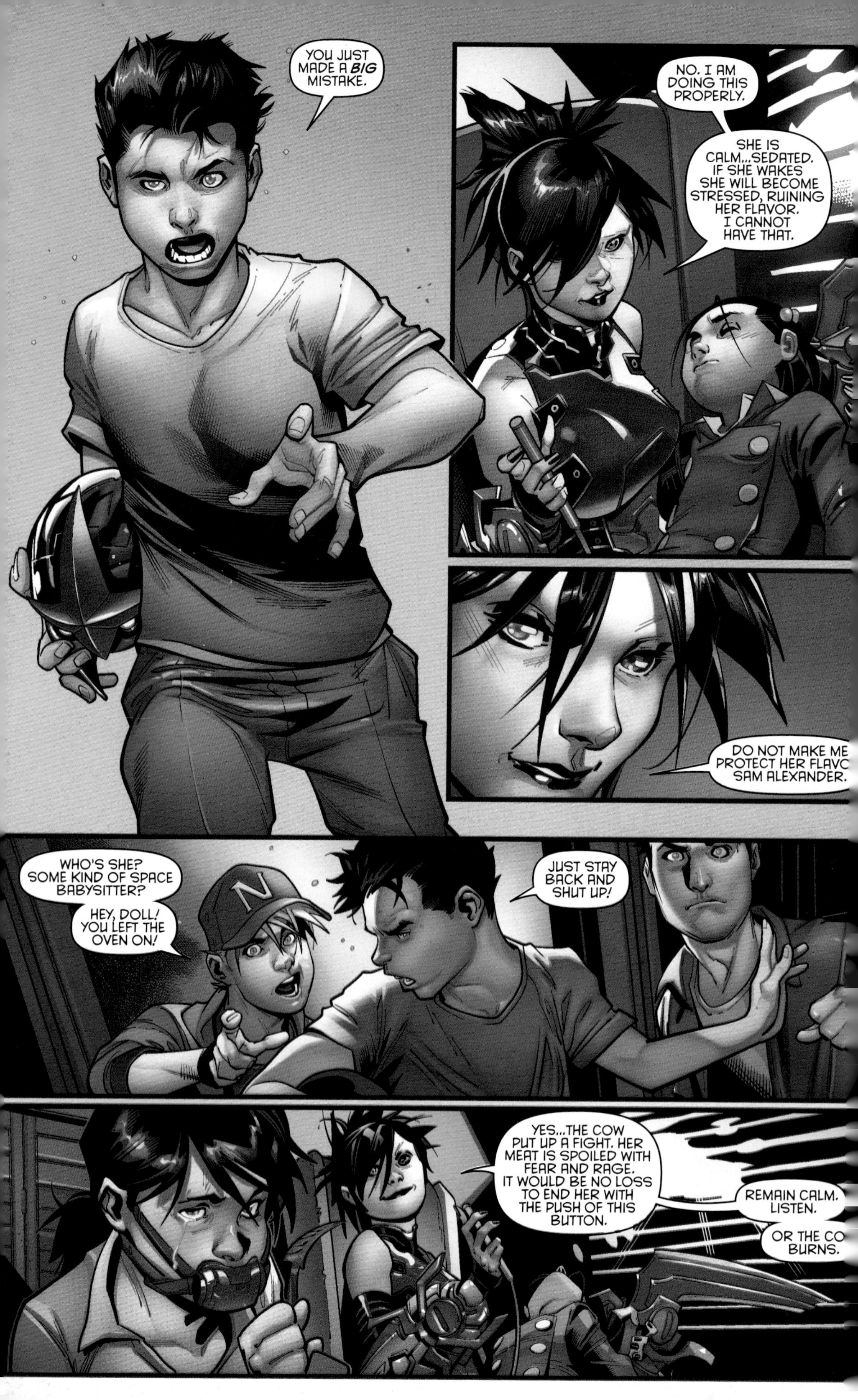
YOU JUST MADE A *BIG* MISTAKE.
NO. I AM DOING THIS PROPERLY.
SHE IS CALM...SEDATED. IF SHE WAKES SHE WILL BECOME STRESSED, RUINING HER FLAVOR. I CANNOT HAVE THAT.
DO NOT MAKE ME PROTECT HER FLAVO SAM ALEXANDER.
WHO'S SHE? SOME KIND OF SPACE BABYSITTER?
HEY, DOLL! YOU LEFT THE OVEN ON!
JUST STAY BACK AND SHUT UP!
YES...THE COW PUT UP A FIGHT. HER MEAT IS SPOILED WITH FEAR AND RAGE. IT WOULD BE NO LOSS TO END HER WITH THE PUSH OF THIS BUTTON.
REMAIN CALM. LISTEN.
OR THE CO BURNS.

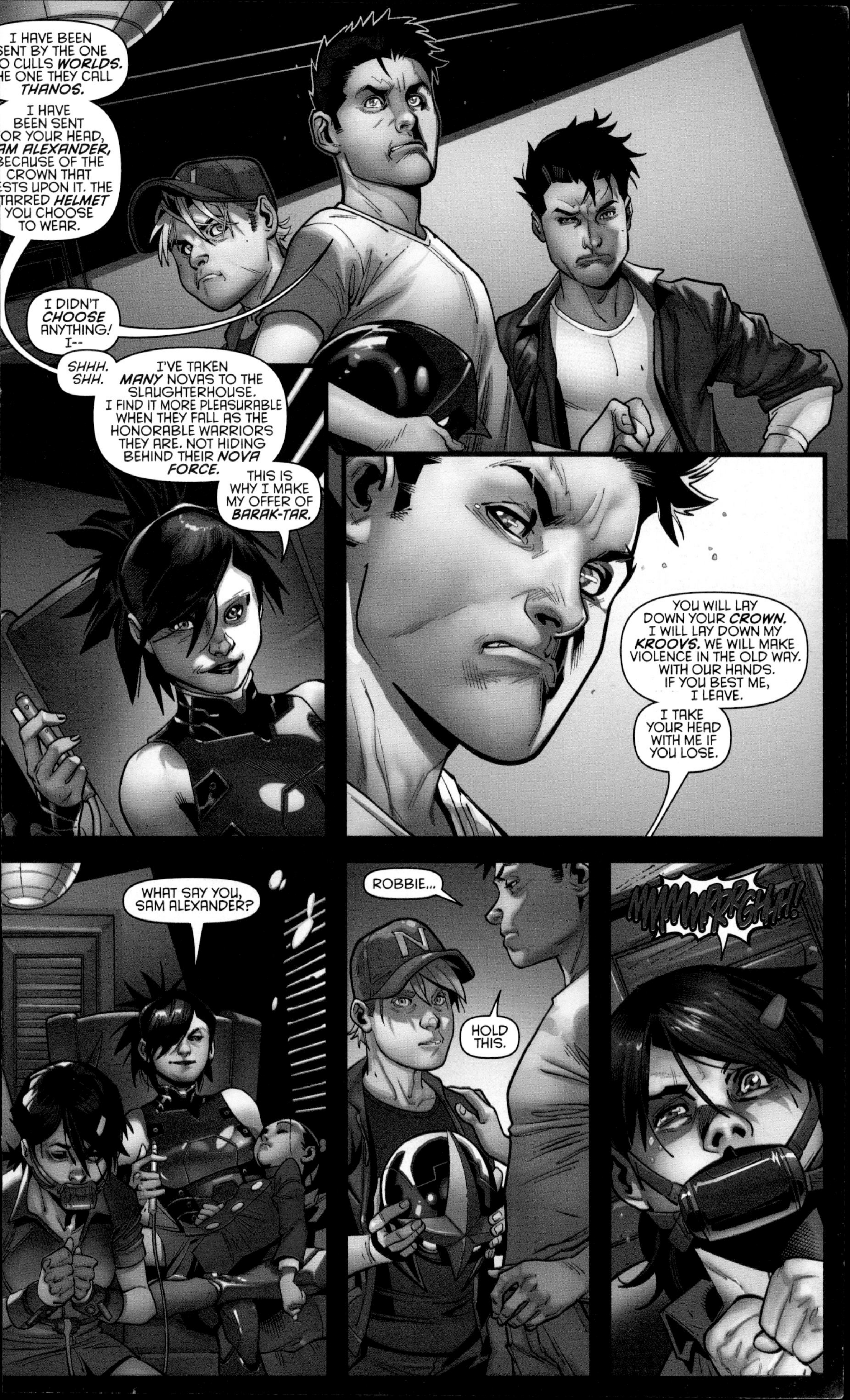

I HAVE BEEN SENT BY THE ONE O CULLS WORLDS. HE ONE THEY CALL THANOS.
I HAVE BEEN SENT OR YOUR HEAD, AM ALEXANDER, BECAUSE OF THE CROWN THAT ESTS UPON IT. THE TARRED HELMET YOU CHOOSE TO WEAR.
I DIDN'T CHOOSE ANYTHING! I--
SHHH. SHH.
I'VE TAKEN MANY NOVAS TO THE SLAUGHTERHOUSE. I FIND IT MORE PLEASURABLE WHEN THEY FALL AS THE HONORABLE WARRIORS THEY ARE. NOT HIDING BEHIND THEIR NOVA FORCE.
THIS IS WHY I MAKE MY OFFER OF BARAK-TAR.
YOU WILL LAY DOWN YOUR CROWN. I WILL LAY DOWN MY KROOVS. WE WILL MAKE VIOLENCE IN THE OLD WAY. WITH OUR HANDS. IF YOU BEST ME, I LEAVE.
I TAKE YOUR HEAD WITH ME IF YOU LOSE.
WHAT SAY YOU, SAM ALEXANDER?
ROBBIE...
HOLD THIS.
MMMMRRRGHHH!

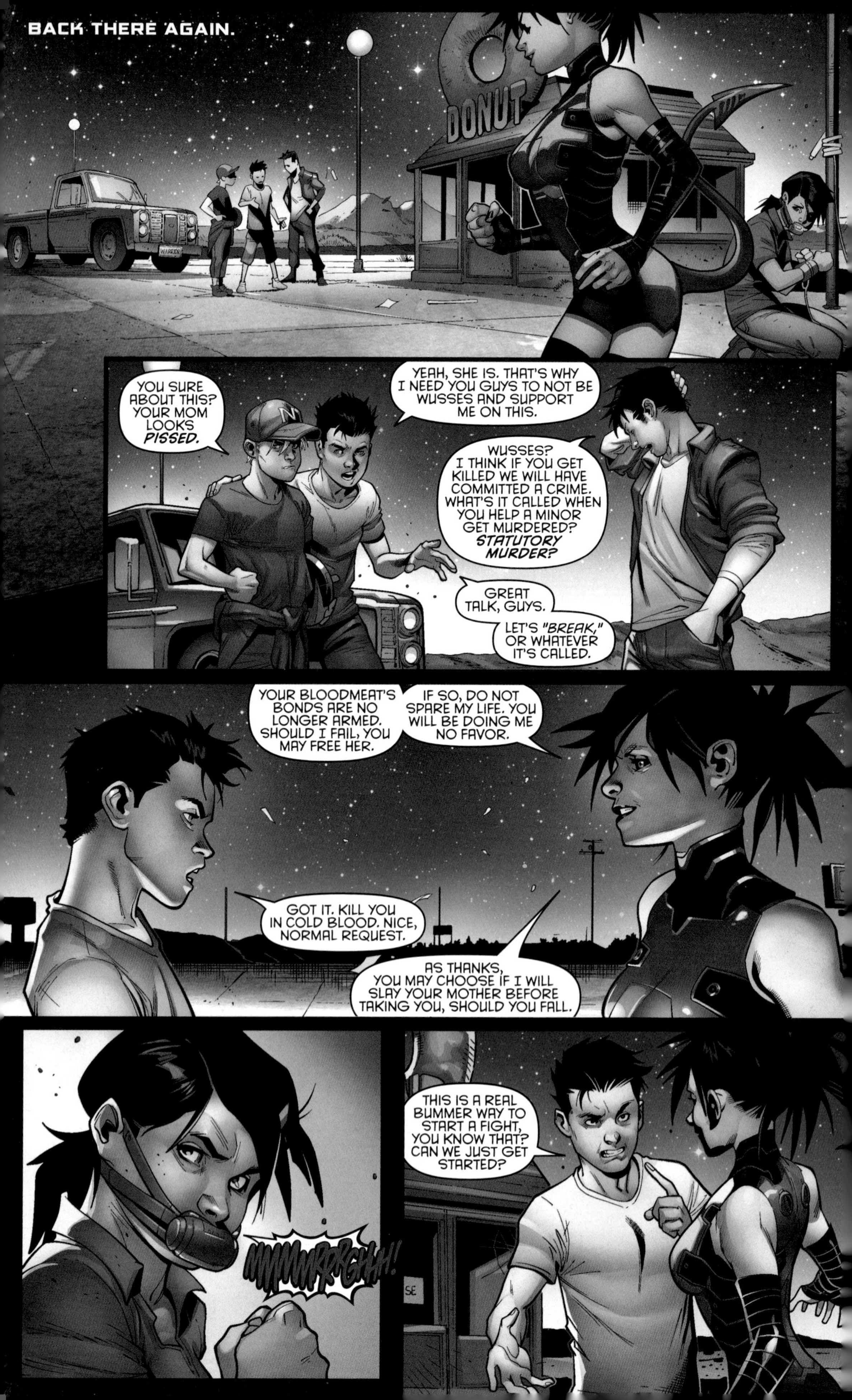
BACK THERE AGAIN.
DONUT
YOU SURE ABOUT THIS? YOUR MOM LOOKS *PISSED.*
YEAH, SHE IS. THAT'S WHY I NEED YOU GUYS TO NOT BE WUSSES AND SUPPORT ME ON THIS.
WUSSES? I THINK IF YOU GET KILLED WE WILL HAVE COMMITTED A CRIME. WHAT'S IT CALLED WHEN YOU HELP A MINOR GET MURDERED? ***STATUTORY MURDER?***
GREAT TALK, GUYS.
LET'S *"BREAK,"* OR WHATEVER IT'S CALLED.
YOUR BLOODMEAT'S BONDS ARE NO LONGER ARMED. SHOULD I FAIL, YOU MAY FREE HER.
IF SO, DO NOT SPARE MY LIFE. YOU WILL BE DOING ME NO FAVOR.
GOT IT. KILL YOU IN COLD BLOOD. NICE, NORMAL REQUEST.
AS THANKS, YOU MAY CHOOSE IF I WILL SLAY YOUR MOTHER BEFORE TAKING YOU, SHOULD YOU FALL.
MMMMRRGHH!
THIS IS A REAL BUMMER WAY TO START A FIGHT, YOU KNOW THAT? CAN WE JUST GET STARTED?

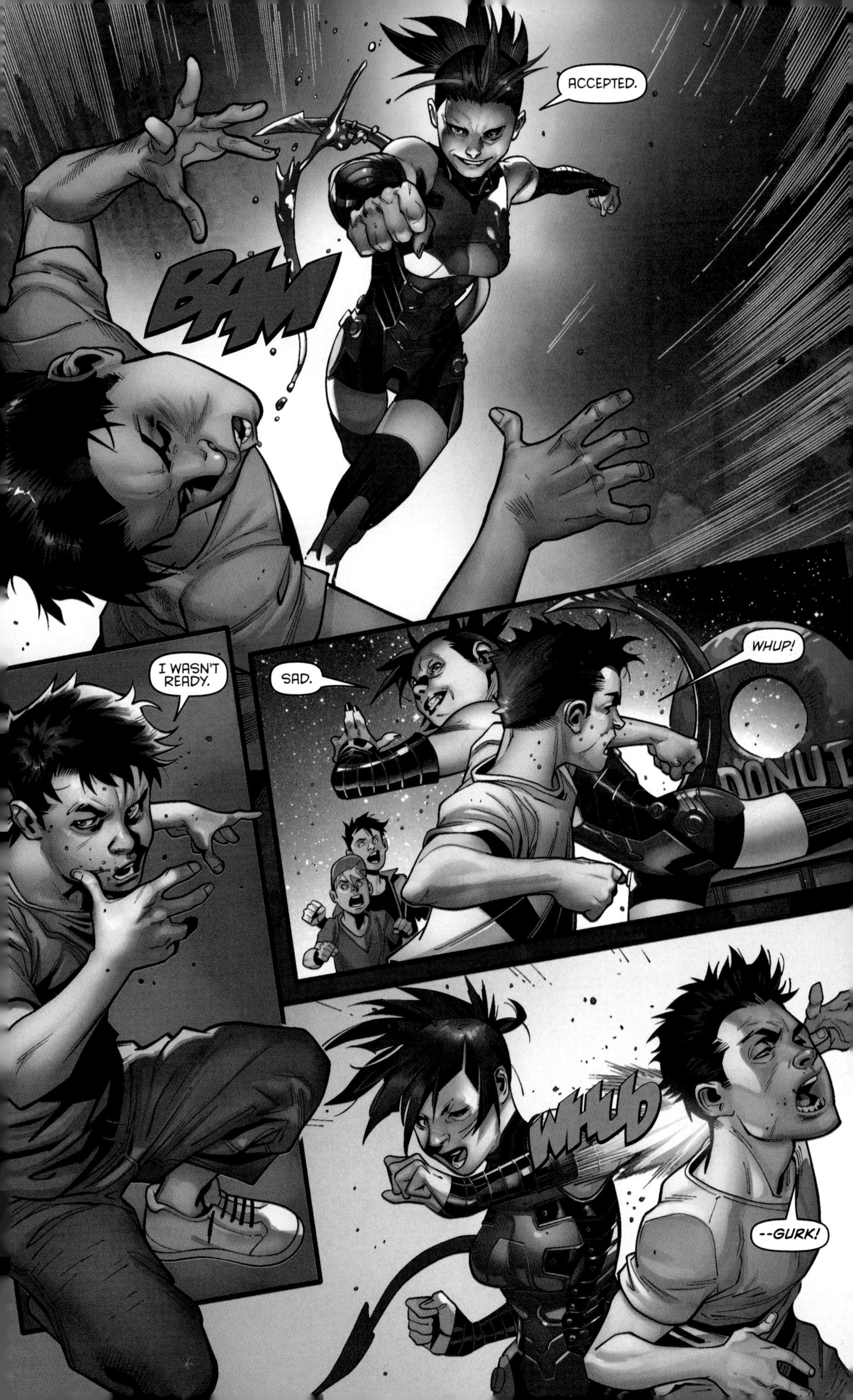
ACCEPTED.
BAM
I WASN'T READY.
SAD.
WHUP!
DONUT
WHUD
--GURK!

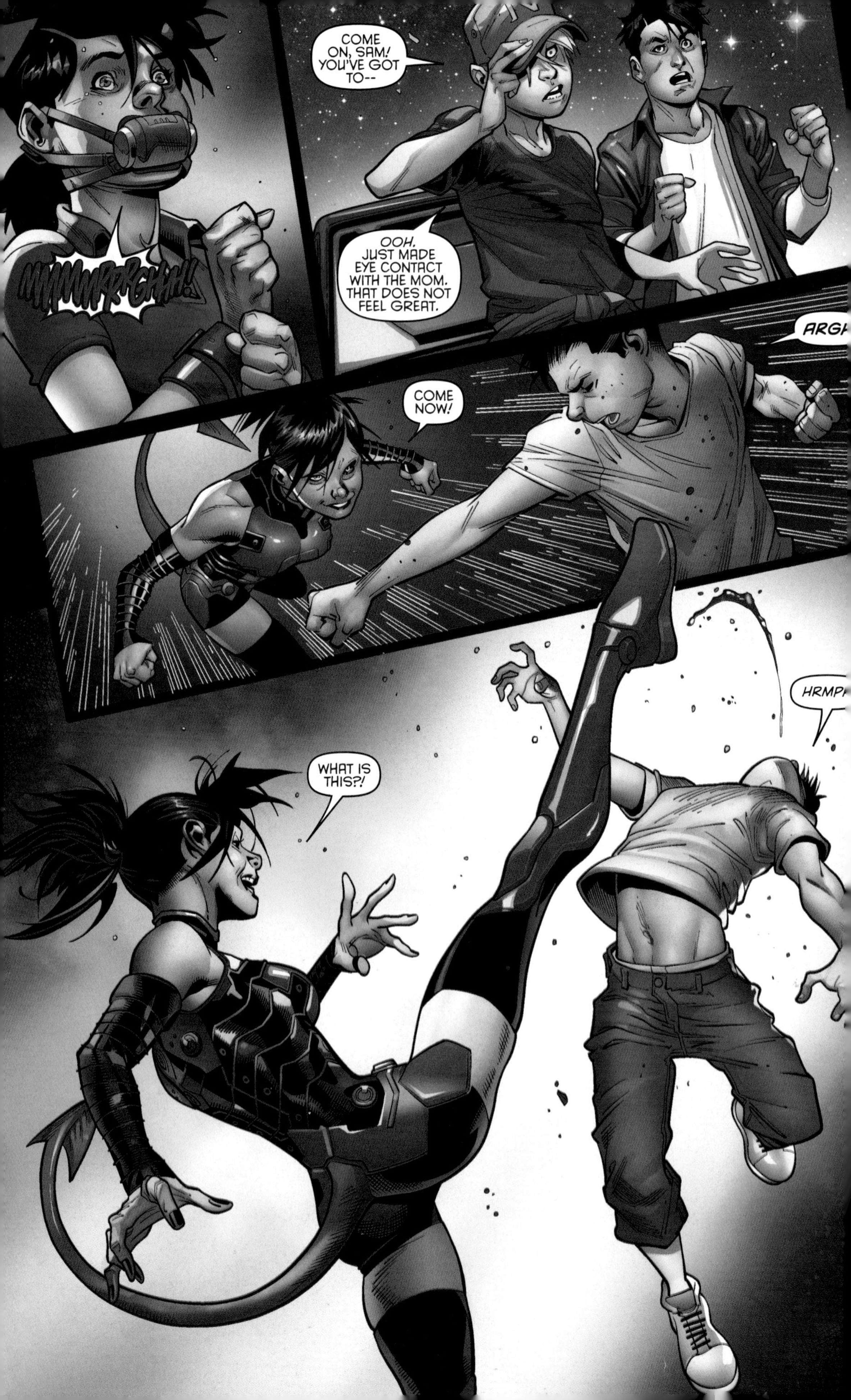
MMMMRRGHHH!
COME ON, SAM! YOU'VE GOT TO--
OOH. JUST MADE EYE CONTACT WITH THE MOM. THAT DOES NOT FEEL GREAT.
ARGH
COME NOW!
HRMPH
WHAT IS THIS?!

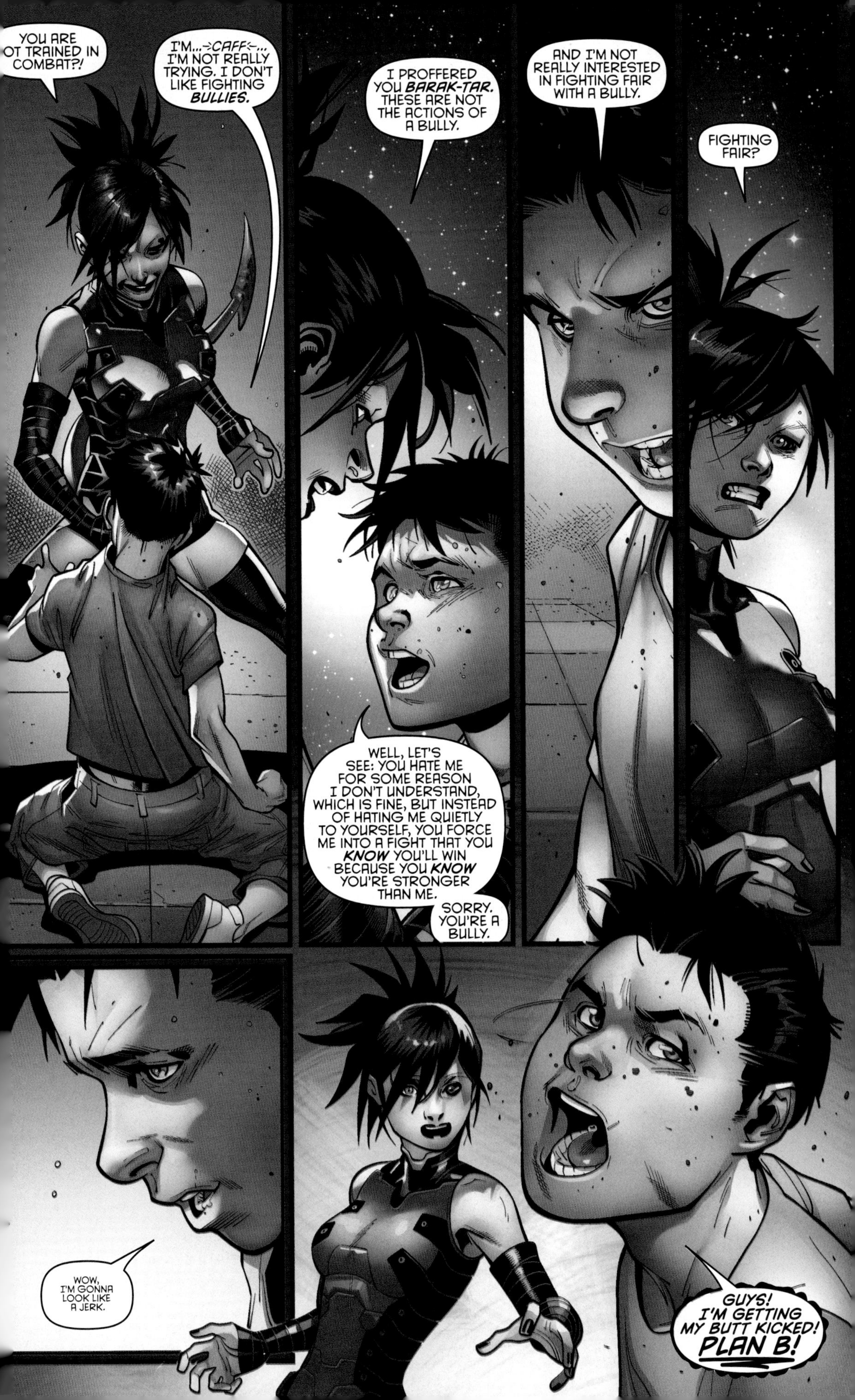

YOU ARE OT TRAINED IN COMBAT?!
I'M... >CAFF<... I'M NOT REALLY TRYING. I DON'T LIKE FIGHTING BULLIES.
I PROFFERED YOU BARAK-TAR. THESE ARE NOT THE ACTIONS OF A BULLY.
WELL, LET'S SEE: YOU HATE ME FOR SOME REASON I DON'T UNDERSTAND, WHICH IS FINE, BUT INSTEAD OF HATING ME QUIETLY TO YOURSELF, YOU FORCE ME INTO A FIGHT THAT YOU KNOW YOU'LL WIN BECAUSE YOU KNOW YOU'RE STRONGER THAN ME.
SORRY. YOU'RE A BULLY.
AND I'M NOT REALLY INTERESTED IN FIGHTING FAIR WITH A BULLY.
FIGHTING FAIR?
WOW, I'M GONNA LOOK LIKE A JERK.
GUYS! I'M GETTING MY BUTT KICKED! PLAN B!

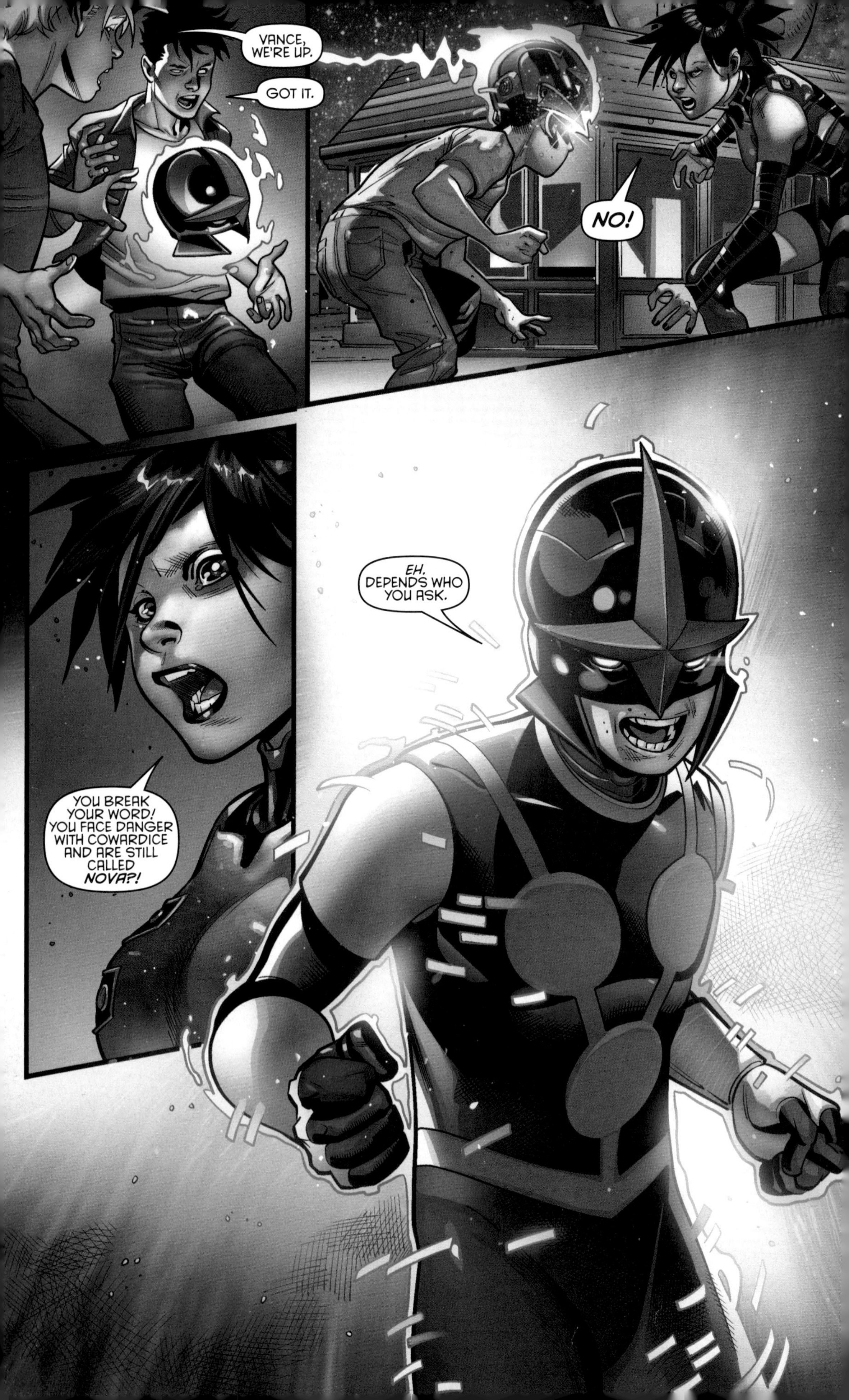
VANCE, WE'RE UP.
GOT IT.
NO!
EH. DEPENDS WHO YOU ASK.
YOU BREAK YOUR WORD! YOU FACE DANGER WITH COWARDICE AND ARE STILL CALLED NOVA?!

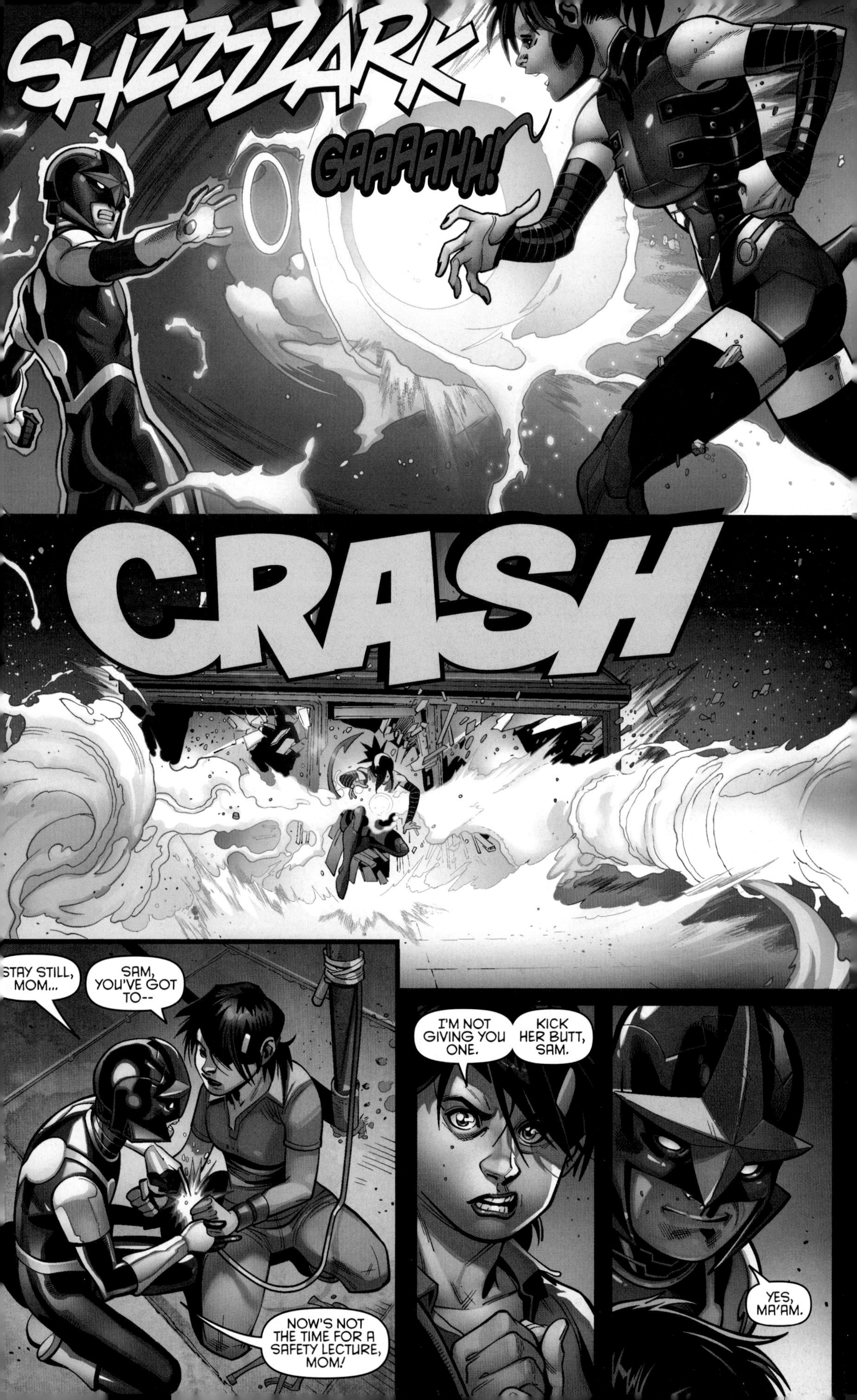
SHZZZZARK
GAAAAHH!
CRASH
STAY STILL, MOM...
SAM, YOU'VE GOT TO--
NOW'S NOT THE TIME FOR A SAFETY LECTURE, MOM!
I'M NOT GIVING YOU ONE.
KICK HER BUTT, SAM.
YES, MA'AM.

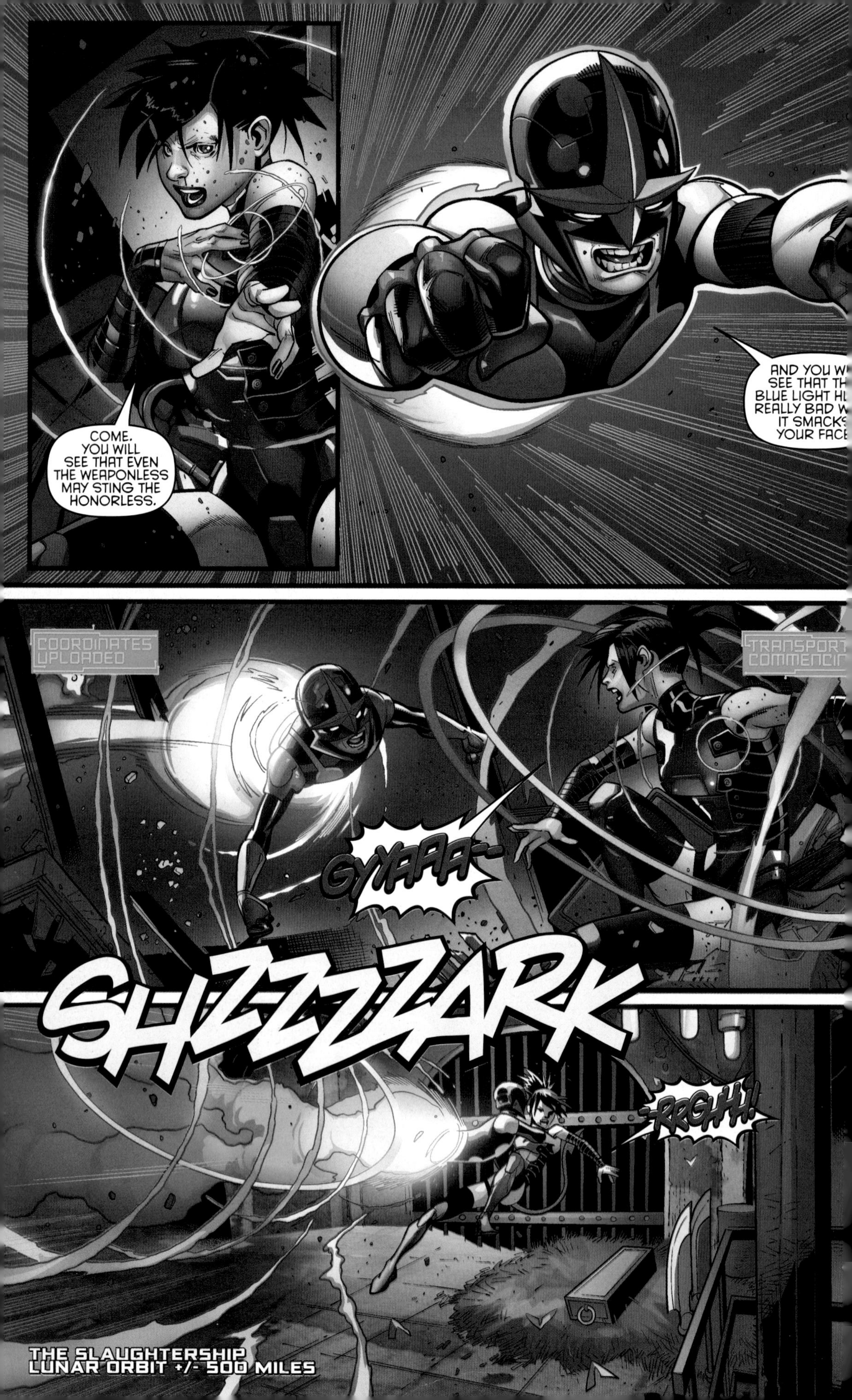

COME. YOU WILL SEE THAT EVEN THE WEAPONLESS MAY STING THE HONORLESS.
AND YOU W SEE THAT TH BLUE LIGHT HU REALLY BAD W IT SMACKS YOUR FACE
COORDINATES UPLOADED
TRANSPORT COMMENCIN
GYYAAAA--
SHZZZZARK
-RRGHH!
THE SLAUGHTERSHIP
LUNAR ORBIT +/- 500 MILES

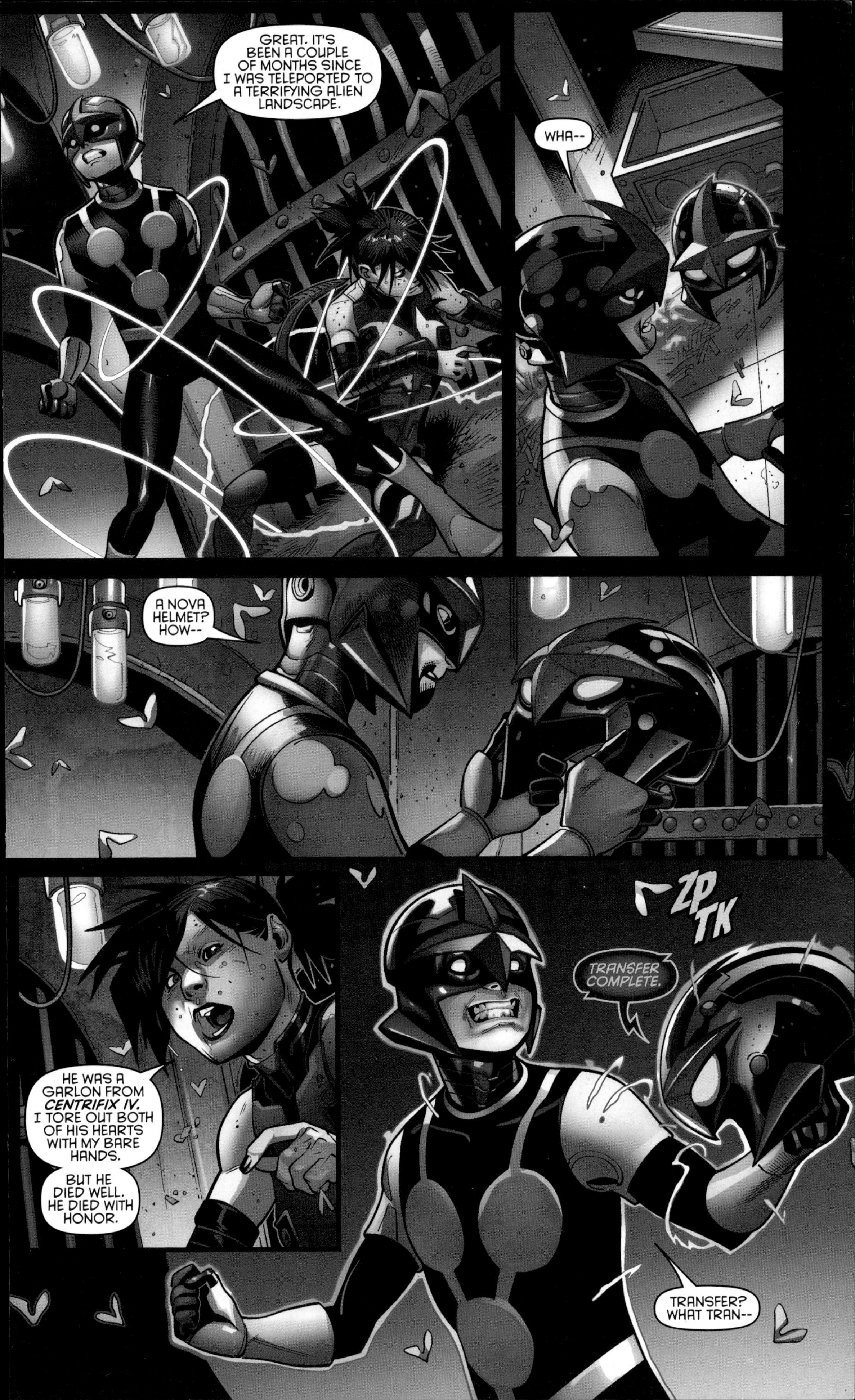
GREAT. IT'S BEEN A COUPLE OF MONTHS SINCE I WAS TELEPORTED TO A TERRIFYING ALIEN LANDSCAPE.
WHA--
A NOVA HELMET? HOW--
HE WAS A GARLON FROM CENTRIFIX IV. I TORE OUT BOTH OF HIS HEARTS WITH MY BARE HANDS.
BUT HE DIED WELL. HE DIED WITH HONOR.
ZP TK
TRANSFER COMPLETE.
TRANSFER? WHAT TRAN--

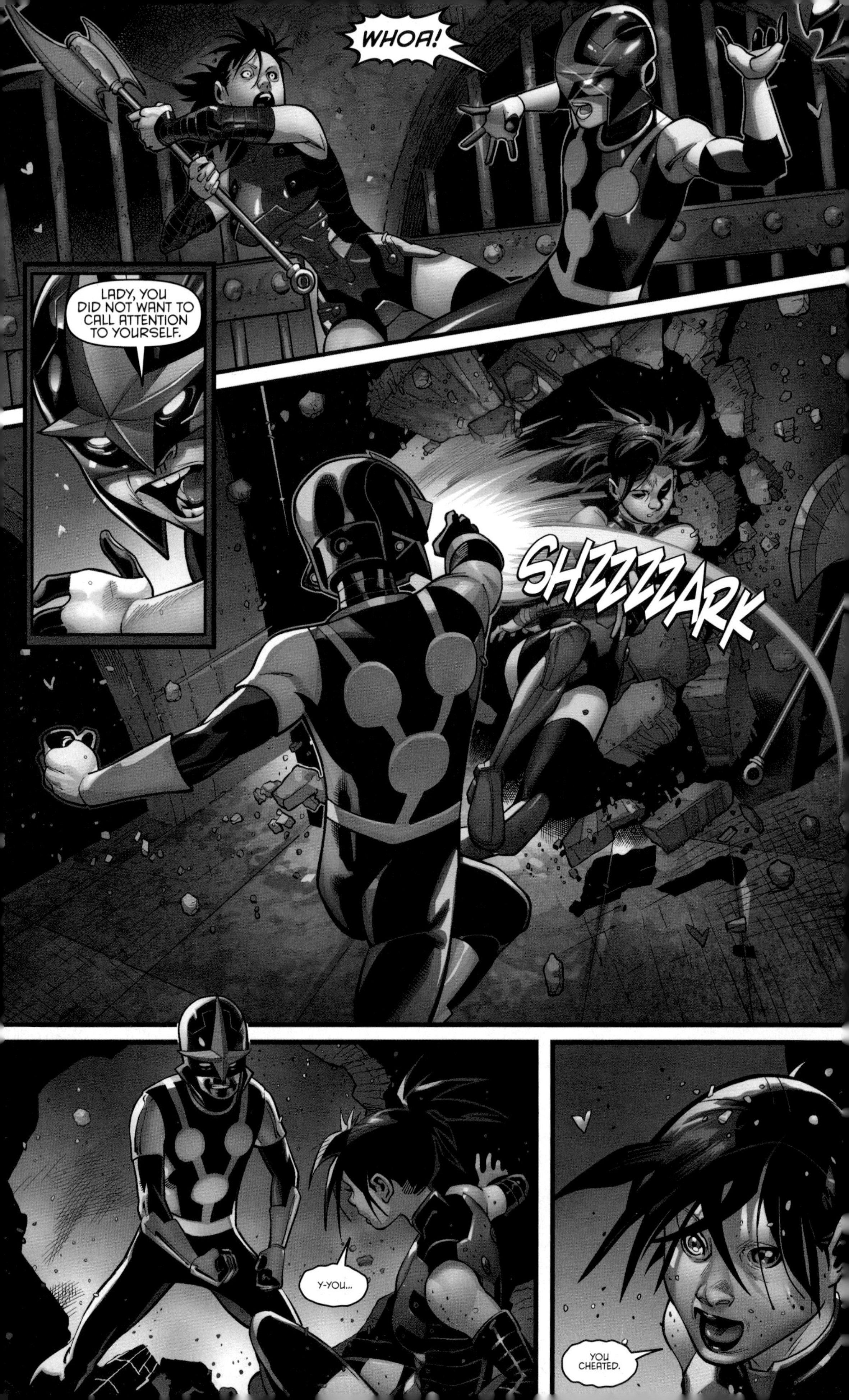
WHOA!
LADY, YOU DID NOT WANT TO CALL ATTENTION TO YOURSELF.
SHZZZZZARK
Y-YOU...
YOU CHEATED.

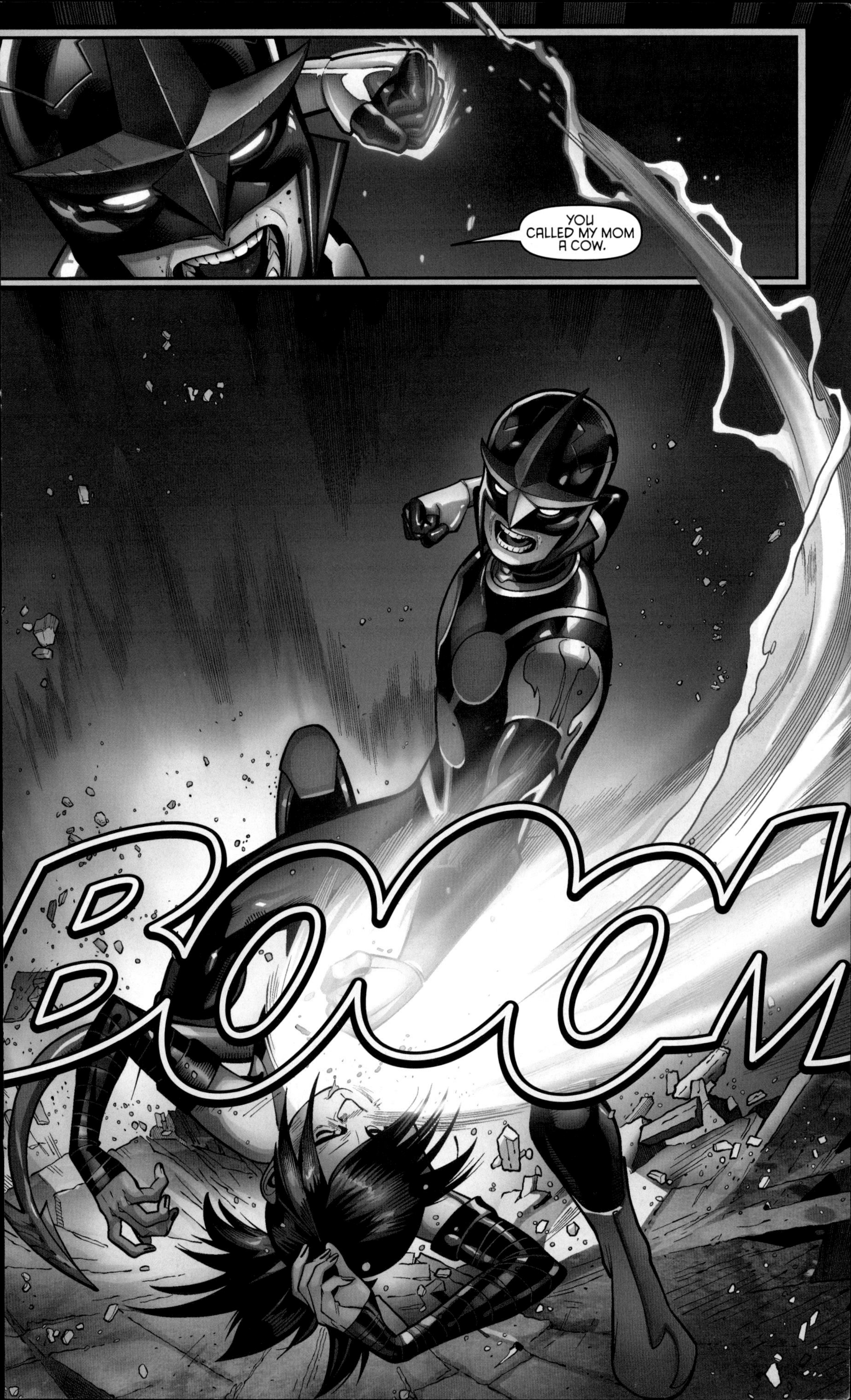
YOU CALLED MY MOM A COW.
BOOM

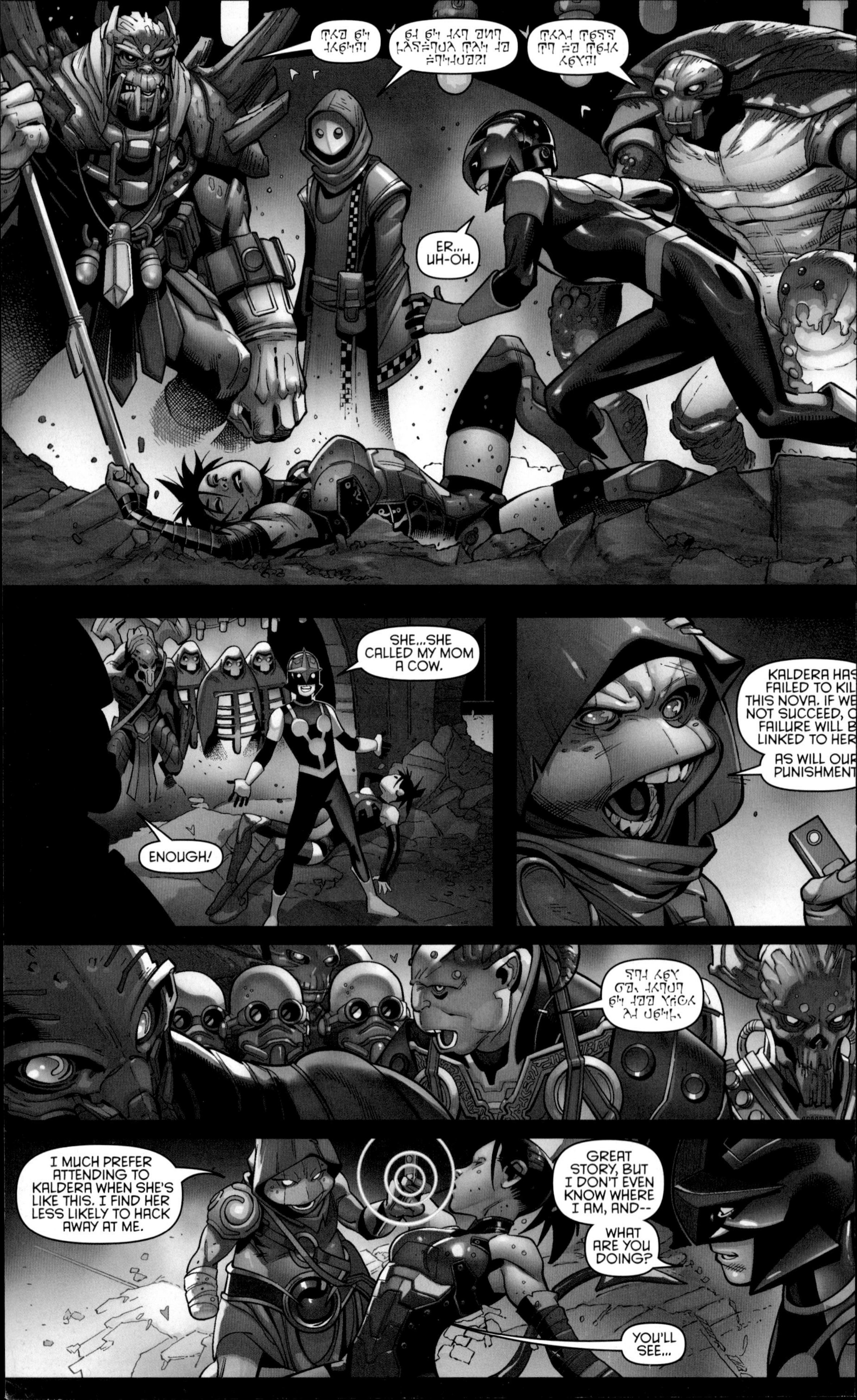

ER... UH-OH.
SHE...SHE CALLED MY MOM A COW.
ENOUGH!
KALDERA HAS FAILED TO KIL THIS NOVA. IF WE NOT SUCCEED, O FAILURE WILL B LINKED TO HER
AS WILL OUR PUNISHMENT
I MUCH PREFER ATTENDING TO KALDERA WHEN SHE'S LIKE THIS. I FIND HER LESS LIKELY TO HACK AWAY AT ME.
GREAT STORY, BUT I DON'T EVEN KNOW WHERE I AM, AND--
WHAT ARE YOU DOING?
YOU'LL SEE...

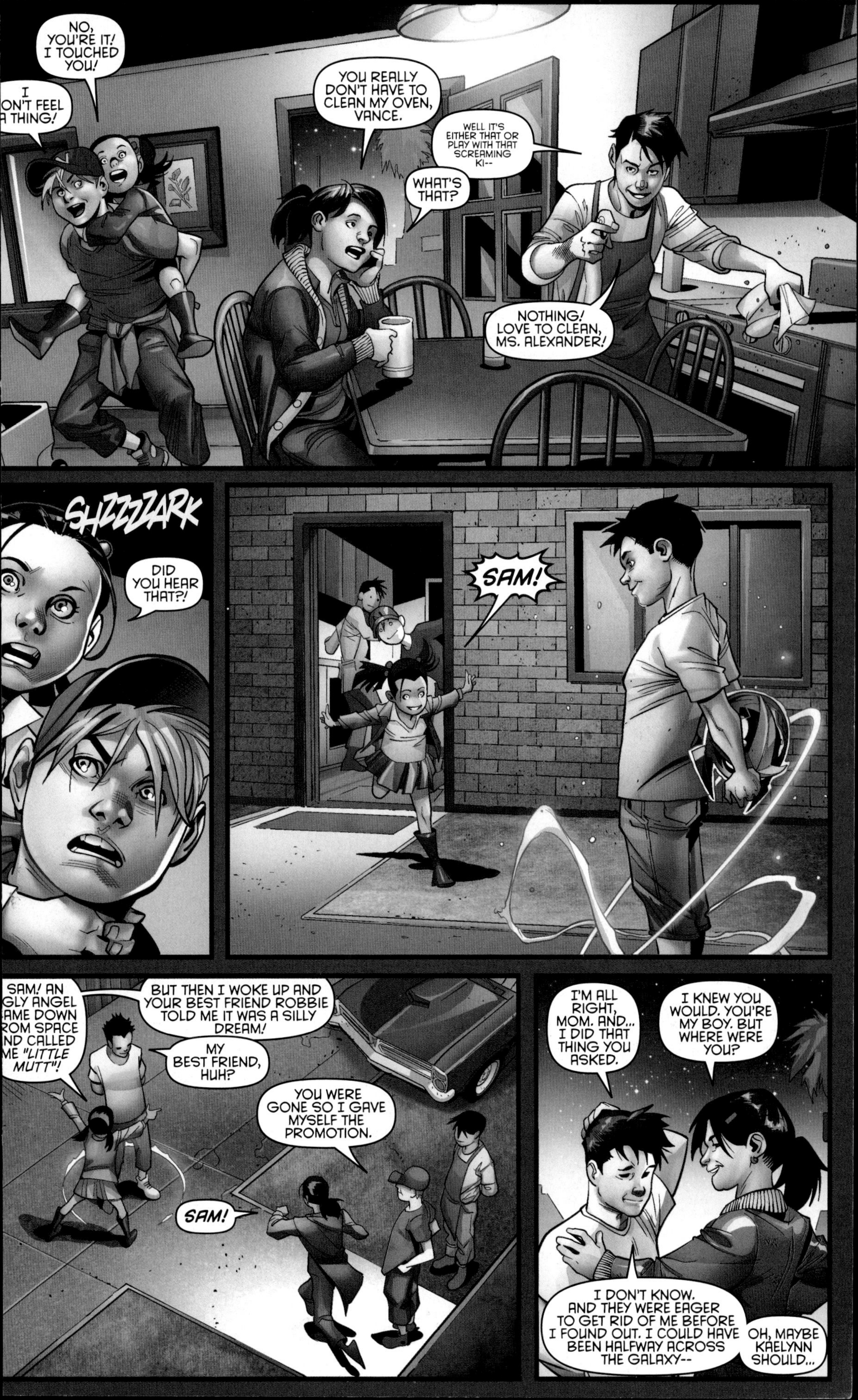
NO, YOU'RE IT! I TOUCHED YOU!
I DON'T FEEL A THING!
YOU REALLY DON'T HAVE TO CLEAN MY OVEN, VANCE.
WELL IT'S EITHER THAT OR PLAY WITH THAT SCREAMING KI--
WHAT'S THAT?
NOTHING! LOVE TO CLEAN, MS. ALEXANDER!
SHZZZZARK
DID YOU HEAR THAT?!
SAM!
SAM! AN UGLY ANGEL CAME DOWN FROM SPACE AND CALLED ME "LITTLE MUTT"!
BUT THEN I WOKE UP AND YOUR BEST FRIEND ROBBIE TOLD ME IT WAS A SILLY DREAM!
MY BEST FRIEND, HUH?
YOU WERE GONE SO I GAVE MYSELF THE PROMOTION.
SAM!
I'M ALL RIGHT, MOM. AND... I DID THAT THING YOU ASKED.
I KNEW YOU WOULD. YOU'RE MY BOY. BUT WHERE WERE YOU?
I DON'T KNOW. AND THEY WERE EAGER TO GET RID OF ME BEFORE I FOUND OUT. I COULD HAVE BEEN HALFWAY ACROSS THE GALAXY--
OH, MAYBE KAELYNN SHOULD...

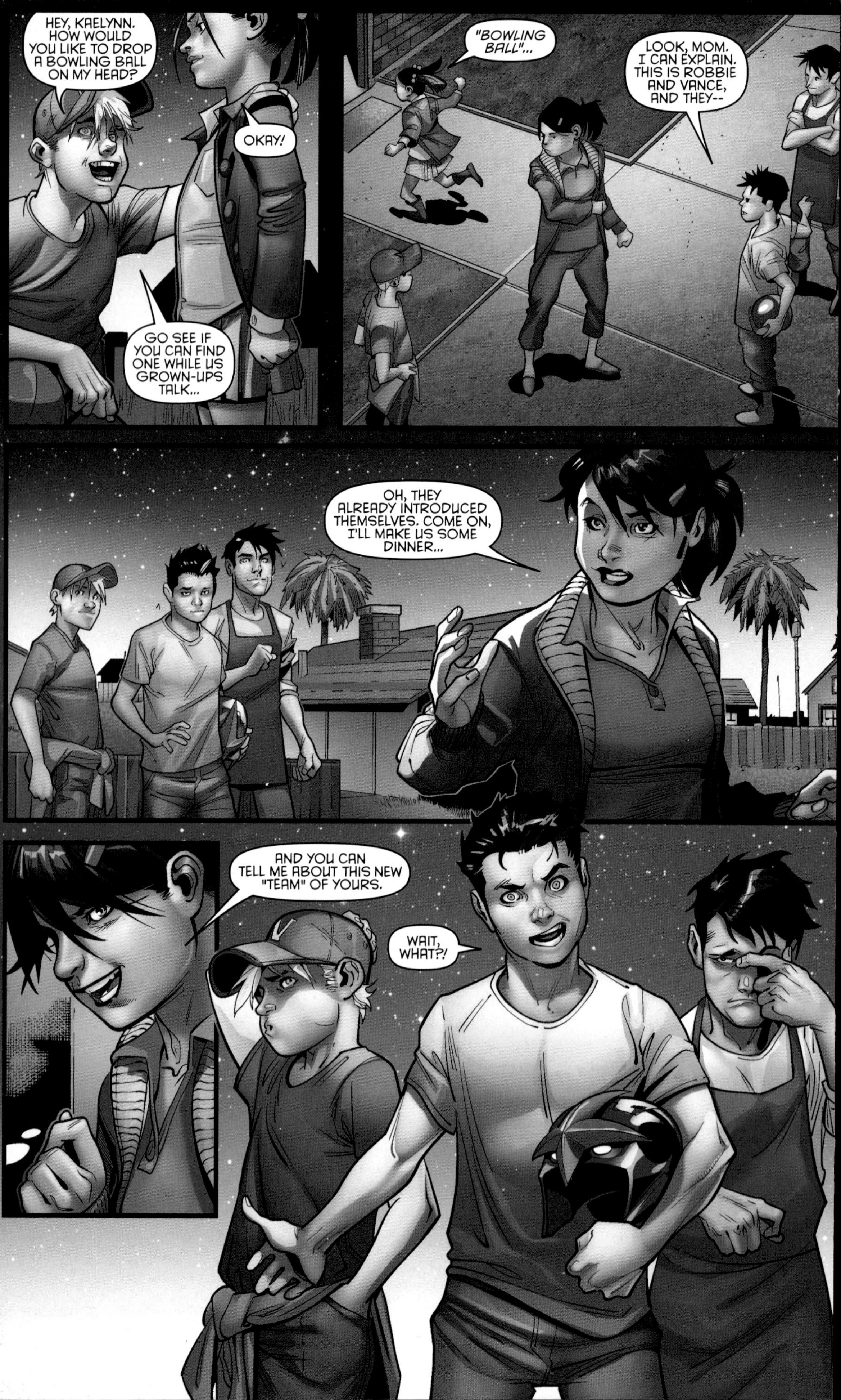
HEY, KAELYNN. HOW WOULD YOU LIKE TO DROP A BOWLING BALL ON MY HEAD?
OKAY!
GO SEE IF YOU CAN FIND ONE WHILE US GROWN-UPS TALK...
"BOWLING BALL"...
LOOK, MOM. I CAN EXPLAIN. THIS IS ROBBIE AND VANCE, AND THEY--
OH, THEY ALREADY INTRODUCED THEMSELVES. COME ON, I'LL MAKE US SOME DINNER...
AND YOU CAN TELL ME ABOUT THIS NEW "TEAM" OF YOURS.
WAIT, WHAT?!

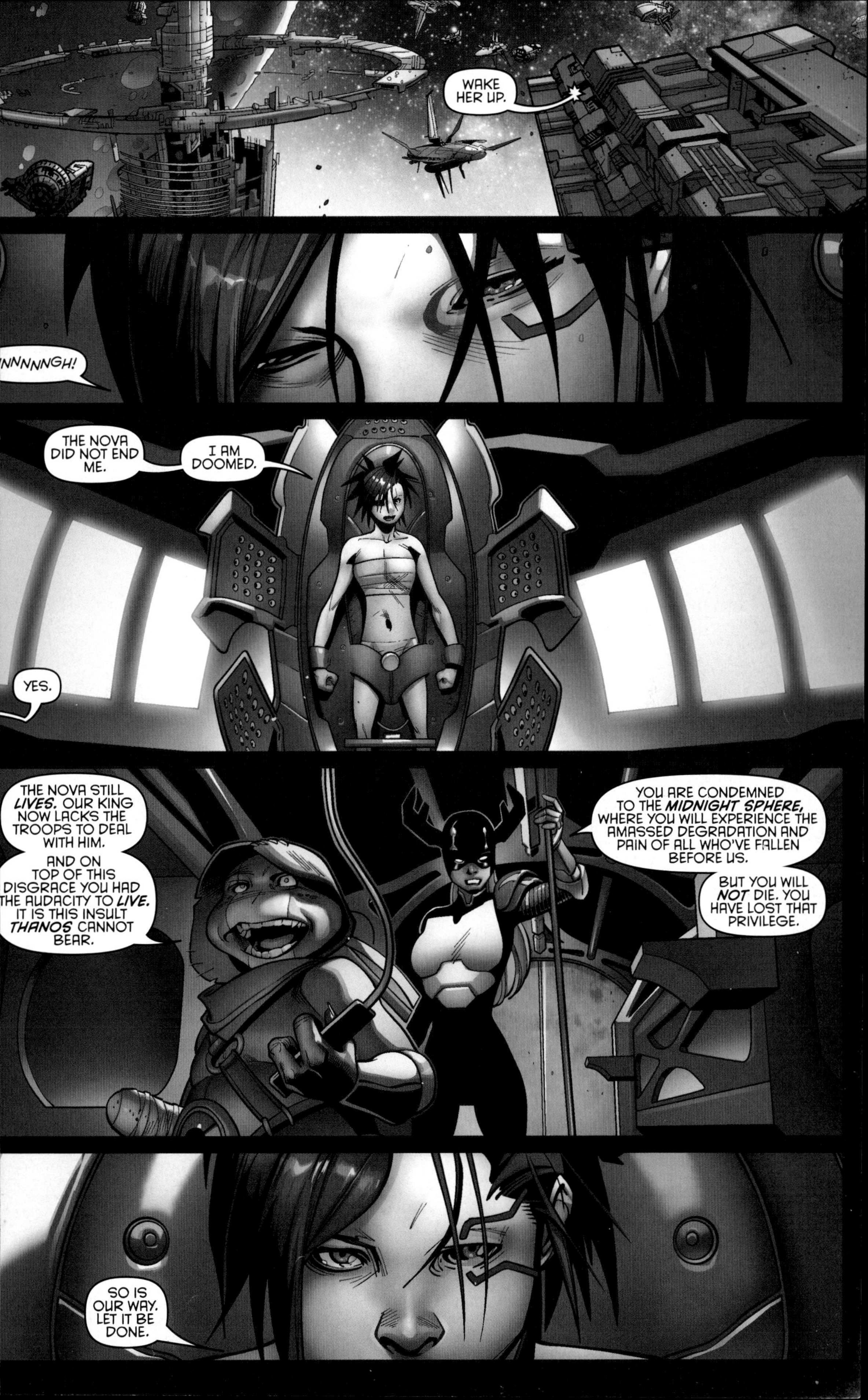
WAKE HER UP.
NNNNNNGH!
THE NOVA DID NOT END ME.
I AM DOOMED.
YES.
THE NOVA STILL *LIVES.* OUR KING NOW LACKS THE TROOPS TO DEAL WITH HIM.
AND ON TOP OF THIS DISGRACE YOU HAD THE AUDACITY TO *LIVE.* IT IS THIS INSULT *THANOS* CANNOT BEAR.
YOU ARE CONDEMNED TO THE *MIDNIGHT SPHERE,* WHERE YOU WILL EXPERIENCE THE AMASSED DEGRADATION AND PAIN OF ALL WHO'VE FALLEN BEFORE US.
BUT YOU WILL *NOT* DIE. YOU HAVE LOST THAT PRIVILEGE.
SO IS OUR WAY. LET IT BE DONE.

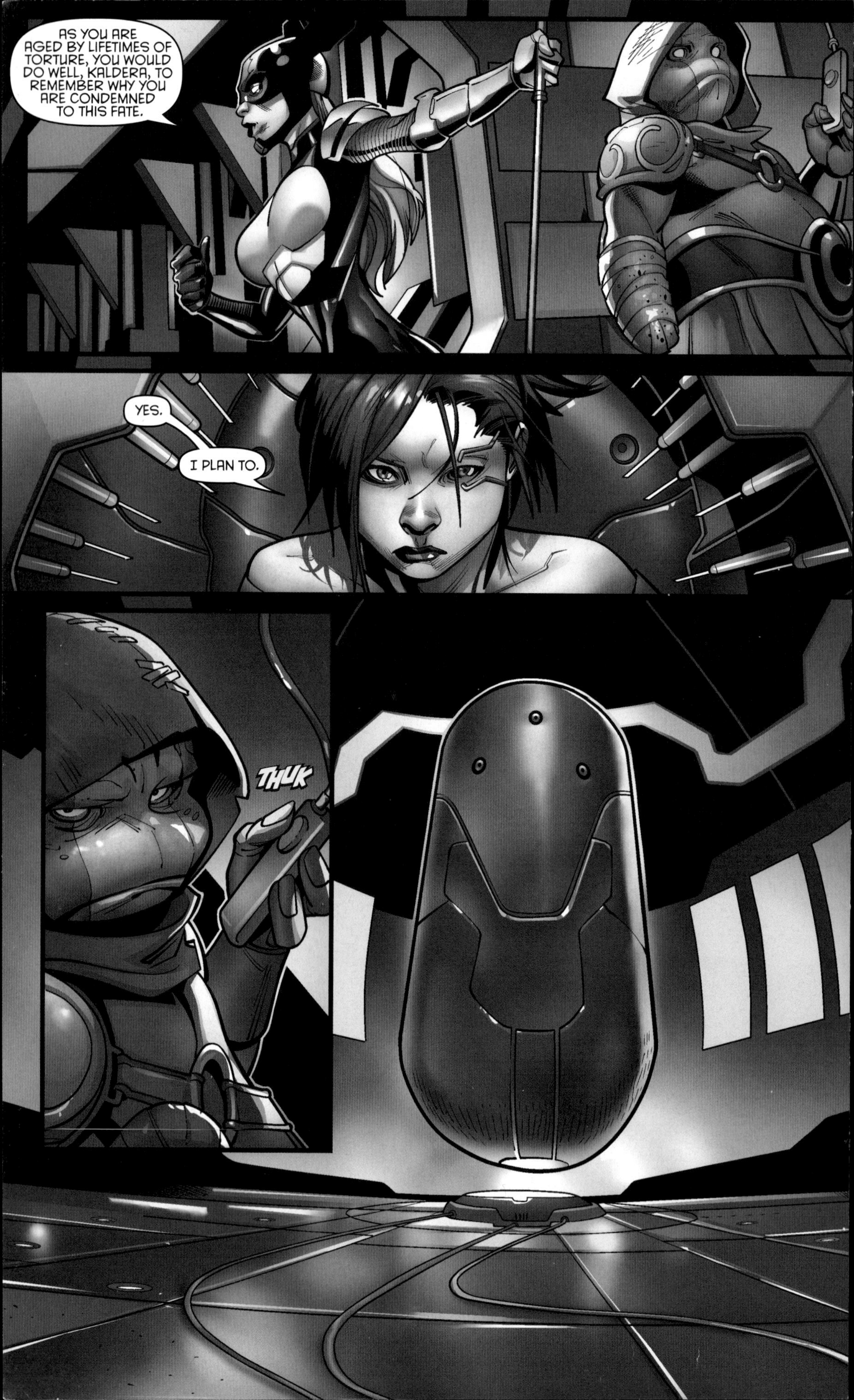
AS YOU ARE AGED BY LIFETIMES OF TORTURE, YOU WOULD DO WELL, KALDERA, TO REMEMBER WHY YOU ARE CONDEMNED TO THIS FATE.
YES.
I PLAN TO.
THUK

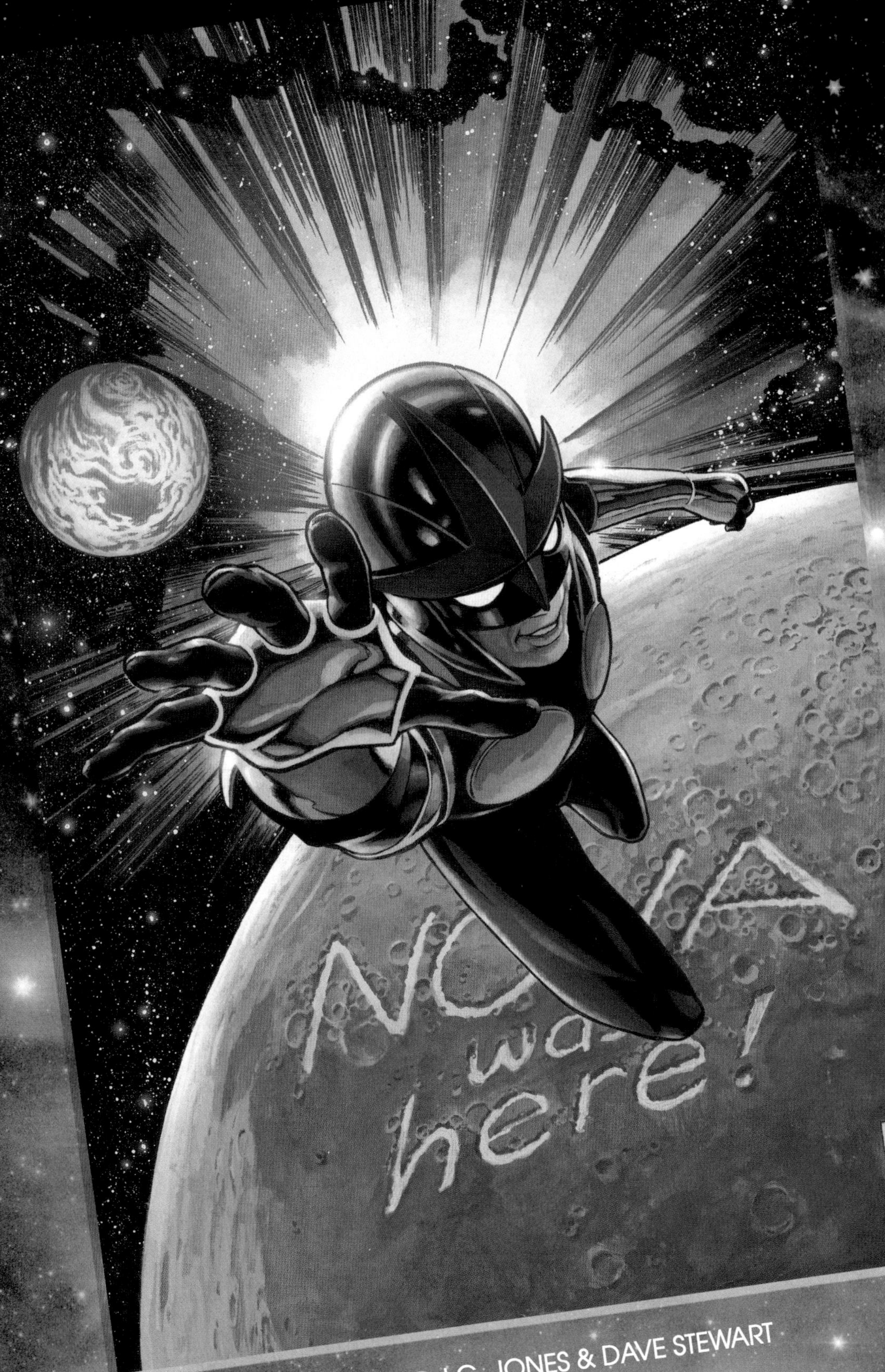
here!

ISSUE #10 VARIANT COVER J.G. JONES & DAVE STEWART

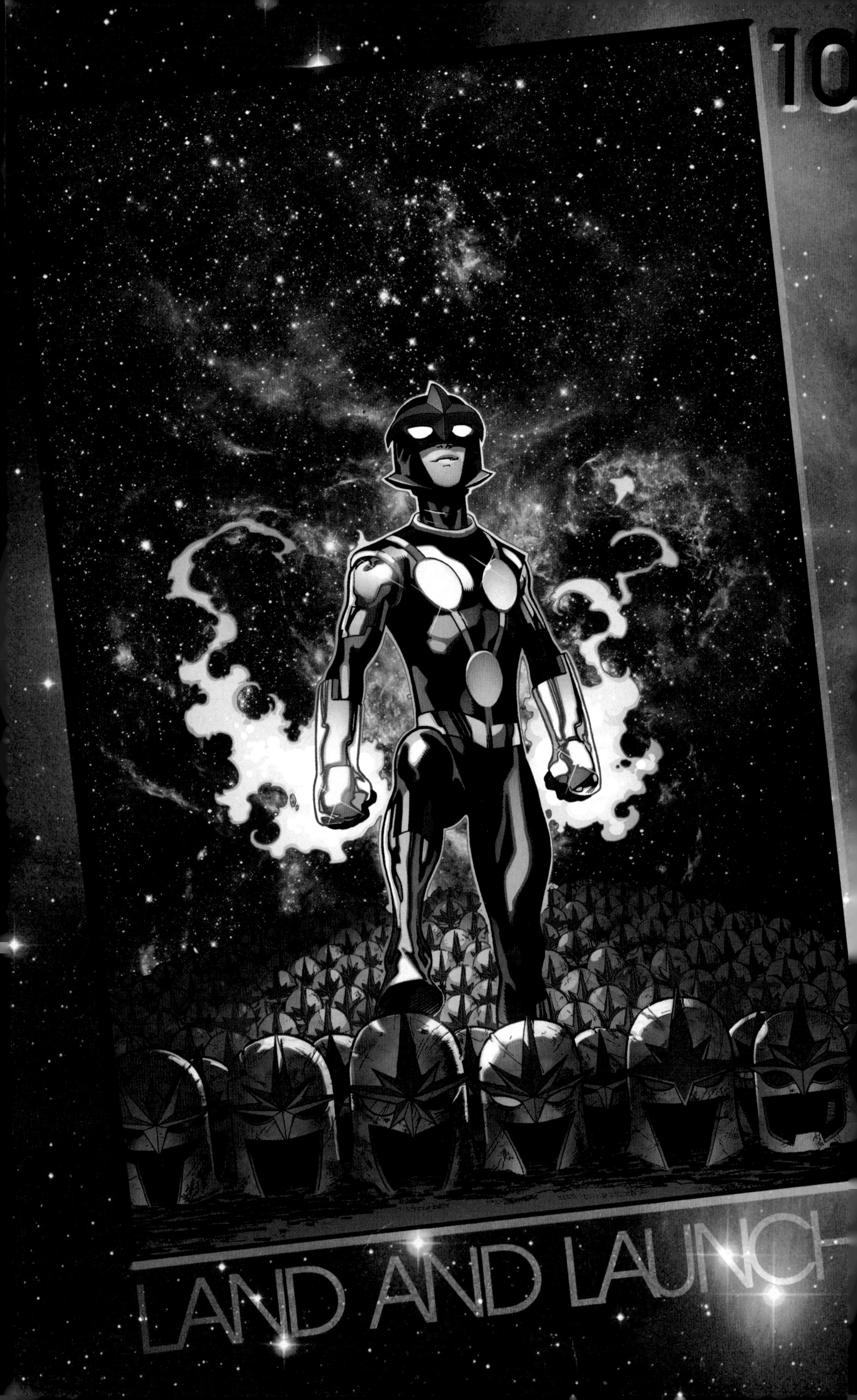
10
LAND AND LAUNCH

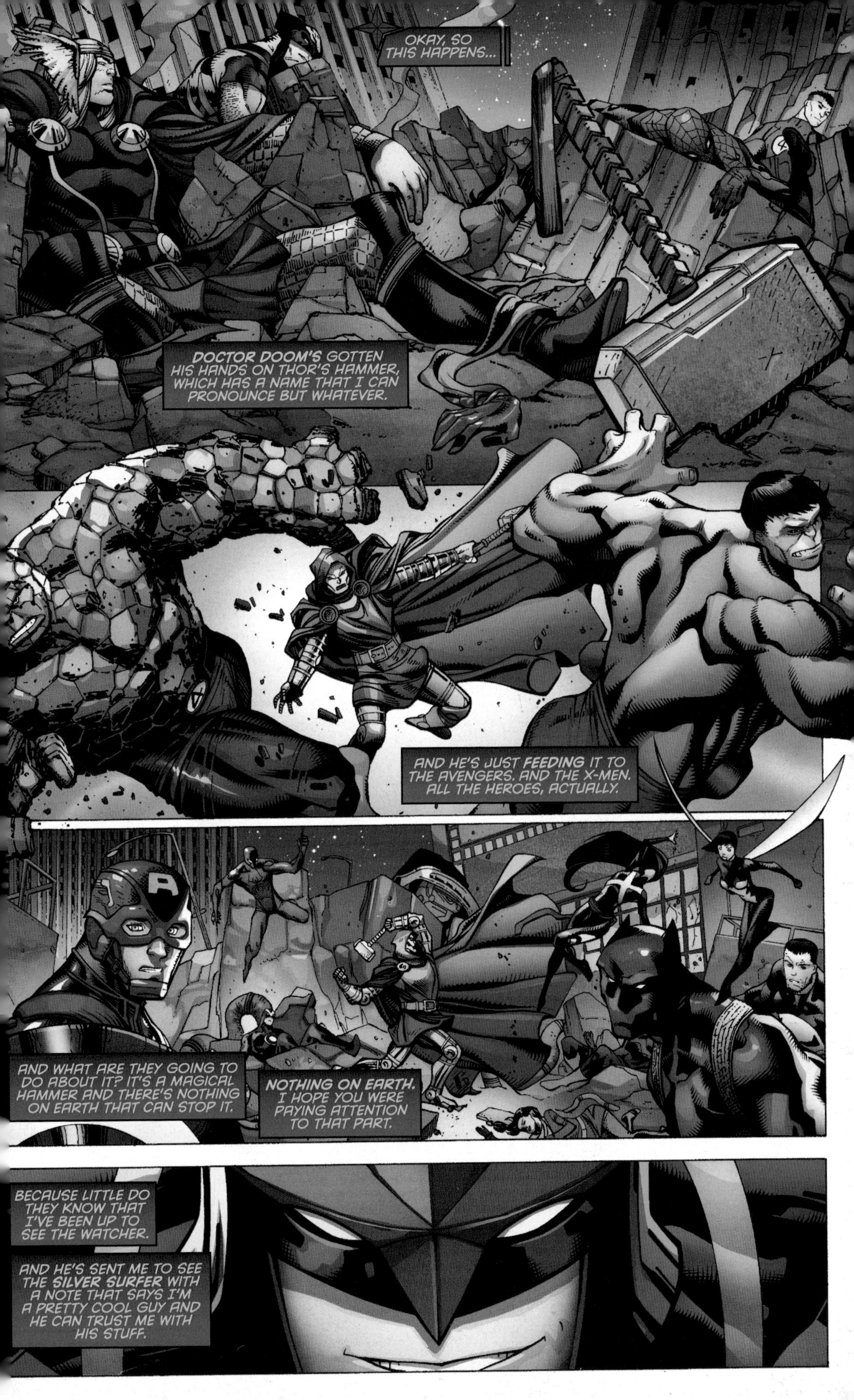
OKAY, SO THIS HAPPENS...
DOCTOR DOOM'S GOTTEN HIS HANDS ON THOR'S HAMMER, WHICH HAS A NAME THAT I CAN PRONOUNCE BUT WHATEVER.
AND HE'S JUST FEEDING IT TO THE AVENGERS. AND THE X-MEN. ALL THE HEROES, ACTUALLY.
AND WHAT ARE THEY GOING TO DO ABOUT IT? IT'S A MAGICAL HAMMER AND THERE'S NOTHING ON EARTH THAT CAN STOP IT.
NOTHING ON EARTH. I HOPE YOU WERE PAYING ATTENTION TO THAT PART.
BECAUSE LITTLE DO THEY KNOW THAT I'VE BEEN UP TO SEE THE WATCHER.
AND HE'S SENT ME TO SEE THE SILVER SURFER WITH A NOTE THAT SAYS I'M A PRETTY COOL GUY AND HE CAN TRUST ME WITH HIS STUFF.

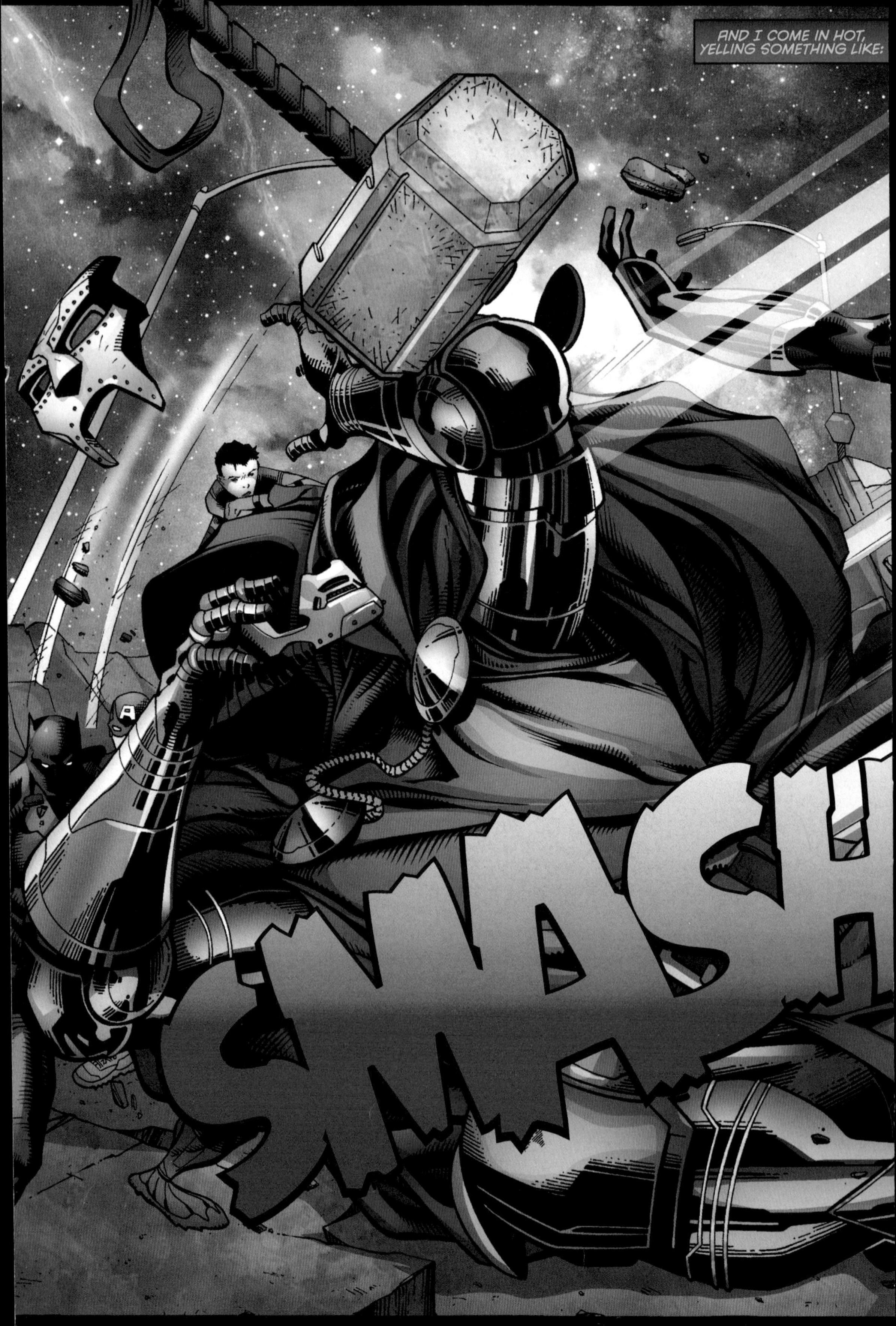
AND I COME IN HOT, YELLING SOMETHING LIKE:
SMASH

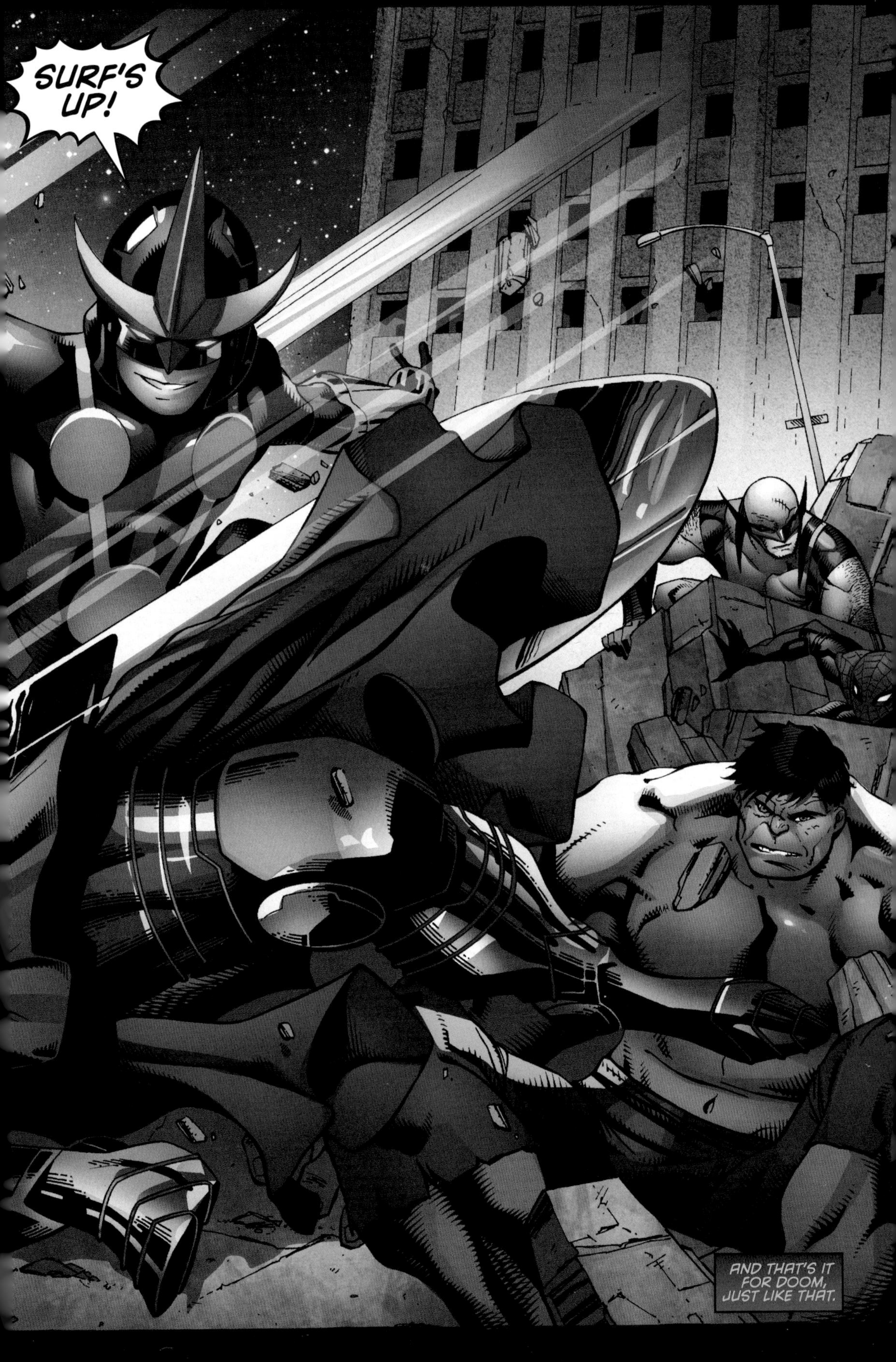
SURF'S UP!
AND THAT'S IT FOR DOOM, JUST LIKE THAT.

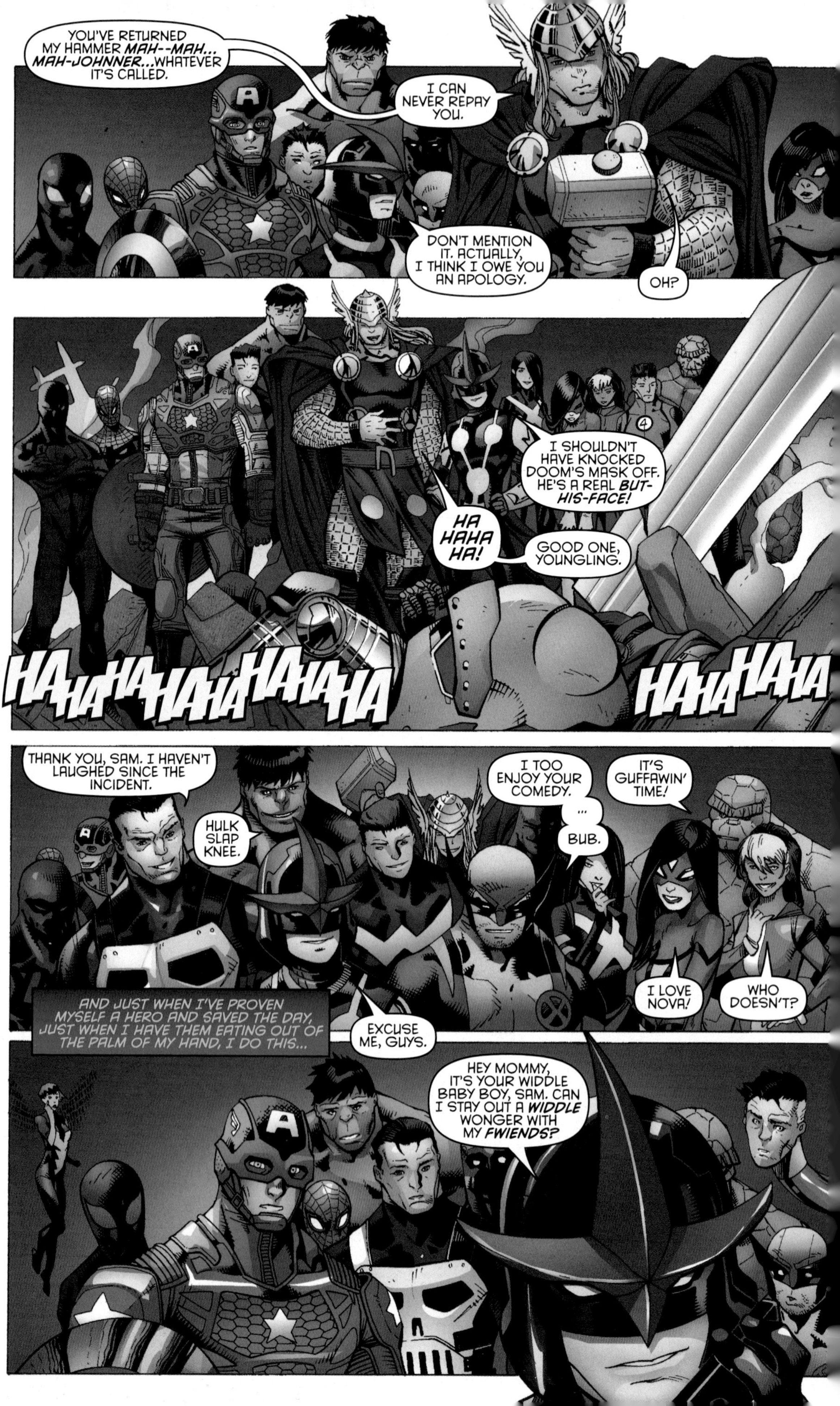
YOU'VE RETURNED MY HAMMER MAH--MAH... MAH-JOHNNER...WHATEVER IT'S CALLED.
I CAN NEVER REPAY YOU.
DON'T MENTION IT. ACTUALLY, I THINK I OWE YOU AN APOLOGY.
OH?
I SHOULDN'T HAVE KNOCKED DOOM'S MASK OFF. HE'S A REAL BUT-HIS-FACE!
HA HAHA HA!
GOOD ONE, YOUNGLING.
HAHAHAHAHAHAHAHAHA
HAHAHAHA
THANK YOU, SAM. I HAVEN'T LAUGHED SINCE THE INCIDENT.
HULK SLAP KNEE.
I TOO ENJOY YOUR COMEDY.
...
BUB.
IT'S GUFFAWIN' TIME!
I LOVE NOVA!
WHO DOESN'T?
AND JUST WHEN I'VE PROVEN MYSELF A HERO AND SAVED THE DAY, JUST WHEN I HAVE THEM EATING OUT OF THE PALM OF MY HAND, I DO THIS...
EXCUSE ME, GUYS.
HEY MOMMY, IT'S YOUR WIDDLE BABY BOY, SAM. CAN I STAY OUT A WIDDLE WONGER WITH MY FWIENDS?

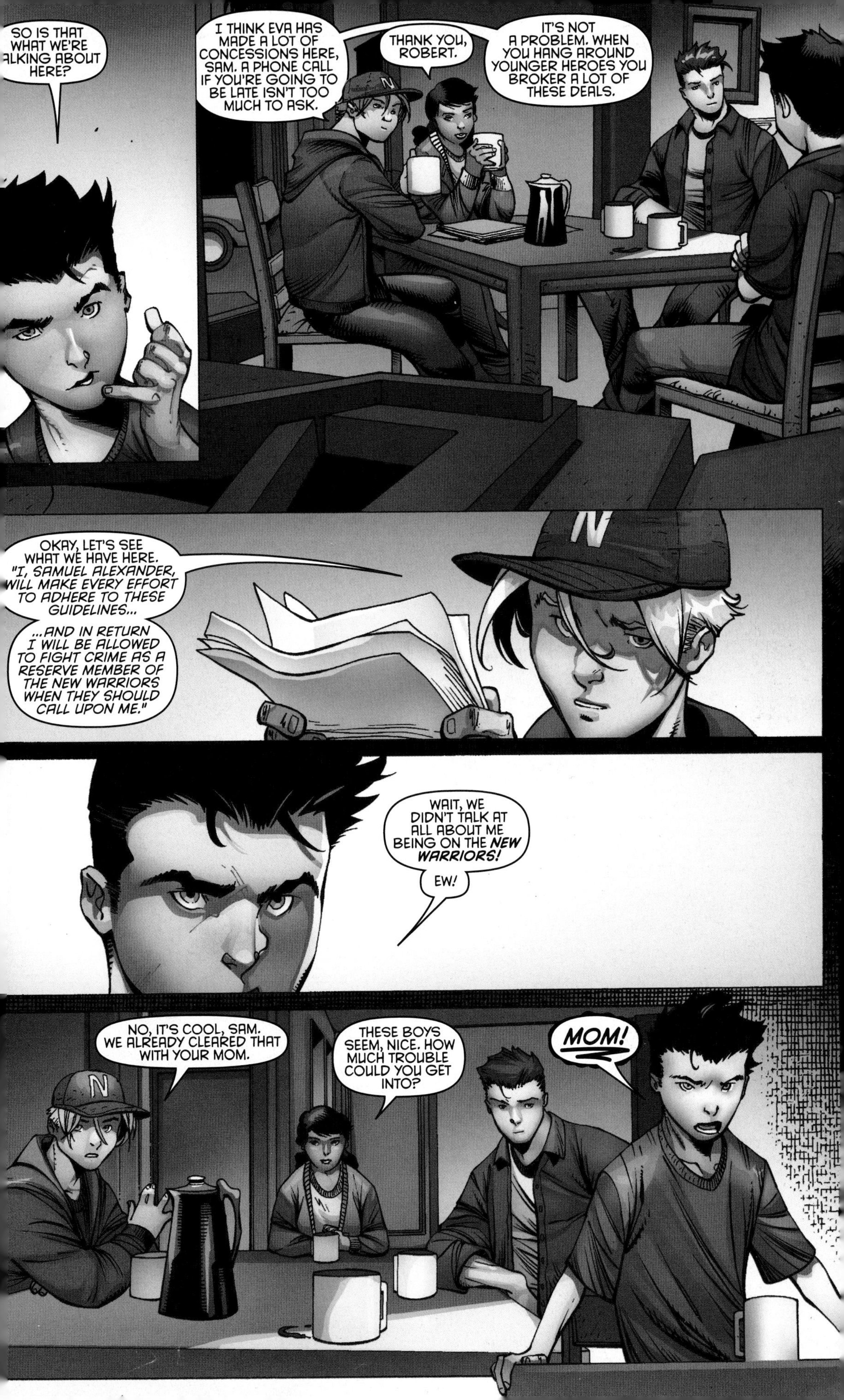
SO IS THAT WHAT WE'RE ALKING ABOUT HERE?
I THINK EVA HAS MADE A LOT OF CONCESSIONS HERE, SAM. A PHONE CALL IF YOU'RE GOING TO BE LATE ISN'T TOO MUCH TO ASK.
THANK YOU, ROBERT.
IT'S NOT A PROBLEM. WHEN YOU HANG AROUND YOUNGER HEROES YOU BROKER A LOT OF THESE DEALS.
OKAY, LET'S SEE WHAT WE HAVE HERE. "I, SAMUEL ALEXANDER, WILL MAKE EVERY EFFORT TO ADHERE TO THESE GUIDELINES...
...AND IN RETURN I WILL BE ALLOWED TO FIGHT CRIME AS A RESERVE MEMBER OF THE NEW WARRIORS WHEN THEY SHOULD CALL UPON ME."
WAIT, WE DIDN'T TALK AT ALL ABOUT ME BEING ON THE NEW WARRIORS!
EW!
NO, IT'S COOL, SAM. WE ALREADY CLEARED THAT WITH YOUR MOM.
THESE BOYS SEEM, NICE. HOW MUCH TROUBLE COULD YOU GET INTO?
MOM!

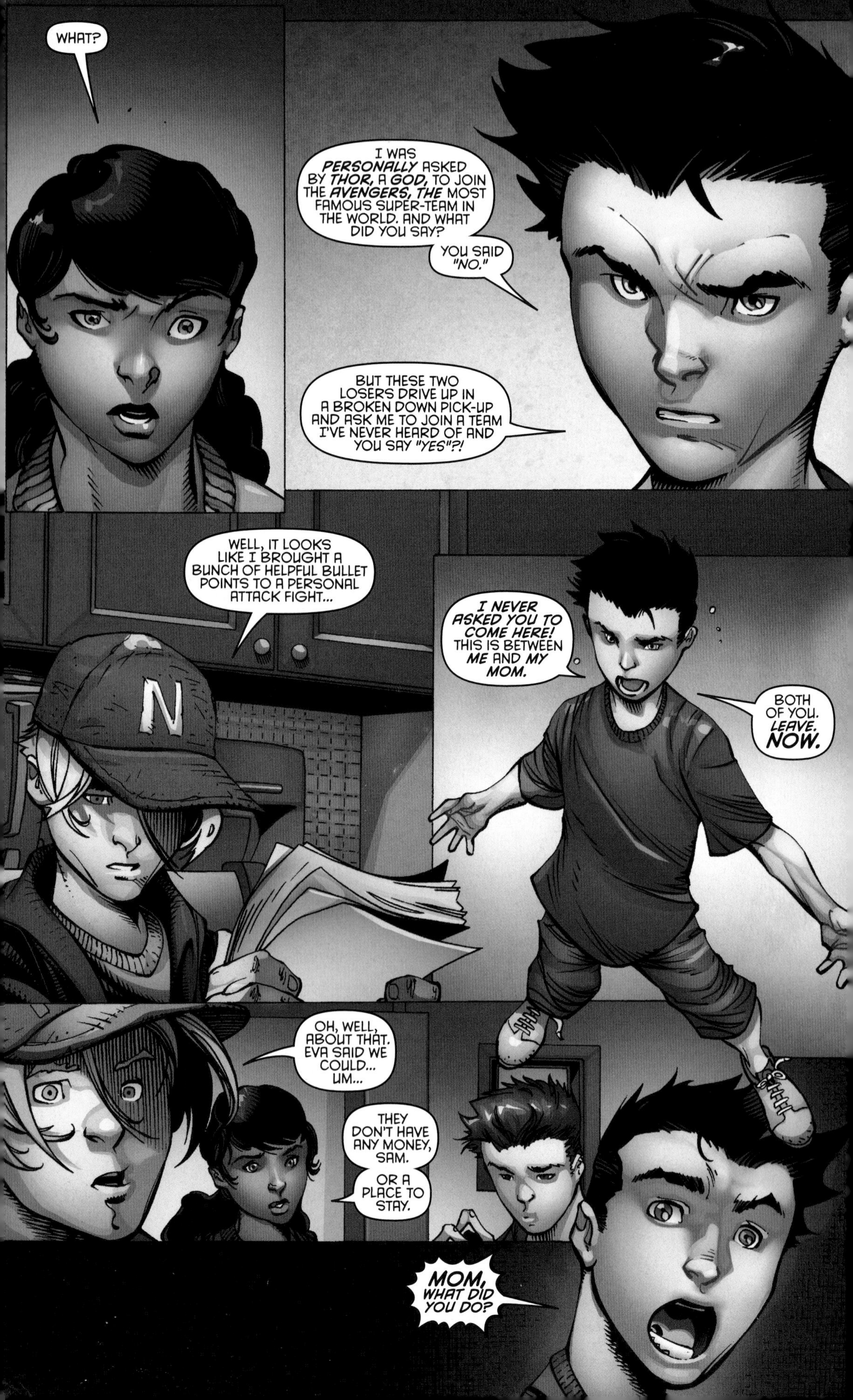
WHAT?
I WAS *PERSONALLY* ASKED BY *THOR, A GOD,* TO JOIN THE *AVENGERS, THE* MOST FAMOUS SUPER-TEAM IN THE WORLD. AND WHAT DID YOU SAY?
YOU SAID *"NO."*
BUT THESE TWO LOSERS DRIVE UP IN A BROKEN DOWN PICK-UP AND ASK ME TO JOIN A TEAM I'VE NEVER HEARD OF AND YOU SAY *"YES"?!*
WELL, IT LOOKS LIKE I BROUGHT A BUNCH OF HELPFUL BULLET POINTS TO A PERSONAL ATTACK FIGHT...
I NEVER ASKED YOU TO COME HERE! THIS IS BETWEEN *ME* AND *MY MOM.*
BOTH OF YOU. *LEAVE.* **NOW.**
OH, WELL, ABOUT THAT. EVA SAID WE COULD... UM...
THEY DON'T HAVE ANY MONEY, SAM.
OR A PLACE TO STAY.
***MOM,* WHAT DID YOU DO?**

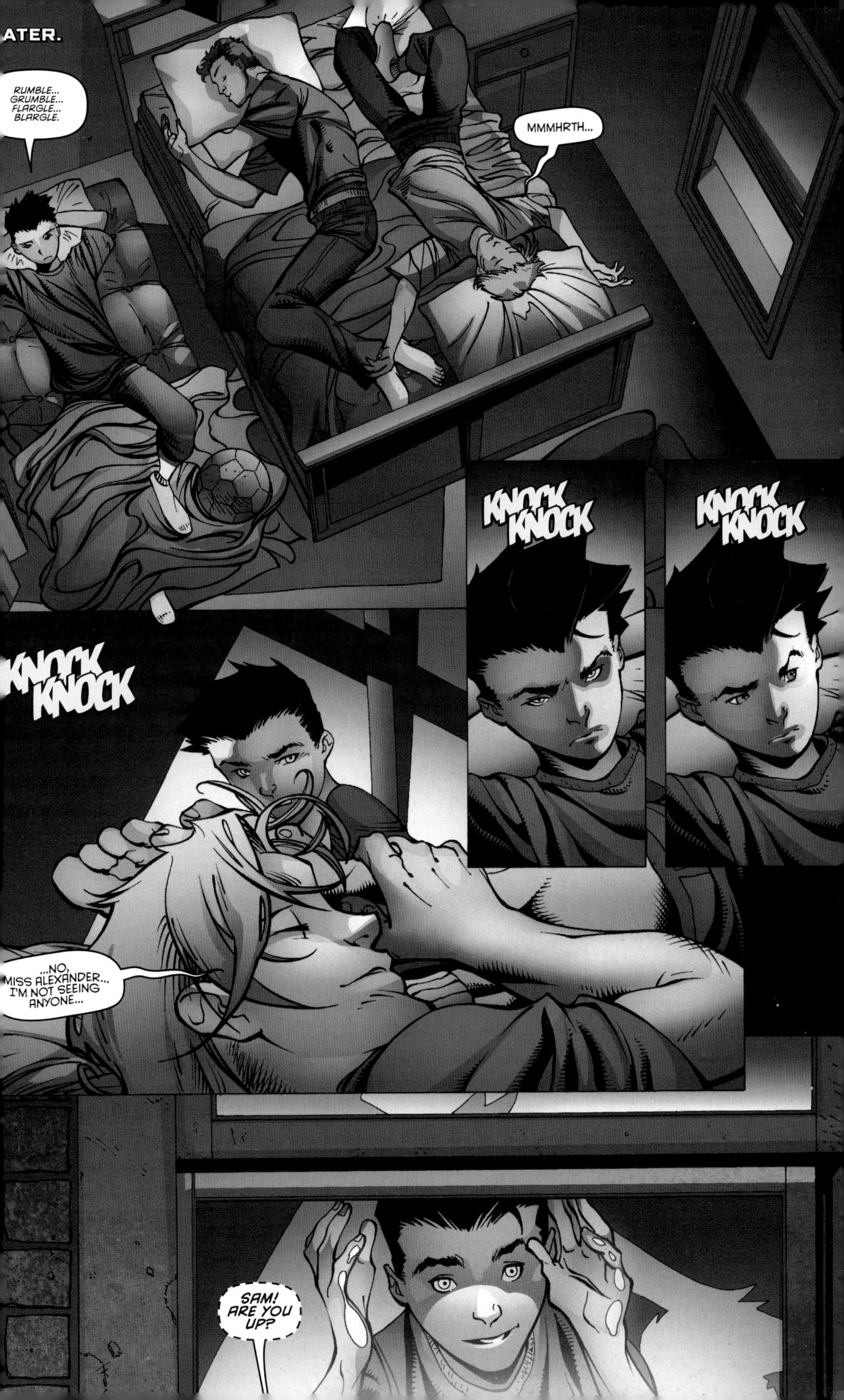
ATER.
RUMBLE... GRUMBLE... FLARGLE... BLARGLE.
MMMHRTH...
KNOCK KNOCK
KNOCK KNOCK
KNOCK KNOCK
...NO, MISS ALEXANDER... I'M NOT SEEING ANYONE...
SAM! ARE YOU UP?

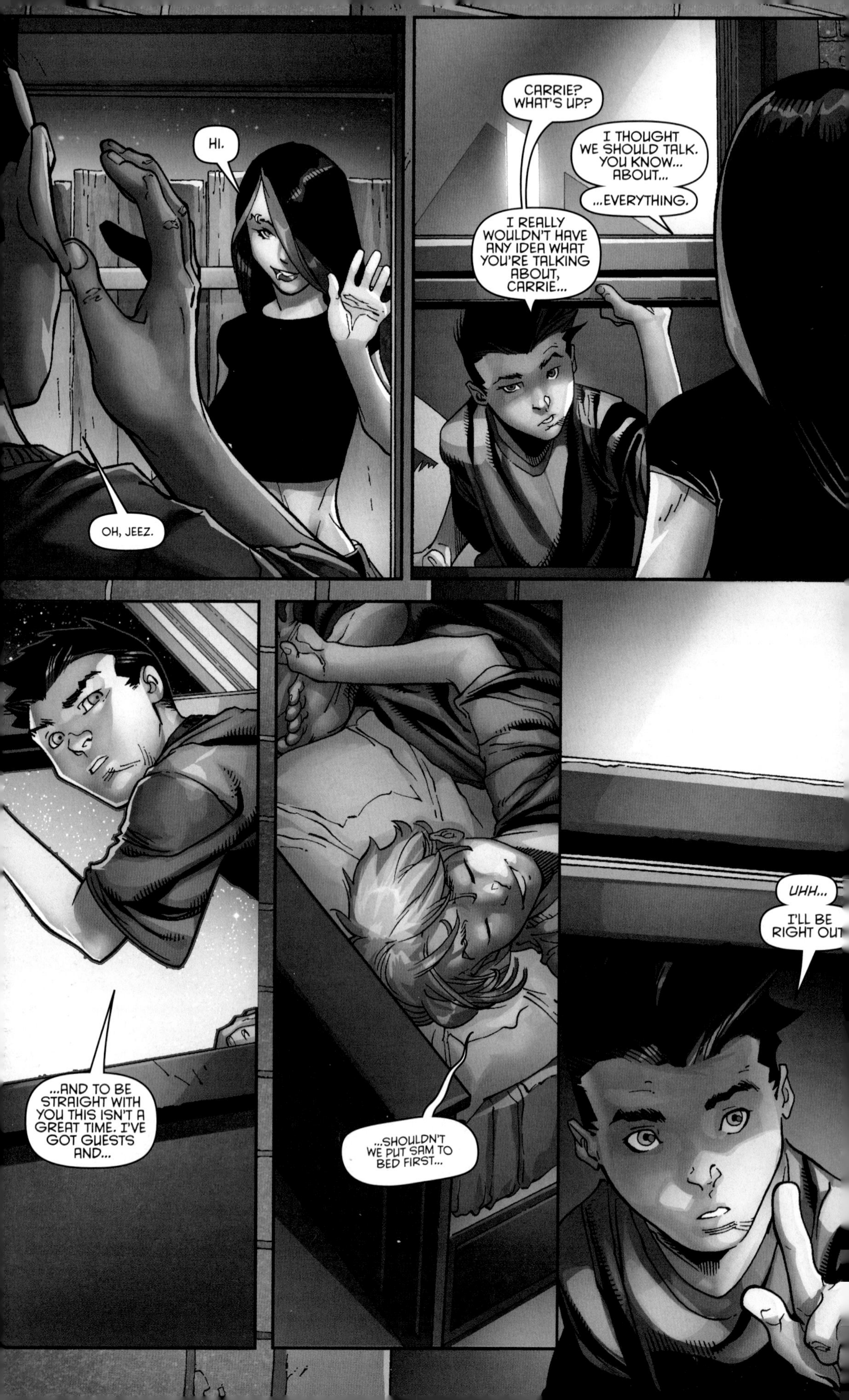
HI.
OH, JEEZ.
CARRIE? WHAT'S UP?
I THOUGHT WE SHOULD TALK. YOU KNOW... ABOUT...
...EVERYTHING.
I REALLY WOULDN'T HAVE ANY IDEA WHAT YOU'RE TALKING ABOUT, CARRIE...
...AND TO BE STRAIGHT WITH YOU THIS ISN'T A GREAT TIME. I'VE GOT GUESTS AND...
...SHOULDN'T WE PUT SAM TO BED FIRST...
UHH...
I'LL BE RIGHT OUT

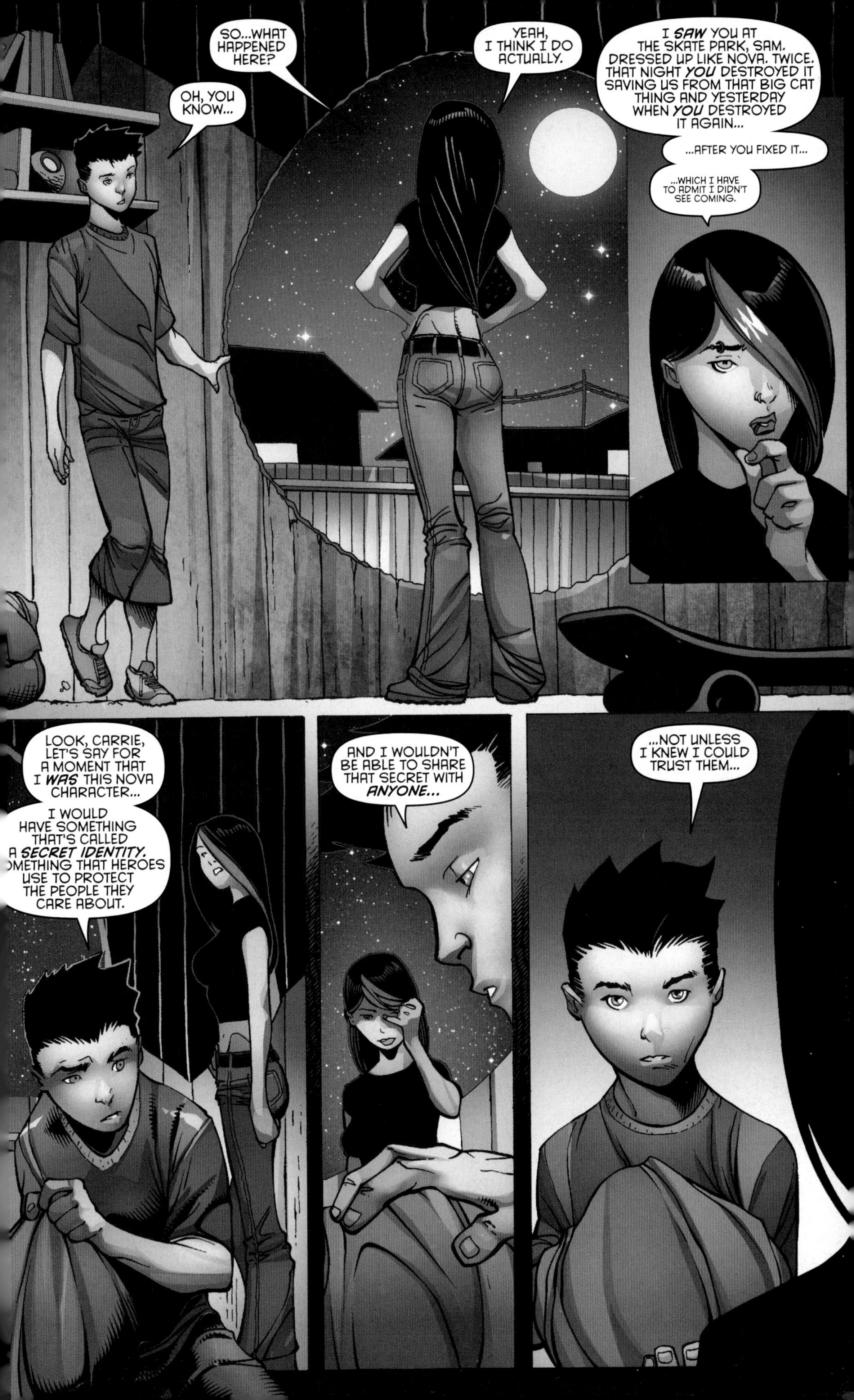

SO...WHAT HAPPENED HERE?
OH, YOU KNOW...
YEAH, I THINK I DO ACTUALLY.
I SAW YOU AT THE SKATE PARK, SAM. DRESSED UP LIKE NOVA. TWICE. THAT NIGHT YOU DESTROYED IT SAVING US FROM THAT BIG CAT THING AND YESTERDAY WHEN YOU DESTROYED IT AGAIN...
...AFTER YOU FIXED IT...
...WHICH I HAVE TO ADMIT I DIDN'T SEE COMING.
LOOK, CARRIE, LET'S SAY FOR A MOMENT THAT I WAS THIS NOVA CHARACTER...
I WOULD HAVE SOMETHING THAT'S CALLED A SECRET IDENTITY. OMETHING THAT HEROES USE TO PROTECT THE PEOPLE THEY CARE ABOUT.
AND I WOULDN'T BE ABLE TO SHARE THAT SECRET WITH ANYONE...
...NOT UNLESS I KNEW I COULD TRUST THEM...

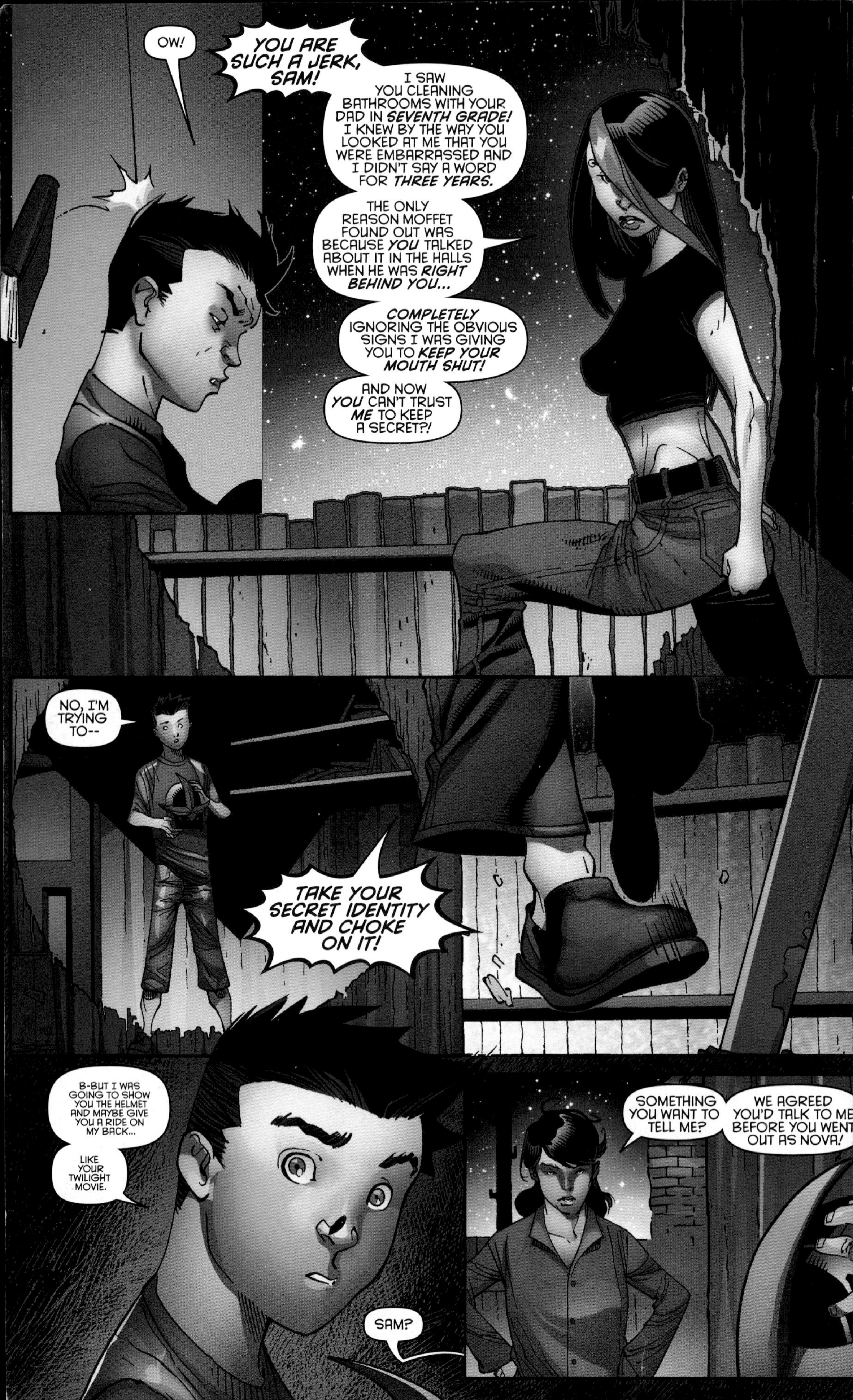
OW!
YOU ARE SUCH A JERK, SAM!
I SAW YOU CLEANING BATHROOMS WITH YOUR DAD IN SEVENTH GRADE! I KNEW BY THE WAY YOU LOOKED AT ME THAT YOU WERE EMBARRASSED AND I DIDN'T SAY A WORD FOR THREE YEARS.
THE ONLY REASON MOFFET FOUND OUT WAS BECAUSE YOU TALKED ABOUT IT IN THE HALLS WHEN HE WAS RIGHT BEHIND YOU...
COMPLETELY IGNORING THE OBVIOUS SIGNS I WAS GIVING YOU TO KEEP YOUR MOUTH SHUT!
AND NOW YOU CAN'T TRUST ME TO KEEP A SECRET?!
NO, I'M TRYING TO--
TAKE YOUR SECRET IDENTITY AND CHOKE ON IT!
B-BUT I WAS GOING TO SHOW YOU THE HELMET AND MAYBE GIVE YOU A RIDE ON MY BACK...
LIKE YOUR TWILIGHT MOVIE.
SAM?
SOMETHING YOU WANT TO TELL ME?
WE AGREED YOU'D TALK TO ME BEFORE YOU WENT OUT AS NOVA!

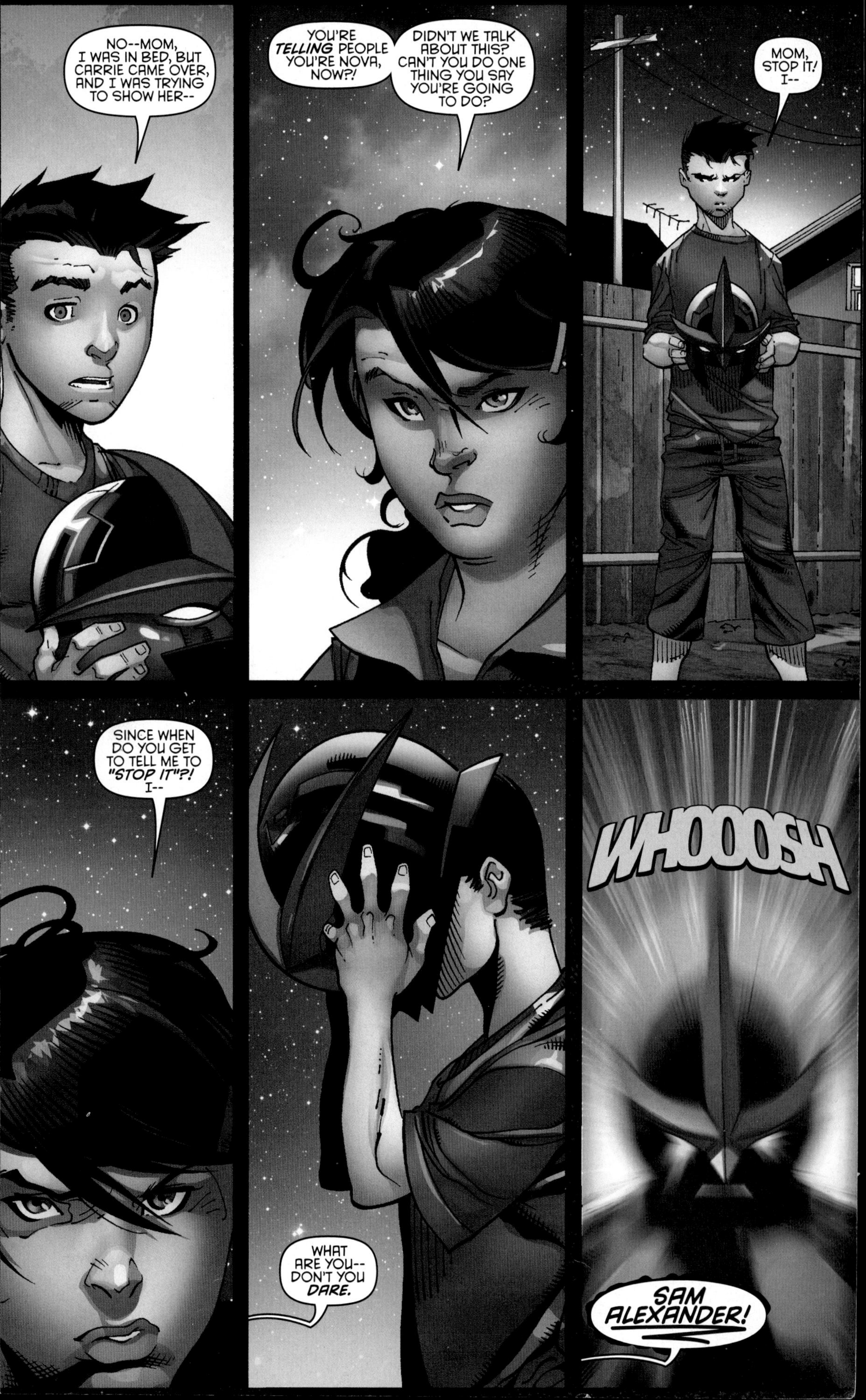

NO--MOM, I WAS IN BED, BUT CARRIE CAME OVER, AND I WAS TRYING TO SHOW HER--
YOU'RE *TELLING* PEOPLE YOU'RE NOVA, NOW?!
DIDN'T WE TALK ABOUT THIS? CAN'T YOU DO ONE THING YOU SAY YOU'RE GOING TO DO?
MOM, STOP IT! I--
SINCE WHEN DO YOU GET TO TELL ME TO *"STOP IT"*?! I--
WHAT ARE YOU-- DON'T YOU *DARE.*
WHOOOSH
SAM ALEXANDER!

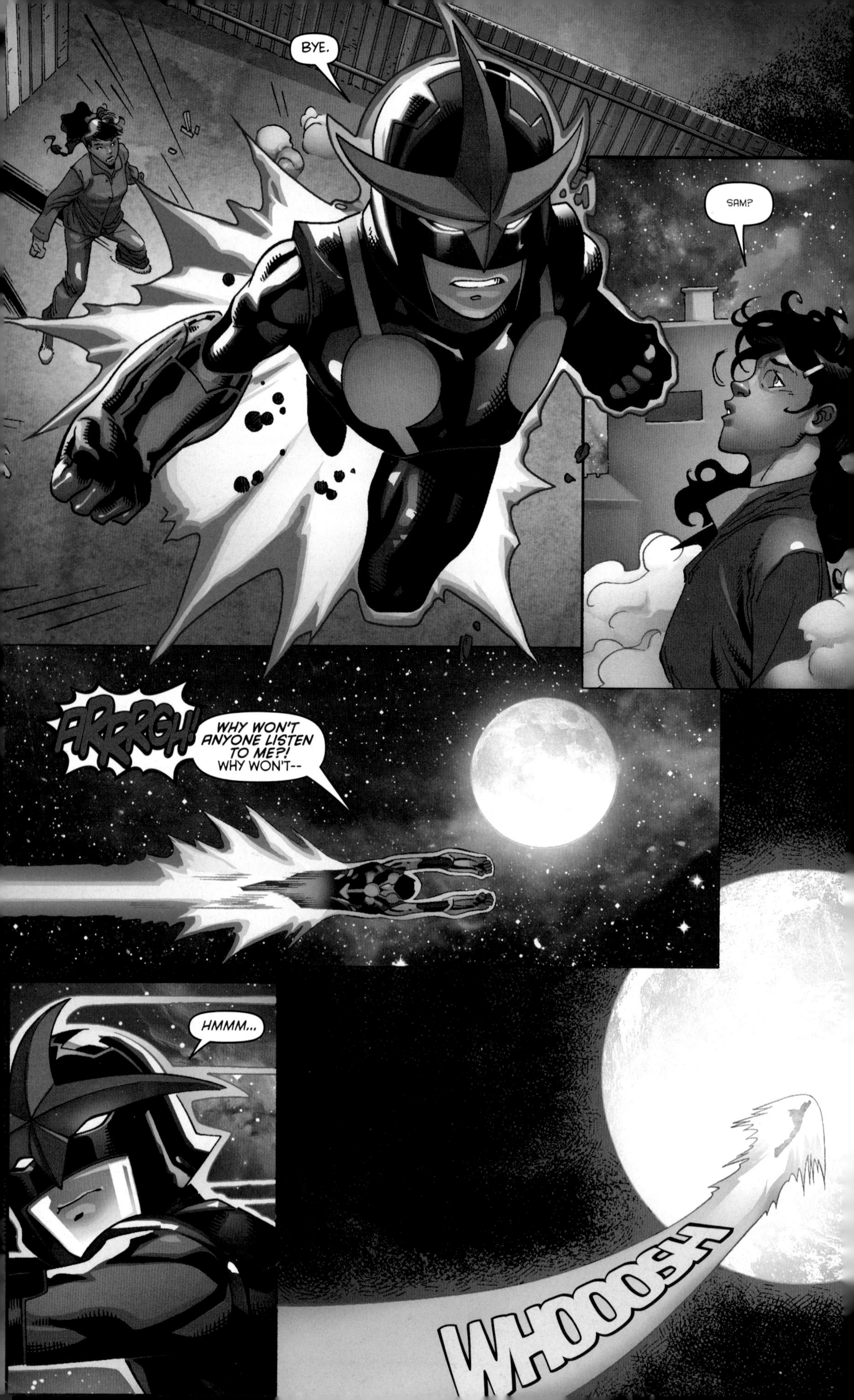
BYE.
SAM?
ARRRGH!
WHY WON'T ANYONE LISTEN TO ME?! WHY WON'T--
HMMM...
WHOOOSH

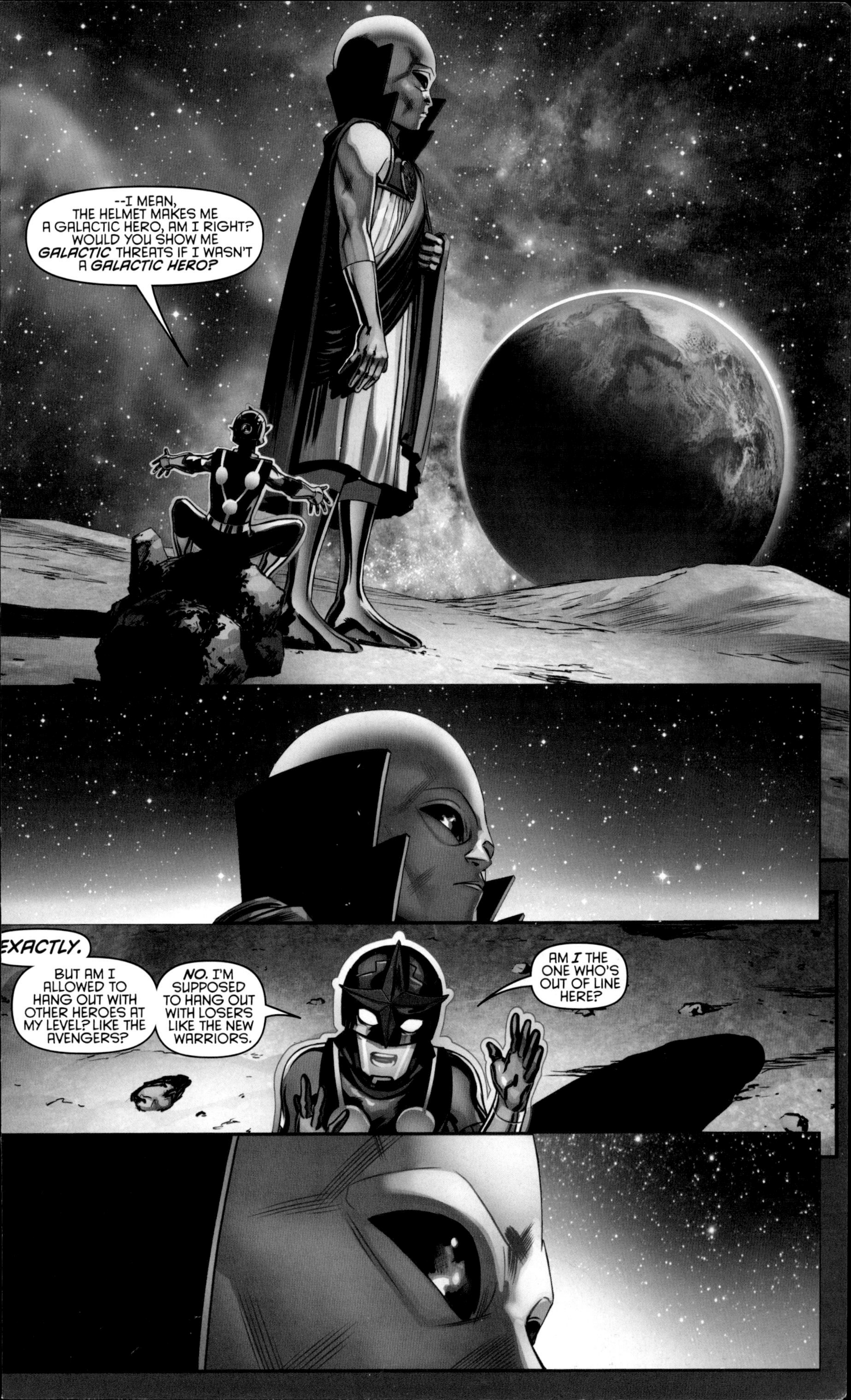
--I MEAN, THE HELMET MAKES ME A GALACTIC HERO, AM I RIGHT? WOULD YOU SHOW ME GALACTIC THREATS IF I WASN'T A GALACTIC HERO?
EXACTLY.
BUT AM I ALLOWED TO HANG OUT WITH OTHER HEROES AT MY LEVEL? LIKE THE AVENGERS?
NO. I'M SUPPOSED TO HANG OUT WITH LOSERS LIKE THE NEW WARRIORS.
AM I THE ONE WHO'S OUT OF LINE HERE?

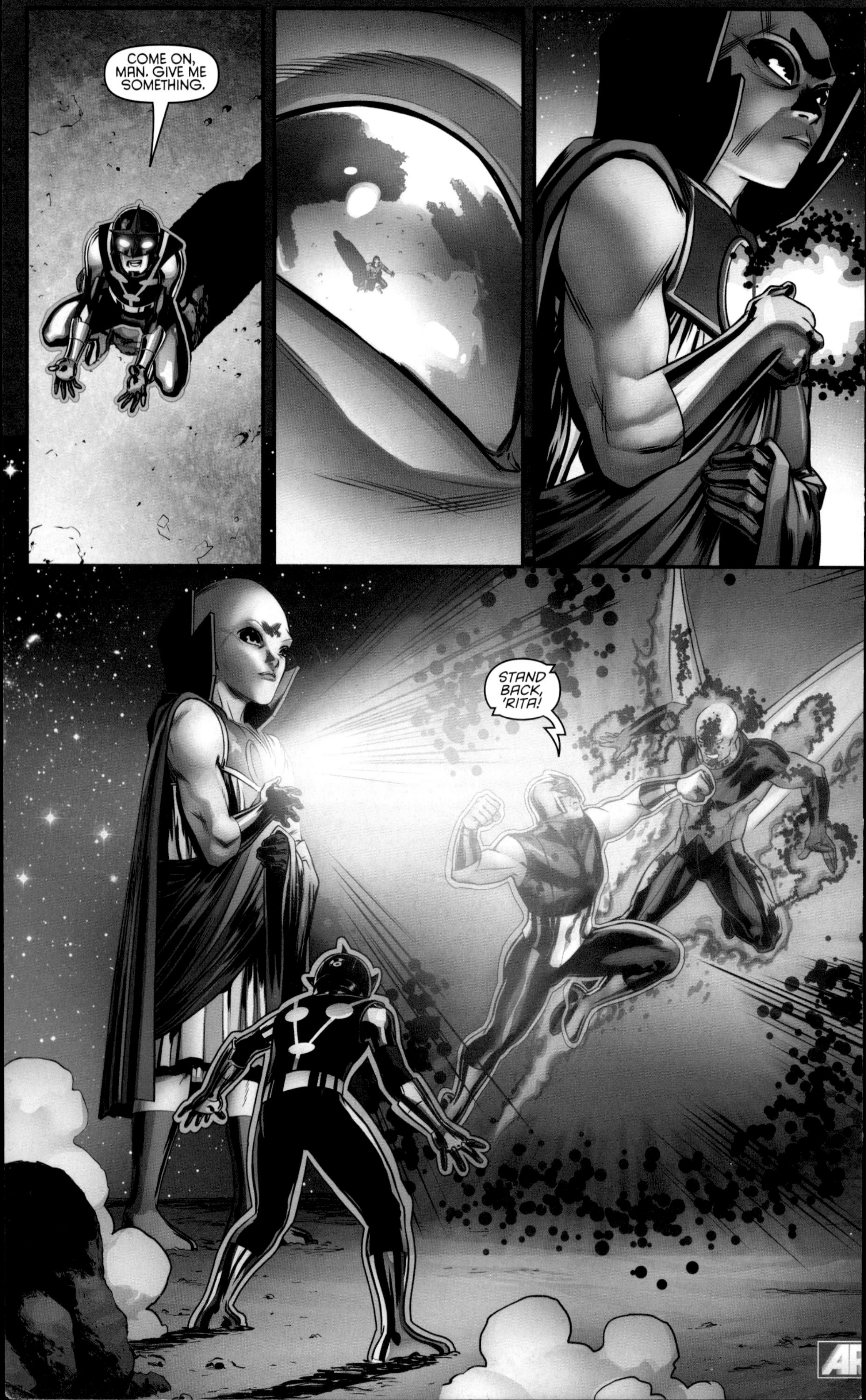
COME ON, MAN. GIVE ME SOMETHING.
STAND BACK, 'RITA!

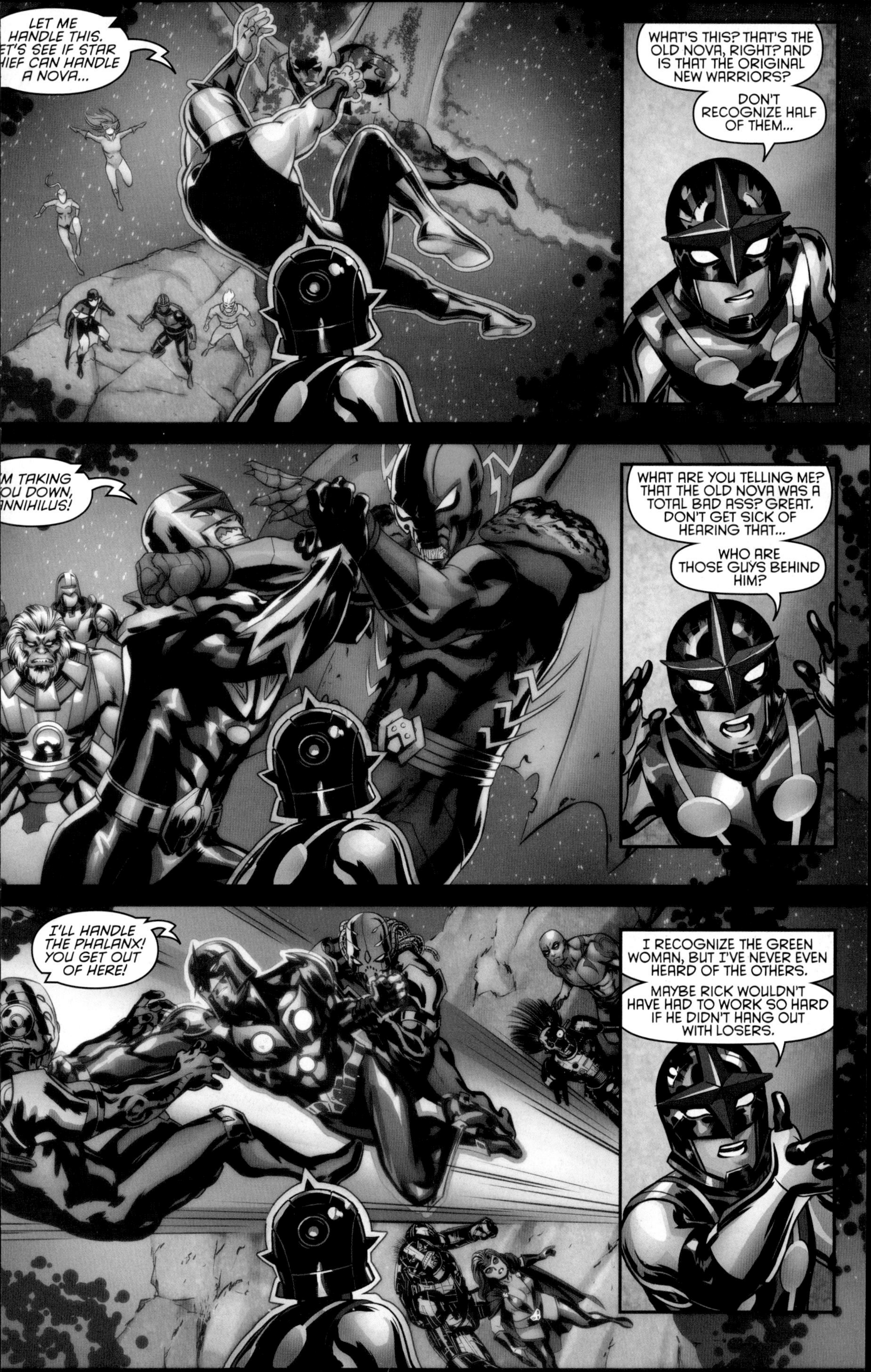

LET ME HANDLE THIS. ET'S SEE IF STAR HIEF CAN HANDLE A NOVA...
WHAT'S THIS? THAT'S THE OLD NOVA, RIGHT? AND IS THAT THE ORIGINAL NEW WARRIORS?
DON'T RECOGNIZE HALF OF THEM...
M TAKING OU DOWN, NNIHILUS!
WHAT ARE YOU TELLING ME? THAT THE OLD NOVA WAS A TOTAL BAD ASS? GREAT. DON'T GET SICK OF HEARING THAT...
WHO ARE THOSE GUYS BEHIND HIM?
I'LL HANDLE THE PHALANX! YOU GET OUT OF HERE!
I RECOGNIZE THE GREEN WOMAN, BUT I'VE NEVER EVEN HEARD OF THE OTHERS.
MAYBE RICK WOULDN'T HAVE HAD TO WORK SO HARD IF HE DIDN'T HANG OUT WITH LOSERS.

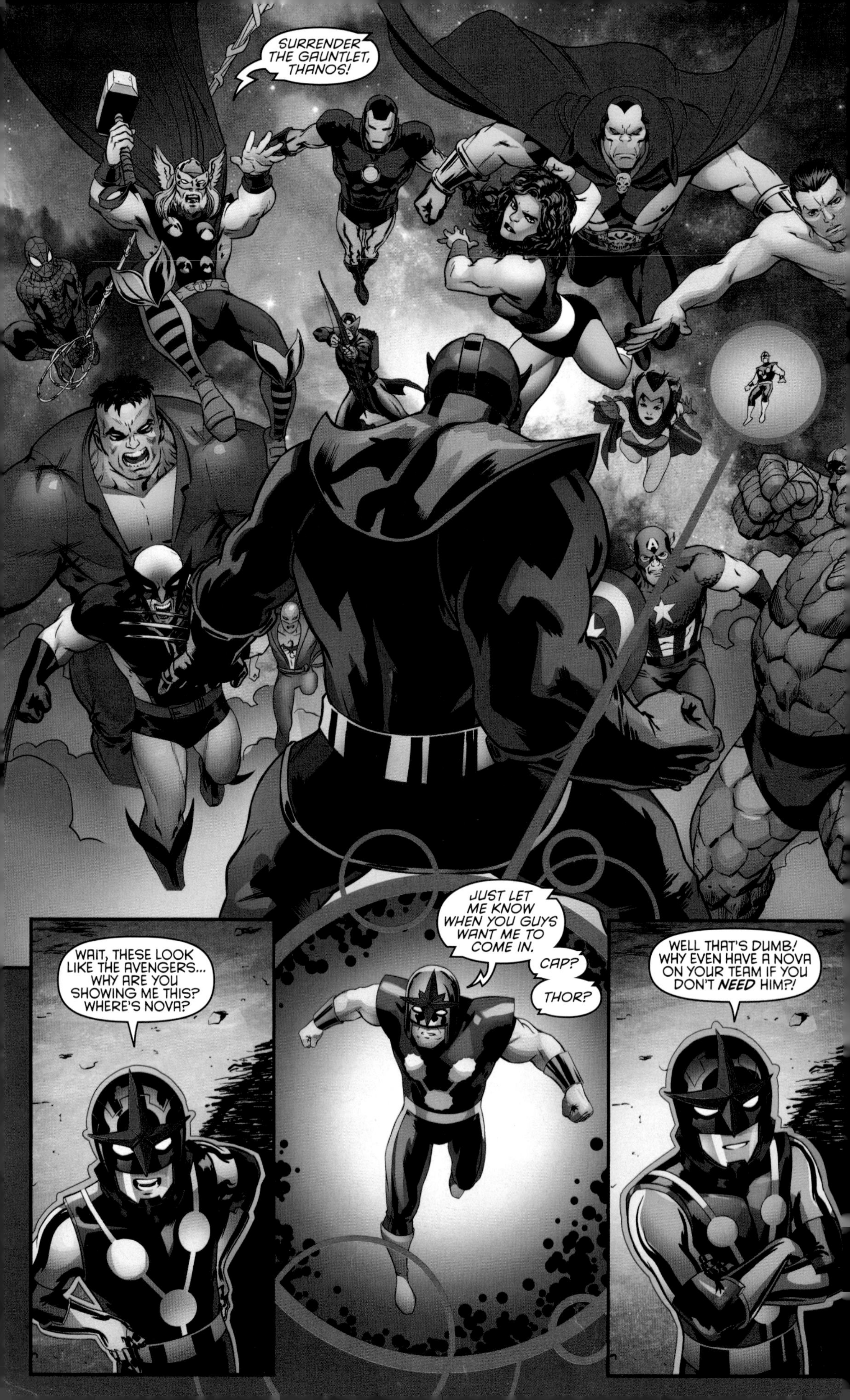
SURRENDER THE GAUNTLET, THANOS!
WAIT, THESE LOOK LIKE THE AVENGERS... WHY ARE YOU SHOWING ME THIS? WHERE'S NOVA?
JUST LET ME KNOW WHEN YOU GUYS WANT ME TO COME IN.
CAP?
THOR?
WELL THAT'S DUMB! WHY EVEN HAVE A NOVA ON YOUR TEAM IF YOU DON'T NEED HIM?!

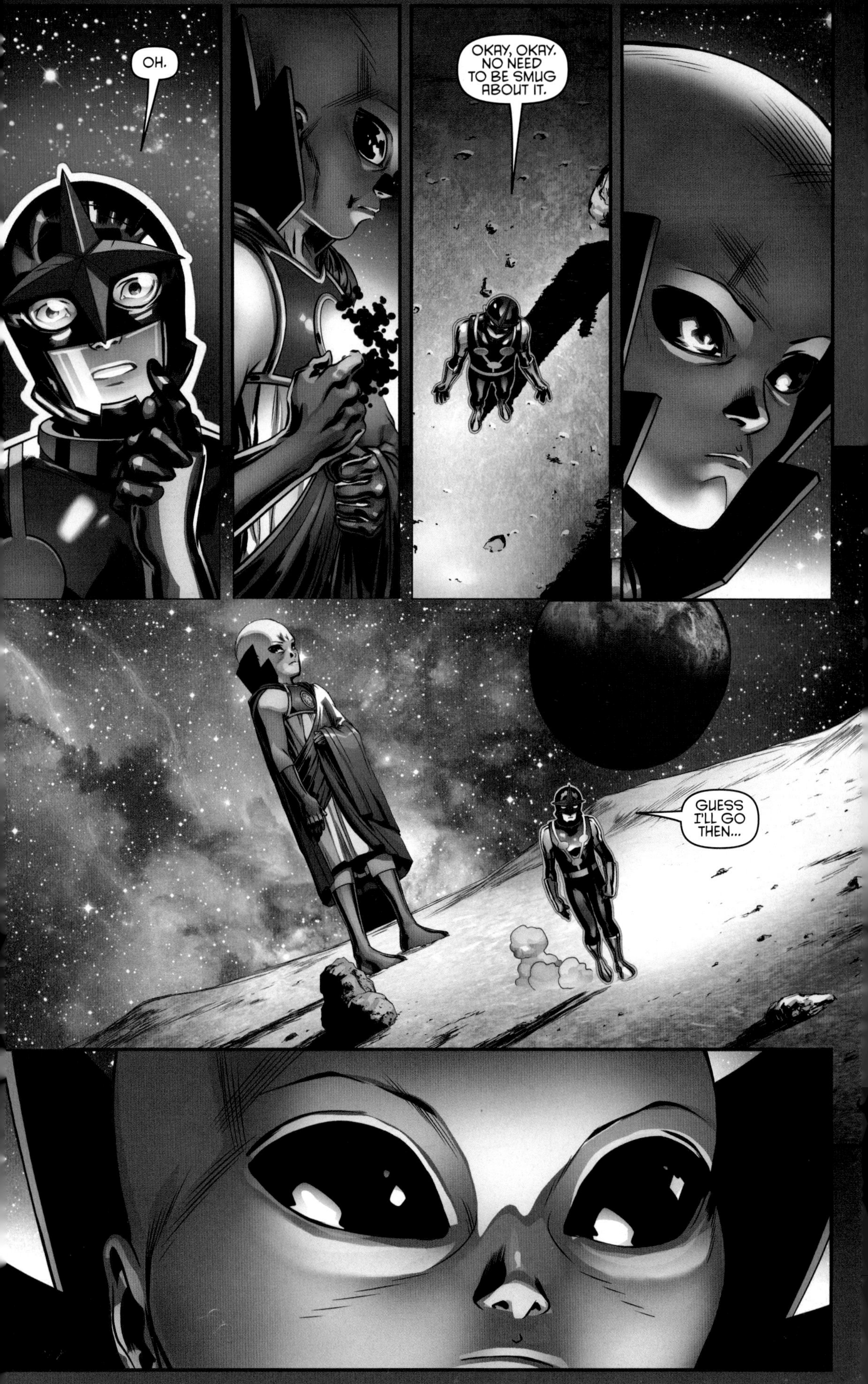
OH.
OKAY, OKAY. NO NEED TO BE SMUG ABOUT IT.
GUESS I'LL GO THEN...

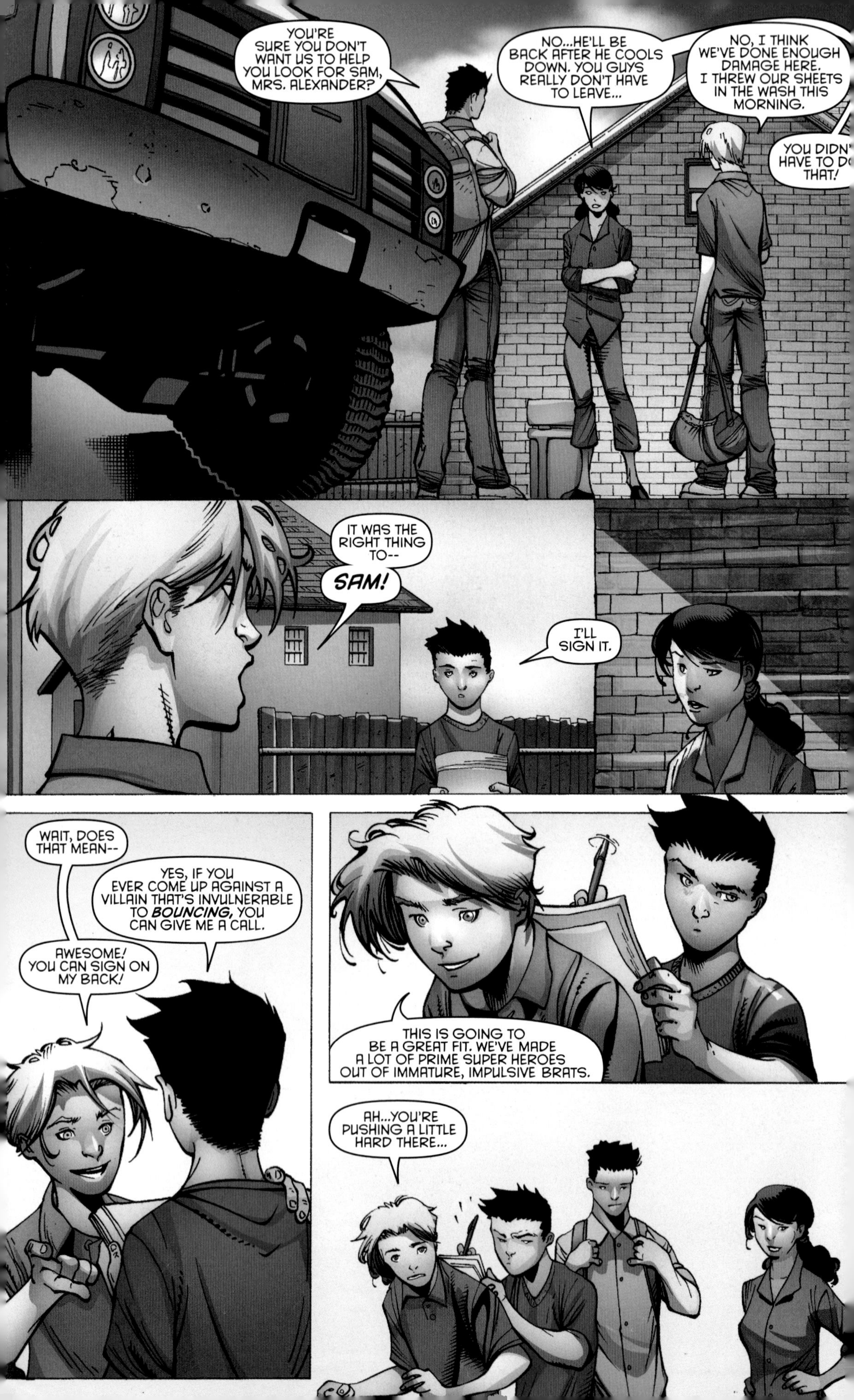
YOU'RE SURE YOU DON'T WANT US TO HELP YOU LOOK FOR SAM, MRS. ALEXANDER?
NO...HE'LL BE BACK AFTER HE COOLS DOWN. YOU GUYS REALLY DON'T HAVE TO LEAVE...
NO, I THINK WE'VE DONE ENOUGH DAMAGE HERE. I THREW OUR SHEETS IN THE WASH THIS MORNING.
YOU DIDN'T HAVE TO DO THAT!
IT WAS THE RIGHT THING TO--
SAM!
I'LL SIGN IT.
WAIT, DOES THAT MEAN--
YES, IF YOU EVER COME UP AGAINST A VILLAIN THAT'S INVULNERABLE TO BOUNCING, YOU CAN GIVE ME A CALL.
AWESOME! YOU CAN SIGN ON MY BACK!
THIS IS GOING TO BE A GREAT FIT. WE'VE MADE A LOT OF PRIME SUPER HEROES OUT OF IMMATURE, IMPULSIVE BRATS.
AH...YOU'RE PUSHING A LITTLE HARD THERE...

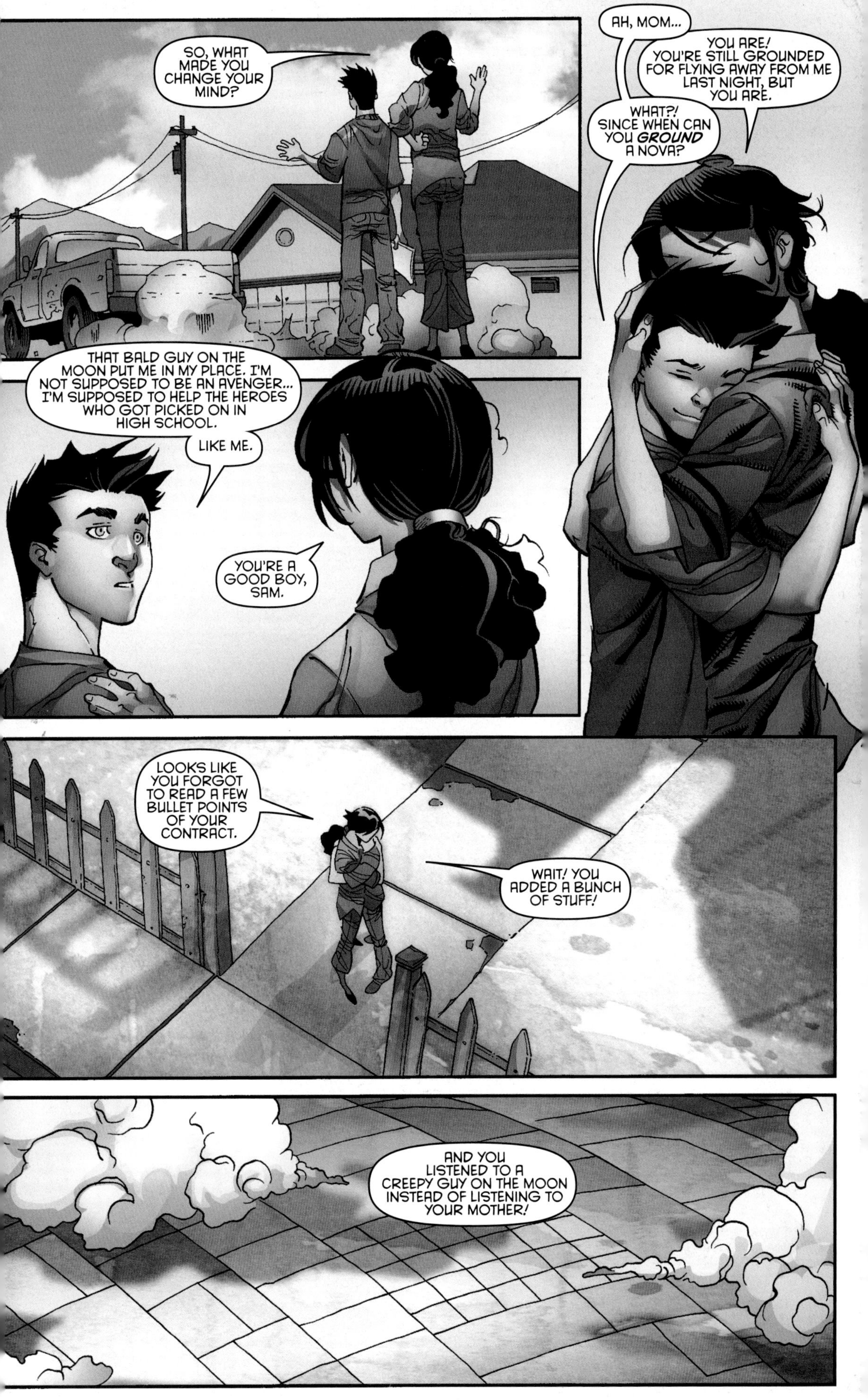
SO, WHAT MADE YOU CHANGE YOUR MIND?
THAT BALD GUY ON THE MOON PUT ME IN MY PLACE. I'M NOT SUPPOSED TO BE AN AVENGER... I'M SUPPOSED TO HELP THE HEROES WHO GOT PICKED ON IN HIGH SCHOOL.
LIKE ME.
YOU'RE A GOOD BOY, SAM.
AH, MOM...
YOU ARE! YOU'RE STILL GROUNDED FOR FLYING AWAY FROM ME LAST NIGHT, BUT YOU ARE.
WHAT?! SINCE WHEN CAN YOU GROUND A NOVA?
LOOKS LIKE YOU FORGOT TO READ A FEW BULLET POINTS OF YOUR CONTRACT.
WAIT! YOU ADDED A BUNCH OF STUFF!
AND YOU LISTENED TO A CREEPY GUY ON THE MOON INSTEAD OF LISTENING TO YOUR MOTHER!

"KIND OF. HE DOESN'T REALLY TALK."

"WELL, I HOPE HE'S HAPPY."

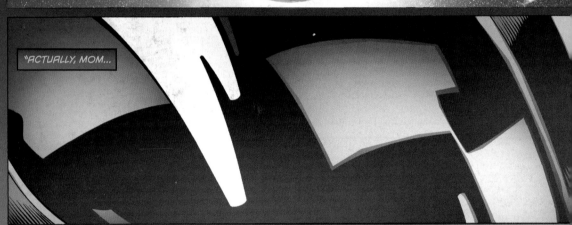

"ACTUALLY, MOM..."

"I DON'T KNOW IF HE GETS HAPPY..."

AR END.

ISSUE #10 VARIANT COVER
SAL BUSCEMA & JOHN KALISZ

ISSUE #10 VARIANT COVER
PHIL JIMENEZ, DAN GREEN & EDGAR DELGADO

TO ACCESS THE FREE *MARVEL AUGMENTED REALITY APP* THAT ENHANCES AND CHANGES THE WAY YOU EXPERIENCE COMICS

1. **Download the app for free via** marvel.com/ARapp
2. **Launch the app on your camera-enabled** Apple iOS® or Android™ device*
3. **Hold your mobile device's camera over** any cover or panel with the **AR** graph
4. **Sit back and see the future of comics** in action!

*Available on most camera-enabled Apple iOS® and Android™ devices. Content subject to change and availability.

NOVA **AR** INDEX